MW00875621

THE SHAKE OFF

THE NEW YORK LIONS: BOOK TWO

LULU MOORE

This book is for anyone who's ever been afraid to ask for what they want

"Love is the most important thing in the world, but base-ball's pretty good too..."

-Yogi Berra

DEFINITION

Shake off: *phrasal verb*

1. To successfully deal or recover from an illness, injury, or negative feeling

2. To free yourself from someone or something that is limiting you

3. A signal in baseball between the pitcher and the catcher

Dear Readers,

Thank you so much for wanting to read The Shake Off, and returning to the world of The New York Lions. It's such an honor to me that you love my characters as much as I do.

This book was immense fun to write, and I've definitely pulled from a few 'real life' experiences for it. Payton has a special place in my heart, and I've written her for every girl who's been with a guy who thinks he's 'all that' - we all know the type… amirite? I didn't always ask for what I wanted, or needed, but I'm hoping now Payton might inspire us all to do so.

Enjoy, and happy reading. I hope you love it.

Lulu xo

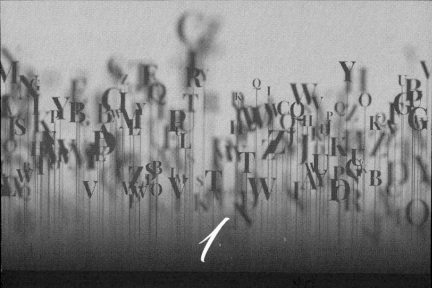

1

Payton

"*O*kay, girls," Kit began as she drained the champagne from her glass and peered around the table at our friends, before her eyes finally landed on me. "I hate to say it, but it's home time. Bell will be awake at six, and I have a full day of classes tomorrow."

I glanced at my watch – nine-thirty on the dot. Gone were the days when my best friend and I would be out drinking until the small hours on a school night, but that's what happened when you fell in love with your boss, adopted his baby daughter, and became a professor of English at Columbia University – her, obvs, not me.

"Hey, any amount of time I get to spend with you, cake, and champagne, in our favorite restaurant, is good enough for me."

She blew me a kiss. "Happy birthday, babe."

"Thank you, and thank you for tonight, all of you. It was perfect." I reached across the table for the remainder of my birthday cake laden with rainbow frosting, and pulled it toward me. This baby wasn't going to waste. "And if you're checking out early, I'm taking the rest of this home to enjoy from the comfort of my couch, watching The Golden Girls. Or, better yet, maybe I'll find someone on the way out who'll come back and feed it to me while I watch The Golden Girls."

That's what Blanche would have done. Blanche was my girl, and I fully intended to be her when I grew up.

"Hey," laughed Beulah, "it's your birthday. You can make that wish come true."

"Oh yeah, where are the candles? I'll try again." My eyes darted around dramatically as I burst out laughing, especially when I caught Beulah attempting to stifle a yawn, and pointed accusingly at her. "I saw that."

"Sorry," she winced. "Not sure what my excuse is. I don't have classes or a toddler."

"You have a squad of baseball players to look after. I'd take a toddler any day over those boys."

"Tell me about it." Her yawn finally made an appearance, and she shook her head in disgust at herself. "Honestly, I don't know how I used to survive on five hours of sleep. Baseball has made me weak I'm telling you. Weak."

Lowe let out a chuckle. "Don't let Penn hear you say that."

"I might be weak, but I'm not stupid."

Penn Shepherd, Lowe's husband, and owner of The New York Lions, where Beulah and Lowe both worked, wasn't known for his sense of humor when it came to baseball.

"How's everything going over at Lions H.Q.?" I asked, finishing off my own glass of champagne as Lowe attempted to signal the waiter for the check. Except, given how busy the restaurant currently was, he was ignoring her, which was his first mistake.

She got up and marched over to him.

"Good," Beulah continued, "though now Spring Training is over, I'm getting less done. The boys have only been back two days, but I swear someone knocks on my door every five minutes. Today I had Ace Watson coming to ask if he could add a clause in his contract about PlayStation and this season's edition of *The Show*, and making sure they got his eye color right this year. Apparently, they weren't blue enough last year." She rolled her eyes. "How is that my job as head of legal? I swear they come up with this shit to fuck with me."

Kit's lips pulled tight as she tried not to smile. "Beats corporate law though, right?"

"Yeah. It sure does," she replied. "It's Marnie I feel sorry for. She had to work with those boys every day."

"Hey, Ace Watson could interrupt me any time. That boy is cute with a capital C. If I was still in college, his poster would be up in my dorm room."

"And he knows it," Beulah laughed. "I swear he could charm his way into Fort Knox with the way he bats those eyelashes."

"I take it you're talking about Ace," Lowe said, sliding back into her seat, check in hand, and fished around in her bag for her AmEx.

"Yeah," I sighed, like I was *actually* eighteen and still in college, but I couldn't help it. Any time The Lions starting pitcher was mentioned, a little sigh escaped.

It was almost a subconscious reaction at this point.

"You might change your mind when you see him. He decided to grow a mustache for Spring Training. He looks like a porn star."

The sigh became a little moan. "That's hot. Like a young, sexier Tom Selleck."

I really needed to stop watching late night TV, but that didn't stop the four of us all sighing at thought of Tom Selleck.

"Whatever it is, I don't think it's done him any harm. You should have seen the girls lined up along the fences at the ground."

The four of us shared exactly the same look – the look that said we knew exactly what that meant and the girls she was talking about – and burst out laughing.

Ace was a key part of a small group of the younger players who'd become the unofficial heartthrobs of The New York Lions. Along with Parker King, catcher; Lux Weston, center field; and Tanner Simpson, short stop, they rarely went anywhere without a trail of women following in their wake. They lined the gates, the fences at practice, and camped outside the hotels.

The four boys each had more social media followers than the rest of the team combined, along with dozens of social media accounts dedicated to them.

They were the same age, had played in the majors for roughly the same amount of time, and according to Lowe, who'd heard it from Penn, he saw them as the future of The Lions. Therefore, he was investing a lot of time and money into shaping them to be the best players they could be. If they were bringing attention to the club, along with a new audience, then they were free to do whatever they wanted, as long as The Lions kept winning.

Because Penn's sole goal was for The Lions to win and lift The Commissioner's Trophy. They'd gotten to the first round of the playoffs last season, and this year Penn was out for more, and nothing would stop him.

I would *not* want to be the poor bastard who got in his way.

"How'd Ace do in Arizona?" I asked.

"His pitching's better since last season already, and he has everyone wrapped around his finger, even Coach Chase. And if he keeps pitching like he does, I swear Penn will sign our first born over to him if I'm not careful," Lowe added, as her AmEx was returned and another waiter brought our coats, passing them around to their rightful owners. "Okay, everyone ready to go?"

Kit picked up the birthday cake, now safely in the box it arrived in, and handed it to me, "Pay, there's approximately eighty yards between us and the front doors. Let's see if we can't make your birthday wish come true."

"And if not, we have Penn's lunch this weekend," Beulah smirked. "There'll be plenty of guys there who'll happily take you home and enjoy your... cake."

"What's the lunch for again?" I asked.

"To kick off the new season. We did it last year, too. The local community is invited, Penn will announce the charity of the year, and give away season tickets." If Lowe could have literally beamed with pride, she would have.

The New York Lions had always been seen as the joke of New York's sports teams, and the Major Leagues, and no one took them seriously until Penn bought them eighteen months ago. Overnight, he transformed them from a club rarely seen above its spot at the bottom of the standings, to one which made the first round of the playoffs. He pumped nearly a billion dollars into renovating The Lions stadium on the Upper West Side, along with the grounds surrounding it, and an overhaul of the players.

In the space of a season, he'd put The Lions back on the

New York map again.

The downside? For eight months of the year – nine if you included the pre-season – our social lives revolved around baseball, because both Lowe and Beulah now worked for the club, along with our other friend, Marnie. Today was the first day we'd been together since the beginning of February. I could find time in my schedule if it meant attending a lunch with my friends, and Penn always threw a good party.

I slung my coat around my shoulders and slowly followed the others out of the restaurant. Leaning forward to Kit in front, I whispered, "Do all these charity functions we're attending these days mean we're officially grown-ups?"

"I think so," she nodded solemnly.

"But there's still cake, right?"

"There's going to be plenty of cake. A whole forty-man squad of cake."

"Count me in then."

She stepped back and looped her arm through mine. "Now you've turned thirty, are we going to be looking for a more permanent type of cake? One without an expiry date?"

"You and I both know that will never happen. I'll like my cake fresh."

"May you be forever single." A knowing little smile curved on her lips as she kissed my cheek, then halted us a second later. "Wait, we were talking about boys, right? Not actual cake?"

I laughed. "Yes, I think so. I lost track about ten minutes ago though. But either way, I have no plans to get myself into a relationship."

"Good, because now the season's about to start, it's you and me again. I need someone to keep me company."

There was that downside I'd been talking about. Our friends would be traveling with the team most of the time, and our regular girls' evenings would consist of just Kit and me, plus Bell, her daughter, even though she went to bed at seven. But Kit and I were both of the opinion we couldn't go to every home game, because – and don't tell anyone – neither of us really liked baseball that much.

Not enough to watch one hundred-sixty-two games, anyway.

"Don't worry, I got you. I'll be your forever buddy."

I opted not to search for more 'cake' as we followed the other two in silence, out of the noisy restaurant for the slightly-less-noisy New York street, where they were all about to head home to the men who'd be waiting for them.

I pulled my coat around me. My bare legs were no match for the cool March air, especially in the evenings once the sun had disappeared. It wouldn't be for much longer though; I could already see the first hint of blossoms coming out for spring. Over the next few weeks, the streets would be lined pink, and the air would become a little bit sweeter from the scent of flowers shooting up in the parks.

It was my favorite season.

We were all hugging goodbye as three black Range Rovers pulled up to the curb in front of us. Beulah hopped into one heading downtown, while the other two were taking Lowe and Kit back to their respective apartments on the Upper East and Upper West sides.

"Pay, get in. I'll take you home!" Beulah called out, holding her door open. "We can go via Midtown."

I smiled at her but shook my head. "No, thanks. I'm good. I'm going to walk for a bit."

Kit peered down at my feet, clad in my new favorite bottle-green Jimmy Choos. "In those heels?"

"Yep. They were my birthday present to myself, and I'm going to wear them for as long as I can. I'll jump in an Uber if I get tired."

"Okay, love you." She leaned in, pressing her lips to my cheek.

"Love you. Give a kiss to my goddaughter for me."

"I will." I slammed Kit's door shut for her and stood there clasping my box of cake as the three cars were swept away into the evening traffic.

I waited until they were out of sight before I retrieved my headphones from the depths of my purse. It probably would have been easier to accept a ride from Beulah, but there was something about walking along the sidewalks surrounded by people, yet in your own private world as you blocked out the sound of chatter and car horns, and whenever I got the opportunity to do so, I snatched it up.

It gave me time to think; to ponder on my life and where I wanted to take it. To mull on my future.

Plus, there was something else I wanted to do.

Taking a left at the end of the street, I marched to the beat of the music as fast as my legs – and new shoes – would carry me. Just as I began to feel the pinch of new leather against my heels, I arrived at my destination; Greyschott Tower; the vast copper and brick building set back from the street on a wide plaza, and home to Simpson and Mather – the world's largest publishing house.

My place of work.

I sat down on the concrete bench in front of it where I often took a mid-morning coffee, but now, nearly twelve hours later, it was a very different place. No one rushing out to grab coffee or a muffin before their next meeting; no one on a call, or sitting on the oversized deckchairs which lined the plaza during the day, and reading the latest book published.

It was quiet.

I craned my neck up and up. My eyes travelled past the thirtieth floor where the H.R. and finance teams sat, past the thirty-fifth floor where the Non-Fiction team sat, past the fortieth floor – my floor – where Children's publishing sat, and stopped on the fiftieth floor; Adult Fiction. The department was actually split over the next five floors because that's how big it was, but I only had eyes for the fiftieth.

My holy grail.

I opened the box containing my birthday cake; one candle had rolled into the frosting and gotten stuck. I pulled it free and licked the excess sugar off the end while I dug around in my purse for the book of matches I'd swiped from the valet desk as we'd left the restaurant. Breaking off a piece of cake, I stuck the candle in the top and lit it.

Taking one last glance up to the fiftieth floor, I closed my eyes and blew.

This was my real birthday wish; not boys or world peace or whatever people wished for. My real birthday wish was that I'd finally make it out of the children's book floor where I currently worked, and up to the adult floor.

It had been my wish since I'd started at Simpson and Mather eight years ago, straight out of Columbia, where Kit and I had studied English together. While other girls dreamed of writing stories, I just wanted to read them. I wanted to be among the words and pages and worlds authors created. I wanted to live in the fantasy of happily ever afters, and love, and make believe that I'd devoured as a kid, and when I realized I could actually do that as a job, my mind was set.

I would work with authors to bring their stories to life, and send them out to live in the imaginations of readers who devoured their words as quickly as a kid with a bag of candy. Simpson and Mather was *the* place to do it.

It was the only place I'd ever wanted to work, and when a recruiter came to Columbia with the opportunity for an internship in the children's department, I did everything I could to make sure I won it. Because as long as I was in the building, I'd be able to move departments, right?

Wrong.

Editor positions are few and far between. Editor positions at Simpson and Mather are even more scarce, because no one ever leaves.

The added problem I had? I'd become quite good at my current job; okay, *very* good. The last three years, books I've edited have been shortlisted for The Children's Book Awards, and my boss was incredibly reluctant to let me go because I made her look good.

But maybe, just maybe, this would be the year my wish would come true.

I stuffed the little piece of cake into my mouth, took a final glance up to my dream floor and stood. It was time to call an Uber.

I was waiting near the curb, clutching my coat around my shoulders and wondering if I should take my shoes off as I watched the little black car move along the road map. I was still thinking about the fiftieth floor, when a blacked-out G-Wagon pulled up.

The window lowered, and the driver leaned out with what could only be described as an entirely devilish look on his face.

My first thought – whoever at PlayStation got his eye

color wrong had to be blind. They were the shade of clear New York skies in the dead of summer. Or the Caribbean Seas. Or Blue M&Ms.

My second – I couldn't blame the girls lining the fences, or gates, or anywhere really. And that moustache definitely added… something.

"Hello there."

I raised an eyebrow, determined not to let out the sigh I always did. Knowing my luck, it would come out as more of a desperate moan. "You're not my Uber."

"No, Babycakes, I'm better."

"Oh yeah? How?"

"I like to provide a more personal service." He turned away, returning a second later and thrust his hand out of the window. "Mint?"

I held my lips together as best I could, and put all my energy into not showing my amusement, but I knew my mouth was curling at the edges. My eyes were definitely creasing. Instead, I looked down at my phone screen, to see my Uber was now circling the block in the other direction.

Fucking Uber.

Ace tipped his chin to the box in my hands. "What's in there?"

"Birthday cake."

"Whose birthday is it?"

"Mine."

"What are the chances?" A deep smile spread wide across his far too handsome face. "I'm obviously your birthday wish come true."

I'd been at the Lions ground dozens of times, but this was the first time I'd ever met Ace Watson in person. Looking at him now with his thick, light brown hair flopping to the side, and his eyes twinkling in amusement as his bicep bulged from the way he propped his chin on his fist while he waited for me to stop focusing on the Uber app, I was amazed Beulah and Lowe got any work done at all.

I wouldn't.

In fact, if Ace Watson was anywhere in my vicinity, I'd get approximately zero work done. The only job I was currently trying to do was get home, and that was proving to be far harder than it should. He was entirely distracting.

"Who said I made a wish?"

"Why else would I be driving past the exact spot where you were looking all lost? It's fate."

"I don't look lost. I'm waiting for my Uber."

Ace leaned out of his car and peered around. "I don't see an Uber."

I glanced down at the screen again to find the Uber was now even further away.

Fucking Uber.

Fucking New York one-way systems.

"He's on the way."

"Cancel it," Ace ordered, with all the confidence of a twenty-something who rarely heard the word 'no'. "I'll take you where you need to go, and you'll have a much better time. I promise."

If my arms weren't full I'd have crossed them. As it was, I pinned him with the same look he'd given me. I wasn't about to let those batting lashes sway me that easily, no matter how much his gaze laved every inch of my body, heating it up until it tingled.

"You want me to get into a car with a strange man?"

"Hey, I'm not strange. This city loves me. My face is already everywhere." He pointed over my head, "see?"

I turned around to find one of the huge New York Lions flags which Lowe had hung all over the city, this one bearing his face, and I let out the laugh I'd been holding. I'd been too busy making my wish that I hadn't noticed the flag flapping next to me had Ace's face printed on it.

"So," he said, when I turned back, "you getting in?"

Fuck it. I was a single woman, and it *was* my birthday.

Why couldn't I have my cake and eat it?

I hit cancel on the Uber, rounded the car to where Ace had pushed open the passenger door, and hopped in.

"Did anyone tell you you're the most beautiful birthday girl they'd ever seen in their life?"

I shook my head with a grin, smoothing down my jacket, which had barely hit my knees, and crossed my legs. I'm not going to lie and say I didn't enjoy Ace's eyes tracking the movement, though when I looked over to him again, he was focused back on my face.

"Good, that means I get to be the first. You are the most beautiful girl I've ever seen in my life," he grinned. "Now, what's our destination?"

*T*his is how it's always gone when I've fantasized about Ace Watson:

The scene opens with him pouring me a drink, in a location that changes depending on my mood. Condensation runs down the glass just as a tiny bead of sweat forms at the base of my throat.

Ace notices.

He's still holding the glass as he leans in and licks it away, dragging his perfect lips up the column of my neck.

Fuck, that mouth could do some damage.

"You're so fucking sweet," he whispers, his breath burning my skin. "You make me so hard, harder than I've ever been in my life, and I can't wait to taste the rest of you."

I'd moan, but I'm struggling to breathe, and my bottom lip is caught between my teeth. I never get my drink because Ace drops to his knees. His lips suction along my skin, my pussy clenching harder and harder the closer he gets to where I desperately need to feel him. Finally, he rips my panties off and proceeds to spread me over his tongue.

Eating like it's his last meal.

The first orgasm rips through me like a tornado, but Ace isn't done. Not even close. Without breaking contact, he lies back on the floor and pulls me with him so I'm straddling his face.

"Ride me," he orders, yanking the neckline of my dress until my breasts pop free. "I want to drown in your cum."

I'm in the hands of an expert; his thumb swiping over my rock-hard nipples with the exact amount of pressure as his tongue stabs inside me as I grind my pussy into his face, and it takes no time before I'm coming a second time.

"Fuck, you're perfect. I wanna make you cum all night," he groans. "Let me do it again. Please."

"Okay, one more, then your turn," I pant, though I'm so breathless it's hard to form words.

But Ace knows.

"No, don't worry about me. This is all about you." He kisses me roughly and flips me over.

His dick is so thick it steals my breath as he plunges inside me for the first time, positioning himself so he hits me right in *that* spot. I'm coiled tighter than a spring, and he's holding me firm enough that all I can do is take it.

His mouth moves along my spine, licking up the sweat from our exertions as he gathers my hair into his fist and really goes to town on me right there on the floor. My toes curl so much that they imprint onto whatever surface we're on, and before long, it results in orgasm number three.

It's usually at this point I fall asleep, worn out by the Ace Watson in my dreams.

Ace Watson, the best sex I'd ever had.

Ace Watson, sex god. A selfless and generous lover.

Ace Watson, perfect specimen of a man.

Tonight did *not* happen like that.

I looked over at the human equivalent of a humping puppy snoring softly next to me, a giant bicep tucked under his head like he didn't have a care in the world. The razor-sharp line of his jaw had shadowed slightly as his stubble made an appearance, but it only enhanced his beauty; smooth golden skin, taut muscles, and thick dark lashes any girl would pay big money for. Even in his sleep, his lashes fluttered against his cheek.

Those goddamn lashes.

Sigh.

I swung my feet out and padded across the hardwood floor to the bathroom in search of my favorite *'any time of day'* toy – the one I'd left in there this morning.

Closing the door, I perched on the rim of the tub and hit the button.

The soft buzzing wasn't loud enough to wake up Sleeping Beauty, but I held in the groan as I placed it right in the spot he didn't quite reach.

This was more like it.

Happy fucking birthday to me.

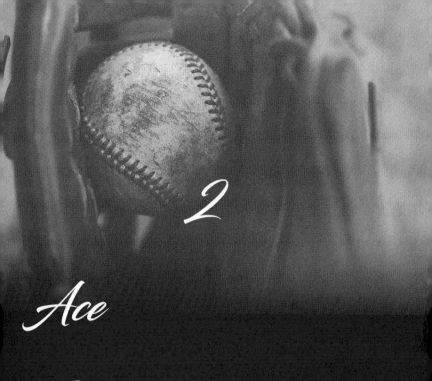

2

Ace

*M*y dick was better than any alarm clock.

I groaned loudly and stretched out of the best sleep I'd had in months. Maybe all year.

It had been one of those sleep-like-the-dead type nights where you woke up feeling like you'd been plugged into a charging station and were raring to go.

I groaned again as my muscles fired up. They were feeling the month of Spring Training in Arizona, and the exhibition game yesterday afternoon, therefore, the massage I'd had last night had been desperately needed, even if it had hurt like a motherfucker. Ivan, The Lions' head PT, took no prisoners when it came to his treatments, but it was worth it, and I always timed it right before bedtime so I could crash after.

I lengthened out and flipped onto my back, freeing my growing boner.

Huh. That's weird. There's no way my bed could h___

shrunk overnight, right? And I was done growing, so why were my feet hanging off the end?

I tapped my toes along the edge of the mattress, and reached behind my head. The wall felt different, and my headboard definitely wasn't this soft. And come to think of it, my bed didn't smell like this; almost soft and floral, like clean laundry and the dryer sheets my mom uses.

It was making me feel cozy and hungry all at the same time.

I stopped feeling around and perked my ears. Silence.

No sound of Lux banging around in the kitchen before switching on the Vitamix and waking the entire apartment.

No loud cries from Tanner or Parker fighting it out on the PlayStation.

Where the fuck was I?

I opened my eyes, immediately screwing them shut again. I hadn't expected it to be so bright.

I tried again, one at a time, easing them open carefully.

From the position I was lying, I could only see white. White ceiling, white walls, white drapes. I was covered in the thickest, softest comforter I'd ever experienced, and lying on the fluffiest, softest pillows.

This is what Heaven must be like.

Oh *shiiit*.

Have I died?

I bolted upright, my heart pounding against my ribcage, and my ears echoed with ringing brought on by my current panic.

Wait. Dead people didn't panic. They were dead.

I glanced around the room I was in; not quite as white as I originally thought, but more cream-ish, although cream was the same as white, kind of. The whole room was creamy white, except for a bright pink scrap of material flung across the chair in the far corner.

And everything came hurtling back like I'd been hit in the head with one of my own pitches, and I wasn't even sure how I'd forgotten, but I was going to blame this bed for sending me into a coma.

That girl.

Holy crap.

I'd been driving down West Fifty-Fifth on the way back from my massage, past that huge brick building across the plaza, and I'd spotted her sitting on the bench outside. She was holding a piece of cake in one hand and trying to light the candle on the top with the other, her bare legs crossed underneath her.

Her long, thick curls were blowing softly in the breeze, and I nearly swerved into one of the trees lining the sidewalk trying to get a better look.

By the time I found her standing on the curb waiting for an Uber, I'd circled the block four times. Even from fifty yards away, under the dim glow of the streetlights, she'd been hot. Up close, she was blinding.

Long legs the color of the bronco my dad started my brothers and me riding on, big brown eyes, and lips I'd be dreaming about in every future fantasy I had. It had been ten p.m. and stopping to talk to her became the highlight of my day, maybe my week.

We'd started on the couch, she'd taken that pink dress off to reveal a smoking hot body, and a pair of tits I wanted to suffocate myself with. We moved into the bedroom, and I proceeded to make her birthday wish come true, twice if I wasn't mistaken.

I'd made mine come true too, and my birthday wasn't for another four months.

Good night had by all, on my estimation.

I sat still, listening for any sounds around me, but was met again with nothing but silence.

Where the fuck was she?

I had enough experience with girls that they always wanted more in the morning, something I was only too happy to oblige, seeing as I always woke up with a boner. If I was lucky, they'd disappear to the bathroom for a freshen up, come back in new underwear for me to take off, and on more than one occasion, their roommate.

We'd go another round before I left for training with the promise to call.

I never called.

But this one? I'd be tempted to call this one.

Fuck. What was her name?

Piper… No. Patty… No. P…

"Babe?" I called out, opting for the safest route. Silence. I tried again. "Babe?"

The lack of response had an adverse effect on my boner.

I threw back the covers, spied my boxer briefs over by the chair and pulled them on.

Taking one last glance around the room to check I hadn't accidentally missed her creepily standing in the corner and watching me – also known to happen – I opened her bedroom door and peered out.

"Hello?"

Nothing. I was definitely alone.

Okay then, I guess there's a first time for everything.

I took a couple of tentative steps and stopped, just in case she suddenly burst back into the apartment. It wasn't big enough for her to be hiding anywhere, because it was just her bedroom, a small hallway, and the living room with a bookcase almost overflowing with books. I thought Lux had a lot, but this chick was housing more than I'd seen outside of a bookstore.

I took one more step, which is when I spied a sticky note taped to the archway leading into the kitchen.

Help yourself to coffee, the door locks automatically on your way out.

Payton

Payton! Yes! That's what her name was. Payton.

Pay*ton*.

I peeled the note off the wall and read it again. And again. Then just about stopped myself from frowning. Something wasn't right.

Where was the *'thanks for rocking my world'*, or *'you're the best I've ever had'*?

Where was the kiss or her phone number with the instruction to call?

Weird.

And it dawned on me I was in a girl's apartment, *alone*.

I should probably get dressed and get out, but my rumbling stomach had me heading into the kitchen instead, and she *had* told me to help myself. I flicked on the coffee machine and went in search of food. By the time I'd opened nearly all the cabinet doors, I'd discovered that Payton wasn't a chef, or showed any evidence of being able to cook.

What I did find was a bag of protein powder, a couple of jars containing random herbs, a pile of envelopes addressed to Payton Lopez, several bags of coffee beans and one of granola, plates and bowls, and in the last door I opened was a pair of shoes.

The type of shoes I'd like her to see wearing with nothing else.

The fridge was no better, bare except for a quart of two percent milk, but at least it would go fine with the granola.

I stood in front of the fridge and ate, taking in the sight before me. It was like standing in a stall of a dive bar bathroom in Atlantic City etched in phone numbers, or graffitied with shitty illustrations of a dick, and messages about Stacey's tits or who Bryony was screwing, and who fucked whose mom.

Except Payton's fridge was heaving with wedding invitations, takeout menus, postcards, notelets from friends saying they loved her, photos of her with babies, and friends, and... I leaned in closer... was that Penn Shepherd?

I put my bowl down on the counter, removed the magnet holding the photo in place while also making sure the other five items underneath it didn't fall, and looked closer.

Yes. That was definitely Penn Shepherd.

The Penn Shepherd, owner of The New York Lions. My boss.

It wasn't an official photo either, like one taken at a fundraiser where she'd met him and asked for a selfie. No, this picture had been taken on a boat, clearly on vacation. Payton was looking sexy A.F. in a black bikini, grinning straight down the lens of the camera while holding a huge Marlin, a blonde girl was standing at the other end, while in the middle were the unmistakable faces of Lowe Slater and Beulah Holmes, and all four of them looked like they were buckling under the weight of the fish.

And there, in the background, was Penn Shepherd, again grinning as wide as he had the night we'd celebrated the end of the season.

I put the photo back on the fridge and moved to the next one. Lowe, Beulah, Payton, and the blonde girl again, plus a baby and a dog. Another one clearly taken at the last game of the season; she was wearing the *I Caught a Lion* shirt, that had been all over social media. And there was one from Opening Day against the Yankees last year.

I'd never seen her at Lions Stadium; there's no way I'd have forgotten her face.

No way.

I stepped away from the fridge and picked up my coffee, sipping it in rare silence.

Who was this Payton chick? Why did it look like she was best friends with my boss?

And, most importantly, why had she snuck out of her own place and left me in bed, without wanting to go for a second round?

*T*he elevator doors opened for me to find Lux wrapped around a blonde like he was trying to resuscitate her. Or maybe she was trying to resuscitate him.

"Oh, hey, Ace," she crowed, unsticking herself from Lux's mouth as I stepped out.

"Hey."

Lux grinned as I walked past and headed down the hallway into the main room of our apartment, from where yelling was getting louder.

It only meant one thing.

"Home run, baby!" Tanner bounced onto the couch cushions, right behind where Parker was sitting and rolling his eyes. "Suck it."

"Hey," I nodded, dropping my bag on the floor and went to the kitchen in search of more food. Payton's granola hadn't cut it. "Losing again?"

"Not yet," Parker replied.

I opened the fridge and peered in. For athletes in their early twenties, it was impressively well stocked. We liked to compartmentalize according to foodstuff: rows of sports drinks and water on the top shelf; eggs and protein on the next one down, followed by vegetables and more vegetables. Lux was in charge of groceries and the delivery arrived last night, but it wasn't helping me decide what to eat.

I grabbed a Gatorade and closed the door. "Who've you got pitching?"

"You," Parker replied and grinned at me. "Wanna play?"

"Is this the new season game yet?"

He shook his head. "No, last season."

"Then no." I twisted the top off the bottle and swigged. "I refuse to partake in that game if they can't get the finer details correct."

"Dude, you can't even tell!" called Tanner, who'd resumed his position on the couch next to Parker, readying himself to send his player around the bases.

Even though he was always trying to fuck with me, I

placed the bottle down on the counter and fixed him with the same look I always did whenever this subject came up.

"I can tell, Tan. I can tell."

He rolled his eyes and went back to the game.

"Anyway…" My stomach grumbled again and I peered around the kitchen; it was usually way more untidy if breakfast had been served, so hopefully I'd made it back in time. "Did Lux make breakfast yet?"

Parker shook his head. "Nope. He was otherwise occupied."

On cue, the great chef himself returned, arms wide open. "Calm down, ladies, I'm here. Now, who wants food?"

"Fuck, yes. I'm starved," replied Tanner, throwing down his controller.

"Me too." I slid onto one of the stools at the breakfast bar as Lux tied an apron around himself – this one covered in hearts, rainbows, and unicorns.

He claimed it was his favorite.

As self-designated house chef, the boys and I had gifted it to him when we moved into our apartment at the end of last season, and every day we had breakfast together, prepared by Lux wearing that, or one of the other dozen aprons we'd bought him since. Tanner had even had one made with his naked body and a strategically placed rolling pin.

We lived on the fifty-second floor of a high rise in Midtown, right by Hudson Yards, in an apartment Tanner had named Casa Greyskull. While it might not have been the penthouse, we were high enough up the building that we had the floor to ourselves, with the elevator opening directly into our apartment. Only those with an access code could stop the elevator on our floor, something which came in handy when uninvited girls tried to slip past the concierge.

"Who was your friend?" I asked as he removed the carton

of eggs from the fridge.

"Kitten with a K."

"A K?"

"That's what she said."

"How else do you spell Kitten?"

"Dunno," he shrugged, pushing the eggs across the counter to me, along with a whisk and a bowl. "Mix these, will you?"

I cracked the eggs and got to work. I didn't bother asking if he was going to see her again, because we were all of the opinion that we would enjoy our lives while we were young enough to enjoy them, and none of us were ready to settle down.

Plus, this apartment would be wasted on a relationship.

"Where did you end up last night?" Lux pulled the waffle maker from under the stove and plugged it in.

"With a girl. Well... a lady. A woman," I replied.

Yeah. Payton was *all* woman. I could still feel her ass cheeks cupped in my palms; the perfect fit.

I couldn't see her standing along the fences at Spring Training, or waiting outside our hotel.

"A woman? Even with that slug on your face?" he grinned.

I smoothed down my moustache and winked at him. "Dude, mock all you want, but I haven't had complaints from any age group."

He grabbed a jar of flour from the cabinet and opened the drawer of spices, scanning down the rows until he found what he was looking for.

"Where d'you meet her?"

"West Fifty-Fifth."

"And you're just getting back now?"

"Yup." I pushed the bowl of eggs over the counter to him. I'd whipped those babies good.

"Nice."

"Yeah." I scratched the stubble along my jaw, thinking about the scene with Lux I'd walked in on, as I watched him mix everything together. "Get this, she was gone when I woke up. Just left me a note."

The batter sizzled as it hit the hot waffle plate, and the scent of sugar and cinnamon filled the air.

"What? She didn't even wake you up with a morning blowie?"

"Nope." I shook my head, wondering if I was overthinking it. Probably. "But that's not the weirdest part. I was making coffee, and found photos of her and the boss."

Lux opened the fridge and pulled out a packet of turkey bacon, laid each rasher out on a griddle, then placed it on the burners. "Springsteen? That's cool."

"No, Shepherd. Penn Shepherd! *Our* boss."

He spun around, looking shocked. "Penn Shepherd?"

"Beulah Holmes was in it too. And Lowe Slater. Looked like they were best friends or something."

Parker pulled out a stool and sat down next to me. "What are you saying about Beulah? You haven't been to see her again, have you? She's gonna ban you from the exec floor if you're not careful."

"What? She's not going to do that," I scoffed with a frown because no one would take me seriously, and it was beginning to piss me off, "but no, there was a photo of her with this girl I hooked up with. Woman, I mean."

"What?"

"I hooked up with a girl last night and found a photo of

her, Beulah, and Lowe this morning."

"And Shepherd," added Lux, as he poured the eggs into another pan.

"You were snooping in a girl's apartment?"

"Don't say it like you wouldn't do the same. It was on the fridge. I was grabbing cereal, and saw it."

"Who was she?"

I shrugged. "I dunno. Her name was Payton."

"Who was who?" asked Tanner as he joined us at the counter, pouring himself a glass of milk like he was ten years old.

I got up and turned on the coffee machine, nodding to Lux, and grabbed four cups. "You tell it."

"Ace hooked up with a girl, and she's friends with Shepherd," he replied, laying the bacon onto a plate while Parker pulled out cutlery and glasses, pouring out juice for the four of us.

"Oh, nice," Tanner responded, holding his fist in front of me for a bump, to which I obliged. "Was she hot?"

"Yeah," I sighed. "Smoking."

"Did she get a one-way ticket on the Poundtown Express again this morning?"

I shook my head. "No. She left before I woke up."

Tanner reached for a slice of bacon Lux had just removed from the griddle, and dropped it because it was too hot. He tried again, blowing hard before he managed to successfully crunch down on it. "Huh. That's why you're in a mood."

"I'm not in a mood."

What is it about someone telling you you're in a mood, that puts you in a mood?

I wasn't in a mood. I might not be in my usual joking mood, but I wasn't in a *mood* mood. I was thinking about Payton, and why she hadn't been there when I'd woken up – or why she hadn't woken me up.

Because the more I thought about it, the more I thought it was really fucking weird.

It didn't help that right then Tanner voiced the exact conclusion I'd been trying not to come to.

"Maybe she didn't have a good time."

"What? What're you talking about? Of course, she did," I scoffed. "They always have a good time."

Parker leaned over and slung his arm around me like the supportive best friend he was.

"Hey, leave him alone. Of course he showed her a good time. He's Ace Watson. Girls line the streets to have a good time with him." He squeezed my face between his fingers just like my grandma did. "Look at these cheeks. How can anyone resist?"

I pushed him away. "Okay, you've made your very accurate point, and I thank you."

But Tanner shrugged. "All I'm saying is if a girl has a good time, they don't leave the next morning. Right, Lux?"

I picked up a wooden spoon Lux had left on the counter, threw it at him, and looked around for what I could use next. "Tan, what are you doing? Are you trying to hurt me?"

Tanner's grin widened, because that was exactly what he was trying to do. Not hurt me, just wind me up enough to get me in a mood.

Mission fucking accomplished.

The four of us liked to fuck with each other as much as possible, and this was likely payback for the plastic spider I put in his bed yesterday, the one left over from Halloween.

Man, I nearly pissed myself laughing when I heard him screaming.

"What did the note say?" asked Lux.

I held my mouth in a straight line before answering. "It said, 'help yourself to coffee'."

Tanner coughed into his milk, spraying himself with it. Served him right.

"Oh, fuck off."

"Is the great Ace Watson losing his touch with the ladies?" he grinned, picking up a paper towel to wipe himself dry.

"No, I'm fucking not!"

"If only there was a chance to ask her so we could settle the debate."

"Well, there isn't. She didn't leave me her number." I took the plate Lux was holding out and loaded it up with scrambled eggs, waffles, and bacon. "And there isn't a debate. She had a great time; I'd know if she didn't."

"You said she's besties with Penn Shepherd, so maybe she'll be at the charity thing tomorrow. You can ask her then," Parker added.

Maybe he wasn't my best friend after all, especially with that shit-stirring grin he was wearing.

"Maybe we'll all ask her," smirked Tanner, throwing his head back in a guffaw as I snarled at him.

"If she's there I'll ask her, and the three of you aren't going anywhere near her."

"We'll see about that," he shot back. "Now eat up. We have to be at the ground in two hours, and I can't be late for batting practice."

But I wasn't listening.

My mind was firmly back on Payton, and the chance that I might see her again.

Not to mention the added task of keeping these three morons away from her.

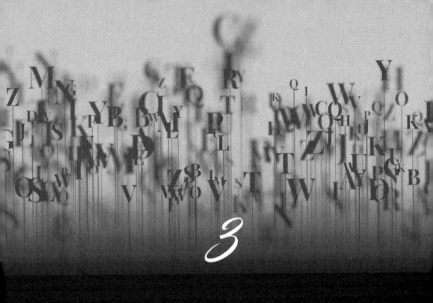

3

Payton

"Excited about seeing your new boyfriend?" snorted Murray, as I climbed into the back of the Range Rover and settled into my seat.

My head snapped around to Kit, my newly former best friend, and I pinned her with my hardest glare. It was a look I'd perfected over the years. It usually resulted in the recipient combusting into a fiery flame, but she'd known me too long and it didn't have the desired effect. She just shrugged and only looked marginally guilty.

"Sorry, I couldn't help it. Murray made me tell him." She held her hands up in defense.

"How? How did he even know you had something to tell?"

Her mouth held in a straight line, keeping up with the guilty expression as best she could, as Murray's driver hit the gas and drove us away.

"I got home right after you told me, and he could tell I had juicy gossip. He forced me."

I rolled my eyes. I wasn't about to ask *how* he forced her. I didn't need any details about their sex life before I'd had a drink, because I knew it involved sex.

"So..." Murray continued, waggling his thick eyebrows at me. "Ace Watson. I've heard he has excellent pitching skills."

"If you're talking about his *actual* pitching skills, then yes."

"Did he let you touch his bat? Did he get a home run?"

"Jesus," I muttered, as Murray snorted loudly and threw his head back with a loud laugh.

"Does that mean it was hard and fast?"

I nudged Kit. "Make him stop. I can't take a whole car ride of this."

"No way," Murray interrupted before Kit could speak. "This is what baseball was made for. Come on, did he show you his curve ball?"

I forced myself not to grin at the expression on his face, the one that said he was inordinately pleased with himself.

"Murray, leave her alone," Kit warned, though I didn't fail to notice the smirk she was wearing as she did.

"I can't believe you told the blabbermouth. You two are as bad as each other," I grumbled as we surged through the set of lights into the next block of traffic.

"Sorry," Kit replied, not sounding the least bit sorry.

"Please tell me you haven't told anyone else." I pinned Murray with the look I'd tried on Kit, to see if it was more effective.

It wasn't.

He grinned at me; a grin that spread wider the longer he held my stare. A grin that was making me seriously want to punch him, until he shook his head. "I haven't told Penn yet, if that's what you mean."

I breathed a sigh of relief. Penn Shepherd was one of Murray's best friends. While I normally wouldn't care about him knowing anything to do with my personal life, when it came to his players, I wasn't entirely sure how he'd react to me sleeping with one of them, especially his Boy Wonder.

I'd likely be hauled over hot coals for causing a distraction, or something equally dumb.

"Thank you. Let's keep it that way, please."

"What's it worth?"

"I'm your child's godmother. It's worth that," I shot back.

Kit kicked him lightly with the end of her shoe. "Murray, stop teasing her."

"Thank you." I smiled at Kit gratefully, even though she was the cause of this in the first place.

But Murray wasn't done. "When are you going to see him again?"

"I'm not. It was a one-time thing."

He clasped his hands to his chest dramatically. "Ah, classic Payton, leaving broken hearts all over the city."

"I doubt that, and we're talking about *Ace Watson*."

"Don't be so hard on yourself, no one can forget you so easily. I'm sure he's been counting the hours until he gets to see you again today."

I rolled my eyes, wishing this lunch hadn't completely slipped my mind until this morning. Or rather who'd likely be on the invite list. "He might not even be there."

Murray stared at me like I'd grown an extra head. "Payton,

it's a lunch for The Lions. He'll be there."

"Well, there's no way he'll know I'm coming, and knowing Penn, he's invited half of New York anyway, so it'll be easy to avoid him." I turned to Kit as she started laughing. "What's so funny?"

"You're probably the only girl in the United States who wouldn't want another night with Ace Watson."

I shrugged mindlessly and turned to stare out of the window, gazing at the Hudson as we headed up Riverside Drive to The Lions ground where Penn's lunch was being held. It was true; I didn't. Maybe if the first time around hadn't been so... anti-climactic as it were... then I'd be tempted if the opportunity arose.

But it had been, so I wasn't.

Truth be told, one-night-stands weren't exactly my style, but they did add a level of convenience, not to mention they scratched an itch that anything in my toy chest couldn't.

Most of the time anyway.

Usually I liked to date; flicking through *Hinge* or *Bumble* or *Tinder* like other people played *Candy Crush*, but for what might have been a first for me, I wasn't currently dating anyone. It was something I needed to rectify immediately. I loved dating. I loved that first little buzz in the pit of your belly when you met someone hot; the butterflies; the sparks of excitement zipping up and down your spine right before you kissed, and boy did I love kissing.

As adults, I don't think we fully appreciate how awesome kissing is if done well, because we're all too busy rushing to get naked. But you can take so much from a good kiss done properly; the neediness, the yearning, the '*I've got to have you now*' feeling. It's a beginning filled with potential, promise and hope, where you can live in the fantasy of what if...

The best bit? It's easy to move on before anyone catches feelings, and New York City was built for dating. There's someone new around every corner.

I pulled the compact from my purse and checked my lipstick. Yeah, I'm sure I could find a new date over the next few hours, so maybe Penn's lunch wouldn't be a total bust.

"Oh good, we're here," Murray said with a dramatic clap of his hands.

I glanced up to find that we had indeed arrived at Lions Stadium, though more accurately, we'd stopped in the line of cars waiting to get past security. Fifty yards away, giant black and gold balloons – the official colors of The New York Lions – adorned the grand arch of stone lions at the entrance to the grounds. Huge flags with The Lions official logo flapped at the top of the posts lining the fences, and two Lionel the Lion mascots were working the crowds, taking selfies and handing out Lions merch.

The car inched forward.

"Penn really goes all out, doesn't he?"

"Yeah. Just wait until we get inside," Kit grinned. "I read The Mets and The Yankees have doubled their marketing budgets just to keep up with him. Someone needs to tell them they'll never win."

Peering out of the window again, I realized the crowds of people lining the outside – the ones I'd thought had arrived on foot – were actually Lions fans waiting to spot guests as they arrived. Posters, banners, and flags were being waved. Homemade cards, little kids holding out baseballs and bats to be signed by any of the passing players, and... I squinted for a better look... a large contingent of girls waiting for The Fab Four - Ace, Parker, Tanner, and Lux - all screaming their names.

Murray raised an eyebrow. "Looks like you've got some competition there, Pay. Your boy, Ace, sure is popular."

"Hey," I returned his grin with a wink, "they're welcome to him. I've thrown him back into the ocean."

"How generous of you."

"What can I say? That's just who I am."

Murray lowered the window as we arrived at the security gates, handed over three embossed gold and black invitations he'd been holding, and a second later, we were waved through.

My mouth dropped. "Jeez."

Kit had been correct; the place looked spectacular. I'd only ever been here on game days, and then the grounds looked great, but today it was something else. We slowly made our way down toward Lions Boulevard which looped the stadium, all the cars in front of us bumper to bumper as everyone was looking out of their windows. The usual Lion shaped hedges and flower beds lining the pathways had been sprayed gold, and glinted in the sunlight. The lampposts were shining with a fresh coat of glossy black paint, at the top of which flew a different flag displaying one member of the team – Jupiter Reeves, Stone Fields, Boomer Jones, Sawyer James, Tanner, Parker, Lux... And there, last in line, was Ace.

Even printed on a flag his face was ridiculously good looking, and that included the stupid pornstache. It was as though God himself had tested his jaw line with a spirit-level for straightness, and his cheeks bones had been freshly chiseled. His light brown hair curled under the rim of his ball cap, and for a second, I remembered how soft it had been to run my fingers through.

He really was a fine, *fine* specimen.

I chuckled to myself; it was clear the marketing team had been under instructions to get his eye color correct, and the bright blue seemed to follow me as we passed by. I could almost feel them boring into me.

I didn't dare turn around in case I found him staring.

Kit nudged me, her lips brushing my ear. "Sure you don't want another night?"

"Quite sure, thank you."

Finally, the car pulled to a stop in front of the stadium entrance, and the doors were opened. Murray hopped out of the far side, and ran around to Kit on the other to take her hand, and I followed.

"I'm going to find the boys. Can I trust you two to stay out of trouble?"

He smacked a kiss to Kit's cheek and took off to meet his friends before we could object.

Kit turned to me. "I guess that makes it you and me. Let's go and find the bar."

"And food, I'm starving."

She looped her arm in mine. "Lead the way."

I glanced around where the car had dropped us off; I wasn't exactly sure where 'the way' was. Even though I'd been joking, it was possible Penn had invited half of New York; we didn't arrive late, and there were already hundreds and hundreds of people wandering around the stadium grounds.

From where Kit and I were still standing, I could see several Official Lions tour guides taking small groups of people around the grounds, giving them all a run down on the Lions' history, and allowing them access to areas of the park usually blocked off to visitors. Set back from Lions Boulevard on the wide stretches of grass, were food trucks serving anything from burgers and fried chicken to lobster rolls and pizza slices, side by side with pop-up bars of Lions IPA and glasses of champagne, plus wait staff passing around trays of drinks.

Kids were lined up for face painters, Lions balloons were being handed out by clowns, and bubbles floated in the air.

It was like the circus had come to town.

"Hey," Kit pointed over to one of the drinks stands, "There's Beulah and Lowe."

They hadn't been far away, yet it still took a couple of minutes to reach them due to the crowds we had to weave in and out of.

"Hey, girls," Lowe greeted, waving her hand in the air as she spotted us. "You made it."

"Yeah, just," I laughed as I hugged her hello. "This place looks awesome. Has your team done it?"

"My team and events. Looks good, right?" she grinned, then let out a wide yawn. "Sorry, Penn's been here since six a.m. making sure everything was right, and I wasn't allowed to stay in bed."

It surprised none of us.

"How many people have been invited?" asked Kit.

"About two thousand I think."

Two thousand might have sounded like a lot, but on game days, tens of thousands of people filed through the stone archway to see the boys play. At the weekends, those who didn't have tickets to the stadium could come and watch on big screens set up on the grass.

In comparison, today was surprisingly intimate.

"Are you two working?"

"Officially, we're networking," Beulah air-quoted, and we all knew what that meant, especially when she stopped a passing waiter with a tray full of drinks and relieved him of four glasses.

"This is my kind of networking." I lifted the glass to my lips and grinned.

"Where's Marnie?" Kit asked.

"She's with Penn somewhere I think," Lowe replied. "He's got her doing demonstrations of the new uniform."

"Rather her than me," she laughed.

Marnie, more formerly known as Doctor Marnie Matthews *PhD,* was a new girlfriend of ours. She'd moved to New York last year after Penn persuaded her to leave her job at N.A.S.A. and come to help him build a winning team. She'd done exactly that. Overnight, she'd created a formula which transformed the players and how they functioned on a daily basis, which in turn made them more efficient players, and The Lions quickly moved up the standings… something like that anyway.

I could never quite follow when she tried to explain it, because Marnie was a super brain and I was not. However, it kept her busy and she was almost as eager to get the boys to the World Series than Penn was – *almost* – therefore, we rarely saw her.

"So, is the team here?" asked Kit in a tone that was far too innocent to fool anyone.

Me, at least. Beulah and Lowe hadn't seemed to notice.

"Yeah, they're all on the field for official photos, then they'll be walking around the grounds. Penn wants them taking selfies with everyone before the season starts."

I stopped myself from stiffening next to her and let out small sigh of relief. There were so many people it was unlikely I'd see Ace, and by the sounds of it, he'd be too busy anyway. Before I could think any more about why I cared, I noticed a guy taking an order of fried chicken, and my stomach grumbled.

"Okay, I'm hungry. Who wants food?"

"Ooh I tried the chicken earlier, it's good. I'm going for the burger next," Beulah replied. "Let's go."

We joined the line, and from the looks of it, everyone else decided on fried chicken and burgers at the same time we had. Thankfully we were at the front of the crowds and not the back.

"Are you guys set for Opening Day? Who's it against?" asked Kit.

"Phillies away. Wanna come? Beulah and I will fly back after the game, you can come with us."

I shook my head. "No, thanks. I'm limiting myself to home games only this year."

"Sensible," Lowe replied, as she stepped up to place our orders, just as my stomach grumbled again.

I should have had breakfast.

She was handing around our food when her eyes focused on something behind me, making her smile. "Photos must be done. Here comes trouble."

I wish I hadn't been stuffing a piece of fried chicken into my mouth as I turned, because the boys weren't only done with their photos, they were making their way over to where the four of us were standing. And the trouble she'd been referring to was exactly the trouble I'd wanted to stay out of.

The future of The Lions – Lux, Tanner, Parker, and Ace – were about to grace us with their presence, and there was nowhere I could hide.

I saw it the split-second Ace recognized me, and his step paused as a grin spread across his all-too-handsome face, one that definitely spelled trouble. It was the same grin he'd given me two nights ago.

"Hey, Payton, long time no see."

Every head except Kit's whipped around to me, then back to Ace. Beulah and Lowe looked confused, while three pairs of eyes belonging to the boys all widened, followed by a smirk, that told me they knew exactly who I was.

Great.

Lowe frowned. "Do you two know each other?"

"No," I replied at the same time Ace said, "Yes."

"No," I repeated firmly. "We just met one time."

Jesus, I was lame.

Even if one of the boys hadn't coughed some indiscernible word into his fist, it was clear I was lying, especially when Ace raised an eyebrow at me.

The eight of us stood there in awkward silence, until thankfully, Beulah broke it.

"Did you boys need something? Or were you coming to say hi?"

"Came to see if you wanted a selfie," Tanner grinned, making everyone laugh except me, because while I was looking at Beulah, all I could feel were Ace's eyes on me, boring into me like lasers. "Nah. Actually, Mr. Shepherd's looking for you both. We said we were heading out to the grounds and he asked us to find you. He said you're not answering your phones."

Beulah rolled her eyes. "Where is he?"

"On the field."

"Thanks, we'll go and find him."

I turned to Kit and handed her my cardboard box of fried chicken. "Can you hold this for me? I need to go to the bathroom."

"Sure," she replied with a broad grin I pursed my lips at,

and took off as fast as my shoes would let me.

"Payton! Wait up!"

I groaned quietly at the deep voice behind me. I should have kept to the safety in numbers, as I turned to see Ace jog slowly toward me and stop.

"Hey, what's up?"

"What's up?" He frowned slightly, thrusting his hands into the pockets of his trackpants. I tried not to stare at the way it made his Lions shirt stretch wide across his chest, or the way his massive biceps flexed.

"Yeah," I took another step. "What's up?"

"I guess I wanted to say hi, and tell you I had a good time the other night."

"Oh, me too," I smiled, letting out the breath I'd been holding as I tried my best to sound as sincere as I felt, because there were certainly worse ways to end an evening than wrapped around a professional baseball player, especially one who looked like Ace.

But you know what they say? Never meet your celebrity crush… or something along those lines.

"Yeah?" he asked, pinning me with those big blue eyes. Up close in broad daylight they were so much brighter, hypnotic almost, and I forced myself to blink before I fell into a trance. "Then how come you left me alone?"

It took me a second to register his words before I burst out laughing. "Because I had to go to work."

"Oh." His shoulders relaxed slightly. "You could have woken me up. I'd have sent you off with a smile."

"Oh… well, you know… I was in a hurry."

His gaze narrowed at me, and I'd be willing to bet all of Penn's billions that Ace was currently in a situation he'd never been in before.

He shifted his feet. "Payton, did you not have a good time with me?"

"Yes," I replied, slowly. "I told you I did."

"Oh, okay. That's good. Good." His head bobbed with his words. It was odd; someone who was usually so brimming with over-confidence he could share it around the entire team and still have enough to spare, was now looking nothing short of nervous. But then he grinned, so maybe he wasn't that nervous. "What're you doing after this? I'll give you a ride home; your place is close to mine."

"Oh. Um… I can't," I started, thumbing in the direction we'd come from. "Sorry, I have plans with the girls."

Ace blinked at me, like he didn't quite understand what was happening. He eased his hand around to the back of his neck and tugged, trying to ease whatever tension had settled. It didn't ease any tension in my own neck however, and I had a feeling this conversation was going to go exactly down the route I didn't want to go.

Running away would have been an option if I'd been wearing the right footwear.

Ace turned his head to the collective group of our friends, all of whom were staring at us. Lowe and Beulah were still wearing confused expressions, while the boys all looked vaguely amused, none more so than Tanner Simpson.

"Okay, look, I'll be straight with you," Ace began. "I told the guys you left me in the apartment, and they've all been joking it's because I didn't show you a good time… and I guess it went to my head. But you said you had a good time, so that's that."

"Yes, Ace. We had fun."

"Right, but you had a good time. You," he pointed to me,

just in case I didn't know who he was talking about. His brows shot up urging me to grasp what he was talking about; except I wasn't quite sure. In the end, he lowered his voice to really make sure I understood, almost at a whisper. "I made you come. You came."

Maybe I could take my shoes off and make a sprint for the bathroom.

"Payton?" Ace snapped, pulling me away from the escape plan I was hatching. "Answer me."

Judging from the look on his face, it probably wasn't the time to tell him he hadn't *asked* me a question. "Huh? What did you say?"

"Did you come?" he hissed.

I chewed on my cheek, then stopped. This was stupid, Ace was a big boy, he could take the truth.

"Actually, no."

"What?" His eyes bulged. Maybe he *couldn't* take it. "You did."

My brows dropped. "No, I didn't."

He grabbed my arm and pulled me nearer the stadium wall, out of the way of passers-by who were starting to gawp. More importantly, it was further away from our friends who were gawping the most.

"You faked it?"

"I faked nothing," I scoffed.

"You were moaning!" he shot back.

"That doesn't mean I orgasmed!"

His face froze like he'd just woken from a coma to the news he'd missed the last five years of his life. Or like he was now questioning every sexual encounter he'd ever had, though we'd be here all night if that were the case, and I didn't have that kind of time.

"Why didn't you say anything?"

"You seemed too focused on yourself, and then you fell asleep."

His mouth opened and closed, reminding me of the goldfish I had as a kid – the one my parents gave me before they told me they were getting a divorce. It used to swim round and round the bowl with its mouth wide open, until one day, I came home to find it floating on top of the water.

Fucking goldfish.

"So that's why you snuck out. I knew you were lying."

"Okay, enough." My arms crossed over my chest. Ace Watson was beginning to seriously annoy me, even more so when his eyes tracked the movement my tits made. "I didn't lie. I left for work, but I'm not going to apologize if your ego wants to take it as rejection. I tried to wake you up, but you may as well have been dead for all the good it did."

It was true, I'd tried.

He'd slept through my shower, the hairdryer, the grinding of the coffee, and several prods to his arm before I gave up and left. If I'd been strong enough to drag him out of bed, I would have.

"I can't believe this! There's no way!" He stared at me, waiting to see if I broke into a grin, or told him I was only joking... Or that he was in fact the God's gift in bed he'd always been told he was.

But I held firm, even when he linked his hands behind his head and began pacing back and forth. Thirty seconds later, he stopped in front of me again.

"Okay, give me another chance," he demanded, like he was seconds away from stomping his foot the way my goddaughter, Bell, was starting to do when she didn't get what she wanted. But from a two-year-old girl it was cute, from a twenty – whatever he was – man, it was borderline comical, not to mention ridiculous.

"For what?"

He looked around, making double sure no one was listening, then back to me with more sincerity than I'd ever seen on anyone before. "To give you an orgasm."

Every muscle in my face tensed and scrunched while I tried to figure out if he was being serious, which all evidence seemed to point toward. I also had to check my own sanity, because I couldn't imagine in what world I'd be standing in front of this seemingly perfect specimen while he begged me to have sex, and I said no.

Oh, wait, it was this world.

"I don't think so."

"Payton…"

But I stopped him before he could beg again, telling myself I was saving him a shred of dignity. I reached out to pat his arm reassuringly, but then stopped myself. This situation was awkward enough as it was.

"Hey, it's really not a big deal. It happens plenty."

"Not to me it doesn't."

"Sure about that?" I smirked, trying to lighten the situation before realizing Ace did not consider it a laughing matter, but this conversation was becoming too stupid for words.

"What's that supposed to mean?"

"What?"

"That comment. Are you saying I've never given an orgasm?"

"No. Noooo, of course not. All I'm saying is… oh never mind." I didn't actually know what I was saying, and more importantly, I really needed to get out of this hole I seemed to be digging. I was definitely not wearing the right footwear for *that*. "Ace, just forget it. We had fun and you're a nice guy, I'm just not interested in a second go around. No big deal."

He muttered something under his breath I didn't catch, and wasn't about to ask.

I thumbed behind me and forced a smile. "I really need to go to the bathroom now. Good luck this season."

He didn't reply, just deepened his scowl and watched me walk away. He was still standing there when I turned around the second time. I might have ended the conversation, but from the look on his face, I had the distinct feeling it wasn't over.

Therefore, I would be hiding in the bathroom for the rest of the afternoon like a mature adult.

4

Ace

I threw a t-shirt into my gym bag; a pair of jeans followed, then a hoodie and my favorite Air Jordans.

The bedroom door clattered against the wall as I opened it with all the annoyance coursing through my body, and marched into the kitchen.

Parker was sitting at the breakfast counter, one eyebrow raised as he watched me dump my bag on the floor and open the fridge. He was still watching as I gulped down half the bottle of Gatorade I'd opened.

"What?" I snapped.

He shook his head, his mouth turning down. "Nothing."

"Why are you up so early?"

"Why are *you* up so early?"

"Couldn't sleep," I shrugged. "Gonna get a workout in before the team meeting."

"Great!" His stool screeched along the floor as he pushed out of it with far too much enthusiasm for my liking. "I'll come too."

My eyes narrowed, because out of the four of us who lived in the apartment, Parker was the one least likely to get up early for a workout. Even him being in the kitchen first was enough to raise suspicion, but whatever. If anyone had to be in the kitchen this morning, I'd go with Parker every single time.

Like most of the players when Penn Shepherd had rebuilt The Lions, we hadn't known each other well before we were all thrown together as a team, but Parker and I had immediately formed a bond it took some guys years to find. He'd already been playing for The Lions, and had finished his first season as catcher, having moved up from the minors the year before. As luck would have it, The Lions' previous starting pitcher was an asshole, and got traded out to make room for yours truly – and so was born one of the best pitcher/catcher relationships currently in the M.L.B., according to several sports journalists who said we were our way to rival Lefty Grove and Mickey Cochrane.

Even though we'd only played together for one season, it was like we'd been playing together forever. Our game was instinctive. Parker and I knew each other; we understood each other, and we trusted each other.

What's more, after The Lions' marketing juggernaut had us appearing on every talk show and magazine spread, New York loved us.

Like *really* loved us. Heart eyes and everything.

"Okay, let's go."

He snatched up his car keys from the old baseball glove we kept them in. "I'll drive."

We rode the elevator down to the parking garage in silence, neither of us looking at each other. At least I didn't think he was looking at me, but I was looking at the floor so I couldn't quite tell. The only thing I knew for certain was that Parker was biding his time, and as soon as we got in the car, he'd start talking.

A hundred bucks said it was about my behavior yesterday, which meant I had approximately ninety seconds to figure out how to answer.

The elevator dinged as we reached the lower ground floor. Parker's black Escalade was parked next to my G-Wagon, which I was very tempted to jump into, but I stepped up into his passenger seat instead and prepared myself for the inquisition.

We made it out of the building and through the first set of lights before he turned to me.

"Well?"

"Well, what?"

"Are you going to tell me what happened between you and that chick yesterday?"

Yep. Hundred bucks to me.

Unfortunately, it still hadn't been long enough for me to figure out how to explain the entire humiliating situation without further humiliation. I was only thankful Tanner wasn't here too.

"There's nothing to tell."

"Then explain why you've been in a mood since she disappeared into the bathroom yesterday afternoon, and why the second we got released from the gala you took off for home, and this is the first time I've seen you since?"

"I was tired."

"Bullshit. What did she say to you?"

I pulled at the wrapper around my Gatorade bottle and began shredding it, anything to buy me some time instead of admitting the truth. The truth that I'd rushed home as soon as I could, flopped on my bed like a sulky teenager, and proceeded to wrack my brains for every girl I'd ever met, while Payton's words flashed in my head like one of those giant neon highway signs telling you to watch your speed.

The problem was, I couldn't remember every girl.

The ones I could remember seemed to have a good time, but I thought Payton had too. So now I didn't know what to think. If I'd kept the number of every girl I'd slept with, I would have spent the night calling them… but I never kept their numbers, so I couldn't.

"She didn't say anything. Why do you care?"

He turned left before we hit Lincoln Square, heading toward Riverside Drive, but we found ourselves in another block of traffic. So much for getting up early, or in my case, tossing and turning all night until I gave up trying to sleep.

"Because you're acting weird. Plus…" Parker shot me a side eye, "you're my best friend. So until you tell me, I'm gonna keep driving."

Of the two of us, I was the talker while Parker was the one who sat back and observed, just like he was doing now, except we were clearly in some kind of Freaky Friday situation this morning because he wouldn't shut up. I groaned, tugging down my ballcap so I could hide my face as much as possible; this would be easier if he couldn't see me.

"Park, do you think you can tell if a girl is faking it during sex?"

Out of my periphery he paused for a second, drumming his fingers along the steering wheel as he thought about it.

One. Two. Three. Four. Five.

One. Two. Three. Four. Five.

"Yes," he answered finally.

I sunk a little further into my seat. Of course he did.

"Yeah, well…" I huffed, "so did I. But then Payton said she didn't come the other night, and she also didn't fake it. And it's making me question everything. Like, if someone's always faked it, how do you know what's real?"

To give him credit, he didn't laugh when I probably would have, and looking at him now, he seemed to be taking my predicament as seriously as I was.

Because that's exactly what it was. A predicament.

"Fuck man, I dunno. Shit."

"What if there are girls going around the city talking shit about us?"

This time he laughed. "They're not."

I spun my whole body in the seat, and nearly strangled myself with my seatbelt in the process. "Parker, they could be. You don't know that."

"Ace…"

"All I'm saying is that everything I thought I knew about women has turned out to be a lie, and something I thought I was really good at now isn't the case."

"You're so dramatic." He rolled his eyes and began laughing way harder than necessary. Hard enough that it was clear he wasn't taking me seriously, so I stared at him in the hopes it was enough to convince him I wasn't kidding. It didn't work. "Dude, please don't tell me this is why you're in a mood."

"Well…"

"Oh, man. Seriously, Ace? Has she really gotten to you that much?"

"Hey!" I protested. "You don't know that it's not the same for you."

He was silent as we drove through the next block, and I glanced out of the window. We'd almost reached Riverside Park. The leaves were thickening on the trees lining the paths surrounding it, and the blossoms were starting to make an appearance. In the distance, boats were sailing up the Hudson toward the George Washington Bridge on the way to who knows where.

"I do know," he said eventually.

"Yeah? How?"

"Because…" he stopped and thought again. "I just know."

"Yeah," I scoffed, turning back to the window, "so did I."

He tutted loudly and muttered something under his breath, though it sounded a lot like 'fuck's sake', "Why d'you care what one girl thinks?"

"I dunno," I shrugged, adjusting my cap again. "Maybe because… what if I'm not that good? What if I'm not the best?"

He shot me a quick side eye before focusing back on the road, with a frown. "Are we still talking about sex?"

"Yes. No. Generally, in general, everything. What if I'm not as good as I thought I was at anything? What if I'm not good at pitching?"

"Jesus Christ. How did we get from sex to pitching? How are you questioning your pitching? The stats speak for themselves. You had a 2.98 ERA over thirty-two starts last year."

"Yeah," I grumbled. Normally hearing my stats made me feel all warm inside, but not today. Not today. "I guess."

"Ace, dude, I'm telling you, you're one of the best pitchers, and the pair of us together will be unstoppable this season. Don't let some girl get in your head because she didn't have a good time. Plus, you forget that my bedroom is next to yours. I've heard them. They're having a good time." From his tone, I could tell Parker was beginning to lose his patience, and he was no longer finding me amusing – but I hadn't found this amusing, period. "Fucking Tanner, this is his fault. He should never have put this in your head. You would never have asked her if it hadn't been for him."

I didn't reply; mostly because he was right, but also because there was nothing to say. And I was done talking about it.

"It's Opening Day tomorrow, and you really need your head in the game," he added unhelpfully.

"I know it is. Can we stop fucking talking about it now please?"

"You're gonna forget about whatever that girl said?"

"Payton. Her name's Payton."

"I don't fucking care." He let go of the steering wheel and threw his hands up. "Just ignore it. Ignore her. Forget everything that happened yesterday."

"Alright!" I snapped, and went back to my sulk.

We continued in silence, though every thirty seconds or so Parker turned to look at me, while I was trying to understand why it had bothered me so much, why *she* – Payton – was bothering me so much. It was like I could almost feel her slipping under my skin, uninvited and unwanted.

Parker drove past the stone arch of lions where lines were already forming for the first stadium tour of the day, or entry into the official Lions store which opened at nine a.m., and continued along the road until we reached the players' entrance. There were no lines formed here yet.

As the season didn't start until tomorrow it was quieter

than usual, save for a small group of girls along one side of the barricades holding up Jupiter Reeves posters, and a family with kids on the other. But on game days, it would be six rows thick with fans, while the overspill would stretch along the outer walls to the Hudson.

We both saluted to Joe, the security guard on duty today, and drove through to the parking lot. The second Parker cut the engine, he turned to me.

"Dude, you gonna be okay?"

"You're the one making a bigger deal about this than me," I grumbled.

"Okay." He held his hands up in defense. "I'm done talking. Now, can we go inside, workout, then meet with the coaches while you rest this bad boy for tomorrow?" he asked and punched me lightly on my pitching arm.

I pushed the car door open, and grabbed my bag. "Fuck, yes."

"Good morning, fellas," greeted Pablo, the guard on the desk. "All ready for the big day tomorrow?"

"Sure are, man," Parker grinned in reply, slinging his arm around me as he did and making sure we walked as quickly as possible past Pablo before he saw the look on my face – or struck up a conversation where I'd spill my woes, and bum out another person as much as I'd bummed out Parker.

He needn't worry, I had no plans to spill my woes or humiliate myself to anyone else.

"That's what I like to hear. Have a good one, boys."

"Thanks, Pabs," Parker called behind him as I shrugged his arm off my shoulder.

Instead of rushing us down the hallway as he'd done to get us through reception, he slowed our steps on the approach to the training facility.

As one, we flung open the swinging doors that lead down to the locker rooms; Parker on the right, me on the left, both of us pretending we were John Wayne.

We did it every single time we passed through here.

I shot him a wry smile.

"There he finally is."

I stopped in front of the fridges lined along the walls of the locker rooms. "Want a water?"

"Yes," he replied, catching the bottle I threw to him. "Thanks."

"You wanna hit the treadmill, then weights?"

"Yeah, sounds good. Remind me to book a session with the PT too, my glutes are still feeling it from last week."

"Sure."

We walked through the locker rooms together, past the couches with TVs set up for video games, past the fully stacked poker table, and past the quiet space in the corner where we could nap if we wanted to, until we reached our lockers. I opened mine and pulled out the fresh gym clothes that had been left for me.

Penn Shepherd had made sure we wanted for nothing when it came to our training – our uniform was new every game, along with our training clothes every time we used the facilities, thanks to his healthy budget and our sponsorship deals.

The locker rooms – including the gym, the pool, the rehab and conditioning suites – were better than any five-star hotel, with a service to match. We were strictly banned from bringing our personal laundry here however, I knew because I'd gotten caught doing it last season. Then an email was sent around to the entire club to reiterate.

I caught a movement in the corner of my eye, and I glanced around to see The Lions third baseman – the great Jupiter Reeves himself – walk through the wide doorway.

While I had only recently started my career in the major leagues, Jupiter was nearing the end. As a kid, I'd never missed a Dodgers game just so I could see him play, witness him smash out one home run after another. I'd wanted to become a baseball player because of him. Even the day I'd been drafted by the Yankees had been bittersweet because it meant I wouldn't get to play with him.

Jupiter Reeves was a goddamn GOAT.

I nodded 'hey' and went back to getting dressed.

"Okay, what's up?"

I pulled my sneakers back on and didn't pay any attention to whatever conversation Jupiter Reeves was having, with whomever he was having it.

He threw his bag into his locker. "Watson?"

"Eh?" My head shot up. "What?

"I've been in here thirty seconds, and you haven't said a word. Normally that would be enough time for you to give me a complete rundown of your evening, and who you'd hooked up with."

I blinked at him. "What?"

"Where's chatty Cathy today?" he asked, switching out his trackpants with gym shorts. "Come on, get it out now so we can all train in peace."

And just like that, my mood returned. I pulled my laces so tight I almost cut off the blood supply to my foot.

"What's with you, Reeves?" I snapped, and shot to standing. "Either I talk too much, or I don't talk enough. Make your fucking mind up."

Jupiter's eyes widened, likely in shock that I'd spoken to him like that, as both a senior member of the team who garnered more respect than I'd just shown, and as a guy I usually hero worshiped.

I turned to Parker, who was also staring at me with wide eyes. "I've changed my mind. I'm going for a run."

Snatching up my headphones, I stormed out of the locker room.

"What's up with him?"

"It's a long story," I heard Parker sigh as the door nearly smacked me in the face from the force I'd used to swing it open.

After stopping to loosen my laces, I took off in a dead sprint. Wearing shades with my hat pulled low, I was going fast enough that no one noticed me as I passed through the pedestrian gates to the Lions ground, and headed along the boardwalk.

The sun wasn't high enough yet, and the stadium rising above the Hudson was still partially blocking it, so I ran in the shadows. Billboards plastered to the sides of the stadium walls had all been renewed over the past two weeks, and now showcased this season's twenty-six man roster. Passing by Jupiter's poster, I could see it already had phone numbers scribbled onto it, but it was too early for the usual group of girls to be taking selfies with it.

By the time I reached Lux and Tanner's billboards, my lungs were on fire and I was beginning to make a dent in the funk which had infected me since yesterday.

This was exactly what I'd needed: fresh New York air, and a run along the river.

Thirty minutes later, by my estimation, I'd hit the six-mile marker. I'd reached the point where I normally turned around, dangerously close to Yankees territory, only running without Parker had gotten me there way, *way* quicker.

Lifting the hem of my shirt, I attempted to wipe some of the sweat dripping down my face.

"Hey, Ace."

I turned around, pulling down my sunglasses to see where the voice was coming from.

Oh, fuck yes.

A blonde, no taller than five four, was standing in front of me, wearing a pair of the shortest shorts I'd ever seen and a bra that one might say was several sizes too small. Her abs were almost as impressive as mine, along with a pair of tits that had definitely been helped along the way. But I was an equal opportunities boob man, real or fake, they were all great to me. Better yet if I could slide my dick between them.

He twitched at the thought.

"Hello, yourself."

"Hey," she repeated, only this time, I swear her voice dropped in the way that made it sound like she was panting. "Good luck for the game tomorrow."

"Thanks, babe. I appreciate that."

"If you wanna meet up after, here's my number." She pulled out a business card from her sports bra and passed it to me. "Sorry, it's a little sweaty."

She giggled bashfully as she batted her eyelashes at me, which was all the more impressive considering she was full of shit. There was nothing bashful about her at all, and I couldn't give a fuck.

"All good," I laughed, leaning in closer. "I love a bit of sweat."

"Me too. And I get really hot and sweaty."

"I'll bet you do."

"Anyway," she sunk her teeth into her lip, "call me."

I watched her jog away, her tight little ass swaying with each stride. I looked down at the card she'd given me. Britnee. I could definitely have a good time with her.

Except the second that thought played out, another one followed almost immediately. One with Payton's face on it saying I was shit in bed, or whatever it had been.

Fuck.

Fuuuck.

Fucking Payton.

Parker was right; she'd not only got into my head, she was making a house there.

I kicked at the grass verge.

Oh, this would not do.

I had twenty-four hours to shake myself out of it before we flew to Philadelphia.

I took off in a sprint.

If I couldn't shake it off, maybe I could sweat it out, because one way or another, Payton Lopez was getting the fuck out of my head.

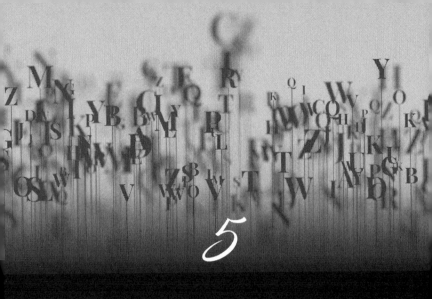

5

Payton

"Alrighty." Kit kicked the door to my apartment shut behind her as she balanced the pizza box on one hand, and held onto the bottle of wine with the other. "I have a large double cheese pizza from Lucky's, a bottle of pinot, and you have the wine glasses."

"And the cork screw," I held them both up, "arguably the most important element."

The aroma of herbs and melted mozzarella filled my tiny kitchen as Kit put everything down onto the counter and opened the box.

"I'm starving."

"Me too," I replied, grabbing the bottle to open. The cork squeaked its way out, ending in a loud pop, then the only noise to be heard was the glug of wine leaving the bottle. Kit reached for a glass almost before I'd finished pouring.

"Mmm," she moaned through the first large sip.

"Rough day?"

"Not really. School was busy, but it was good. Bell threw a tantrum before I left because she didn't like her pajamas, so she went to bed in her fairy tutu and wings. I honestly couldn't be bothered to argue, because I swear that child is as headstrong as her father."

I smirked through my first sip of wine. Murray *was* headstrong, but he was no match for Kit. Even if Bell wasn't Kit's biological child, with the way she took after her, you'd never know it.

"Thank God for carbs and alcohol then."

"Exactly!" She lifted her glass and gently knocked it against mine.

"Okay, let's get cozy."

I opened a drawer and grabbed a pile of paper take-out napkins – something I always had in abundance, seeing as I never cooked. It wasn't a gene I'd been gifted with, and had reached the point in my life where I could probably name my local delivery guy as one of my best friends.

I picked up the wine and followed Kit to the couch, where she was already on her second slice of pizza, and plopped down next to her. I peeled off a slice, blowing away the steam on top.

"Did Murray take over bedtime?" I mumbled through a far too large bite.

Kit shook her head. "No, he's gone to the game tonight. He and Rafe flew down after work."

Of course they had. I should have already known the answer; it was Opening Day, and the boys wouldn't miss supporting Penn and cheering on the Lions to victory. Murray, Rafe, and Penn were three best friends since college days, who did everything together, even now in their mid-thirties. Not long after Kit came along and fell in love with Murray, so followed Beulah, and Lowe. The six of them were a perfect little group that I'd somehow managed to infiltrate because Kit was my best friend.

Reaching for a napkin, she wiped the pizza grease off her fingers and picked up the remote. "What channel is the game on?"

I shrugged. "Dunno. Try them all."

We hit the jackpot on the third attempt. The camera panned out from the Phillies field where the Lions boys were warming up.

"Do you think we'll win?" Kit mumbled through a giant mouthful of pizza, only the cheese was still too hot and she couldn't close her mouth.

I sat back and sipped my wine, trying to figure what she'd just said. "Do I think we'll win?"

She nodded.

"Maybe. Beulah seems to think so, and Marnie has been busting her ass since Spring Training…"

Simultaneously, wine and air were inhaled too quickly and down the wrong way as Ace's face filled the screen. My eyes watered profusely, tears streamed down my face, and my attempt at coughing it away wasn't working, so I had to stand up and get my lungs back to normal function.

It was quite the spectacle.

As I sat back down, a broad grin spread over Kit's face. She said nothing, but stretched out her leg and prodded me with a perfectly manicured toe, which reminded me I'd missed my appointment today.

"Shut up."

"God, Pay," she laughed, "his face when you walked off the other day. I thought he was going to cry."

"As if…" I replied, using the sleeve of my hoodie to mop up my still watery eyes. "Probably the first time anyone turned him down, that's all."

She rolled her eyes. "Boys. Such delicate egos."

"Yeah."

Our focus went back to the screen as the camera panned around the field and stands. Unsurprisingly, it was a full house today. The Phillies red and white colors were almost matched in volume with the Lions black and gold, and it was almost impossible to see where one fan base ended and the other began.

Next, we were treated to a close up of Jupiter Reeves throwing and catching with Stone Fields, the same for Lux Weston and Tanner Simpson, while the commentators began their back and forth; discussion ranging from injuries and expectations, to new players brought in from the trade, and the phenomenal season the Lions had under Penn's first year of ownership.

And then there he was, standing in the tunnel next to the Lions coach, August Chase.

"That man is handsome," announced Kit. "I don't think it gets said enough, but he's a fox with a capital F O X."

I nodded. "I think it gets said plenty. I'm sure the camera stays on him so long to bring in the female demographic."

Kit chuckled under her breath. "I have to say, Penn has picked out a good-looking team."

"Yeah, and there's something about the all-black uniforms… it's hot. Makes them look a little dangerous."

"I agree," she nodded. "I think Lowe helped design it from pictures she'd found in the Lions archives."

The camera zoomed in on Ace again, this time he was in close conversation with Parker King, pulling down on his cap as he dropped his head and nodded slowly. I couldn't say I'd never seen him look so serious, but I didn't think I had. Even from the way his jaw was working back and forth as he chewed his gum, you could see the tension running through it. It was almost popping, along with the little twitch under his eye as he nodded at whatever Parker was saying to him.

"He's cute, Pay. Looks like he's about to dislocate his jaw from that gum chewing though." She sat back, wine glass in hand, and I could feel her eyes on me. I guessed she was expecting me to agree with her.

"Yep."

"Was it really that terrible?"

"Nah, but I had high expectations, and the fantasy didn't live up to the reality." I giggled, with a shrug. "He needs to get some more practice in."

The camera was still on Ace, and the pair of us watched in silence as his tongue stretched out the gum in his mouth, then disappeared again.

Dear Lord, that scene should have come with a Pay-Per-View fee.

I rubbed hard at the goosebumps which shot across my body, though I don't think it helped. I wasn't cold and I didn't need warming up. I was hot enough after that spectacle.

Next to me on the couch, I could almost feel Kit vibrating before her giggle burst out. "He looks like he could do some damage with that."

"I wouldn't know."

"What? You mean he didn't..." Her eyes widened

knowingly.

I shook my head slowly. "Nope. It was not an event where *I* was the focus."

Kit picked up her nearly empty wine glass and drained it. "Wow."

"Look, it wasn't terrible. I've definitely had worse. I guess I just thought he'd be…" I waved my hand around as I tried to come up with right word, but I got nothing. "Oh, I dunno. I mean, he almost tipped me over the edge a couple of times, but didn't push hard enough if you know what I'm saying."

Kit responded with a nod. She looked too shocked to form words.

"And I don't think it's too much to ask that if I'm having sex with a guy, he paid at least fifty percent of attention to me too, instead of focusing on himself. It was like he was doing me a favor by letting me suck his dick."

"Wow, that bad?"

"No," I smirked, "he has an excellent dick."

Kit picked the wrong moment to take another bite of pizza, because her gasp of amusement soon had her choking through her laughter, just like mine had, only I was kind enough to get up and grab her some water. I also gave her a good whack on the back.

"Oh my God," she giggled, as tears poured down her face, though that could have been because of the choking. "That's so funny. Imagine if he's like that with all the girls."

"He must be, but maybe they are all grateful to suck his dick. You've seen them at the gates." I grinned, emptying the remains of the bottle into Kit's glass and went to get another. "I'm just bummed I didn't even get to show off any of my own repertoire because it was like he was in a sprint to the finish line; except he was the only one racing."

"No wonder he fell asleep," Kit managed to wheeze out and wiped away another tear.

I smirked back at her and gripped my fist around an imaginary headboard. "I was just hanging on – and not in the good way."

I placed the new bottle on the table and slumped onto the couch as Kit snickered and shook her head, then decided if we were going to watch the game, I could kill two birds with one stone. I reached into the drawer under the coffee table and pulled out my box of nail polishes I kept there for emergencies.

On the screen, the players all started making their way off the field.

"Okay, I'm going to pee now so I don't miss the first pitch." Kit jumped up and ran to the small half bath by the front door.

My apartment might be a tiny one bed, but thankfully, my landlord had the foresight to add a half bath into what used to be a hallway closet, so guests didn't have to traipse through to the bedroom. Though maybe I'd be tidier if they did.

Probably not.

I peered into the box of polishes, and called to Kit, "Hey, can you grab me some cotton rounds and polish remover while you're up, please?"

"I thought you had a pedicure at lunch," she said, returning two minutes later with the items I'd hollered for and put them on the table.

"I was supposed to, but I had a meeting run over with my boss."

"Is she letting you go yet?"

I shook my head with a groan. "Nope."

"Oh, that sucks." She reached for the corkscrew and the new bottle of wine. "Have you talked to her about it?"

"Not for a while. I think I need to quit and start over somewhere else."

Kit stopped pulling on the cork. "Isn't that a little drastic?"

"I don't know what else to do," I shrugged.

There was another loud squeak as she eased open the bottle. "Pay, you're good at your job. Your boss loves you."

"She loves that I do all her work for her," I snapped. "I work my ass off, but I don't get paid nearly as much as I should do for the amount I do. I've fallen into a trap of being indispensable yet cheap, and no woman should ever be cheap. Plus, I don't want to edit children's books forever. There's only so many fluffy bunnies chasing a carrot I can take."

"But I love all the fluffy bunny books," she grinned, "so does Bell."

"Well, if I ever get to move, I'll keep you in grown up books instead." I smiled, though I could feel the annoyance starting to rise at thought of never getting out of the fortieth floor. "Want a rom-com? Thriller? Historical?"

"Oh, I'll take historical for a thousand," she replied, in her best Jeopardy contestant voice.

"You got it," I said, soaking a cotton round in polish remover. "What are you teaching right now?"

"Virginia Woolf and Sylvia Plath."

"Oh God, depressing. No wonder you need wine."

Kit and I had met on our first day of college at Columbia. I was moving into my dorm room and found Kit sitting on a chair – on the left-hand side – having already unpacked, made her bed, and added her retro posters of Shakespeare and Charles Dickens book covers to the wall. She'd also tidied her desk, setting out all her note pads and Post-its in color order, and put all the pens in a pot by a plant that lasted a month when we both forgot it needed watering. I promptly dumped the large box I had under one arm on the floor, left my suitcase by the door, and suggested we go to the nearest bar which would accept our fake IDs, and get to know each other better.

Before the first drink arrived, we discovered we were both English Lit majors, and have been inseparable since. The only difference between us, aside from the obvious that she's the neat freak whereas I can always find something better to do than tidy, is that Kit knew from our first year she wanted to pursue teaching, whereas I wanted to be a book editor, and I couldn't think of anything worse than sitting through a semester on Sylvia Plath and Virginia Woolf.

"Tell me about it," she winked, and glanced at the television. "Ooh, the game is starting."

I let out a gasp, nearly dropping the polish remover all over the floor. "Holy shit, is that President Andrews taking the first pitch? How did I not know this?"

We both watched Emily Andrews, the small, blonde-haired President of the United States, walk out onto the Citizens Bank Park field. Even sitting at home on the comfort of the couch, you could tell that this woman meant business – dressed in her sports jacket and ball cap bearing the Presidential seal, and a pair of jeans and sneakers. Her features were schooled into that steely but smiley expression she always wore, like she'd order your assassination but give you a mom hug first.

It never faltered.

President Andrews conducted every aspect of her life the same way; from winning the election in an almost state-wide sweep last year to the determination she exuded when taking on Congress, and the world. This woman fought to win, and most of the time, did exactly that.

We watched as she stood on the mound, right where Ace usually positioned himself, and leaned back. The ball flew out of her arm and straight into the Phillies pitcher's glove to a deafening cheer and encore of the Star-Spangled Banner.

"Jeez, she must have been practicing. That looked powerful."

"Yeah. She's probably had the team at The White House all week showing her how to do it," Kit replied with a nod. "Hey, did I tell you Radley Andrews is considering Columbia for the fall?"

I turned to her with wide eyes. "Radley, her daughter? No. That's cool."

"Yeah, there are a couple of other schools she's looking at, but everything is under NDA for security, so I only heard from someone else who'd heard it."

"It would still be quite cool if that happened, the President's daughter at our Alma Mater."

"Speaking of mothers, have you heard from yours?"

I shook my head. "Nope. She's on a cruise with Joe."

"Don't tell me she forgot your birthday again!" Kit fumed.

I nodded. I couldn't bring it in me to get as annoyed as Kit; I'd had years of both my parents forgetting my birthday. Twelve years in fact, because once I'd left home for New York, it was like I didn't exist. That might be a slight exaggeration, but it wasn't far off.

When I was ten years old, my parents sat me down and announced they were divorcing. As divorcing parents do, they assured me nothing would change. They still loved me, and loved each other, but they were going to be friends instead of husband and wife.

That was their first lie.

It quickly became incredibly messy and acrimonious. I was frequently used as a pawn in their fights, and for my teenage years when I should have been at the mall with my friends, or kissing boys, I'd had to deal with my parents and their self-absorbed games of one-upmanship. If my dad found a new girlfriend, then my mom had to find a new boyfriend. If my mom bought a new car, then my dad would go on a spending spree to make it clear she wasn't getting any more of his money.

When I was fifteen, my dad finally stopped playing games and met a lady he could truly love – Cynthia – and they started their own family, and I finally got the sisters I'd always wanted. Except my dad finding happiness left my mom so incensed she went on a mission to find a new husband. Joe is currently her third.

The moral of the story is, if you have parents who care more about fighting with each other than the welfare of their daughter, then you can't expect to be remembered for important occasions. It also instilled in me the hard truths that you can't expect anyone else to make you happy, and love will only crush you in the long term.

A few college boyfriends tried to change my mind, but the damage had already been done.

I'm a child of divorce. Fifty percent of marriages end in it, and I have no intention of being included in that statistic, however cliché that makes me.

Dating apps would forever be the life for me.

Kit reached over and squeezed my thigh, taking care not to jolt me while I applied the first layer of *Essie Licorice* black polish to my toes. "I'm sorry, Pay."

"Eh, what you gonna do? I'm thirty now, they're never

going to change."

"Nope, but you have Murray, Bell, and me. We can adopt you into our family."

"Hey," I turned and smirked, "we're all for adoption."

"Damn right," she grinned, though it dropped as she glanced to the television. "Hey, what's going on?"

I peered up at the screen. Ace's face was so close up, it made the tension in his jaw even more pronounced than it had been. The first Phillies player was jogging to first base.

"Turn it up, what's wrong with him?"

I snatched up the remote and increased the volume, though we both still leaned forward to listen to the commentary.

"Wow, Aaron. That's four balls all missing the strike zone, and the Phillies get a walk on the first batter. Penn Shepherd isn't going to like that as a start to his Lions' Opening Day."

"None of the team is, Mark."

"Looking at Ace Watson now, he doesn't seem too happy either. Unsurprising really."

Kit and I stayed silent as Ace took the mound again. This time the ball was hit, but the batter only made it to first base.

"This isn't what we expect from the Lions' golden boy on Opening Day," continued the commentator, while Ace looked more thunderous, though it was nothing compared to Penn's face when the camera found him.

"You're right, Mark. He had a great first season with the Lions. The chemistry between him and Parker King was a big contribution to how far the Lions came last year from the year before – moving from the bottom of the standings to the first round of the post season – but he just doesn't seem to be there today."

The screen changed to a wide shot of the field, or more

accurately, the diamond where there was now a Phillies player on every base.

"This doesn't look good," muttered Kit, as she reached for another slice of pizza.

"Well, Aaron, would you look at that? The Phillies have got a runner on each base. If Bryce Harper hits big now, the Phillies are going four up in the first innings, and no coach wants that for their Opening Day game.

Ace leaned back, his knee raising up as he pitched his arm. The ball flew out of his hand on the way to where Bryce Harper was waiting.

Crack.

The ball soared *high… high… high…* through to left field, and into the Phillies home crowds screaming so loudly we could probably hear them from a hundred miles away. The four Phillies players all made their way around the bases and back to the dugout.

The Lions were down 4-0 before the end of the first inning.

Kit reached for the wine and topped up our glasses. "Oh shiiit."

I blew over my toes and resumed with applying a second coat of polish. "Yeah, happy we didn't go. There's no way I'd want to be around Penn and the mood he's going to be in now."

"Yeah, it's definitely safer to be here," she nodded heavily and picked up another slice of pizza. "If this doesn't get better, I might have to pretend to be asleep when Murray gets back, then I won't have to listen to him complaining about either the game or how Penn was steaming with rage all night long."

The game didn't get better. By the third inning, the Lions had a home run courtesy of Lux, but the Phillies were up another three. The commentary didn't get better either.

"I'm telling you, Aaron, if August Chase is sensible, he'll pull him out. This is an embarrassing start for the Lions, and for Ace Watson."

"You're right. There's no reason for this. I haven't heard about any injury, but maybe we'll find out in the post-game press conference, because questions need answering."

"Something's got in his head, that's for sure."

Kit returned from the bathroom, where she ran off again during the next team change, and dropped back on the sofa with a grin. "That's you."

"Huh?"

"You're the one who got in Ace's head."

Rummaging through the box of polishes, I found the top coat I'd been looking for.

"This isn't because of me."

Kit's tongue poked against her cheek as she side-eyed me.

"He's a professional baseball player. He has to have the ability to compartmentalize, not accounting for the fact he'll have forgotten our conversation the second he laid eyes on another woman."

"Yeah, you're right." She stretched her arms over her head and yawned. "Okay, well, I can't watch any more of this blood bath. I think I'm going to go home and get in an *actual* bath, maybe put a face mask on before Murray gets home."

"Ooh, face mask. Awesome idea! I'll do the same; I have one somewhere."

I followed her to the kitchen, walking as slowly as I could on my heels, so my newly painted toes didn't smudge before they'd dried properly.

"Thanks for the wine and pizza," I said and wrapped my arms around her, squeezing her into a tight hug. "I'll come over this weekend and we can take Bell to the zoo or something."

"Yeah, she'd love that." She kissed my cheek as she grabbed her coat and made her way to the front door. "Okay, babe, talk to you tomorrow. Love you."

"Love you."

After clearing away the empty pizza box and napkins, I fell back on the sofa and finished the second bottle of wine. I gave up on watching the game after Ace was switched out for a new pitcher, and instead, found a face mask in the bathroom cabinet and settled in for a bedtime episode The Golden Girls.

I must have fallen asleep, because the next thing happening was me falling off the couch having been woken by a loud and very persistent banging on my front door, which was more annoying than my alarm clock.

"What the fuck?!" I rubbed my bruised elbow, then winced as my face stung and cracked at the same time. "Fuck, my face! Ouch."

Bang. Bang. Bang.

"Hang on!" I screeched, "I'm coming!" But instead, I went to the bathroom to wash the mask off my face, which was doing a good impression of dried cement.

Bang. Bang. Bang.

"Jeez." I swiped the towel from the rail and patted my face dry, trying not to make it any redder than it currently was, though I still resembled a tomato.

I was gripping the door handle when it dawned on me that I had no idea what time it was, or who was demanding entry into my apartment.

"Who is it?"

"It's Ace. Open the fucking door, Payton!"

It was more out of shock and disbelief that I opened the

door as quickly as I did, because I needed to see for myself that it was, indeed, Ace Watson.

And he did not look happy.

I must have been asleep for longer than I thought if they'd already made it back to the city, and I could have sworn they were staying in Philadelphia.

"What are you doing here?"

"You fucked with my mojo," he snarled.

Under his black Lions ballcap, his eyes had narrowed so much I could barely see them, and the dark stubble which covered his jaw and those famous cheekbones only added to the effect. I'd been right earlier – he did look dangerous.

"Your what?"

"My mojo. I totally choked tonight."

I grimaced in sympathy while also rubbing sleep from my eyes. "Yeah, I saw. I'm sorry."

One of his thick fingers was jabbed in my direction. "And it's your fucking fault."

I blinked once, twice, then again as I tried to understand his words, but honestly, I was still groggy from being woken up so suddenly and having to wash my face at lightning speed.

"It's my fault you played badly?"

"Yes."

"How'd you figure that, exactly?"

"Because you told me…" he looked around to see if anyone else could hear, but my neighbors were away, and old Mrs. Kellerman upstairs was deaf and usually went to bed at eight. He pushed me into the apartment and closed the door. "You told me I was shit in bed. You've given me the yips."

My arms crossed hard over my chest and my nostrils flared in outrage, because how dare he!

"Excuse me? I've given you no such thing. We used protection."

He frowned, his brow dropping so it almost forced his eyes to narrow further. "You have. I couldn't play tonight. I've got the yips and it's because of you!"

"What the fuck are yips?!"

Ace took a step back from the volume I'd yelled, but really, again... how *dare* he?

"It's a death sentence!" He threw his hands in the air, but it still didn't explain or make sense of anything he was saying, something he figured after he took one look at my face. "I couldn't throw tonight. It was like my brain and my arm couldn't connect. My mojo. It's gone. It's the yips."

I sighed in relief at not having to make the emergency trip for antibiotics I was plotting ten seconds ago.

"Oh. Well, I'm sure it'll come back for your next game."

His head dropped low and his shoulders slumped almost in defeat. "Why did you have to tell me that?"

"Tell you what?"

"That I was shit in bed!" he snapped, like saying it as quickly as possible made it not so real.

I pursed my lips, wondering how much longer I was going to have to entertain this ridiculous middle-of-the-night interruption.

"I never said that," I enunciated very slowly. "I said I didn't orgasm."

"Same difference," he huffed with a deep eye roll.

"Jesus Christ, the size of your ego is insane! If you're so bothered about a woman not orgasming, then maybe you should make more of an effort in the future to ensure she does!"

"The fucking President of the United States was there. The President, Payton. She saw me choke. It's your fault," he repeated like he hadn't heard a word I said, which was likely, seeing as he was clearly the most self-obsessed human being that walked the streets of New York, and that was coming from someone who was raised by my parents.

"Okay, we're done here." I opened the door and shoved him back out into the hallway, easier than I expected, which says something for the level of annoyance I was feeling. "And don't bother coming back."

I slammed the door in his face before he could say another word.

As I bolted the lock, I glanced down at my feet; *Essie Licorice* had smudged everywhere.

Fan-fucking-tastic.

6

Ace

*D*o you know what it feels like to get booed by twenty-five thousand fans? No? How about cheered by twenty-five thousand, but by the team you *don't* play for?

You're probably unfamiliar with that feeling also.

I wish I could say I was.

Let me describe it to you. It's like someone is jumping up and down on your chest, each time flattening it a little bit more. Your stomach is rolling back and forth like you've been on one too many rides at the state fairground, and your head is pounding because you're trying your hardest to block out the volume of chants reminding you that you suck, and you're fucking up so badly that your lack of ability to do a job you're paid millions for means the other team wins.

The other team wins purely because you couldn't do your job; not because they did theirs well.

Let me spell it out again. You lost. They didn't win.

All you need to do is tune into your brain and focus on the job in hand.

All you need to do is throw the ball and get it in the strike zone without your opponent hitting it, or, if he does hit it, make sure it's not very far. Not enough for a home run, barely enough to reach first base.

You just need to throw, something I no longer seemed capable of.

"Fuck! Fuck. Fuuuck!"

The bucket of balls went flying as soon as my foot made contact. As I watched each one soar through the air, it dawned on me that I was almost better at kicking a baseball than I was at pitching one, at least this week anyway. I'd been out in the pitching cages for the past two hours, and out of the seventy-five balls I'd pitched at the make-shift strike zone and cardboard cut-out of Jupiter Reeves someone had left, I'd hit the mark six times. Six fucking times out of seventy-five balls.

I didn't know what percentage that was, but it wasn't very fucking many.

I couldn't even bring myself to laugh at the fact one of the balls from the flying bucket had hit the red dot in the middle of the wall; the center of the strike zone.

Rolling my shoulder back, I squeezed the tendons and muscles along my arm in an attempt to ease the tension which had been gradually building since Opening Day, or the day before Opening Day. Six days ago, to be precise.

I couldn't even blame it on the rigor of pitching for the majority of a game, because I hadn't done that since Spring Training. No, because all I'd pitched during Opening Day was three disastrous innings, before I'd suffered the humiliation of being pulled off the field.

Three fucking innings.

Riley Rivers, a new relief pitcher Penn Shepherd had brought up from the minors for this season, had stepped into my place and managed to get us through the next four innings without the Phillies scoring, while we hit three home runs.

It had been announced this morning that Riley would be the starting pitcher in tonight's game, and all the ones I should be starting in. Everyone knew what that meant – Riley Rivers would take my place until I'd sorted myself out.

The bucket was still upside down where it had fallen, and I slumped onto it – or tried to. Instead, I misjudged the space, fell back on my ass, and smacked my head on the floor.

Fuck's sake. I couldn't even manage to sit down properly.

I was nothing more than a pathetic overpaid lump.

I flung an arm over my eyes to block out the brightness of the spotlights, though if I really wanted to admit it, I was also attempting to stop the tears from forming.

"Dude, what're you doing on the floor?"

My head fell to the left to see Parker walking toward me. He stopped by my feet and held his hand out. I didn't take it; I should probably stay here. I was as much use on the floor in the corner of the pitching cages as I was on the field right now. And at least here I wasn't getting in the way.

"Contemplating my life choices," I grumbled.

"Well, stand up and do it." Parker flicked his hand at me again.

This time I took it, because knowing Parker, if I didn't, he'd only bend down and heave me to standing. Or yank me up. Something, anyway, but whatever it was, I would find myself standing soon because if Parker decided he wanted something to happen, he would find a way to get it. The man did not give up.

I wish he could find a way to get my throwing arm back.

"I've been calling you," he said once he'd succeeded in bringing me to standing.

"Don't have my phone on me," I shrugged.

"You always have your phone on you."

"I don't today," I replied, bending down to pick up the bucket. "It's in my locker."

Parker sighed heavily and looked around. It was clear I'd thrown a lot of balls, just like it was clear the cutout of Jupiter had been eviscerated when he should have been intact. Even the space on the back wall marking the spot where Parker usually crouched was intact, save for a few scuffs.

He picked up a couple of balls and dropped them in the second bucket. "I would have come in with you this morning. You should have woken me up."

I tossed a ball from where I was standing. It hit the side of the bucket and rolled onto the floor.

Of course it fucking did.

"Ace, how long have you been out here?" Parker continued.

"Dunno."

"Judging from this, I'd say a few hours." He gestured his hands toward the bucket. "Dude, you need to get your shoulder iced and rested."

I rolled my shoulder again; it had been aching for most of the morning, like I'd slept badly on it. Though seeing as I'd slept for a total of eight hours in five nights, that couldn't be the cause of the ache. I wasn't even sure if pitching continuously for the past two hours had made it worse, but without practicing, I wouldn't get my arm back, so I was in a catch twenty-two.

"Yeah. I'll go in a bit, just want to get through another

bucket."

I looked up as Parker laughed, because it wasn't his usual laugh of amusement; it was more of a deep scoff.

"What?"

"You're not serious?"

"Serious about what?" I snapped.

"About another bucket of balls." He dropped two more into the bucket by his feet. "You need to rest your shoulder."

I looked at him, a deep, *deep* frown creasing my brow. "I'm not playing tonight. Rivers is starting, and Coach will keep him in for the whole game while I warm the fucking bench."

"Dude, you'll be playing."

"No, Parker, I'm not. Read your emails. I've fucked up and Coach has pulled me. I'm supposed to go for more X-rays later, in case they missed something the first time. Fat lot of good that will be. They need to be X-raying my head, not my shoulder. You should leave. You don't want to catch the yips from me."

The tightness which had been sitting on my chest and squeezing my ribs together suddenly became too much, and before I could stop it, the pressure barreled up. I tried to hold in the sob, but it was like trying to get toothpaste back in the tube: impossible.

"Oh, buddy." Parker wrapped his arm around my shoulder and pulled me into him while my frustration and humiliation flowed out of me until I became a sniveling mess. "Dude, we can fix this."

"How?" I wailed, praying there was no-one in the vicinity to hear me, or witness me ugly cry.

Parker read my thoughts as I glanced toward the door to the cages. "No one's around. Yours was the only car in the lot when I drove in; everyone else stayed in bed."

"Sensible."

Wiping my sleeve across my nose, I caught the disgusted look on Parker's face as he peered down at his tear-and-snot-soaked shoulder. Only then did I manage the first smile I'd given all week.

"Sorry, man. I'll get you a clean shirt."

"Don't worry about it," he grinned back at me. "We have more important things to do, like figuring out how to fix your pitch."

I sighed, falling back into my funk. "Yeah, good luck with that."

He spun me around and grabbed both my shoulders. I braced myself for a slap to the face, but it never came. "Ace, we're gonna fucking fix it. I don't care what we have to do, but we're fixing it."

"Parker, I hear you. I do. It's been five days, and I'm getting worse. I can't seem to get it out of my head."

I nearly, *nearly* said Payton, but it didn't matter because we both knew exactly what I was talking about, and Parker's argument was exactly the same as it had been the last fifty times we'd talked about this.

"Dude, just go and find another girl to sleep with. You're Ace Fucking Watson. I passed ten signs on the way spelling it out in big black letters, and right now, they all want to console you and make you feel better, so please just let one do it, and you can go back to being the genius pitcher we all know you are."

I looked at him with exactly the same expression I'd worn the last fifty times. "I can't. It doesn't work like that."

"How? How do you know? This has never happened before."

"I don't know how I know; I just know. Payton was the cause of this, therefore only Payton can fix this." It might have been skewed logic that only made sense to me, but I'd never been good at math.

"Then go and talk to her again."

"She slammed the door in my face."

"I know. That's why I said *again*. And this time, don't do it by sneaking out. You're lucky you didn't get caught."

I moved Parker's hands off my shoulders and gripped his instead. It had only been three days, but I also knew that it wasn't just me affected, it was Parker, too. If Riley became starting pitcher, then Parker would need to build up a relationship with him like we had together. They'd need to learn new plays, new signals, body language, and that didn't happen overnight.

"Parker, I'm sorry man, I really am. I'm trying to figure it out."

"Please figure it out sooner rather than later." He picked up his bucket, and pointed at the one I was still filling. "Come on, let's get out of here. Whether you're pitching tonight or not, you still need to ice your shoulder."

I nodded and did what I was told because I didn't have the energy for a fight.

"Did the others come in with you?" I asked, following him out of the cages and leaving the buckets of balls neatly lined up along the wall with the rest.

Parker shook his head. "Nope. Lux was making breakfast, and Tan hadn't woken up yet. He feels bad, you know."

"What?"

"Tan, he feels bad about this. Thinks it's partly his fault."

I scoffed. "Why?"

"Because if he hadn't been teasing you about her, then none of this would have happened." It took Parker a second to realize I'd stopped walking next to him, and spun around to find me staring at him. "What are you doing?"

Pushing my ballcap up, I gave my head a good scratch. "This isn't his fault, it's mine." I didn't add, *'and Payton's'* like I had been doing, because I wasn't altogether sure it was her fault – not after the way she'd yelled at me when I'd stormed over to her place. It had been loud enough that her words were still ringing in my ear.

"He thinks it's his, too."

I sighed. It was one thing for me to live under my own black cloud, it was quite another for anyone to join me. I knew my mood was affecting Parker, but I hadn't accounted on it affecting the rest of the boys, or even the rest of the team. I needed a fix to this problem, and fast.

"I'll tell him it's not."

"Good." He thumbed over his shoulder. "Now, can we keep walking?"

I grinned. "Yeah."

We pushed through the doors leading away from the batting cages and training facilities into the main building through the reception, where Pablo was manning the desk.

I nodded to him and smiled, the same as I had when I'd walked in with my head down while also giving him a wide berth. It was embarrassing to walk the hallways after my performance, and even more so when I saw the pity on everyone's faces.

There was nothing worse than pity.

"Ace, come here."

"Oh, Pabs, dude, I'm in a hurry."

"No, you come here." His finger hit the counter right in front of him, and the big signet ring he was wearing glinted in the light.

Parker raised his eyebrow, his head tipping to where Pablo was now standing with his arms crossed. "Go on."

I stepped over to him. "Hey, Pabs."

"Ace, you gotta hold your head up, man." Before I could stop him, he slapped a meaty palm around the back of my neck, and his eyes bored into mine. "You're a Lion. A New York Lion. You think you're the first Lion to ever have a shitty game? You're not. This club was built on shitty games, but you know what? Every single player before you held their head up when they walked through the door, so pull your finger out of your ass and pride yourself on the fact you're a Lion, and we face adversity head-on and come through the other side. You understand?"

It took me second to break out of the shock from seeing this new side to the security guard I always considered like a cute grandpa-type figure, but now I wasn't convinced he couldn't be at home in an Upper West Side gang. Or the mafia. I also wondered if I was supposed to answer this question, seeing as he didn't give me a chance to answer any of the other ones he'd asked, but this time he stayed silent.

"Um, yeah, Pablo, I understand." I blinked and tried to ease away, but his grip tightened.

"Do you understand?"

"Yes. Jeez. Yes, I understand. I understand."

I'd never found him intimidating before, but from the way he was grinning at me, I could safely say that was no longer true. More surprisingly though, while the delivery wasn't the most reassuring, I did take comfort in his words. It was true; the Lions used to be the worst club in the league, and they'd never shied away from the humiliation.

And we'd certainly come through the other side now Penn Shepherd owned us.

"Good, now go and ice your shoulder," he added, nodding to the monitors under the counter, "or we'll be having more words."

I always forgot there were security cameras in every inch of this building, and he'd probably been watching me all morning.

"Will do. I'm on the way now. Thanks for the talk, Pablo."

I was turning back to Parker when Pablo called over my shoulder.

"Good morning, Mr. Shepherd, Mr. Reeves."

I groaned quietly, my entire body tensing. If there was anyone I didn't want to run into, it was Penn Shepherd. Coming in a close second would be Jupiter Reeves.

But luck was on sabbatical it seemed.

"Good morning, Pablo. How's it going?"

"Not bad, Sir. Just having a chat with young Ace here." He nodded to me.

I spun around to where they were walking across the entrance foyer to see Penn's head snapping up in my direction as he swiped his pass over the entrance gates. "Ah, Ace, good. I'm glad you're here."

I readied myself for another lecture, though grabbing me around the neck wasn't really Penn's style. Come to think of it, that's probably why Pablo was employed in the first place.

"Morning, sir."

"Walk with me." He gestured forward, and I did my best to follow at the same pace. For someone who wasn't a professional sportsperson, he sure was fast. "Parker, you too."

I took the stairs two at a time, just as Penn had, Jupiter and Parker close on our heels. By the time we'd reached the fourth floor, where the owner's suite was, I'd almost broken out in a sweat whereas Penn had barely raised his heartrate from the looks of it, as his long strides ate up the stretch of hallway leading to his office.

I stopped momentarily in the doorway and took in the view. I'd never been in here before. I wasn't sure I'd even seen the field from this angle. The rich terracotta dirt fanned around three bright white bases, and home plate.

And there in the middle was *my* spot. If I could still call it that.

"Whoa," exclaimed Parker as he reached the office, right behind Jupiter who'd marched straight in and sat down. "Nice view."

"It is," Penn grinned, then looked at me. "Do you want coffee?"

"No, thank you."

"Okay." Penn rolled his lips and perched on the edge of his desk, his stare never straying from my face.

I wasn't sure if I was supposed to speak, so I didn't. Instead, I clenched and unclenched my fists, anything to distract myself. Silence made me uncomfortable, and right now, I was really fucking uncomfortable.

"Think that's the longest you've ever kept your mouth shut," chuckled Jupiter after what felt like hours, when it was probably only ten seconds.

My eyes flicked over to his with a scowl, making his grin widen.

"What's going on, Watson?" asked Penn. "Are you okay?"

I shuffled my feet. I'd already had a talking to from Coach Chase and Coach Willis, my pitching coach, and hoped I'd be able to avoid one from Penn Shepherd, because this felt a lot like being hauled into the principal's office… except I'd walked in freely.

"Yes, sir. I'm fine. I just had an off day."

"We can't afford to have off days, Ace," he replied, matter-of-factly. "Is it your shoulder? The X-rays have come back negative, but we can have it looked at again."

"It's not my shoulder, sir, I just couldn't focus. It was a bad day. I can't blame anything except myself."

"Coach Chase is starting Rivers tonight."

I nodded. "Yes, sir."

Penn took a deep breath, his nostrils flaring as he did. "Get your head back in the game, Watson. I want to see you out on the mound with the fire you had last season."

I nodded again, because there's no way I could argue against it. This man owned my job, and if I wanted to keep it, I needed to do everything within my power to get my pitch back. *Everything*.

"I'm fixing it."

I didn't dare turn around to where Parker was standing, I didn't even want to look at Jupiter or his raised brow, making it clear he wasn't sure what exactly 'fixing it' entailed, but had every intention of finding out.

Jupiter Reeves knowing about any part of this situation would only be happening over my dead body.

"Okay, you can go. Have you been to see Doctor Benedict?"

I stilled. I thought I might have gotten away without the club psychologist being mentioned, but it was something Shepherd had been hot on last season; we'd all had to make sure we were mentally fit as well as physically fit – except this wasn't a subject I wanted to discuss with anyone, especially when I knew what was wrong.

Doctor Benedict couldn't help me with this problem.

I shook my head. "Not yet."

"Go and see him today, and ice that shoulder."

"On my way to, sir."

I took one last look at the view; at The New York Lions diamond. That was *my* diamond, *my* home. I belonged on that mound, and I'd do whatever it took to get back there.

Now I just had to figure out how to get Payton's number.

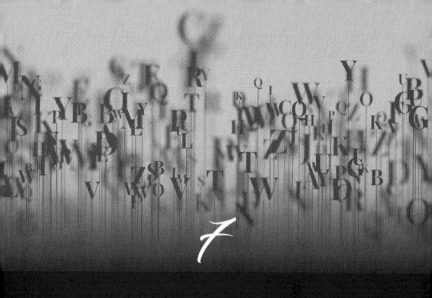

7

Payton

Payton: *How did you get this number?*

Ace: *I'd rather not say… I need to talk to you.*

Payton: *We have nothing to talk about.*

Ace: *When are you free?*

Payton: *I'm not.*

Ace: *Please, Payton, I need your help.*

Payton: *I'm really sorry your game is off right now, but I can't help fix it. I don't know anything about baseball.*

I watched the little blue dots float on my screen, disappear, pop back, then disappear again. It was pointless replying; not only did we not have anything else to talk about, but I had more important things on my mind – like figuring out what

The phone landed at the end of my office couch and bounced onto the floor with a soft thud. At least the carpet stopped the screen from smashing, because that really would put the cherry on the top of my day. I was just resting my head back when the sound of footsteps marching down the hall had me jumping back up, because I knew exactly who those footsteps belonged to.

"Payton, you-hoo! Are you there?"

Let me introduce Susie Van Marin, my boss, and the only person left alive who still used the greeting 'you-hoo'.

I groaned and plastered on the smile I'd had eight years of practice for.

"Hi, Susie, how are you?" I asked as her head appeared around the door.

"Oh good, you're here." She pushed the door wider, marched in and sat down on the couch I'd just got up from.

The entire time her dark brown bob never moved, like it wouldn't dare step out of place. The woman didn't own one wrinkle, either.

"How can I help you?"

"There's a new author I've heard about and want you to get hold of. We simply must have her in the S&M family. I'd do it myself, but I am swamped right now. As you're the very best of all my editors, Payton, I thought you could go out and get her. I want to present her in the divisional meeting next week and tell everyone we've signed her."

I looked at Susie, wondering if she realized I wasn't as dumb as she clearly thought I was; that laying the compliments on thicker than mustard on a hot dog no longer worked, because I was no longer a green, highly ambitious intern, desperate to climb their way up the ladder.

I grimaced. "I'd love to help you out, Susie, but I'm swamped too. There are book awards coming, not to mention the other submissions you gave me last week."

I gestured to the coffee table which was filled with manuscripts and prototypes for books with all the added extras, like a fluffy bunny tail or a honking nose.

"I hear you, Payton, I do." Her nose crinkled up in a way she obviously thought was cute and caring, but her tone said she couldn't give a single shit about my workload. "But I just don't trust anyone else. I need you to do this for me, and it'll be great for your career come promotion time."

Give me strength.

The problem was two-fold: my boss was fucking lazy, and I'd fallen into the trap of bringing in too much money to her division. Therefore, if I left for a new division, she'd have to do some work of her own, something Susie and I both knew, but she loved to hold the promotion over my head anyway.

Though maybe I was the dumbass for letting her.

"Send me the details and I'll see what I can do. I'm not promising anything."

Susie's face lit up. "Oh you're the greatest, Payton. What would I do without you?"

Get fired, I thought to myself.

"Okay." She stood up, smoothing down the linen of her dress. "Must dash. See you this afternoon."

"See you." I waved, and waited for her to leave before dropping my head on the desk.

Weak. That's what I was.

Kicking off my shoes, I got up and resumed my position on the couch just as the subtle vibration of another message came through. I smothered my phone with a cushion; it was ten-thirty a.m. and I'd already had my quota of Ace Watson for the day.

I added 'find out who'd given him my number' to my list of things to do, because as soon as I did, I'd be paying them a little visit.

Leaning forward with a groan, I peered at the giant stack of manuscripts that I needed to go through but really didn't want to, and reached for the first one off the top; *The Sad Bunny...* and threw it to one side. Nope. The next one didn't fill me with any more hope; *The Owl Who Lost His Hoot...* and had my cheeks puffing in frustration. It landed on the bunny. The pile now featured a puppy – *toss* – then horse – *toss* – a kitten, a fish, a donkey... and finally a lost tortoise – *all toss*. Where was the misunderstood hyena? Or the spider who'd worked her butt off building a web, but still couldn't get moved off the broken tree branch and into the cozy, warm house? What about her? Where was the relatable children's book in that pile?

I needed more caffeine for this, and – clutching my stomach as it rumbled – some breakfast.

Snatching up my purse and heels, I headed out of my office, along the plush carpets of the hallway to the elevator. I was still slipping my shoes on when the doors pinged open, so I didn't immediately notice that someone else was already standing inside.

The woman, in turn, was looking at her phone, so she didn't notice that my mouth was now hanging open and my eyes were in danger of falling out of their sockets from how far they'd widened.

Holy *shit*. Stay cool, Payton. Stay cooool.

In my eight years of working at Simpson and Mather, I'd only seen Nathalie Cheung at company-wide meetings, or reporting on the quarterly figures, or on board panels discussing the newest trends in publishing. And all those times had been over Zoom, or from the back of the giant auditorium on the lower-ground floor of this building and over the heads of the two-thousand other people who worked here, or in the latest copy of *The Reader*.

Even in *The New York Times*.

I'd never seen her up close, and I'd never been in an enclosed space with her.

Come to think of it, the execs on the sixtieth floor had their own high-speed elevator which opened directly there… but not today it seemed.

C.E.O. of Simpson and Mather for almost ten years, Nathalie Cheung was a powerhouse in her own right. She'd led the charge in changing the way books were read; specifically female targeted books. She'd brought romance into the mainstream markets as a genre to be proud of, and she'd taught a previously men-only board what it was like to work with women. She balanced motherhood, fought for equal pay and longer vacation time, for maternity *and* paternity leave, and sat on boards across New York, championing equality and women in the workplace.

And while she'd been doing all that, she'd quadrupled profits at Simpson and Mather, brought in big name authors, world leaders, and celebrities for their autobiographies. The current jewel in the crown was an access all areas biography of President Andrews during her Presidential campaign trail.

I might have always wanted to work in publishing, but the woman standing in front of me had been the sole reason I'd wanted to work at Simpson and Mather.

In short, Nathalie Cheung was my idol.

I stepped inside, positioning myself as far away from her as possible, in case I had the sudden inappropriate urge to hug her or something. As it was, my heart was pounding so hard that I was convinced she could hear it, but thankfully she was still focused on her phone screen, and from the way she was looking at it, wasn't happy.

That was fine. If she didn't look up, I could stare longer.

I slid my hand over the elevator wall to press the button, trying not to make any sudden movements in case I startled her.

Think, Payton. *Think.* All these years you've dreamed of what you'd say if you ever saw her, and now your mind is cotton-candy. Think.

She glanced up from her phone and smiled.

"Hello." I smiled back, hoping she couldn't tell I was only just managing to hold my shit together.

"Hey there." Nathalie Cheung went back to her emails.

She didn't need to introduce herself. If I didn't know who she was, then I had no right to work in this building.

The red numbers above the door flashed and lowered as we moved down the floors. I prayed no one else would get on and ruin this moment I was having. As luck would have it, they didn't.

Luck had different plans.

I jolted back slightly as the elevator ground to a halt with a judder. The numbers stuck on twenty-three.

"Um…" I reached and pressed the lobby floor again. And again. Nothing happened.

I looked over to Nathalie who seemed indifferent to the entire situation, so I opened the wall panel and picked up the phone.

"Maintenance," said a voice at the other end before it even rang. Or maybe elevator phones didn't ring.

"Hello? This is…" I scanned down the instructions fixed to the panel door, "the north bank elevator three."

"Yeah, we got you. We're just fixing a fault; we're getting to you as soon as possible. Sit tight."

I blinked. "Sit tight?"

"Yeah, sit tight. We won't be long."

I took the deepest breath I could muster, but it didn't seem to help. I wasn't usually claustrophobic, but I'd seen enough episodes of Chicago Fire to know this might not end well. "Are we going to plummet to our death?"

"I hope not."

I assumed that was some kind of elevator maintenance humor, though I didn't find it particularly humorous.

"Sit tight, sweetheart. You're going to be fine. It's not the cables, it's the electronics."

It was hard not to panic about dying, but also remain calm and collected in front of Nathalie Cheung. I dug deep into the acting classes I'd taken in ninth grade, and attempted to channel my best 'unruffled elevator passenger'.

"Well, please hurry. Thank you," I added, and hung up.

I slumped down to the floor, and looked over at Nathalie, still standing against the railings and appearing far calmer than I felt. She would though, she was Nathalie Cheung.

"He said it's an electronics issue, they're fixing it. Won't be long."

She nodded. "It's this whole building. The express elevator was broken for the same reason yesterday. They're working on it now."

"Oh," I replied, unsure of what else to say, especially as she went back to her phone.

I pulled out mine and sent off a text to Kit.

Payton: *I'm stuck in an elevator. How's your day going?*

Payton: *It's with Nathalie Cheung though, so if we're stuck in here long enough, I might be able to build the courage to ask her for a job. Ha ha.*

I watched the screen for a reply but nothing came, she was likely giving a lecture on the influence of Shakespeare in our daily lives, or something along those lines.

I was just about to open *Tinder* when Nathalie sat down opposite me. "Which floor do you work on?"

"The fortieth. I'm in children's editing."

"You look familiar, what's your name?"

"Payton. Payton Lopez."

She frowned, her red lips pursing slightly. "Did you edit a book last year… *Flash the Wonder Dog*? Was that yours?"

Holy shit. Nathalie Cheung knew my name. She'd heard of me.

My eyes popped wider with each nod I gave. "Yeah, that was mine."

A smile stretched across her face. "My kids love that book. We had to buy a second copy because the first one got used so much that some of the pages fell out. It's still chosen as the first book of the bedtime reads."

"Yeah, it's a great book. Ellie Norris is a wonderful author. It was fun to work on." I grinned back at her, and the excitable nervous energy which had been shooting around my veins calmed. "Next time, come to the fortieth floor. I have some spare copies."

"I'll take you up on that. Thank you."

"You're welcome."

"You like children's publishing?"

I nodded, genuinely. "I do. It's where I started my career,

but my plan is to move into adult fiction soon. That's my hope anyway."

Crap.

My breath caught as I realized what I'd just said, especially as Nathalie Cheung raised one perfectly sculpted brow at me. I also had the feeling she was about to say something, but her phone pinged again and I lost her attention to whatever was going on, at whatever was making her sigh in frustration.

"Everything okay?"

She glanced back up and shook her phone at me. "Yes... no, actually. It's my youngest's birthday in a couple of weeks and he's recently become obsessed with The New York Lions. I've been trying to get a personalized birthday card or shirt from the team, but it's next to impossible. I thought they'd sell them in the store, but they don't. I've pulled all the strings I have. I even bought season tickets to see if that would help, but it didn't."

"Oh, yeah. Penn doesn't allow the players to do anything like that, unless it's on the gates before or after games. He thinks it takes their focus away." I snorted loudly, remembering vividly how that conversation went with Lowe. She had wanted to add it into her marketing plan, to hold organized signings or have personalized memos or cards sent to avid Lions fans. She wanted to humanize the team more, but Penn wouldn't budge. He didn't want them accessible. He wanted them to win. "Dumb, if you ask me."

"Penn?"

I nodded. "Penn Shepherd, owner of The New York Lions."

"But you said his name like you know him."

"Oh," I chuckled, "yeah, I do. He's married to one of my best friends."

Nathalie Cheung didn't break eye contact as she put her

phone down and shifted forward on her knees, and I suddenly had a new understanding of why she was so successful and got shit done. Even though I wasn't the easily intimidated type, and probably had thirty pounds on her, this was kind of intimidating.

"You have direct access to The Lions?"

"Um…" I shrank back as much as the elevator walls would let me. "Well… I mean, kind of."

"Payton, can you do this for me? Can you get something personalized? I'll take anything, shirt, poster… even if it's only Ace Watson, I'll take it."

I swallowed hard, trying to push down the air that had stuck in my throat.

"Ace Watson?" I croaked.

She nodded. "He's Chester's favorite player, though he hasn't had the best start this week, apparently. It's all that's been talked about at family dinner."

I stopped my head from falling back against the cool metal of the elevator, though it would probably help with the throbbing in my brain.

This woman that I desperately wanted to impress needed my help – except my help involved asking a favor from the one person I *really* didn't want to talk to.

"Please, Payton, at this point I'll do anything." She chewed on her lip nervously. I'd never imagined Nathalie Cheung to be nervous, but here she was, waiting for my answer. "I can move you up into adult fiction. You're a good editor, and I'm sure you'd fit right in. I've loved your work."

I blinked. I mean, come on. Why? Why did it have to be this?

"Nathalie…" I started, then stopped. It felt weird calling her by her first name. Though I wasn't sure what else to call her. Ma'am? Ms. Cheung? Oh, whatever. "Nathalie, are you saying you'll move me into adult fiction if I deliver signed memorabilia from Ace Watson?"

She nodded, way too eagerly. "Yes. I know they're looking for a new editor because the entire division had a shuffle around last quarter, and there's space. I wasn't kidding when I said you'd fit right in. I looked you up after I saw your name on *Flash*. You've been nominated."

My teeth gritted. Susie Van Marin had told me there was nothing going right now. Un-fucking-believable.

Now here I was being presented with the opportunity to have everything I'd ever wanted... Except it came with a catch; I knew what Ace would ask for in return.

Was it a no-brainer? The future of my career in exchange for showing Ace how to give an orgasm.

I mean, it could be a worse assignment.

Maybe I'd even get a lifetime membership to The Sisterhood for services rendered.

I opened my eyes to find Nathalie's pleading at me.

Oh, crap

"Okay, as soon as we get out of this elevator, I'll go and see him."

Her eyes bugged like mine had when I'd first stepped in and saw her. "What? You can go and see him, just like that?"

I nodded with as much of a smile as I could conjure. "Yeah. I'll see if I can get it for you now."

She held her hand out to me. The CEO of Simpson and Mather holding her hand out *to me*. "You have yourself a deal, Payton. Boy, am I glad this elevator broke."

I didn't want to question why the elevator started moving again the second I shook her hand.

I sucked in a deep breath and stood staring at the executive entrance to The New York Lions. Behind it, the glossy black walls of the stadium rose high and foreboding against the backdrop of the Hudson, with New Jersey in the distance. The sunlight bounced off its curves, making it look even more impressive than usual, or maybe ominous was a better word. The all-black façade and spears crowning the top of the stadium certainly added a little foreboding, even with the bright, cloudless day.

Or maybe it was just me.

Since the last time I'd been here, a giant Lions logo etched in gold had been hung over the huge doors. It was a warning to all who entered; reminding them they were about to go into battle, like Roman gladiators entering The Colosseum.

I'd almost rather face a pack of lions than this particular one.

I reached into my purse and pulled out my phone, clicking into Ace's stream of messages. The last one had been left unread.

Ace: *You know it's not baseball I need help with.*

I paused over the keypad – ugh – here goes nothing. Typing out a message, I pressed send before I could change my mind.

Payton: *Okay, I'll talk. I'm in the parking lot.*

I wasn't expecting to wait long for a response, but one

came back immediately.

Ace: *What parking lot?*

Payton: *The Lions' parking lot.*

Ace: *What?*

Payton: *I'm outside, Ace.*

I checked my watch wondering how long it would take him to find me. It was less than five minutes before he walked through the door. Sauntered was a more accurate description, each step holding a little more attitude than the last.

When he'd dropped by my apartment the other night, I'd been so dazed that I hadn't fully registered how incredibly handsome he truly was. On any other day, Ace Watson was a total American-cut cutie-pie. But in a bad mood and fired up, like he appeared to be now, Ace Watson became a smoke-show.

A very hot, smoldering, smoke-show.

His hair looked darker this morning, though on closer inspection I could see it was damp; tendrils curled along his collar as they dried. The black Lions t-shirt emphasized his tanned skin, stretching tight across his broad chest, and I had to remind myself I'd already been naked with this man. I knew what was underneath.

Maybe this wouldn't be so tough.

He was still a couple of yards away when my nostrils were assaulted with the scent I'd been trying to forget; of lakeside forests in June and camping under the stars, or sailing across the bay while the breeze floated around you. It was oaky and sweet, all wrapped up in that distinctive man smell you could never quite describe.

He stopped before he was too close, and his scowl

deepened. "How did you get through security?"

"I smiled at the guard."

For some reason my answer seemed to annoy him, based on the way his jaw clenched even tighter. "Yeah, of course you did."

I wasn't sure if he required a response, but from the way he was still staring at me, I'd hasten to add that it didn't.

I cleared my throat. "How's the mojo?"

"Still missing," he snapped. "Come to rub it in further?"

I frowned, not really appreciating this heartless monster he seemed to think I was. "No."

"Then what are you doing here, Payton? We've got a game tonight and I need to focus. It's bad enough I haven't started in two weeks."

I shifted from one foot to the other and uncrossed my arms, trying to give the impression I was totally chill, when I'd rather be anywhere else. I also tried not to think about whether this was bordering on solicitation.

"About that… I think we can help each other."

Ace narrowed his eyes and leaned back ever-so-slightly. "What does that mean?"

"You need my help, and I've come to ask for your help with something. I'm proposing an exchange of services."

"What?" he frowned. "You want me to help you with sex?

It took a great deal of effort to hold in the scoff I wanted to let out. "No. I don't need help with sex."

"What then?"

I took a deep breath. "Do you know who Nathalie Cheung is?"

His mouth drew into a hard line, and he shifted back with

a stamp of his foot. "No. Is she also saying I was shit in bed?"

"What? No…" I shook my head. "She's the CEO of Simpson and Mather…" My gaze moved over Ace's face, but there was no recognition there. "The publishing house? It's where I work…"

"Oh," he frowned, "okay."

"She's a big deal, Ace." I stopped myself before I waxed lyrical on Nathalie Cheung, because it was clear it would be lost on my current audience. "Anyway. She's a big Lions fan, or her kid is…" I gestured to him with a smile, "of you actually, and she's been trying to get a signed birthday card…"

"Shepherd won't let us," he interrupted.

I drew in a long breath before I lost my patience. "I know. I was thinking, if you could sign something maybe just from you… then I'll help you with the… um… the sex thing."

His eyes narrowed in suspicion. "What do you get out of this?"

"I get to move out of my job in children's publishing and into adult fiction"

"Oh." He pushed his hands deep into the pockets of his trackpants. "And I only need to bring you a signed birthday card?"

"Maybe throw in a photo, too. No, make it a shirt with your number on. And a cap. All of it," I blurted. I wasn't about to chance losing this job opportunity.

His blue eyes fixed on mine, narrowing again. "And then you're going to let me give you an orgasm?"

"I'll let you try."

"Fuck's sake." He dropped his head with a shake. "I can't believe I'm having to bargain with someone to have sex with me."

This time it was my jaw gritting. "Yeah? Well, there's your first problem."

"What?"

"Stop acting like you're God's gift. You're not. You think being better at sex will help your game? Consider that your first lesson."

He held his palms up. "Alright, I get it. Believe me."

"Good. What time do you finish playing tonight?"

He shrugged. "Should be done by ten."

"Be at my place by eleven."

"What? Tonight?"

I nodded. "You want to start playing again, don't you?"

"Fuck, yes."

"Then be at my place later, and don't forget to bring me that stuff." I held out my palm to him, just like Nathalie had done to me. "We have a deal?"

"Deal." He gave my hand one hard pump that nearly pulled my arm from the socket. "See you later."

I tried not to look at his butt as he jogged back to the entrance doors, before he disappeared out of sight without a second glance.

I stood there for a minute contemplating what I just done, and whether it was down the end of the more stupid stunts I'd pulled.

Unfortunately, the jury would be out on *that* verdict for a while.

8

Ace

*T*his has to be the weirdest booty call ever.

If you could even call it that.

I'd never had clammy hands and a gut swirling with anxiety; I was usually too focused on the semi in my pants.

I did *not* have a semi this evening.

I wiped my hands down my shirt, then stuffed them into my pockets. Nope. That wouldn't work. I puffed out a deep breath; my tongue was still burning slightly from the toothpaste I'd sucked down on my way here in an attempt to disguise the acidic taste from all the nerves.

I'd also showered after the game, because it was the polite thing to do before you had sex with someone, not that I'd exerted myself *at all* tonight, but showering had killed time.

I raised my fist to the door, and knocked hard.

I was about to knock again when I heard light footsteps

on the other side, and then the door swung open. The simple 'hey' I'd been about to give her immediately fell out of my brain as I stood there staring at Payton, wondering if maybe I hadn't looked at her properly before. Or at all.

She was wearing a pair of navy sleep shorts which curved around the tops of her thighs and made her legs look ten feet long. The matching top was falling off her shoulder, just shy of revealing a very pert, round tit, and a stretch of skin so soft-looking I clenched my fists before I stroked my finger along it.

"Hey," she breathed out, her voice catching like she just woken up.

Something, I think, was confirmed when she rubbed her eyes and tugged up her top, only for it to fall back into its previous position.

I didn't need to touch it to tell it wasn't made of the silk or satin or whatever girls normally wore when they opened the door to me.

It was that soft cotton, like the lumberjack shirts Lux had in every color.

I'm sure we were supposed to have sex. I'd been absolutely positive that's what we agreed earlier, yet she hadn't made the slightest bit of effort, and... I peered closer... she wasn't even wearing make-up.

None of this was playing out like I was used to.

Payton was *nothing* like I was used to.

Even for a strong swimmer, it had become abundantly clear I was well out of my depth.

My heart thudded again, and not in the good way. The way that reminded me there was a ball of anxiety bouncing in my belly and getting bigger by the day.

"What's wrong?" she asked as she wiped the corner of her

mouth. "Why are you staring at me like that?"

Instead of answering with something dumb, I thrust the bag I'd brought with me at her; the one containing my home and away uniform, a New York Lions ball, and cap, and a poster – all signed by me.

Payton opened it up, her eyes widening as she sorted through everything.

"Wow, Ace," she breathed in a way that woke my dick up. "This is amazing. Thank you."

She looked at me and smiled, which only made me frown deeper. Maybe she'd forgotten why I was here. Maybe she'd meant I just needed to bring over the bag, then we'd have sex or whatever a different day.

Maybe that's why she looked all... nah, she looked sexy as fuck, and the semi growing in my pants agreed.

She stepped to one side. "Are you going to come in?"

"Oh. Yeah."

She walked off, so I followed mutely and closed the door behind me.

I knew I'd been in her apartment before, twice if you counted when I came over the other night to tell her she'd ruined my life, but my mind was completely blanking.

I could not remember a single thing about it.

Except this... I remembered standing in the kitchen.

She placed the bag on the counter and turned to me with a smile. "Hey, how was the game? The Lions won, so that's good, right?"

I stared at her. And stared some more. I wasn't sure what game she was talking about, but it didn't sound like anything I'd taken part in. Except the winning. Not that I'd contributed to that, in any way, *at all*.

"Did you watch it?"

"Some of it." She lifted her shoulder up, like that explained everything, especially when her eyes lit up. "I saw you pitch. That was great."

I frowned again, so deeply I felt it right between my eyes. The only pitch she saw me make was a wild one, and it absolutely was not great.

It was possible I was standing in front of the only person I'd met who couldn't reel my stats off with a click of my fingers. Or name every play I made, or ball I threw.

She probably didn't even know the different types of throws.

Or that there *were* different types of throws.

"So," she pressed on, "how was it? How did it feel?"

I leaned back against the kitchen counter, standing opposite her, and crossed my arms. "Do you know anything about baseball at all?

She shook her head and grinned widely. "No, not really. I like watching it when we go to the stadium, and I'm watching it more now, you know, because of…" she paused and glanced at her feet, "um… my friends."

"Penn Shepherd?"

Her dark brown eyes darted back to mine, a smirk curved up her lips making them appear even fuller. "You know that, huh?"

"How d'you think I got your number?"

"What?" she spluttered. "Penn gave it to you?"

My eyes widened as far as hers had. "No! Fuck, no. No. Beulah Holmes did. I saw the picture of you all."

Her gaze followed my finger to where it was pointing at the fridge. "Oh. I'm surprised Beulah gave it to you."

Now it was my turn to look at my feet.

In an act I wasn't entirely proud of, I'd gone up to Beulah's office and stayed there until she'd given Payton's number to me. I'd talked and talked *and talked* about the yips, until she couldn't take it any longer. In the end, she'd written the number on a Post-it and tossed it at me, asking for me never to return.

"I had to promise not to bother her for anything ever again."

"Oh, okay, phew." She pressed a hand to her chest before she continued, "And the less Penn knows about this, the better. I can't cope with a lecture on breaking his boy wonder. Or any subject, if I'm honest."

I huffed a small laugh. I was well acquainted with Penn Shepherd's lectures. "Me either."

She stood staring at me, and I remembered why I was here in the first place, and all the nerves came flooding back. I tried to find some words, but I had nothing.

Normally when I was with a girl, I knew exactly what to do.

Charm oozed out of me, and they lapped it up with a coy little giggle while batting their lashes. But not this one. I wasn't flirting; I wasn't even sure I knew how to flirt with her.

If I tried, she'd probably shoot me down on that, too.

I didn't want to smile; I didn't throw her a wink. Nothing.

I'd been stripped of my powers. They were all gone.

This is how Superman must feel. Payton is my Kryptonite.

Whatever she was, the longer we stood here in silence, the more awkward as fuck it was getting, and if my career didn't rest on it, I'd be running for the door.

It was like she read my mind. "Do you want a drink?"

I didn't drink during the season, but I was about to make an exception. "Sure, waddya got?"

"Shot of tequila?" she grinned, and for the first time throughout this entire shitshow – including, and especially, the last two weeks – I found myself genuinely laughing.

As she reached behind me for the bottle, her arm brushed past me, and the scent of roses and clean linen – the same scent I'd woken up to twelve days ago – floated under my nose and lingered in the air.

I rubbed against my chest as it tightened.

Payton picked up two shot glasses, poured out the tequila, and handed me one so full it dripped onto the countertop.

"You seem uptight."

The tequila burned all the way down to my belly. "I feel like I'm starting my first day of school."

She looked up at me, her big brown eyes twinkling under her thick black lashes, and a sly grin crept over her face. "Maybe it is."

I coughed out a laugh. "It's not funny. I'm under pressure. I fucking choked this week. I'm going to ruin the entire season, and my career."

"Are you always this dramatic?" She poured out another shot, throwing me a hefty eye roll as she did. "Actually, don't answer. Penn is exactly the same."

I groaned. "Can we not talk about my boss?"

"Sure." She lifted the shot glass to her lips and knocked back the pale gold liquid. "What d'you want to talk about?"

I looked away as her pink tongue darted out and licked a stray drop from the corner of her mouth, reminding me of what else that tongue was capable of. My cock stirred again, and I couldn't decide whether it was wrong to be attracted to someone who'd ruined my life.

Two shots of tequila didn't normally warm my blood so quickly, but I'd been surviving on two hours of sleep a night, and not much food, because my appetite was also on hiatus. The nerves I'd had walking in here suddenly didn't feel so present.

"Well, I guess, how we're going to do this?"

"You mean, you want me to explain to you about the birds and the bees?" She smirked, *again.*

I scowled, *again.* I wanted to wipe that smirk right off her beautiful face, along with her refusal to take this situation seriously.

"Stop being a dick," I snapped. "You know what I mean."

But she just stood there, arms crossed over her chest, with one thick dark eyebrow arched pointedly. I thought I'd get away without mentioning the 'O' word, but I'd been wrong.

"I need to know what was wrong with… before… apart from…"

"The lack of my orgasm."

"God," my teeth gritted. "Do you always just say whatever's in your head?"

She shrugged. "No point lying, is there?"

I huffed in response because I didn't have anything verbal to offer. It was true, though her truth was what had gotten me into this mess in the first place. Payton must have read the annoyance in my expression because her smirk disappeared and her eyes softened, only to be replaced by something gentler.

"Okay… there wasn't anything *wrong,* wrong, but… what do you remember of it?"

I shrugged, praying that she couldn't tell I hadn't been

going over and over *and over* it in my head. But it didn't matter how many times I replayed it; I still couldn't figure it out.

"I dunno. We made out, had sex. I thought we had a good time."

"It started well, very well…" she closed her eyes and took a deep breath. "All that kissing got me really fired up. I fucking love kissing, and you weren't bad."

Fucking *kissing*? Girls were so weird. I didn't even remember kissing her that much.

"Kissing?"

I swear she let out a little moan.

"Mmm, yes. Good kissing really turns me on. You know what else I enjoyed?"

"What?"

"Your fingers, but sadly I only got to experience them for a very short time." Her plump bottom lip curled into a deep exaggerated pout. "What did you enjoy?"

I didn't have to think long or hard… I'd been trying not to think about it at all, but it was my turn to almost moan. She might like my mouth on hers, but I liked hers on my dick, and the memory of her lips wrapped around it momentarily pulled me out of my sulk. "You sucking my dick was a highlight. You were very good. Skilled." The visual of her on her knees swam into my brain. "Fuck, you'd have been swallowing my come if I hadn't pulled you off."

"I enjoyed it, you have a very nice dick. Unfortunately, after that, it's all you were focused on."

"What?"

One shoulder lifted up in a half assed shrug. "You coming."

"Oh, I… well…" My words froze and I frowned deeper as

hers sunk in. "If you hadn't been so good at sucking my dick then I wouldn't have needed to come so badly."

"Oh no," the dark polish on her long nail shone under the spotlights as she wagged it, "don't try and turn this around on me with a back-handed compliment. Haven't you heard of staying power?"

"I… I…" My mouth opened, then closed, but any explanation I had vanished from my brain. In all the hours and *hours* I'd spent analyzing every second we'd been together, I'd never noticed that one glaring and important detail. I'd been so wrapped up in myself I'd just assumed she was having a good time, like every other girl.

Except she was not every other girl.

I wouldn't be in this situation if she was.

"You fell asleep almost the second you'd finished, and I was left needing… more."

Fuck, she was right. I'd been completely spent. I couldn't have moved even if I'd wanted to. Without trying, she'd stripped me of power – in more ways than one.

Didn't make this situation any less embarrassing, though.

"I'm so sorry, Payton. I didn't realize."

"It's okay," she grinned. I'd never have regarded her as a sadist, but she was clearly enjoying my torture. "I helped myself."

Images of her touching herself swam into my brain, and I let out a small groan as my eyes closed. When I opened them again, she was much closer than she had been. I hadn't realized it, but as we'd been talking, she'd stepped nearer. Her thumbs inched under the elastic of her sleep shorts easing them down until they dropped to the floor.

I caught a flash of emerald green lace between her legs.

"You want to try again?" She held out her hand for mine, but I didn't take it.

If she wanted to teach me, then I was here to learn. I wouldn't get this opportunity again, so I was going to learn the fuck out of her.

I was going to be an A+ student.

"I've got a better idea – let's play show and tell. You know, seeing as this is my first day of school and all."

Her neck craned back as she looked up at me. "You want me to show you how I make myself come?"

I nodded. "Yes, so I can do it next time."

A hint of pink crested her cheeks, but it wasn't out of shyness. No, it was challenge, and a hefty dose of arousal which turned my semi to full-mast in less than a second. I could just make out the peak of her nipples hardening through the soft cotton shirt as her hand slipped downwards and under the scalloped edging of her panties.

"Wait, I can't see." I placed my hands around her waist and lifted her onto the counter pulling her forward until her ass was resting on the edge. Smoothing my palms along her soft thighs, I hitched one up to rest on my hip and spread her wide. "Much better."

Her bottom lip caught between her teeth, holding back a smile, and she followed my eyes down to where they were now glued – right between her legs and the darkening patch of green silk.

Propping herself up on her left hand, her right moved lower, but I still couldn't see.

This was supposed to be show and tell, after all.

I reached out and hooked a finger under the silk, easing it to the side for a better view. Her rich brown eyes flared bronze, and her breath caught as my knuckle grazed against the neat little patch of hair and held back the elastic. My heart was hammering and my dick was so hard it would have the imprint of my zipper against it, but I'd take the pain if it meant I got a front row seat to this show.

I didn't want to blink in case I missed a second of it.

"Holy shit, you should see how sexy you look."

She looked up at me from under thick black lashes. "Yeah?"

"Fuck, yeah, so hot. Now show me how you like to be touched."

My free hand gripped onto her thigh, widening them as far as I could, and desperate to join in as her fingertips slipped between her legs spreading her wetness everywhere. Her gaze fixed on mine as her index slid over her swollen clit, then with a quiet moan, her eyelids fluttered closed, and I lost her.

All the girls I'd been with before had been confident, one-night-stand level confident to put on show and give me what they thought I wanted, but I was beginning to learn something: Payton was a whole other level of confident.

That *I-don't-give-a-fuck* type of confident.

And it was the sexiest fucking thing I'd ever seen.

The pink on her cheeks soon spread across the rest of her skin giving her an almost radiant glow, and as I watched her fingers slide around her glistening clit, I realized I'd never seen someone so totally comfortable with who they were and what they wanted.

I was torn between wanting to watch her finish, and wanting to be part of the show. My fingers were digging into her thigh so hard they would leave a mark, but the decision was made when her eyelids flickered open and she looked at me through heavily hooded eyes.

"Put your fingers inside me."

She didn't need to ask twice, and the 'good' she'd awarded me earlier I was determined to upgrade to 'excellent'. She was so wet I slid in two straight up to my palm, curling them around and pumping them inside her, while she kept up the rhythm of her fingers.

She reached out and grabbed my shoulder, squeezing it so hard I nearly yelped.

"You like that?"

"Oh fuck. Yes. God, Ace, don't stop that."

A freight train couldn't have stopped me, and I increased the pressure, stroking against her until her breathing became short, sharp, bursts. I was so mesmerized with her fingers working over mine, that when she breathed out my name, my eyes shot up.

"Wh… what are you doing? Don't stop," she gasped.

"That noise… make it again." I pushed a third finger inside her and twisted it up. "Say my name *again*. Say it, Payton."

Her head fell back, and her fingers started moving faster than my hand could. "Oh fuuck. Ace. Ace. Fuck, I'm coming."

My fingers suctioned inside her from every powerful contraction of her pussy. Over and over she came, even as her fingers slowed and her lungs filled with air. I'd never seen anything like it; I think my brain was about to combust. I don't know what realm I'd been in that night we'd had sex, or how I thought she'd come if this is what she looked like when she really did.

I'd never been so close to my own orgasm while remaining untouched and fully clothed, but I was too desperate for a repeat show to think about my dick.

"Holy shit." She caught her breath, easing back on the counter and leaving a silvery trail in her wake. "That was… good."

"Oh, we're not done." My hands slid under her top and pulled it over her head. The tits I'd been dreaming about for two weeks bounced free, big and luscious. "I want to hear you make that noise again."

She watched my thumb stroke over her nipple and roll it between my fingers. "Let's see if I learned anything shall we? And don't fucking lie to me this time."

"Ace?"

I answered by pushing her back onto the counter, yanking down her panties and widening her thighs again.

If I was honest, I loved eating pussy, but I rarely did it. There was something too intimate about being that close to someone you'd only met an hour before. Yet right now, I was almost salivating at the thought of it.

She tasted exactly how I thought she would; sweet, salty, and faintly of the roses I kept smelling on her as my tongue flattened over her sensitive clit.

I peered up to find her watching every move I made, her eyes glimmering and her jaw slack. With the tip of my tongue, I flicked against her hard little nub and she groaned deeply.

"You like that?"

She managed a nod.

"Tell me how you like it. Hard, like this?" I dipped down and took one long lap, and halle- fuckin -lujah, heard *that* noise again. "Or soft, like this?"

"Both," she breathed out. "I want both. Your stubble… fuck…"

I resumed my position between her legs. Her nails scraped along my scalp, fisting my hair, as I rubbed my face all over her pussy, grazing my stubble over the most delicate parts of her. I learned that when my tongue speared inside her, her grip tightened, and when I ran my tongue along the outside of her lips, her thighs trembled. But it was when I suctioned onto her clit and flicked gently that her entire body shook like she was the epicenter of an earthquake.

Maybe we both were.

Yanking my head away so hard I was convinced she'd left a bald patch, I stood to find a sheen of sweat covering her entire body. A smirk crept up my lips until it was a full-blown grin.

I'd been nominated for the Cy Young Award. I'd won several Pitcher of the Years though college, and Rookie of the Year during my first season in the majors, but seeing Payton spread on the counter in front of me, a dripping, panting mess, I really felt like I'd achieved something… and I don't think my dick had ever been this hard.

"Holy shit," she rasped, "how did I not get you to do this before?"

I wiped my hand across my mouth. "I don't do it often."

"Why?"

I tore my eyes away from her chest heaving and the single droplet of sweat rolling between her tits. "I never know where my mouth's going."

"That's a little hypocritical. You couldn't wait for me to suck your dick."

"I know where my dick's been," I grinned.

She eased up onto her elbows, her frown slowly disappearing into a smile until she was laughing hard, and the way her boobs jiggled as she did was almost hypnotic.

"Oh my God, that's such a boy thing to say."

"Are you complaining again?"

One of her brows arched high. "No."

"Good, because now you have a choice. I can leave and you can go to bed, or we continue your lesson and go for a hat trick."

She tapped a long black nail against the corner of her lips before answering, "Every day's a school day."

"Just as I thought." I scooped her up, carried her under the archway leading into her bedroom, and kicked the door open wider. She was still laughing as I threw her back onto the bed, her tits bouncing again as the mattress sprang against her.

I stood there watching her. The streetlights outside her apartment were peeking through the blinds and making her body appear like it was lit with gold. I'd never spent much time – or any time – looking at the women I was with. I was always far too busy...

"Why are you smiling?"

"I was just thinking that..." I shook my head. "Never mind, no reason."

I wasn't about to tell her that I was thinking how sexy she looked, or that I'd never seen anyone like her, or met anyone like her. Because if I had paid attention to the girls I'd been with before, then I wouldn't be here now.

And right now, I couldn't think of anywhere else I wanted to be.

She narrowed her eyes. "Well, while you're smiling, perhaps you could remove your clothes so I'm not the only one naked."

I'd never stripped quicker.

It was only when I unzipped my fly that I remembered it was restraining my dick, and it bounced back with enough force to wipe the smile off my face.

Her eyes dropped, hungrily scanning along my chest, my biceps, my abs, and lower. She stopped, her head tilted. "I was correct, you do have a very nice dick."

I gripped around the base and stroked up; I was rock

hard. After her performance in the kitchen, I was so close to coming that if I wasn't careful, I'd make the same embarrassing mistake as I did before.

I was 2-0 tonight, and I planned on making it 3-0.

"What would you like to do with it?"

The tip of her pink tongue darted out and licked across her bottom lip. I had to hold in the groan I could feel deep in my balls, which were tightening more with every second I stared at her. No matter how much I wanted to feel that warm, wet mouth wrapped around me, it would be game over for both of us.

Even thinking about her mouth had my entire body tingling, and beads of precum dripping from the end.

I took another long tug, trying to ease some of the pressure.

"Payton, while you decide, I feel I should point out that you've been naked for the past forty-five minutes, and I'm…" I stopped while trying to find the words to explain without sounding like I was complaining.

Because I definitely wasn't complaining.

"Ready to burst?" she smirked.

I nodded, firmly. "Yep."

"Poor, Ace. We'll have to do something about that, then." She patted the bed next to her. "Lay here."

In less than a second, I bounced on the bed next to her, making her laugh loudly. She reached over to her nightstand and took a condom from the drawer. Ripping it open, she knelt next to me, but I snatched it from her.

If she touched my dick, I wouldn't be held responsible for what happened.

"I'll do it."

Instead, her hands slid over my abs, tracing along the

outline of muscles. "What was it you wanted? A hat trick?"

Before I could answer, she straddled my thighs. I didn't think it was possible for me to be any more turned on than I already was, but I was wrong; she was so fucking wet, her pink pussy dripping, and my balls twisted another notch.

My dick thumped against her belly as her hands flattened over my stomach so she could steady herself. She hovered over me, making my dick flex as she rubbed against it, and with a wicked twinkle in her eye, sank down and took me in one long, hard stroke.

There was no way I was going to last.

"Oh fuuuuck." The groan I let out could have been heard over at the Lions' stadium.

I swear it echoed off her bedroom walls.

Black stars shot through my vision. My brain throbbed, my dick throbbed... every goddamn muscle in my body throbbed.

For the second time, I laid in Payton's bed and wondered if I'd died.

"Fuck, you feel good," she moaned, arching her back with a roll of her hips which shot another bolt of electricity down my spine. "You really do have a perfect dick."

"Yeah," I groaned, "and my dick thinks you have the perfect pussy. Oh. My. God."

Her thick, dark brown waves tumbled over her shoulders, brushing across her nipples, and I wanted to do nothing but twist it around my fist. But I was smart enough to know that Payton was running this show, and I was going to do exactly what I was told.

She circled her hips again, adjusting to the size of me, and my brain nearly broke from the sensation. "Oh yeah, that's so good."

I could only grunt in response as I watched her rise above me, using me for her own pleasure. It was the most incredible thing I'd ever seen.

Lacing her fingers with mine, she guided my hands until they were either side of her hips. "I like to be touched. I want your hands stroking me, squeezing me, playing with me, and I want to hear you telling me how good I feel sliding up and down on your massive dick."

I didn't even have to think about it, especially when she slowly lifted her hips until she'd almost removed herself from me entirely, then sunk back down with such a deliberately leisurely pace that it was excruciating.

"Payton, you feel so fucking good. I've never felt anything like it in my life."

"You bet your ass you haven't." She groaned again, and with another thrust of her hips, sank down even further. "Just think, you could have done this two weeks ago."

I didn't want to think about that.

"Tight and wet," I gritted out. "So goddamn tight and wet."

My hands found her ass, squeezing hard as I adjusted myself with a swivel of my pelvis which had her eyes rolling back. My fingers slid up her spine, through the slick of sweat, until I could grip the back of her neck.

"Kiss me," she ordered.

She might have only been an inch away, but I yanked her mouth to mine until I surrounded her. Teeth clashed as my tongue thrust into her mouth, stroking along hers to match the pace our hips had set, and I knew she could taste herself on me. I could *still* taste her. Another squeeze of her ass had me swallowing a moan, and I now understood what she meant about kissing.

This might be the best kissing I'd ever experienced.

"Ace… harder… I'm going to come. I need…"

"Tell me," I growled, a tone I'd never heard before. "What do you fucking need? Because whatever it is, I'll give it to you."

I pushed her back and sat up, bending her knees until I could lift her, ignoring the bolts of pressure tightening my balls. With one hand splayed across her hips, my thumb reached for her hard little clit and began stroking exactly how she had. In seconds she was riding me like a bronco, bucking against my thrusts; then her thighs quivered, her chest flushed red, and her breathing almost stopped as my name fell from her lips in a way it had never done from anyone before.

I'd been holding on so long for this moment that my balls were quicker off the mark than my brain. With her first convulsion I exploded inside her, emptying myself and jerking with so much force I thought my dick had broken.

That hadn't been an orgasm: that was the world shifting back onto its axis.

I was still floating above my body when she eased off me, patting my shoulder as she collapsed face first into the pillow next to me. "Congratulations. You got your hat trick."

It was the last thing she said before her breathing settled and she fell into the deepest sleep, while I was still watching her eyelashes flutter and wondering what the fuck just happened.

I might need to grow my balls back.

If that was how sex was supposed to go, thank fuck I didn't keep the numbers of every girl I'd slept with, because I had a lot of apologies to make.

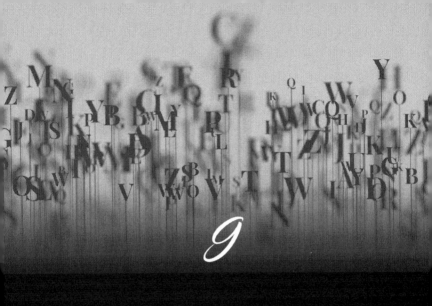

9

Payton

I flicked through my clothes, making the hangers screech along the rail as loudly as possible. It was worse than nails down a chalk board, enough to have goosebumps erupt across my body, but the sight behind me remained unchanged.

The sight which I'd been trying very hard not to stare at.

The sight which had already made me late for work because a. I hadn't wanted to get out of bed in the first place, and b. it was very distracting.

I wasn't even sure he'd moved in the thirty minutes since I'd finally slipped out, showered as quickly as possible, then pulled on a bra and panties – a new pale pink pair I'd bought last week – all while I watched him sleep; but not in the creepy way, more like the 'how has he not yet woken up yet?' way.

I nudged the end of his foot again, but it didn't make a

difference. I'd learned the first time that dead people were easier to wake up than Ace Watson.

I knew he was alive, even with his face pressed into the heavy bicep flung over his head; I could tell from the soft rise and fall of his smooth, golden back, and the way his muscles contracted ever-so slightly with each quiet inhale. One of his thighs was curled around the comforter, stretching the fabric along a fading tan line and the curve of his ass.

Unfortunately, I didn't have time to stand here all day and stare at him, or think about his dick, or fingers, or... Jesus, his *tongue*... so I walked back into the bathroom in search of my makeup.

It was as I curled my lashes that I realized the reflection peering back at me wasn't the one I usually saw. I mean, it was me... but it also *wasn't* me. It was like me five years ago, not the me I saw yesterday; the one who had me vowing to start getting earlier nights. If I didn't know better, I'd swear I'd already spent an hour contouring my face – something I would never do, because I had neither the patience nor the time for contouring. But there was... *something*.

I picked up the blush, then put it back down. My cheeks were already rosy enough. Instead, settled on a slick of eye pencil, a lashing of mascara, and a coat of my favorite berry red lipstick, followed with a quick brush of my hair and a run through with the curling iron. All done in under five minutes.

I could be accused of a lot of things, but high maintenance would not be one of them.

Thankfully, I didn't have to make another attempt to wake Sleeping Beauty because when I walked out, he was sitting up in bed, the white comforter across his lap only emphasizing his ridiculously stacked abs and setting off his tan further, and making him look so impossibly handsome that I stopped in my tracks.

Jeez, who *seriously* woke up looking that good? Even with that moustache…

I briefly wondered how many college girls had his poster in their dorm. If I'd had him on my wall, I'm not sure I'd have ever left the room.

"Good morning." A broad grin split his face, showing off perfectly straight white teeth. "Sleep well?"

"I did, thank you." I smiled back, because I couldn't help myself. His smile was infectious. "I don't need to ask if you did…"

He stretched his arms over his head, lengthening his body back down the bed. His biceps flexed as he opened and closed his fists. I also didn't fail to notice the impressive tenting in the comforter right where his dick was, and averted my eyes. I could still feel where that impressive tenting had been less than eight hours ago, and tried my best to ignore the heavy throb between my legs, just in case I needed reminding.

I didn't.

Focus, Payton.

"I did. It seems I sleep very well in your bed." He yawned before continuing, "Do you always get up so early?"

"It's not early. It's eight a.m."

I could feel his eyes on me as I crossed the room to where I'd hung the clothes I'd picked for today – a white silk shirt and grey pencil skirt, with a pair of black Manolos Kit had given me for Christmas. I'm not going to lie and say I didn't take my time as I stepped into my skirt and slowly zipped myself up, knowing full well Ace was watching every move, but I peered up to find him looking at me with an expression I didn't recognize. It was almost curiosity, especially when he sat up straighter and propped a pillow behind his head.

"Why are you looking at me like that?"

He shrugged. "I've never seen a woman get dressed before."

I shouldn't have asked, and dropped my head so he didn't see the smile I was wearing.

"Seems you've had a lot of firsts lately," I shot out before I could stop myself, but he merely laughed. It was the same laugh I'd heard the night I met him when we'd driven back here together, the one that had gotten me into this mess, along with – you know – the rest of him looking exactly like that.

"Yeah, you're right," he grinned, "I have, and you won't find me complaining about it."

I slipped my arms into the shirt sleeves, and buttoned it one by one. Ace's mouth slackened as his eyes fixed on my fingers.

"Why don't you have a boyfriend?"

Okay, good mood ruined.

I turned around to finish the last two buttons without an audience. "Why are you assuming I want one?"

"Because you're every guy's wet dream. And girl's too, probably. I don't know how you haven't been snatched up yet. Lucky for me though."

"Again, don't I get a choice in the matter?"

He scooched up the bed, and reached out to take hold of my hand. "Come back to bed."

I glanced down at where his thumb was tracing back and forth over my knuckles, and eased my hand free. "No."

"Please," he begged.

"No," I shook my head. "Plus, there's no need. Your curse has been broken, or whatever you called it. You made me come, three times if you remember. Congratulations."

"But what if it hasn't been broken?"

"Ace," I rolled my eyes and stepped back. "Next time you're with a girl, just remember she's there too, and it's not all about you. Then you'll be fine."

He grinned, making me wonder how long women usually held out against him. Not that I had a great track record when it came to saying no to Ace Watson.

"I think we should try again just to make sure."

"We had a one-time deal." I held onto the closet door and stepped into my heels one at a time. "I'm leaving now. You can let yourself out again."

"Hang on. Don't I get a kiss goodbye? I thought you loved it."

"In the right time and place, which now isn't, especially as I'm already late for work."

He jumped out of bed, wrapping the comforter around him like a Grecian God and followed me to the front door.

"Want me to come and sweet talk your boss so you don't get into trouble?"

"No, thanks," I replied, picking up the bag of signed Lions merch he'd brought over, and reached for the doorknob. "And thank you, again, for these."

"Payton, wait."

"What?" I sighed.

Ace leaned in and softly pressed his lips to my cheek. "Thank you."

I blinked. I'd never been thanked for sex before, and I was trying hard not to blush; trying even harder not to breath him in. How did he smell *this* good, like he'd just walked through a forest or something?

"You're welcome."

He opened the door for me and I tried not to watch his

bicep flex as he gripped the frame, but failed miserably. "See you around, Babycakes."

I could still hear him laughing to himself as I ran down the steps and out into the beautiful morning sunshine, where I finally allowed the grin to spread across my face.

I hadn't even had coffee yet, so why did it feel like I'd been mainlining caffeine since sunrise?

"*Why* are you staring at me?" I found myself asking for the second time today.

Kit shrugged. "Dunno, you look different. Did you have a facial before you came to meet us?"

"Don't be silly." I shook my head. "It's probably the ridiculously flattering lighting in this place. How can you not look good in here?"

"Yeah, probably," she grinned, and plopped herself down on the couch next to me. "We both know you'd drop from a ten to a five as soon as we walked onto the street and the natural daylight hits."

I stuck my tongue out at her.

We were currently in the den of Kit and Murray's mega apartment, as I liked to call it – the one with six bedrooms and a view of Central Park, a terrace that was big enough to have trees on it, and an entrance foyer that could double as an art museum if it wanted to. Flattering lighting kind of went with the vibe here. It was the type of lighting that made you look like you wrapped yourself in cashmere and got twelve hours sleep every night.

I snuggled into the couch and pulled one of the cashmere blankets from the backrest, throwing it over my lap just to prove a point to myself.

"Did Bell go down okay?"

"Yeah, she's got her favorite stuffy and Barclay in bed with her, so she'll fall asleep in no time," Kit affirmed, picking up the bottle of wine that she'd brought in with her. "He'll be in here the second the food arrives though."

I hadn't had the most productive day today, but it *had* been fun. I'd arrived at work with all the expectations of Nathalie Cheung being so beside herself with excitement that I'd brought her the entire Ace Watson signed merchandise range, that she'd move me to the fiftieth floor immediately. But when I went up to find her, her P.A. informed me she was out at a conference in D.C. for the next three days, the same one Susie Van Marin was attending.

I'd left the bag with the P.A., and promptly walked back out of the office to play hooky. I'd met Kit and Bell, and their Labrador, Barclay, in the park. Then we'd come back here to hang out for the rest of the afternoon. Murray had gone to the Lions game; Kit and I had bathed Bell and put her to bed.

It was something I tried to do at least once a week, being the godmother and all. It was usually on the nights Murray was out with his boys, so Kit and I would get to have some girl time together. I also felt it was my duty to spend time with Bell and make sure she had someone to teach her about proper footwear, seeing as her mother seemed to live exclusively in sneakers. Bell might only be two, but it was never too young to start them early.

The other benefit of spending time here was Murray's wine cellar, because while I liked wine, he was a borderline professional and ordered it by the very-expensive case load. The cork in the bottle we had planned to drink tonight, however, didn't seem to want to move.

"Let me try." I took the bottle and stuck it between my knees. The corkscrew eased out slowly with a loud pop just as the door buzzed.

"Yes!" Kit cried, jumping up and sprinting out of the room.

I finished pouring the wine, and ran back to the kitchen for plates when she returned, her arms laden with our delivery, Barclay hot on her heels. Whenever we had a night together, we always ordered the same thing from our favorite deli – the best lemon spaghetti I'd ever had in my entire life, a big salad, and three portions of fresh asparagus, because we always had to get extra for Murray.

My stomach rumbled and my mouth filled with saliva as the smell of butter and citrus filled the air from each box opening. Kit passed me the spaghetti tongs and I scooped up a big bowl for each of us.

"Yum, thanks," she replied, taking one from me and twisting a forkful into her mouth before she'd properly sat back down.

She snatched up the remote and switched through the channels until she found The Bachelor reruns.

"We're not watching baseball?"

She glanced up at me. "Yeah, just seeing what else is on."

I leaned forward and picked up my glass of wine, trying to keep my voice way more casual than I felt. "Let's see what's going on with the game first. We already watched The Bachelor."

"Sure, okay." She flicked back through until she found The Lions game.

It was already top of the second inning; the score was

still zero to both The Lions and The Red Sox, which was an improvement on the previous games so far this season – especially the opener.

The Red Sox were pitching, so it wasn't clear whether Ace had started. Lux Weston stepped up to the home plate and hit a line drive to third, but the Red Sox third basemen wasn't quick enough and it slipped through his fingers, continuing its journey to the outfield. As Lux ran around the bases and back into the dugout, the camera panned along the benches. Riley Rivers was sitting where Ace usually sat, which likely meant Ace hadn't pitched yet.

I tried to ignore the way my chest tightened.

Stupid superstition.

But at least now the Lions had made it on the score board.

The Lions took the field, and Riley Rivers walked slowly to the mound. I tried to ignore the sinking in my stomach. The commentators started up while the camera followed the teams change over, and I stabbed my fork through the salad leaves.

"The Lions seem to be coming back on form in their home field, Aaron, after the shocking opening series in Philly. Shocking. I'm still thinking about it."

"You're right, Mark. It'll be one for the record books, but Penn Shepherd and August Chase have been making the decision to start Riley Rivers both times when Ace Watson would normally have been on the mound, and it appears to be the right one. I'm going to go out and say it, I think we're looking at an early contender for Rookie of the Year."

"That is bold, Aaron, but you predicted it two years ago with Watson, so I'm not going to bet against you on this one either."

"Speaking of Ace Watson, we've heard he will be pitching

tonight. We don't have confirmation on which inning, but we do know that August Chase will be sending him out to the mound."

I let out the breath I didn't realize I'd been holding, and looked down to find I'd twisted almost the entire bowl of spaghetti onto my fork. I shook it free, and started again with a frown.

"And what are you expecting to see from him tonight, Mark?"

"We all obviously want to see Ace back to his usual form, but…"

I grabbed the remote and turned down the volume, not wanting to listen to any more talk about Ace.

"Hey, do you know what the yips are? Had you heard of them before all this?" I asked as I waved my hand at the screen where the Red Sox batter was up.

He swung and missed the first pitch, and got back into place for a second attempt.

Kit leaned forward and picked up her glass. "No. I hadn't. Had you?"

"I thought he was talking about an STI."

She turned and grinned at me. "Weird how it suddenly happens, comes out of nowhere, and they almost never recover at full strength."

The Red Sox batter made contact on the second swing, and the ball went flying straight into Tanner Simpson's glove. He hadn't even made it to first base.

"What? Where d'you hear that?"

"I overheard a couple of students talking about it today, so I asked them."

"What did they say?"

"That it can finish careers, it can be completely debilitating. Affects catchers and pitchers, mostly, in baseball anyways." She reached for the box of asparagus, tipped a couple into her bowl, and handed one to a slobbering Barclay. "Seems to be what keeps sports psychologists in jobs."

"Um... so what causes it?"

"No one knows." She shrugged, then shot me a sly side-eye coupled with an equally sly grin. "Not your vagina, I'm sure."

"Shut up." I nudged her hard, letting out a hefty snort as I did and took the asparagus box. "Just seems odd that something can completely change overnight; everything you thought you knew."

I could feel Kit staring intently at me, but thankfully decided against saying whatever she was going to say, and turned back to the television.

The Red Sox now had two guys around the diamond, one on first and one on third. Riley Rivers drew his arm back and pitched the ball. The Red Sox batter swung hard, and the ball rose high over the field, heading toward the stands on the left where the crowds had jumped out of their seats hoping to catch it.

All three of the Red Sox players sprinted around the bases and back to their dugout.

"Did we win yesterday?" Kit asked.

"Yeah. I only saw the end and I can't remember the final score, but it was a win."

By the time the game reached the bottom of the fourth, the score was still Red Sox three to the Lions' one. I watched the teams change over and the camera zoom into Coach Chase deep in conversation with one of his players. I didn't need to see the player's face to know it was Ace.

This time Riley Rivers wasn't the pitcher walking to the

mound.

I stood up abruptly and picked up our empty plates. I didn't want to watch Ace, and I didn't want to listen to the commentary.

I didn't want to see his first pitch in case he fucked up again.

I didn't want to see his first pitch in case he didn't.

I wasn't sure which I wanted to see less.

"I'm going to get some ice cream."

I walked slowly to the kitchen, my ears straining for any type of cheering which might indicate how Ace had thrown, and placed the dishes in the sink.

Slowly, I opened the freezer and ran my finger along the enormous selection of ice cream tubs until I found the ones I was looking for – mint choc chip, cherry, peanut butter, and vanilla. Slowly, I scooped out each flavor into two bowls, then placed the tubs back in the freezer and slowly carried the bowls back out.

The camera had zoomed into Ace's face. Even from the brief five minutes I'd seen of the game last night before he'd come over, I could tell he looked completely different. Relaxed, almost. It wasn't the Ace I remembered from last year; the one with the almost arrogant, gave-zero-fucks quirk of his lip right before he powered a ball toward his opponent at a hundred miles an hour, but it was a far cry from the guy with tension and worry carved into his features... the one I'd seen since Opening Day.

"He's pitching much better," mumbled Kit through a mouthful of ice cream.

"Yeah?"

"Look." She nodded to the screen where Ace was in position; his knee raised and his arm back. The ball flew out of his hand, straight into Parker King's glove. "That was ninety-seven mph."

"Huh."

"You took so long getting ice cream you missed his first throw. The Red Sox guy only got onto first base after Ace's third pitch. He's going for the fast ball tonight."

I spooned a mouthful of cherry ice cream. "Oh, okay then."

"See? Maybe he didn't have the yips. Something seems to have worked, anyway." She reached for the remote again. "Can we watch The Bachelor now?"

I picked it up before she could. "No, wait, let's just see Ace finish pitching."

"I thought you didn't care about Ace." She turned to me with a frown. "What's going on?"

"Nothing."

Kit spun her entire body around until she was facing me and crossed her legs, determination radiating from her. "What's going on?"

I sighed; she would only keep asking. I don't know why I was feeling so weird about it. I always told Kit everything, but for some reason, this felt a little... private? No, wrong? No. That wasn't it either.

Dumb. Yeah, dumb is exactly how it felt.

"Okay, but try not to judge too much, and can you keep it to yourself this time? I don't want big mouth Murray telling Penn."

"What did you do?"

"I had sex with Ace Watson."

She stared at me, a confused expression on her face. I swapped my bowl of ice cream for my glass of wine.

"I mean, *again*. I had sex with him *again*."

She would have won an award for the gasp she let out. "What? When?"

I cringed. "Last night."

"How? You said it was terrible the first time."

I held a finger up to her. "No, I never said that. I definitely didn't say it was terrible. I said it needed refining."

"Then what happened?"

I took a large sip of wine, and recanted the series of events which lead to me doing something I said I'd never do again. Kit's mouth dropped a little more as my story continued.

"Was it worth it?"

"Oh, yes," I nodded slowly. "Very much so. Ace Watson is one eager learner. He was really gunning to be teacher's pet."

Kit let out a loud snort. "So has lesson time finished then?"

I nodded, putting my glass down. "It was a one-time deal, and it looks like he's got his game back now. Plus, I've dropped off all the signed merch to Nathalie Cheung's P.A."

"Still can't believe you met her," she sighed.

"I know," I replied with a grin.

"Anyway," she waved her hand at the screen, and Ace, "this is only his first inning. He could crumble again."

"He's thrown well. He'll go back to charming his way around Manhattan, only better this time."

"Pay, you realize what you've done?" she giggled.

I frowned. "No, what?"

"If Ace really thinks you've been responsible for his bad pitching or whatever, then you have sex with him and he miraculously goes back to playing like he did, all the credit will go to you."

"Don't be stupid. I'm not telling anyone about this, and

you promised not to either."

She zipped her fingers across her lips and handed me the invisible key. "I promise I won't. But who's going to tell Ace?"

"Tell him what?

"That you don't have a magical vagina."

I rolled my eyes. "Now you're the one talking crazy."

She picked up the remote and turned up the volume, just as Ace threw a fast ball which clocked in at almost a hundred miles an hour.

"Whoa, Mark, would you look at that? Ace Watson goes from his performance so far this season where he could barely make the strike zone, to this."

"You're right, Aaron. Whatever's turned his game around, I wanna bottle it and sell it for millions."

Kit turned back to me with a grin so wide it was in danger of splitting her face.

"I'm not sure what point you're trying to make, but last night was a one-time deal. I'm not having sex with Ace Watson again."

"Want to bet me a lot of money that you're wrong?"

My eyes flicked back to the screen where Ace was walking back to the dugout. His head was down, but no one could miss the broad smile, or the way Parker King flung his arms around him for a big hug. He looked relaxed, happy.

He looked like the guy who'd walked me to the door and kissed my cheek this morning. The guy I hadn't been able to stop thinking about all day.

I couldn't have had less conviction in my response if I'd tried.

"No."

10

Ace

Jee-zus. I could pull a hamstring trying that.

I turned the page ninety-degrees adding a head tilt; didn't make it look any easier.

"You could pull your hamstring trying that."

I slammed the magazine shut, but it wasn't quick enough for Parker's lightning fingers. Or maybe it was my slow reflexes, seeing as he'd just scared the shit out of me, and my mind was elsewhere.

"Give that back."

"Not until I see what it is." He grinned annoyingly wide, dropping into the seat next to me, and turned the magazine over to look at the front cover. His expression changed to the one I'd predicted he would wear, which was exactly why I hadn't shared anything about my new reading material. "Cosmo?"

I snatched it away, placing it back into the confines of G.Q. which I was also reading, just reading more openly.

"Expanding my literature."

He peered over and pointed to the headline of the page it had fallen open at, letting out a loud snort. "That says cliterature."

"Shhh," I hissed, stuffing the offending materials into my bag. "Will you shut the fuck up, Parker?"

"I will if you tell me why you're reading a girl's magazine."

I held my hands up, my head snapping around right and left to make sure we weren't overheard. "Okay. But can you hear me out before you judge?"

"Sure."

After I'd been pulled from starting pitcher and it became obvious to everyone in the club I had the yips, all the boys aside from Parker, Lux, and Tanner, had been giving me *way* more space than usual. It was why I was sitting down the far end of the plane on my own for the short flight to D.C., or had been before Parker interrupted.

But for the first time ever, I was more than happy with being alone. It meant more time for me to think without people yapping in my ear.

More time for me to read.

More reading equaled better pitching.

"Okay." I took a deep breath. "We both know that I've been pitching like shit since the beginning of the season."

He nodded solemnly, which was the closest he'd ever come to saying it outright. Parker was supportive to a fault, and I knew for a fact my 'current pitching situation' as he called it, had been almost as hard on him as it had been on me. And as much as I wanted to get my throwing arm back, I wanted it back for him just as much.

Parker was an excellent catcher, and had worked well with Riley Rivers in the short time they'd had together, but that was just it – short – they hadn't built up a relationship like we had.

"Then the second game against the Red Sox I came on and pitched a fast ball. It wasn't the fastest I'd ever pitched but it was hard, and compared to what I have been throwing, it was unexpected."

He nodded again. This time looking a little more curious, and now I had his attention. Neither of us had expected that fast ball to be quite so fast, especially as Parker had signaled for a curve ball. But I'd felt it, deep in my bones, that a fast ball was the ball needed…

And I'd been right.

"If Coach had kept me in for more than three innings, I think I'd have almost been back on form by the end of the game."

"Totally," he agreed and nodded with a grin, punching me playfully in the shoulder. Aside from being my best friend, Parker had been the only one who steadfastly refused to take the yips seriously. "You had a few off weeks, dude. You'll be back as starting pitcher in the next series, just see. I told you it was nothing."

"Parker," I shook my head. "No, it wasn't nothing."

I fixed him with a look, and to his credit he didn't roll his eyes like he had done before, or told me I needed to forget about Payton. He just sat there and gestured for me to continue.

"Okay, then what was it?" he asked, smiling up at the Lions' steward handing out bottles of water. "Thanks, man."

I chewed on the edge of my thumb. As far as Parker was

concerned, Payton had never replied to my first messages, but after she had, I'd been too nervous to tell any of the boys in case my theory didn't work, and I had to find another way to fix my throw.

"I went to Payton's for a do-over."

His hand contracted around the plastic bottle, which unfortunately no longer had the lid screwed on. Water shot up like a geyser, soaking the pair of us.

"What?" he yelled, shaking himself dry. I got up to grab some towels from the galley, handed a couple to him, and dried myself with the rest. "When did this happen?"

"The other night."

"Before yesterday's game…" His brows dropped as he did some quick calendar math. "Doesn't seem like you fucked things up worse."

"Not possible," I laughed. "Nothing could have gotten worse."

"Ace…"

"Parker, I had to try something."

He got up and moved to the dry seat opposite me, throwing the wet towel on the floor to mop up the puddle, and leaned forward.

"So, what? You had sex and now it's all better?"

I closed my eyes and began running through the little mental inventory I'd started yesterday morning – head, *check*; body, *check*; arm and shoulder, *check*. It all felt… normal. Back to normal. Or rather, I felt different to how I had been feeling. I'd felt different the moment I'd woken up.

Hell, I'd felt different the second she'd fallen asleep, and I'd laid there listening to her breathing. And the more I thought about it, the more I was certain that I didn't just feel different,

I felt *better*.

All day I'd been testing myself to see if the fog I'd been living in had returned… but it hadn't.

I'd tried not to get mad when Coach Chase had announced Riley Rivers as starting pitcher, because I wanted to test my theory. It had been hard, but I understood. Coach wanted a winner. Instead, I'd sat there on the bench waiting to be called, and the strangest thing happened.

For the first time since the beginning of the season, I hadn't been consumed with doubt and worry and anger that something was wrong with me. I hadn't been comparing my last season's stats, I wasn't thinking about what I'd do if my career tanked and I was dropped by The Lions before this season ended.

I was thinking about Payton, and that noise she made. That I *made* her make.

If I closed my eyes, all I could see was her face contorted in ecstasy as her pussy clamped around my fingers, before it morphed into her riding my dick like she was going for Olympic gold, and then she was appearing in the bathroom doorway, wearing only that heaven-sent bra and panties set. I'd never seen anything like it.

It was the most perfect thing I'd ever seen, until she started getting dressed.

If anyone had asked me whether watching a woman get dressed was sexy, I'd have answered with a loud laugh and an *'are you crazy?'* but Payton Lopez had firmly changed my opinion on a lot of things in the last twenty-four hours, and getting dressed was one of them. From that point on, my brain ricocheted between that noise and what she was wearing underneath her demure little skirt and blouse, and whether she always wore it. All day long – *moan*; her walking around New York, *moan*; taking meetings, *moan*; talking on the phone.

It was fucking hot.

And the best thing about it? My brain didn't have room for anything else. No anxiety, no nerves, no panic.

Nothing.

When I walked to the mound, my mind was clear.

It was only as the Red Sox first batter made his way to home plate so slowly he almost got a time penalty and Parker signaled for the pitch he wanted, did everything suddenly slot back into place.

For the first time in nearly two weeks, I could breathe properly.

I could feel myself coming back.

The dark clouds shifted; my muscle memory returned. Out of habit, my neck cracked left and right, and my spine re-aligned. I stood tall.

My hand gripped the ball inside my glove. I stepped back, and my knee raised.

The ball shot through the air; the Red Sox batter swung… and missed. The ball was safely inside Parker's glove.

I did it again. It was only on the third pitch that he managed to get off home plate and make it to first.

The crowds cheered. There wasn't a boo in earshot.

When I returned to the dugout at the end of my innings, Coach Chase had slapped me on the back and thanked me for finally *pulling my finger out*, which was the most praise I'd be getting.

I looked at Parker and shrugged. "I'm not sure yet. That's a theory I plan to test."

"Want to share this theory?"

"I…" I paused. Parker and I shared most things. Or everything. But I suddenly didn't want to share any part of Payton with him. Any part of what Payton and I shared. "Okay… this is all I'm going to say, but after I went to her place… best sex I've ever had."

His eyebrows shot up. "Really?"

"Yup. It's like I've had a… what's that word?" I snapped my fingers while I waited for it to drop off the tip of my tongue. "Epiphany. I've had an epiphany."

"And this time, it was the same for her?"

His face contorted with a grimace. Actually, not a grimace, a wince, and he was looking kind of worried about my answer.

"I don't know if it was the best she ever had, but I do know she had a good time."

"Dude, you thought that before. Are you sure she's not going to turn up at the grounds again and tell you otherwise?"

I nodded. "Yeah, I'm sure. This time, I hit the jackpot."

"And this is what turned your game around last night?"

I nodded again. "Something like that."

"Great, so can we all get on with our lives now, and things can go back to normal?"

I leaned forward. He was close enough that I could clasp the back of his neck and kiss him Godfather style, so I did.

He shoved me away with a laugh.

"Yes, we can go back to normal. Thanks for sticking with me, Park."

"Dude, it's been two weeks. You're such a drama queen."

I shrugged. "A long-ass two weeks."

Parker nodded, got up without saying another word, and returned with two bags of mixed nuts and two chocolate protein shakes.

"You haven't gotten to the bit where you tell me why you're reading a girl's magazine."

"Well…" I reached over and picked my bag up, pulling out both magazines. "There's a news stand on the corner near her place, and I wanted to get the paper. You know… see what was being said about me. While I was paying, I saw this." I held up G.Q. and pointed to the small pull quote in the middle left of the front cover, which had caught my eye.

"How to Give Your Girl Better Orgasms."

Parker took it from me and flicked to page ninety-seven; the article in question. His mouth hardened into a straight line and his eyebrows rose higher the longer he kept reading, until he finally looked up at me.

"It says here, according to a *Cosmo* sex quiz…"

I swept my hand out in front of him. "And that's why I have *Cosmo*."

He pointed to it, still in my hands. "Has that got the sex quiz in it? Did you take it?"

I shook my head. "Nah, it must have been a different issue, but I found these instead."

I flipped through to the article I was reading before Parker interrupted, and handed it to him.

17 of the Best Sex Positions for Intense Orgasms

He tapped the page on top of a cartoon couple twisted into a shape I'd been trying to figure out when he'd walked over. I wasn't sure I wanted to try it either, no matter how intense an orgasm it promised.

"This could do some serious damage."

I nodded.

"Have you ever done stuff like this?"

I shook my head. "Not really. Definitely not that. What about you?"

"Nope." He glanced over drawings one through ten. "I had a girlfriend in college, and we might have tried a couple of these. Maybe we did this one." He tilted his head and tapped number eight, which looked like you needed a certification in gymnastics to attempt. "Couldn't be sure though."

"But this is my point. It's all new. And if I can come back from the yips in one game after a night of amazing sex, what if I can really improve my game by getting better at all this?" I tapped the edge of the magazine.

But Parker was reading through the pages and not listening to my theory. "Have you seen this? Are you good or bad in bed? There are questions."

"What?" I pulled down the edge of the page so I could see what he'd found. I'd been so engrossed in the cartoon people I hadn't read beyond it. "What are they?"

"Foreplay. For or against? That's it, that's the whole question."

"What's the whole question?" asked Lux, dropping down in the seat next to me and shooting straight back up. "Ugh, why's it wet?"

"Spilled water," I replied, while also trying to consider my answer.

"Oh." He moved to the seat next to Parker. "Anyway, what's this question?"

I shot Parker a sly grin, and nodded. Including Tanner, the four of us were all very similar when it came to women, or so I'd always thought, because I realized we never really talked about girls. They were in the apartment more often than not; a fuss free revolving door.

But maybe this quiz would be interesting in more ways

than one.

"Foreplay, are you for or against?" Parker replied.

"Foreplay? Like in sex?"

I nodded.

"Where'd this question come from?"

Parker stuffed *Cosmo* down the side of his seat, out of sight. "Doesn't matter."

Lux's gaze flicked between the two of us. "What are your answers?"

"We haven't answered yet. You arrived as Parker asked it. Well?"

He scratched through his stubble and thought for a moment. "How much time do I have for the sex?"

My brows dropped into a confused frown, "What? You have a normal amount of time. A night."

"Okay, is this with a girl I met after a game, or a girl I really like?"

"What difference does it make?"

"I'm going to make more effort with a girl I really like," he replied in a tone that made it clear he thought it should have been obvious.

I sighed deeply. The man had a very valid point.

Which is perhaps where I'd been going wrong all along. I had nothing against foreplay, I think I'd perhaps forgotten the value of it. And when it came down to it, if I thought hard, it had been so long since I'd met a girl I really liked that I seldom bothered.

While I might be familiar with the casual-sex game, so were the girls I was having sex with, and more often than not, the reason they were with me in the first place was so they could say exactly that; that they'd had sex with Ace Watson.

Parker nodded, like he'd been thinking the exact same thing.

"Okay," I said, "next question. Kissing. For or against?"

"What?" laughed Parker. "Just kissing?"

I nodded. "Yep."

"Pass, unless it's leading somewhere," replied Lux.

"Isn't that the whole point of kissing?"

I shrugged. "Dunno. That's what we're trying to figure out."

Until two nights ago, kissing had always been a pointless appetizer before the main course. One of those tiny things handed around on trays that you ate because you were starving but it didn't even touch the sides. But then Payton had ordered me to kiss her while I was fucking her, my tongue thrusting inside her while she was riding my dick, swallowing her moans until they hit deep in my balls.

My mind on kissing had been changed.

Lux sat up straighter. "Seriously, where are you guys getting these questions from?"

Parker pulled *Cosmo* free from where he'd stuffed it and handed it to Lux, who looked just as confused as Parker first had.

"Why are you reading this?"

"Because G.Q. said there was a quiz in it."

"A quiz about what?"

"Orgasms."

Lux looked at Parker, then at me, then back at Parker. "Okay, next question."

I snorted, taking *Cosmo* and thumbing to the quiz, only for Lux to stop me before I got there.

"Jesus, how do you do that?" He pointed to the cartoon

drawing and leaned in closer like it would help him figure it out quicker.

"We're not sure." I flipped to the quiz page. "Okay, here's one. Being tied up. For or against?"

"Who's tied up? Me or her?"

I looked back down at the question. "Doesn't say."

They both sat back in their seats. Parker drummed his fingers against his cheek, while Lux smoothed down his beard.

My mind drifted back to Payton, *again.*

I could see her tied up, wearing that pink lace, while I ate her pussy until she made *that noise.* The one where my name became an affirmation.

If I had one goal for the rest of my life, it would be hearing it again. I shifted in my seat before I got a full-on boner.

"I'm for it," Lux said finally, a smirk growing from the corner of his lip. "There was this girl I was screwing once, she loved being tied up. She also loved being told she was a good girl."

Parker snorted. "What? Like put your hands behind your back, like a good girl."

"Yeah, exactly." He picked up the nuts from the table rest between us and tipped the entire bag into his mouth. "She fucking loved it."

"Did she tie you up?"

He nodded with a grin. "Yeah, one time, but it wasn't that good."

Parker's mouth dropped open as he stared at Lux, and his head fell back with a loud laugh. We all knew why – Lux was a big guy, at six foot five it would take a lot to restrain him under any circumstance.

"What happened?"

"She lacked conviction," Lux shrugged.

"Oh, dude. That's fucking funny." Parker shook his head and looked at me. "Next question."

But my eyes caught a different movement; Riley Rivers was walking down the gangway to our seats. I flipped *Cosmo* shut and tossed it to Parker who shoved it back down the side of the seat rest.

"Hey, man, what's up?" I nodded to him.

He glanced around at the three of us, noticed the weirdly guilty expressions we were all wearing, and frowned slightly. "Coach and Mr. Shepherd want you. They're down at the front."

"Cool, thanks. On my way." I turned back to Lux and Parker, pointing my finger at them. "Don't go through any more without me."

I stood up and followed Riley to the front. Even though this was a short flight, some of the guys were already napping. Saint Velasquez looked like he was meditating while wearing a pair of giant noise cancelling headphones. I passed Jupiter, Stone Philips and Boomer Jones playing poker with a couple of the PTs, but mostly the plane was quieter than it usually was on a longer journey.

It was as I reached two thirds down that I realized I needed to pass Beulah, Lowe, and Marnie Matthews who were sitting on one of the sectionals along the side, though thankfully they were deep in conversation, and I walked quick enough they didn't notice.

Coach Chase and Penn Shepherd were sitting with Coach Willis, one of the pitching coaches.

"Coach, sir," I nodded. "You wanted to see me?"

"Ah, Watson," Coach Chase greeted as he looked up.

"Please sit down."

I sat.

"How are you feeling?"

Up to the point where Riley had come to fetch me, I'd been feeling great. Now, with three pairs of inquisitive eyes on me, my hands became slightly clammy again. I tugged down on my ball cap and concentrated on keeping my heart beating at its usual pace, instead of where it felt like it might break one of my ribs.

I cleared my throat. "I'm feeling good, thank you. Looking forward to tonight."

"You really turned the game around last night," Penn nodded. "Seemed like we had Ace Watson back. That was some impressive pitching, even more so considering you barely made the strike zone the last time you were on the mound."

I ran my hands along my thighs, stopping any jittering before it even started. "Yes, sir."

Coach Chase took off his glasses and pinned me with narrowed eyes. I'd never noticed before how piercing they could be, especially when they were staring right at me. "Think you can do it again if we start you during this away stretch?"

"That's the plan," I nodded, and tried to summon as much conviction as I could. "I know I fucked up the beginning of the season. It was my fault alone, but I'm feeling good now. I'm back in the game."

The four of us glanced up at the steward as he passed by our seats. "Gentlemen, we'll be arriving in approximately fifteen minutes. Please prepare for landing."

"That's your cue, Watson. Go and sit back down."

"Thank you." I stood up and turned to walk away, only for Penn Shepherd to call my name.

"Whatever you did to help get your focus back so quickly, keep doing it."

I tried to hold in the smile. "Yes, sir."

I made my way to the back of the plane as quickly as I could to find Tanner was now in the wet seat next to mine, but he looked far too engrossed in what the three of them were reading to have noticed.

"Hey, I said wait for me," I grumbled, sitting down and reaching for my seat belt.

"We only just started."

"What's the next question, then?"

Lux's eyes flicked down to the page. "What's your go-to sex position?"

"Ass up," Tanner and Parker announced at the same time, throwing a high five out as they did.

"And what does it say about that?" I asked.

Lux went back to the answers and snickered loudly enough to have Parker snatching *Cosmo* from him. His face fell as he read the answer. "That we lack intimacy and romance."

"Works for me," grinned Tanner. "It's easier to get away the next morning, or better yet, the same night."

I snorted and glanced out of the window as we made our descent into Dulles. In the distance, I could just make out the Washington Monument. Beyond that would be Nationals Stadium, where we were playing tonight. Coach hadn't gone outright and said it, but with any luck I'd be back starting in the next series, and I needed to make sure I was back permanently.

Therefore, I needed to ensure my game hadn't just returned, but improved immensely.

I pulled out my phone.

Ace: *Hey, Babycakes, I'm sure you saw my game was better last night… and my boss just ordered me to keep doing whatever I've been doing.*

Ace: *As I've been doing you, I guess we're going to be seeing more of each other *winky face**

I didn't wait for a response. Next to me, Lux was packing up his bag. I turned as he tapped me on the shoulder with a rolled-up *Cosmo*.

"Can I borrow this?"

"When I've finished with it," I grinned, taking it from him and stuffing it into my backpack.

I had homework to do.

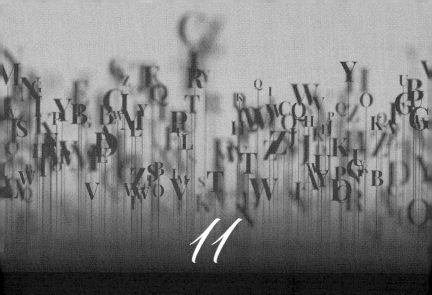

11

Payton

*T*equila before nine a.m. is acceptable, right?

"Mom, I don't know what dad's doing, I haven't talked to him." I banged my head repeatedly against the couch cushion.

"Well, you tell him that I know what he's up to. Every year I host Memorial Day Weekend, and now he's decided he's hosting too? He's doing it on purpose. How are our friends supposed to decide which party to go to?"

"You don't have any of the same friends anymore."

"We have some of the same friends," she snapped. "You tell him…"

"Mom, you're a grown-ass adult woman. You tell him," I snapped back. "I have a job and I need to go and do it. Sorry, Mom, I gotta go. Hope your party is good."

I hung up before I could hear any more about how her

party would fail, or how my dad was a selfish asshole, and tried to ignore my guilt creeping in.

I remember when I first moved to New York, I thought I would be free of the hatred my parents had for each other, but I'd been wrong. After the first month of being away, they'd called me more times to complain about each other than they had to hear the voice of their only child. I used to attend support groups for kids of divorce, and for the life of me, I couldn't figure out why I'd stopped. I needed to find a new one.

The buzzing of the intercom halted my train of thought.

"Ms. Lopez, your nine o'clock is here."

I scowled at the offending announcement and quickly brought up my calendar, because a nine o'clock meeting was both new to me and unwanted.

I scanned through today's date. Nothing, I knew it.

"I don't have a nine o'clock," I replied.

"He's quite insistent, ma'am."

"He? Who is it?"

The receptionist didn't need to answer however, as over the faint muffling of the speaker I heard a voice I recognized immediately, and three things happened:

My heart leapt into my throat.

My belly sank.

And my pussy throbbed.

It was all very confusing, nor did I have time to think about it, because the next voice on the intercom was his.

"Good morning, Babycakes. Let me up, will you? I have a present."

I couldn't decide whether the giggle of the receptionist made this situation worse, or if I'd already hit rock bottom.

"What are you doing here?"

"Told you, I have a present."

"Ace, I'm at work. You can't just show up here." I didn't know why I was bothering to explain, because even if I said no, he'd somehow still make it up to my office within the next five minutes.

Another giggle from the receptionist told me as much.

"Too late," he replied, and I knew if I could see him, he'd be wearing that shit-eating grin again, the one he'd worn two nights ago when he'd pitched the fifth inning against the Braves without any of the three batters making it to first base. He'd walked off the field with a swagger he could have only learned from Jupiter Reeves. It was almost like the first few weeks of the season hadn't existed.

Except, *except*, I knew they had.

If they hadn't, I wouldn't be so distracted all the time – even more so than usual.

If they hadn't, I wouldn't be falling asleep every night in an Ace Watson fantasy induced post-orgasmic haze, based on very real-life experiences.

And if they hadn't, then I wouldn't have approximately seven hundred tabs open on my computer screen, all trying to find new snippets of news about his performance during the Lions away series. All of them were saying the same thing – that Ace had turned around his game overnight, and was on his way back to playing like he had done last season, and whatever had caused his blip seemed to be well and truly over.

I'd tried not to think about me being the blip; both causing it and being the solution, or – worse – whether he'd been practicing his new techniques with other women; the girls that followed them on tour, the ones that waited outside his hotel and made sleeping with them as convenient as possible.

It was ridiculous. Why should I care in the slightest whether he'd been with anyone else? It was none of my business, it was what I told him to do. It was what I wanted… and I certainly didn't like the twisting in my belly at the thought of it.

"Payton?" he tried again. "Are you gonna let me up, or am I going to have to figure out another way to see you?"

I was almost tempted to see what he'd try, but I knew it would probably cause me more hassle in the long run. Not to mention Giggles would likely stick the news of his visit on the building's Slack channel the second she let him through the barriers.

"You've got five minutes," I sighed, ignoring every alarm bell ringing in my head, least of all the one that sounded like Kit betting me I'd sleep with him again.

The second I heard him whoop I grabbed my purse, rummaging around for the hand mirror to check out the current state of my face. Thank God I'd washed my hair this morning. I tidied up the stack of manuscripts I'd been reading through and slipped my feet back into my heels.

I got up and perched on the edge of my desk – no, that looks too sexy secretary…

I ran back around and sat down in my chair. Better. Now there was furniture between us, which lessened the likelihood I'd throw myself at him.

Holy crap. What was wrong with me?

I didn't have time to debate that because in the next breath, he was standing in my doorway. It was the last breath I took for a while.

The last time I'd seen him, he'd been wrapped in my comforter, and now he was once more clad entirely in black. Lions black. Over the past week I'd been watching the games and wondering if he was growing his beard out, and now with him standing here smiling his perfect smile, it was almost impossible to imagine him without it.

It was like he'd aged overnight, like a fine wine. Or grown another three inches, tall and wide.

My office wasn't big, but as Ace strode across to my desk and took the seat opposite, it felt almost suffocating. Like the ventilation had been cut off and the oxygen was slowly being sucked out. He filled the chair, his huge shoulders taking up all the space as his legs stretched out in front of him.

"Hello," he said, placing a small turquoise and white striped bag in front of me.

My focus, which had been entirely on him, and how, again, I seemed to have forgotten quite how good-looking he was, suddenly switched allegiances. Sugar and Bean was my favorite coffee shop in New York. Even seeing the store bags had a Pavlovian response on my taste buds.

"What did you bring me?"

He nodded toward the bag. "Open it."

I didn't need to be told twice, and reached across the desk for it. Inside was a to-go cup of coffee and a little blue and white striped box. I almost didn't want to open it, because there's no way I'd be able to resist whatever was inside. There was a reason I only allowed myself to go to Sugar and Bean once a week, and that was mostly because I was scared of the dentist. My sweet tooth could do some serious damage if I let it.

A bright red cupcake with pink frosting and little gummy hearts was inside when I eased open the lid, and I couldn't hold back the smile as looked up at Ace. The ridiculously proud expression on his face, smug almost, made my smile even wider.

"Thank you. These are my favorite."

"I know," he grinned, only for my brows to furrow in question. "I saw a note on your fridge saying you loved them."

"Oh." I peered down at the box and fastened it up. "Well, it's very kind of you. Do you want to tell me what you're doing here?"

"I wanted to see you."

"Why?"

He shrugged. "Do I need a reason?

I glanced over at the door, which he'd left open enough that anyone walking past could see or hear him, and got up to close it. I stayed where I was. A room between us was better than a flimsy desk, but I didn't count on Ace also standing up, though he turned and sat his ass on the desk instead.

"I've been pitching better; have you watched?"

I tried to pretend the question hadn't been asked, or how I should answer… Maybe if I stayed silent, we could both pretend he hadn't asked it. Then I wouldn't have to say no instead of yes – I've watched every single second of every game, hoping to catch a glimpse of you. But I wasn't that lucky.

"Payton, have you been watching the games?"

I shook my head, hoping he couldn't see the heat creeping up over my cheeks. "No."

His head tilted ever-so slightly, and I wasn't sure if he believed me or if he was disappointed. "Really?"

"No," I frowned. "My life doesn't revolve around you. I have work, you know."

The problem with lying is that it's always going to bite you in the ass. I didn't think this particular lie would be proven quite so easily, but as he shifted on my desk, the movement nudged the computer mouse, which woke my screen up – my very large computer screen which was turned enough that I could see it very clearly, along with what I'd been reading all week.

He didn't immediately notice, but as my eyes widened in horror and darted away, he only needed to turn around to see exactly how big of a lie I'd just told. A lead weight dropped in my belly, a direct contrast to the slow, steady grin spreading from cheek to cheek on Ace's face, and lighting him up like a sunrise.

I could do nothing to stop it.

His face stared back at us.

More specifically, an image of him running into the dugout last night at the end of the final game against The Braves. The Lions swept the series. Last night, Ace had been starting pitcher and stayed on until the seventh inning. Every sports page and publication was saying he'd made an unexpected come back after the worst Opening Day in Lions history, and that included the four decades before Penn bought them, where they stayed exclusively at the bottom of the standings.

Before I could stop him, Ace guided the mouse, flicking through enough tabs that he could see they were all about him, and turned to me with an expression that made me dearly wish the ground would swallow me whole, or the ceiling would cave in.

Anything so that I wouldn't have to live through what was about to happen next.

"Were you checking up on me?"

"No."

"Your computer screen says different."

I looked away, only for him to push off the desk, and in three large strides he was standing in front of me. I took a step back and hit the wall.

Goddamn wall, why did it have to be *there* of all places?

Ace gently took my chin between his fingers and pulled me back to his blue eyes, boring into me so hard they'd be able to see every secret I had and every lie I'd told. Those blue eyes I'd been seeing every time I closed mine. They were hypnotic.

"Payton, we talked about this. Don't lie to me."

"Fine, you've been playing well."

"So you have been watching me?"

"Hardly," I scoffed. "I saw a couple of minutes the other day."

Yeah, way to save face, Lopez.

He continued staring at me so intently that if I didn't know better, I'd swear he'd stripped me naked. My heart was beating in every cell of my body. Blood whooshed in my ears firing up my synapses, and each vicious spark hit dead center of my clit.

The air became hot, stifling almost. I'd barely caught my breath back from when he'd walked in, and now it was gone again.

He'd stepped forward and spun his ballcap around.

"Wh… what are you doing?"

"I'm going to kiss you, unless you say no."

My eyes fell to his lips; his plump, pouty lips, which were currently far too close for me to make any kind of sane decision. Or decision, period.

Instead, I let out a moan – a fucking *moan* – like I was some dribbling, wanton hussy who couldn't control herself. His blue eyes flared.

"I'll take that as a yes."

I don't know how, given there was no space at all between

us, but he moved another step closer and pinned me against the wall.

I could feel the calluses on his palm as they cupped my cheek. I hadn't noticed them before, but now it seemed my body was hyper aware of everything about Ace Watson. All I knew as his nose ran along my jaw and his tongue brushed my earlobe, was that I was on the verge of hyperventilating.

It wasn't until his lips made their way along the column of my throat that I realized I'd tilted my neck back to give him better access. He could have all the access he wanted. I wasn't sure what game we were playing, but I'd surrendered the second he'd walked in here like he owned the place, and all I could do was wave my white flag.

I'd always thought I was stronger than this with an innate ability to say no, but by the time his mouth found mine, I was a quivering, trembling mess. As his lips engulfed mine and his tongue slid across my tongue, a loud groan escaped and I could barely stand. My entire body went limp until I whimpered.

All from a goddamn kiss from a guy who couldn't find my clit with a map and a headlamp three weeks ago.

At some point my thigh hitched around his waist, and his big hand hooked under my knee as they continued stroking over my body, squeezing, caressing, and pushing up my skirt until it resembled more of a belt. It was becoming impossible to focus on any one sensation when his tongue was still so insistent in my mouth.

I barely noticed as his fingers slipped under the elastic of my panties and he eased two inside me.

Oh *shit.*

I wasn't sure if the moan I swallowed was mine or his.

"Fuck," he mumbled, "you're soaking."

My head fell back, only for him to grip my face and bring me back to where he was looking at me so intently, and I couldn't stop a second moan barreling up my throat.

"Oh, yeah," he growled. "There's that fucking noise. I haven't been able to stop thinking about it. Make it again."

"I don't perform on command, Ace."

All I got in return for snapping was that irresistible boyish grin, and his palm cupped harder, grinding down against my clit. "What if I tell you you're being such a good girl? Do you like that?"

Oh *God*. Maybe I was his slave. I think every cell of my body clenched around his fingers.

"Oh, you do." He chuckled softly, and his voice dropped to a whisper. "What a good girl. What a perfect pussy you have."

"Wh… where did you hear that?" I managed to breathe, though it wasn't enough to stop the black spots from clouding my vision. I needed more air, yet Ace was stealing it all. "How did you know?"

"I've been studying. Wanna see what else I've learned?"

"No," I groaned.

His eyes roamed over me, finally settling back on my face, his fingers never letting up on their insistent twisting, scissoring, and curling. And then his thumb rubbed against my clit and my brain nearly disintegrated.

"Oh… Ace. I'm…"

His hand slapped over my mouth.

"Shhh, Babycakes, we're in a professional working environment. Can't have you screaming the place down. Save it for later. Now, let me feel you squeezing the life out of my fingers and wishing it was my cock."

It wasn't an explosion; it was an *implosion*.

My entire body caved in on me from the pressure under his fingers. His magic, *magic* fingers. Every contraction spasmed through me until I was shuddering uncontrollably from the force of my orgasm, and only his grip on my ass stopped me from crumbling to the ground. As it was, I couldn't be sure he wasn't holding me up entirely.

His mouth found mine again, but this time, he wasn't keeping time with the power of his fingers. He was bringing me back down to earth, his tongue gently stroking against mine until my body was ready to hold itself up again.

When he finally pulled away from me, he looked so unbelievably pleased with himself that I couldn't hold in the laugh.

What the fuck had just happened?

"You know something?" he grinned. "You were right. Kissing *is* good."

"Oh, man." My eyes started to roll just as his thumb brushed over my clit, and instead, they rolled back. Without his hand clamped over my mouth, a loud groan escaped before I could stop it.

"Be careful, Payton." He eased my leg off his thigh and placed it gently on the ground, bending as he did so he could straighten my panties and my dress. When he looked up at me, I swear his eyes were pure lava. "I'm going to get addicted to you and that noise you make. I'm very competitive, especially against myself."

The smile died on my lips. The thought of him making me come like that on a regular basis was enough to set waves of panic crashing through me.

I'd never survive.

The grin soon bounced back like a Golden Retriever puppy. That's what he was, a puppy who never tired. That's why I couldn't hold out against him; he had too much energy.

"Have you ever had sex in your office before?"

"No."

"Do you want to?"

"Christ, I've created a monster," I grumbled, slipping my foot back into my shoe.

"Yeah, and I can't wait to eat you up." He snapped his teeth, though even the grin and the way his hair curled under his ball cap, or the deep sparkle in his sapphire eyes couldn't stop him from looking wholly dangerous.

"Okay." I stepped away, he was far too close, and I was clearly incapable of making any type of sound decision in his presence. "You need to leave now."

He chuckled again, but thankfully moved toward the door. "Are you going to watch the game tonight?

"Maybe."

"You'll be able to tell me what you thought of it when I come over to your place later. I'll finish what we just started. I've got some moves I want to try."

I was just about to tell him he wasn't going to be coming over later to try any moves when the rest of my reality decided to kick me up the ass, just in case it hadn't done enough of a number on me already this morning.

"Knock knock." The door pushed open.

"Nathalie," I gasped, stepping even further away from Ace in case she realized exactly what we'd been doing and fired me, while trying really hard not to check if Ace's dick was still hard in his pants.

If my window had opened, I'd have probably jumped out.

There's no way she couldn't smell sex in the air.

But Nathalie had walked in, and the first thing she'd seen

had been Ace smiling so naturally he was all she had eyes for. Mine, however, rolled so hard they almost stuck.

Was there no one unaffected by him?

I quickly glanced down at his pants, where thankfully nothing seemed too obvious, or maybe the black trackpants were hiding them.

Nathalie's head moved between Ace and me. "I'm so sorry, did I interrupt?

"No, not at all," Ace answered before I could, with that smile that ensured he got whatever he wanted. "I just swung by on the way to practice to bring Payton her favorite cupcake."

Oh dear God.

Nathalie's mouth dropped open. "How kind. I'm Nathalie."

"Payton's boss. I've heard so much about you. It's great to finally meet you."

My lip curled in disbelief. He was laying it on thicker than… actually, I dunno if there was anything thicker than the way he was smiling at Nathalie right now. If we were in a Disney movie, a little sparkle would have hit his tooth while he was backlit by a rainbow.

"I hope you got the bag of merch Payton brought for you."

Nathalie's eyes widened, her head still flicking between the two of us. "Yes, yes I did, thank you. It's why I came down; I've been out of the country. It's so generous, I can't thank you enough."

"Happy to help, just let Payton know if there's anything else you want. If you ever need tickets…"

She clasped her hands to her chest in a way that I never imagined Nathalie Cheung would do. I almost wanted to shake her or slap some sense into her. Both even, especially when she started giggling like a schoolgirl.

This woman had met world leaders, academics, pioneers of industry, and yet here she was, drooling like a twelve-year-old at a Harry Styles concert.

"That's very kind. Wow, I never expected… anyway, I came down here to say thank you, but also to let you know you're being moved this week."

Maybe I wouldn't jump out of the window after all.

My eyes widened and I forgot Ace was standing there. "You're moving me to the fiftieth floor?"

She nodded, with a smile.

"Thank you so much, Nathalie. This is amazing news, I'm so grateful to you."

"H.R. will touch base today, but I wanted to give you the heads up."

I grinned as widely as I could. Ace might be annoying, but I wouldn't have my promotion without him. "Thank you, again."

"I'll see you around," she smiled, glancing over to Ace one last time, and paused with her hand on the door frame. "In fact, my husband and I are having a small get together at our house next month, we do it every summer when the kids are in camp. It's casual, we fire up the grill with some friends, have some drinks… Why don't you both come? Payton, we can talk plans for your future."

I grabbed the edge of the chair behind me, right before I blanked out.

I couldn't be certain – except I was absolutely certain – I'd just been invited to the Nathalie Cheung's legendary summer soiree. I'd never met anyone who'd attended, so anything I'd heard was the stuff of legend, but safe to say it was attended by the literary elite.

As I hadn't heard from Nathalie since I'd dropped off the

signed memorabilia last week, nor had I checked with her P.A. to see if she'd gotten it for fear of looking too needy, I'd slowly been convincing myself of the possibility I wouldn't be moving anywhere.

Now here I was, minutes away from the most intense orgasm of my life, and I'd been invited to Nathalie Cheung's for her summer soiree and I was moving to my dream job.

Maybe there was something in this mojo thing of Ace's.

However, Nathalie Cheung's plus Ace equaled a recipe for disaster. Thankfully, baseball players never got any time off.

"Yes, I'd love to, though I'm sure Ace will have a game, but please count me in."

Unfortunately for me, Ace didn't pick up on the heavy hint in my tone that he *really* needed to have a game.

"What date is your party?"

"May 18th, it's the third Saturday, five p.m. onwards."

Ace turned to me with a grin, tapping a finger against his head. "You're in luck, The Lions are at home on the eighteenth, and we'll be done by five. *We'd* love to come."

My insides twisted together in a little ball; twisting and knotting and churning. May 18th was nearly a month away.

"Wonderful. I'll send Payton the details." She checked her watch. "I've got to scoot. Thank you again for the merch, I can't wait to show Chester. I'll win mom of the year for this."

She waved behind her as she walked out, leaving me kind of speechless and Ace looking like… well, Ace. Only the stupid grin on his face had widened.

"Ace… that was…"

"I know who she is. I looked her up after you told me about her. I wanted to know who I was getting this merch for."

"Oh."

"Anyway, looks like my work here is done." He leaned into my cheek and kissed me. "See you tonight, Babycakes."

I was still standing there a minute later, wondering if hurricanes were less destructive, and wishing I'd remembered to tell him to stop calling me Babycakes.

Especially because it was growing on me.

12

Ace

Giving someone an orgasm really works up an appetite.

I snatched two protein bars from the shelf without breaking stride. If there hadn't been possible witnesses, I'd have added a hop, skip, and a jump as I made my way into the locker room, because it had been that type of day already.

I found Lux sitting on the far bench tying his sneakers, which really sealed the deal on my morning, because without knowing it, he'd come through for me today.

"Hey," I greeted and rubbed my hands together as I stepped over to where he was sitting. "Just the dude I was looking for."

He peered up. "Yeah?"

"Yeah." I sat down next to him and slung my arm around his giant shoulder, pulling him in for a smooch.

"What the fuck, Ace?" he grumbled and pushed me away while rubbing his head where I'd kissed him. "What d'you do that for?"

"Just showing my appreciation."

"You want to tell me what for?"

"No, not really." I shook my head. "Just know that I love and appreciate you, and that I listen to what you have to say."

He stood up, throwing me a very confused look. In my defense, we'd lived together long enough by now that my behavior shouldn't take him by surprise. "Can you make your appreciation a little less sloppy next time, please?"

"You got it, bud," I grinned, peering around the empty locker room. Through the windows into the gym, I saw a couple of the rookies were stretching out, but apart from that, the place was empty. "Where is everyone? Where's Parker and Tan?"

"They were both still in bed when I left… in fact, I thought you were too. I left breakfast out." He frowned and shrugged. "A couple of the guys were called for early practice, but it's only ten-thirty."

"Huh." I flipped my wrist around to check the time. "So it is. I thought it was later."

I laid back on the bench, folding my arms behind my head. Truth be told, the only point this morning when I'd known the time was when I'd arrived at Payton's office, before events escalated.

Holy shit, had they escalated.

You know that old saying – absence makes the heart grow fonder, or whatever? Well, it really fucking does. I hadn't talked to her in a week. She never replied to my text message about Penn – not that I'd expected her to – but I had needed to see her again, if only to discuss making a new deal of some kind, and get to work on all the skills I'd been reading about.

Practice makes perfect, and all that.

I was determined that a week spent reading would not be a week wasted.

However, I was also aware of the delicate nature of the situation, given how she'd reacted to me the first time I'd asked her to help me, so all I'd planned was a little thank you; a cupcake peace offering if you will, where I would politely ask if we could renegotiate terms. I might not know that much about women, but I knew enough that they really didn't like it when you ordered them to have sex with you – even if it's what your boss had inadvertently told you to do.

I also knew Payton would likely punch me if I came outright and said it.

Therefore, my plans to see her had been completely innocent, and the five minutes she'd allotted me would have been more than sufficient.

I swear, your honor.

That all went to shit the second I laid eyes on her.

I'd spent a lot of time over the past week thinking about Payton and that noise she made. Mostly about how fucking hot it was. Which led me into thinking how hot *she* was.

But I'd been way off base.

I'd knocked on her door, and my heart had come to a shuddering stop.

It had only been a week since I'd last seen her, but in that week, she'd turned from smoking hot to… I dunno, whatever was hotter. Volcanic? Inferno hot? Those goddamn chili peppers Tanner kept in the fridge that melted your skin if you so much as looked at them?

She was the type of hot that set off forest fires, that should come with a flashing warning to be kept away from incendiary devices.

She was a Saturday night New York ten, who rolled into

a lazy Sunday morning ten too. She was the girl who walked through a bar and fights broke out in her wake over who buys her first drink.

The girl you'd hand your soul over to, just so you could watch her wrap it around her pinkie.

I stared and stared at her, then she'd looked up at me.

No one had ever looked at me the way she'd been looking at me as I walked into her office. Not in the two years I'd been playing in the major leagues, or the two years before then in the minors. Or in college as star pitcher.

Never.

She didn't look away, not even to blink as I strode to her desk with all the purpose I could summon. I had to remember to blink myself.

It was thankful there was a chair, because she'd put me on my ass.

I hadn't been able to remember a single second of my life before I sat down, and all I could focus on was her mouth and kissing it.

Kissing *her.*

I'd put the cupcake on her desk and gave a silent prayer she wouldn't eat it in front of me. I didn't want to see her lips covered in frosting as she bit into it, or her tongue licking the sugar away. I wanted to run.

But when her computer screen fired up and I found myself looking at everything that had been written about me over the past week and more, my dick took over. She'd been checking up on me, and her denial only made it hotter. I became deaf to everything except hearing that goddamn moan again.

So no, I had zero clue what the time was because my morning had revolved around Payton.

"Are you okay?"

I opened my eyes to find Lux standing over me with a frown, and I returned it with my biggest smile. Here's the thing about Lux; he might look like he could snap you in half with one hand tied behind his back, but looks could be deceiving, though the bright pink hoodie and trackpants he'd just changed out of should be enough to give it away. It had taken us a few weeks to figure out, but of the four of us, Lux was the secret romantic. The sensitive one. The one who liked to read poetry, and take bubble baths.

Bubble baths, I tell you. By himself.

To each their own, but it all added up to someone who'd be far too invested in my new-found interest with Payton. Up until this morning, I would have sworn blind it was just about perfecting the sex and getting my game back, but now I wasn't so sure, and until I figured it out for myself, it needed to stay my little secret.

"Never better, my good friend." I jumped up from the bench and opened my locker for a fresh pair of shorts. "Never better. Want to go for a run? I thought it was later than it is."

He picked up his ball cap from the bench and tugged it on. "Come and spot me first, then I'll run with you."

I stretched my arms out as I thought about it. "Yeah, okay. You've got a deal."

"Hurry up and change then." He reached up and pulled a copy of *Cosmo* from his locker, and sat back down.

"Is that mine?"

He shook his head and opened the pages. "No, the new issue came out today so I got it delivered to the apartment. Wasn't going to be seen buying it, was I?"

Huh. Delivered. I hadn't thought of getting it delivered. Reading it from the comfort of my own home, without having to hide it… very smart indeed. You could even take notes if you were so inclined, and no one would ask what the fuck you were doing.

"We should add it to the subscriptions."

"Yeah," Lux nodded, "good plan."

"Anything in there?"

I stripped out of my sweatshirt and tee, pulling on one of the new workout shirts we had to wear. Along with our game uniforms which were lined with sensors, our workout performances were now being monitored to make sure we all stayed in peak fitness.

"More of those cartoon positions, and a guide on masturbation."

I raised an eyebrow. "Interesting."

"Yes, it is," he looked up with a grin, "and I have a date after the game where I'll be trying it out."

"Oh yeah?"

"Yeah," he nodded, hitting the back of his hand against the page. "Don't know why you started reading this, man, but I think it's probably the best idea you've ever had. This shit is gold."

I dropped onto the bench to tie my sneakers, but threw my arm around him again instead. "I think you might be right."

Lux chuckled and went back to reading.

"There you are!" Our heads shot up to see Parker walking into the locker room. "I've been texting."

"Have you?" I snatched my phone up to find he had indeed been texting. A lot.

The Powers of Greyskull: Group Chat

Parker: *Anyone awake?*

Parker: *What's for breakfast?*

Parker: *What time are you leaving for the ground?*

Parker: *Srsly. Anyone awake?*

Tanner: *I am now you've woken me with all your goddamn texting*

Parker: *Put your phone on silent, you dipshit*

Parker: *Okay, I'm getting up*

Parker: *Srsly. Where is everyone?*

"Oh, dude," I grinned, "did you have FOMO?"

"No," he huffed, in a way that made it clear he did. "But where were you?"

Lux was too engrossed in whatever bit he'd got to in the masturbation guide to look up at Parker, thumbing to the next page as he replied, "I messaged to say I was coming for an early workout, and I left you breakfast."

Parker's eyes flicked to mine. "What about you?"

I bent down to finish tying my sneakers. "I had an errand to run."

"What sort of errand?" Parker asked as he opened his locker door, retrieving a glove and ball. "You don't run errands."

"A none of your business errand."

"Oh," he snorted, "that sort of errand."

I looked at my watch. If I was correct, my little secret had lasted all of twenty minutes, because any second, Lux would want to know what we were talking about. The dude missed nothing. He was also the nosiest person I'd ever met.

Lux snapped *Cosmo* shut and looked up at me. "What are you two talking about?"

"Payton."

"Who's that?"

I sighed. "Remember when I came home after I'd hooked up with that girl, and she'd left me in bed?"

Lux nodded, his eyes widening when I didn't offer up any more information. "Her? The yips chick?"

"Yep."

"Heads up!" Parker called from where he was now standing on the other side of the locker room, and tossed me the ball. "She's the reason why we've all been reading lady magazines."

"What?" Lux peered down at the *Cosmo* on his lap. "I'm so confused."

"Make some sense, will you?" I grumbled, lobbing the ball back to Parker. "And I didn't hear that girl complaining about it in D.C."

"You're right, she didn't," Parker grinned, because Lux wasn't the only one who'd been trying to hone his bedroom skills.

The ball flew through the locker room again. Lux's hand shot out and caught it before I could.

"Time out."

I sighed and removed the ball from his fist. "The very essence of my manhood was questioned, and it affected my pitch."

"And this girl who broke you has helped you find it again? That's how you got your pitch back?"

I held Lux's confused stare and nodded. "Bingo."

"And what's that got to do with this?" He waved *Cosmo* in front of my face.

"If I excel at sex, then I'll excel at pitching," I replied simply, expecting him to scoff at my theory, but he didn't.

Instead, he sat back, his head resting against the locker. "Interesting. That's very interesting."

"Yeah? You think?"

"Yeah. Have you got anything to back it up already?"

"Only the game when Coach put me back in for the final Red Sox game and I threw those fastballs."

"You had sex before the game?"

"The night before, but more specifically…" I glanced around the locker room to check it was still only the three of us. "I gave her an orgasm. A big one."

"And that's where you were this morning?"

I nodded, and tossed the ball back to Parker. "Yes."

"Giving her another orgasm."

"Yup."

"Interesting," he repeated, his head bobbing slowly as his brows knitted together. I stood there watching him. You could almost see the cogs turning as his brain fired up. "Very interesting. You know, I think we can test this theory of yours properly. Let's see what happens tonight, and I'm hooking up with that girl after. We can see what happens in tomorrow's game too."

I caught the ball, crossing my arms over my chest, and squinted at Lux to see if there was anything to indicate he was about to start laughing, but I couldn't.

"You don't think I'm crazy?"

"No. Fuck, no. It makes sense. You suddenly tanked overnight. You had us all worried, man, especially Park." He nodded over to where Parker was waiting for the ball with his hands on his hips, like he was Superman or something. "But if this chick was the reason, then getting her to fix it is the logical solution."

"Oh," I replied. "Yeah… thanks. I thought so. But can we keep it an apartment secret? Not sure Coach or Shepherd needs to know about this."

"Of course they don't. Besides, we have to prove it first," he replied in the same tone I imagine scientists would use when they were on the verge of a life-changing breakthrough, like the cure for cancer, or life on another planet. But then he stood up, throwing *Cosmo* to the back of his locker. "Now can we please go and work out?"

"*A*ce! Ace! Ace!"

I turned to the small pack of reporters waiting in their designated spot just inside the locker room. I hoped I might be able to get away without the questions, just like I had last night, and I'd be able to sneak past without them noticing me, which is why I'd walked in on the other side of Lux who was more like a human wall.

But no, Lux walked too quickly to get showered and out to his date.

"Ace, can we have a word? Ace?"

I tugged down on the peak of my ball cap as half a dozen microphones were thrust in my face, and I was half blinded from the light of the camera. "Sure."

I wasn't expecting the same brutal assassination I'd been subjected to the last time I'd had to go against this lot for questioning – right after Opening Day – and even though I'd pitched well yesterday – okay, better than well – if I was given a choice between this and having my fingernails pulled out, I'd definitely have to think about it.

"Quite a difference in your game over the last few weeks. Can you talk us through your game last night?"

I nodded and cleared my throat. Every single one of them leaned forward, desperate to hear my response. "Yeah, the start of the season was rough. My job is to execute a pitch as best I can, and unfortunately, that didn't happen for me the way I wanted it to."

"Did you agree with Coach Chase's decision to reinstate you as starting pitcher? Are you ready?"

I tried hard not to roll my eyes, but come on… what a dumb question.

"Coach is the coach for a reason. He's here to win a game as much as the rest of us. We respect his decisions, and I'm not going to complain about being starting pitcher. It's hard staying out in the bullpen."

"But talk us through what happened yesterday, because you were like a completely different pitcher out there compared to Opening Day. Did you feel it?"

I tugged on the back of my neck out of habit, only right now, there was no tension to ease away. This *ESPN* dude was right; I had been like a completely different pitcher.

Parker and I had been on fire from the first inning. He'd read the play perfectly, and called the balls.

"Good. I felt good going in. We had a strong start. There were some hits which we could have done without, but The Lions won at home, and that's what counts."

"The strikeout of the leadoff hitter, Alex Stanley, was impressive. Had you planned it?"

I chuckled. "As much as you can plan anything. I want to

say I was lucky, but Parker and I work well together, and I followed his lead with that call. Stanley's a hard hitter, and a fast ball doesn't always translate well on that type of swing."

"That first pitch was over a hundred miles an hour. What mechanics did you adjust to get back to your usual speed?"

"I'm not where I want to be yet, but I'm closer than I was at the start of the season."

A low rumble of laughter rolled through my audience.

"What's changed for you over the last three weeks?"

"I'm hanging out less in the bullpen, that's for sure. My ass isn't quite so numb from sitting on the bench."

This time the laughter was a little louder, especially as Tanner and Parker walked by at that exact moment, Tanner offering up a "He's got a great ass though."

"Anything else? What's been the turnaround for you?"

My mind blanked. Blank except for Payton. For the entire game, whenever I needed to block out the noise, she became the central point I held onto.

She'd become the calm in my chaos.

My focus.

"I reevaluated what I needed to do to achieve what I wanted. I had some strong words spoken to me, and I listened."

"Can you elaborate on that?"

"Not really." I shook my head, using a response I'd learned from years of watching Jupiter deal with the media. Not that he ever really offered up more than a grunt, but sometimes words came out. "Now if you'll excuse me, I need to hit the showers."

Smoothing my fingers over my beard, I held my cheeks in place so the broad grin I could feel escaping didn't give me away. I didn't think Payton would appreciate it if I mentioned her name.

She probably wasn't watching anyway.

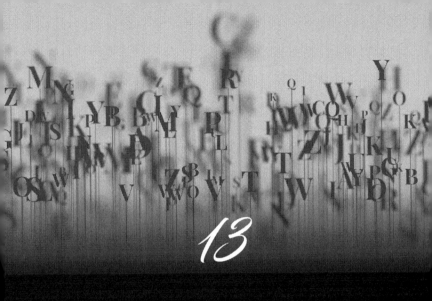

13

Payton

"*Y*es. Yes, I saw his press conference." I sighed for what felt like the fiftieth time. "I saw it live, and I saw it again when you sent it to me the next morning, and every day since."

"He's crediting her for turning his game around," Kit called from the confines of the dressing room to any one of our friends who were listening.

Who am I kidding, they were all listening.

I rolled my eyes. To be fair, I was surprised it had taken this long for the subject to be brought up, but we hadn't seen each other for a couple of weeks, and sometimes more important things took priority over a friend's sex life – namely shopping. I wish she'd keep her voice down a notch though, but she was replying to Beulah who was two dressing rooms over.

Me? I was sitting on the giant ottoman in the middle of the changing room, refereeing this conversation. I'd given up shopping an hour ago, which was unusual for me because it used to be one of my favorite ways to relax, but nothing had quite hit the spot today.

"No, he's not," I interrupted. "He said he listened to some strong words. That could be August Chase for all we know."

"They were your words," Lowe said as she opened her dressing room door, wearing a long, white maxi-dress covered in large blue flowers, and twirled in front of the floor to ceiling mirror on the other side of the room. "What do you think of this?"

"It's beautiful. It suits you," I smiled. "What do you want to wear it for?"

She shrugged. "Penn and I have a ton of parties to attend this summer, and I realized this week that I don't have anything to wear."

"I doubt that," I grinned, "but you should still get it."

Lowe had an enviable wardrobe, and a limitless budget. I'd seen that dress she was trying on when we'd walked in, and the price tag was more than my monthly rent. The only place I came close to rivalling her was my shoe collection, but that was because I spent all my money on shoes and had nothing left for anything else.

"Seriously, I haven't been shopping like this since last year." She twirled in the mirror again, checking out the crossed straps at the back. "Okay, I'm getting this. Anyway, what were we saying about you saving Ace's game?"

"We weren't. And might I remind you all he was also the one who accused me of breaking his game in the first place?"

"Semantics!" someone called, possibly Kit again.

Marnie walked through from the front of the store, her

arms laden with clothes which were swiftly relieved by a store clerk, and hung in a dressing room lest they wrinkle. The staff in here were far too efficient for their own good, although not efficient enough to have refreshed the glass of champagne they'd handed me when I sat down.

"Statistically speaking," Marnie began, "he has been pitching better since you guys started sleeping together. Therefore, it's the logical conclusion, unless there's another variable we don't know about."

"We're not…" I stopped talking, because I was about to say I wasn't sleeping with Ace.

While we might be the only ones currently shopping in this particular store in Greenwich Village, the staff were hanging onto our every word, and I'd rather not discover my news in the next edition of Page Six.

Also, I couldn't exactly deny it after I confided in them at brunch that I'd had sex with Ace six times in the past two weeks, seven if you counted what happened in my office. I tried not to cringe at the wanton harlot I'd become, or the way my pussy convulsed whenever I thought about him – which was far too often, or whenever he texted me – also far too often – or whenever I looked up his latest game reports – not even admitting to how much I'd done that.

Every morning I'd woken up, looked at him sleeping soundly, and stopped myself from tracing my fingers over the curves of his muscles. Every morning I made a promise that time had been the last time. But then he'd send me a text and I'd cave, or, like two nights ago, he'd turn up unannounced, and I'd have to let him in before any of my neighbors saw.

At least I'd made him promise not to turn up at my office again, which I was taking as a win.

I don't even know how it happened; how I'd gone from a very average one-night-stand which I had no intention of repeating, to possibly the best sex of my life with the same person over and over again. In the morning, I'd leave to go to work and he'd go to the stadium, or wherever it was he went first, then later he'd either rock up on the mound and throw a couple of balls or watch from the bench while he was rested, but he'd always be back at my place before I'd have a chance to get through my late-night episode of The Golden Girls.

The better The Lions played, the more fired up he was when he arrived.

Yesterday, I barely managed to close the front door before he'd ripped my panties to one side and began eating me like his life depended on it. Every fantasy I'd ever had about Ace was coming true. If I kept a diary with my deepest, darkest secrets, I'd swear he'd been reading it.

"You're dressing room is ready, ma'am," the store clerk said and smiled at Marnie.

"Thank you," she replied, trotting off into the open stall, but she clearly wasn't done adding to our conversation, unfortunately. "He threw two clean innings yesterday."

I groaned, though it wasn't as loud as it should have been, given this conversation. I already knew about his clean innings because he'd told me as his hand inched into my panties. He'd described every last detail excruciatingly slowly while he curled his fingers inside me, adding more and more pressure until I was screaming for release. "*This* is how I curl them around a fast ball," he'd said.

I shouldn't be finding baseball this sexy.

"You're making me sound like I'm one of those little green goblins at the bottom of a rainbow."

"You mean a lucky charm?"

"Semantics!" I shot out.

Beulah dropped down next to me on the ottoman, and

another store clerk ran over to take the clothes she'd brought out with her.

"Can we wrap these for you?"

"Please," Beulah nodded, and leaned into me as the clerk walked off. "You could say no to him, you know."

"What?" I placed my empty glass down on the floor, I'd given up on having it refilled. I guess if I wasn't spending thousands, I only got one drink. "Like you did when he kept turning up to your office to ask about PlayStation and got my number instead?"

"Yes," she winced. "Sorry about that. I honestly didn't think you'd mind. If I'd known why he wanted your number in the first place I wouldn't have given it to him, but he seemed so sad, and he's very persuasive."

I chuckled. "I'm fully aware of how persuasive he is."

"Is that why you're buying those?" She tipped her chin down toward the bra and panties folded in my lap. The very sheer black bra and panties that I happened to notice as I walked in, and thought would make a good addition to my underwear drawer.

"Coincidence," I grinned.

"Yeah, I'm sure."

"Is Ace really that bad?" asked Marnie, walking out with only one pair of jeans from the approximately seventeen she took in with her. "I've always thought he's pretty fun. He makes me laugh anyway. Or maybe that's more to do with how much he annoys Jupiter. He'd probably be fun to hang around with for a bit."

My eyes widened at the thought of spending time with Ace outside of the bedroom. "God no. We don't hang out. We have sex. We barely even talk unless it's to do with... you know, sex." *And baseball*, I nearly added.

"And the sex is bad?" She frowned, looking almost as confused as I felt.

"No, that's the problem. He's excellent. It's like overnight, he suddenly became an expert in all things regarding the female anatomy, because he believes it'll make him better at pitching. Thank God they're leaving for an away stretch tomorrow. My vagina needs a rest."

I huffed loudly, making Beulah grin. She arched one of her perfectly shaped eyebrows, and if eyebrows could talk, hers would be shouting 'Just Say No'.

But I seemed to have lost my ability to say no, and I couldn't explain why. Just like I couldn't explain how the sex with Ace had gone from zero to OhMyFuckingGod.

"How can you be so down about having great sex?"

"I dunno. It feels a little… transactional. I'm his experiment, and he's helping me get a job I want because I don't seem to be able to get it on my own," I grumbled. "I'm still pissed about this party I got invited to, but only because Ace decided to turn up to my office. I can't have him hanging around every time I want to get ahead in my career."

"Can't you go without him?"

I shook my head. "I daren't. It's a big deal. It's the type of event people cancel vacation plans to attend. She hosts it every summer. It's always at her townhouse, and it's like thirty of the most influential people in publishing and literature. Nobel Prize winners and laureates, that sort of thing. I'm sure I only got invited because of Ace. If I say he can't go, I'll get disinvited."

"Really?" frowned Lowe, walking out of her dressing room. "It's *that* big of a deal?"

I fixed her with a look so she could see exactly how serious I was. "This is my Met Gala."

Lowe's eyes widened, and her mouth dropped open. Now she understood. "Okay, say no more. We definitely have to go shopping for it then. When is it?"

"In a few weeks."

"You only have to sleep with Ace until then?"

"I guess," I sighed.

Beulah threw her head back and laughed at the expression on Marnie's face. In fact, the expression on all of their faces. Even I couldn't help but crack a little smile.

"It's just such a long time!"

"This is only because it's the longest you've ever spent with one guy since college," Kit remarked, picking up the store bag of her purchases, tied together with a neat little black ribbon.

Marnie's brows shot up. "You've never had a long-term relationship?"

I shook my head. "Nope. Not since my college boyfriend, Deacon, but that was never going to go anywhere so it felt okay. But we're older now, and after seeing what my parents went through... are still going through..." I shuddered. "No thanks. My motto is have fun, move on. I don't want a marriage that ends in divorce."

Unfortunately, the champagne I'd drunk this morning caused the rest of my thoughts to surface, the ones I usually shoved as far down as possible. Aside from Kit and my therapist, no one here needed to know that I avoided relationships because I wasn't sure I had the capacity for them. The capacity to love someone.

Because if I don't ever allow myself to fall in love, then I won't ever get hurt.

Marnie smiled softly. "I can empathize. Hopefully my first one will counter-balance Jupiter."

I always forgot Marnie had been married before she'd come to New York; before Penn set in motion the events which brought her and Jupiter back together. I picked up her left hand, bringing her huge engagement ring to the light so it sparkled even more than it normally did, and smiled. "I'd say this counter-balances divorce. Now can we change the subject, please?"

"Sure, what do you want to talk about?" Lowe asked, handing her credit card over to a very smug looking clerk who was clearly on commission.

I shrugged. "Anything except Ace Watson or baseball. They're off limits for the rest of the day."

The four of them looked at each other, like they were having difficulty thinking of a subject besides Ace Watson and baseball. Then Kit's eyes lit up, and she leaned forward with a whisper.

"I have something, but let's wait until we've paid and we're outside."

Ten minutes later, we walked into the bright New York sunshine, store bags swinging from our hands, except for Lowe, who'd bought so much it was being delivered to her apartment later this afternoon. The Saturday streets were now bustling with shoppers and brunchers, and those who'd clearly only just surfaced for the first time after too much partying the night before.

April was turning into May, bringing with it the start of warmer days, and I whipped off my sweater which had been protecting me from the store's intense A/C setting.

"Come on then," said Beulah, nudging Kit. "What's this news?"

"Oh, yes." Kit peered over each shoulder to double check there was no one nearby to hear her. "Radley Andrews is starting Columbia in the fall."

It wasn't what I thought she was going to say, but it beat talking about baseball.

"That's cool they confirmed. Go Columbia. What's her major?"

"English," Kit grinned. "She's going to be in one of my classes. The Secret Service came around this week to assess the security systems, and what needs to be upgraded."

"Holy shit! That *is* cool!" I put my arm around her shoulder and squeezed tight. "You're going to be teaching the President's daughter. That's huge."

She grinned. "I know."

"I like her," nodded Lowe in approval, as we all stopped in front of *another* store window, then followed her inside. "Whenever you see pictures of her, she always seems sensible."

"Terrible choice in boyfriends though."

She chuckled. "Yeah, but it can't have been easy with her parents being the President and Secretary of State. I know all about difficult parents and rebelling, and mine just have regular jobs. Can't imagine the pressure she's under."

"How do you know who she's been dating?" asked Marnie, flicking through a rack of exclusively white items of clothing, and pulled a dress off. "This is cute, it would suit you."

I took it from her and held it out as I stood in front of the mirror. She was right, it *was* cute. The price tag wasn't, however, and I put it back.

"It was in the papers last year, and all over social. How did you miss it?"

Marnie shot a wry smile in Lowe's direction. "I work for Penn Shepherd."

"Touché," she smirked. "She was only seventeen. He was a

senior at Georgetown, and was using her to get into politics and get to her parents. She broke up with him, and somehow pictures of them naked together made their way onto the internet."

Marnie's face dropped in horror. "Oh my God, that poor girl."

Beulah nodded. "Yeah, it was bad. It was during the election campaign as well. It was why she deferred her college year last year."

"Was it the boyfriend who did it?"

"Nothing was ever proved, though I think everyone assumed it was him."

"What a dick. What happened to him?"

"Nothing. He's still riding the coattails of being Radley Andrew's ex. He's working for a lobbying firm in D.C."

"She'll find someone better at Columbia. Columbia boys are hot." Kit picked up the white dress I'd put back on the rack, and held it against her.

"What're you talking about? She'll be far too busy writing essays on sixteenth century poets, or which is the superior Shakespeare play, to mess around with boys."

"You're right, she will be. I'll have her up to her eyeballs in manuscripts."

"You make me almost thankful we had Professor Grady teaching us," I chuckled. Grady was not a teacher anyone ever messed with, though Kit had always been her favorite while she merely tolerated me just because I was Kit's best friend. "And speaking of manuscripts, I think I've found my next novelist. Like a proper one; not one who writes about carrots and farmers, and the naughty bunny."

Beulah's eyes lit up. "Oh, who? I really need a good book to read."

"Her name is Gracey Jackson. She's unsigned right now, but I think I'm going to sign her. She'll be my first signing for adult fiction."

"Hang on," Lowe blurted and spun around, the blue striped shirt she was holding whipping through the air. "You've moved out of children's books? When did this happen?"

I winced. "A couple of weeks ago. It's tied into this whole Ace situation."

"What d'you mean?"

"This lunch I've been invited to."

"The Met Gala one?"

I nodded, again with a wince, because now I remembered exactly why I hadn't given the more salient details to Lowe. "Yeah. It's Nathalie Cheung's lunch. She likes Ace, and I happened to mention I wanted to move into adult fiction. She said she'd help me if I could get some signed stuff for her kid. Please don't tell Penn."

She rolled her eyes. "I don't tell Penn everything. He'd probably send you a case of champagne if he thinks you're the reason the Ace is pitching so well."

"Not if he knows I'm the reason Ace broke in the first place," I grumbled.

"Your secret is safe with me. Plus, Ace is free to sign anything privately, Penn just doesn't want it to be an official event. You know, like turning up to functions... things like that. But congratulations! This calls for celebration." She pulled me into a big hug, which I gently eased out of. "Aren't you happy about it?"

"I am, but I feel like I don't quite deserve it because it was handed to me, even though I've been busting my ass for Susie for eight freaking years."

Susie Van Maren, in fact, could not have been more

supportive at the news of me leaving. Fake supportive, but considering she sent an intern down to help me pack up my office last week, I was taking it. I couldn't swear the intern hadn't been sent to spy, but I also couldn't have given less of a shit if she had because I hate packing, and the intern was good at it.

Annoyance flashed across Beulah's face. "Sometimes people will keep you down because it's a benefit to them, not you. You grab any opportunity you can, and if that means you also get to have awesome sex because of it, then I say you fucking rock. We should all be that lucky."

I turned to her, my forehead creasing. "You *are* that lucky. Your boyfriend is hot."

"Yeah," Beulah grinned dreamily, "he really is."

"Okay," Lowe began and placed the shirt back on the rack, clapping her hands together, "let's go and celebrate Payton and Kit. We've done enough shopping."

"Sounds good to me," I grinned.

"But…" Lowe pointed a finger at me, "Beulah's right. You have to grab this opportunity and be excited about it. Both of them," she added with a wink. "The boys are leaving tomorrow night; I say you give Ace a send-off tonight that'll have him pitching his way into the Hall of Fame."

I rolled my eyes but couldn't help laughing at the way Lowe's face had lit up as she gave a little wiggle of her brows.

"You're as bad as he is."

"No, I'm just married to Penn, and I want the Lions to win this year for purely selfish reasons. Therefore, I vote you take one for the team."

"I'm still not sure this isn't the dumbest theory ever," I laughed, opening my purse for my sunglasses. As I did, my phone screen lit up.

Ace: *See you tonight, Babycakes.*

I looked down at the store bag swinging from my other hand. Maybe I could give him a send-off, and it would be a shame to relegate such pretty lingerie to the back of my underwear drawer so soon.

"Hey," I leaned into Lowe before I could think too much about it, and dropped my voice, "You couldn't get me Ace's address, could you?"

She grinned and pulled her phone up, her fingers flying over the screen. "The Lions will thank you for this one day."

I wasn't sure I shared her enthusiasm.

Out of interest, was it possible to die from too many orgasms?

14

Ace

*Y*ou can never find a vibrator when you need one.

I tossed the couch cushions up and ran my fingers along the underside to see if it had gotten stuck, praying I wouldn't come across anything sticky… or worse. I found nothing except a PlayStation remote Parker hadn't been able to find yesterday, and candy wrappers Tanner had stuffed down there.

No vibrator though.

"What are you looking for?"

"Nothing." I grabbed another handful of wrappers, and held them up to Tanner. "Can you put these in the trash, Tan? Seriously? I know we have a housekeeper, but she can't only clean up after you."

He grumbled something I didn't catch and huffed off to his bedroom as I moved to the other sectional. I don't know why I was bothering, I never had it out here anyway. I clearly remember opening the package as I came in from the elevator then walked to the kitchen... and straight to my bedroom, and...

I snapped my fingers – I knew where it was – just as the elevator buzzer signaled a guest was on the way up. That'll be for... I dunno. One of the boys. We'd all rushed home after the game, and I wasn't the only one of us with plans for a good night's sleep.

"Why are you here, anyway?" asked Parker from the comfort of his kitchen stool where he'd been watching me flail about, but hadn't once bothered to get up and help.

Don't worry, I noted it for the next time he needed *my* assistance.

"I'm not here. I forgot something before and had to come back for it," I replied, sprinting into my bathroom where, hiding on the countertop behind a bottle of aftershave, was the little black box I'd ordered on rush delivery yesterday.

According to *Cosmo*, it contained the most powerful bullet vibrator on the market. It had been awarded five explosive emojis in a survey of vibrators. Ten thousand readers had voted, so I figured it was good enough to try out, and hopefully the person I intended to use it on was waiting for me at her place in that cute little sleep number I enjoyed. Or maybe in some of those panties she liked to parade about in every morning, the ones which always had me desperate to drag her back to bed.

There was always a chance she'd play the 'I-forgot-you-were-coming-over' game, and answer the door with a yawn and a loud huff, but it only took me a minute to wake her up. Especially if that minute involved my lips on her neck.

Fuck *me*.

My dick thumped at the idea of her splayed out beneath me while I pinned her thighs apart with mine, and buzzed it over her pussy. *Cosmo* said to tease the sensation, and I planned on teasing her for hours, edging her closer until she strangled my cock with how hard she came. I'd have her screaming louder than she screamed last night, and last night I was surprised the neighbors hadn't complained.

I was pulled out of my little fantasy by a loud shriek, but at least it jolted me enough to take off again once I'd readjusted my pants. Snatching up the box, I stuffed it in my backpack and sprinted back down the hallway to the kitchen where I came to screeching halt.

I'd been wrong when I thought the shriek was just the boys fucking around. Very wrong indeed.

Oh crap.

My eyes popped, but the rest of me froze, unsure of exactly what I should do. Picking my jaw up off the floor would be good place to start.

What did one normally do when the girl you were sleeping with turned up at your place wearing sky high heels, and a raincoat she was hugging to herself so tightly it was clear there was nothing underneath? And given the way the coat wasn't fastened, I'd be willing to bet she'd walked in here with it wide open, especially as Parker and Lux were staring at her like all their fantasies had come true.

I knew how they felt.

The pancakes on the griddle were starting to smoke. It was only when Tanner ambled down the hallway and slid to a stop with his mouth open that I jumped back into action.

"Payton? What are you doing here?" I asked quietly, praying that I didn't scare her back into reality.

Her eyes darted around at each of the boys before settling back on me.

"You have roommates?" she hissed.

"Yeah," I nodded. "I thought you knew."

"No, I didn't," she gritted through her teeth, waving a free hand the length of her body. "Clearly."

"Looks acceptable to me," snickered Tanner into his fist, not even bothering to try and disguise it with a cough.

Payton's head snapped around with narrowed eyes and a snarl fit for a Doberman. It was an expression I'd only been on the receiving end of once, and when I'd been too angry for it to take full effect. On Tanner, however, it had the desired result, and the smirk dropped off his face quicker than a fast ball.

Then she turned back to me, like this entire situation was all my fault.

Five minutes ago, I'd been on my way to another night of unbridled passion and several orgasms. Now, there was a very real chance I'd have to jerk myself to sleep tonight, and that was not something in my immediate plans. Therefore, I had to fix it fast.

I held my hands up before anyone could say another word. "Everyone! Turn around!"

Lux grinned, letting out a hefty eye roll as he did, like I was overreacting or something. But I didn't fucking care.

"Dude, we've already seen…"

"TURN AROUND!"

The three dipshits did as they were told, though I didn't miss Tanner taking a quick second peek.

"Thank you." I let out the breath I didn't realize I'd been holding. "Now if you'll excuse me, I'll be taking my guest to my room, and we don't want to be disturbed. I shall see you all in the morning."

Parker chuckled, his head dropping with a slow shake as

I passed him and slowly walked over to Payton to take her hand. I tugged her to follow, but unfortunately, she held firm, and she was strong.

How had I not realized how strong she was?

"Ace..."

"Payton, come to my room. It's fine..." I opened my mouth to tell her we always had girls over and the walls were thick, but then thought better of it. I tugged again, but she still didn't move. "Come with me... or we can stay here if you prefer."

Her response to that was clasping her hands tighter to her neckline, so instead, I changed up my approach. Wrapping my arm around her waist, I kind of pushed her forward, past the kitchen where the pancakes were now full-on burning, and guided her silently to my room as quickly as I could until she was safely inside.

"Lux, your pancakes...."

"Fuck!" was the last thing I heard any of them say before I closed the door behind me, blocking out the chaos, and focusing on the reality that was now in front of me.

I hit the dimmer switch so we weren't standing in the dark or the eerie blue casting shadows around us from the lights of the city, and took the deepest breath I could. I wasn't the world's tidiest person, but given I'd spent every night this week at her place, my room was tidier than usual. Thankfully, the housekeeper had also been by, and I had clean sheets. The bed was made way better than I normally managed; all the empty Gatorade and water bottles that I left on my nightstand had been thrown in the trash; my laundry was clean and neatly put away instead of discarded on the floor where I'd stepped out of them.

In fact, looking around, my room might be the cleanest I'd

ever seen it.

I never normally cared what a girl thought about my room. It never crossed my mind to care. They weren't usually in here long enough to notice, and if they did, they never said anything. But I realized I cared what Payton thought, especially as she was standing in the middle of the room, statue-still, as she silently peered around my space. I ignored the stab of self-consciousness as her eyes moved along the bookshelves which ran the length of one wall.

They might have been bookshelves, but as I didn't have that many books, they'd been used to store other things, like the ball from the first home run I'd hit after I was signed to The Yankees AAA team. The ball from the first game I'd pitched starting for The Yankees. The glove I'd been wearing the day I was drafted. An old Yankees bobblehead next to my Lions one, which she tapped on my nose as she passed, setting them both off in their little wobbly dance.

She finally stopped in front of one of the framed photos of my brothers and me, with our golden retriever, Wednesday. It had been taken last Thanksgiving, back home on my parents' ranch. We were all dressed up in the pajamas my mom made us wear, even the dog, and standing in front of the roaring fireplace in their log cabin. The snow had been three feet deep that day, and we'd spent all morning sledding down the hillside like we'd always done as kids.

When she spoke, her tone was quiet, not quite a whisper, but quieter than I'd ever heard it before, and it was missing the usual assertive tone it carried; the one that always had me doing her biding.

"Is this your family?"

"Yeah." I stepped next to her, the scent of fresh laundry and flowers wafted up my nose and settled on my chest. "I have three brothers – Coby, Travis, and Stevie. And that's

Wednesday Watson the Wonder Dog. I'm the youngest."

"That figures; it's why you don't take no for an answer." She placed the photo back down before continuing. "How come you got Ace for a name?"

I chuckled. "Actually, my name's Justin, but when I was a kid, I was always getting out of trouble, or never getting into it in the first place. My brothers took the heat, mostly because they weren't as quick as me. They started calling me Lucky Aces, which became Ace."

She didn't say any more, but I could see the start of a smile curving the edge of her lips, only for it to drop as her eyes flicked to the next image. "Are these your parents?"

"Yup. That's Bill and Ellen Watson."

"And they still live together?"

I frowned. "What? What do you mean?"

"I mean…" she paused and her knuckles whitened as she gripped her raincoat. "Your parents are still together?"

"Oh," I chuckled, "yeah. My dad's a cattle farmer, and they have a ranch in Montana. It's where I'm from."

She spun around, her eyes brighter than they had been, a hint of amusement sparkling behind them. "Your dad's a cowboy?"

I nodded. "Yeah."

With her heels on, she was much closer in height to me than she normally was. It also occurred to me we never really spent any time talking. I knew next to nothing about her except for where she worked, and who her friends were. Oh, and I'd read up on that boss lady of hers I'd met. But outside of sex, we'd never been *this* close together for *this* period of time while we still had our clothes on. Also, all this information was easily searchable, so no one ever bothered to ask. Any girls I'd had in my bedroom already knew it all, but as I answered her questions, I realized I *liked* answering.

It made me feel as though she was interested in me, getting to know me for more than just my dick. And it had me wondering what else I could find out about her, though it didn't seem like she was done with her questions.

"How did you end up in baseball, if you were a farming family?"

I grinned. "My dad loves baseball. I think he figured he already had three boys to pass the ranch on to, and so I was the one he pushed into sports – especially as I'm not great with blood. Birthing calves? No thank you." I shuddered dramatically, making her smile.

She really did have the prettiest smile. It lit up her face better than any spotlight, and I wanted to see it again.

"Do they come to watch you?"

I shrugged halfheartedly. "They come to the Midwest and West coast games more, but it's hard for them to get away. Ranching is twenty-four/seven, but they watch every single one at home – or my pop listens on the radio while he's out on the Big Green."

"What's that?"

"A tractor. A big one he uses for building fences or moving shit."

"It's nice that you have a family who supports you like that."

Her tone made me want to wrap her up and ask if she was okay, but then her gaze moved over my shoulder. The next thing I knew, she was holding up the latest copy of *Cosmo* I'd taken from Lux, and was flicking through the pages.

The problem with this was the relevant pages – the ones with the quizzes on and the cartoon sex people – had all been earmarked. Lux had even scrawled through diagram three on page fifty-seven and scored it two out ten in a red Sharpie. The word 'unrealistic' was next to it.

I held in my grin as I remembered him coming home on Wednesday following that episode. He'd spent all morning in the bath, we'd needed to restock on Epsom salts afterwards, he'd seen the PT before warmups, and then again after.

She turned around and I held my breath. This was about to go one of two ways, and I prayed a storm-out wasn't on the cards. I *really* wanted to see what was under that raincoat.

"Why do you have this?"

"Um…" I smoothed along my moustache, although it had now completely disappeared into my beard. I debated lying, but I wasn't quick enough to come up with something convincing. "I've been reading it."

"Why?" she frowned.

"For you," I shrugged. "For my game."

Her frowned deepened, and I already knew her well enough that it meant I needed to provide more of an explanation.

"Since I've been reading that, I haven't just been improving on the start of the season, I've been improving on last year too."

"Because of us having sex?"

"Yes," I replied simply, ignoring all the skepticism in her voice, because I had no other explanation. "My average for earned runs last year was just under three for the season. If you don't count the beginning of this season, it's nearer two point seven… since we've been having sex."

She nodded, but I wasn't quite sure she was following me. "And is this where you've been getting everything from? That thing you did with your tongue the other night?"

"Yep."

The smirk reappeared in the corner of her mouth, adding a level of amusement to her eyes that turned the dark brown a caramel color. I could almost see little flames burning behind them, and my shoulders relaxed measurably.

"Impressive."

"Thank you." I removed *Cosmo* from her hands, and tossed it to the side. Out of sight, hopefully out of mind. I was done with the talking portion of the evening. "Now, you want to show me what's under that coat of yours?"

Her eyes widened like she'd just remembered why she was here, and loosened her hold on the raincoat until it fell open. Her bottom lip caught in her teeth as she looked up at me, and slowly allowed the coat to drop from her shoulders. My cock was hard before her coat hit the floor. My fists clenched and my heart hammered so hard against my rib cage, I was convinced I was on the verge of a heart attack.

This was nothing like what I saw her wear in the mornings. If it had been, I'd never have allowed her to leave the apartment.

The thinnest, silkiest, black ribbons were tied in little bows on the edges of her collarbones, running down to tiny triangular cups of the sheerest black lace. So sheer and delicate the goosebumps pebbling her body were on full display, and I wanted to congratulate it for doing such an awesome job at holding up her incredible tits in a way that seemed to defy gravity.

Between them hung a long pearl necklace, unnecessarily drawing my attention straight to her cleavage. Unnecessary, because I couldn't tear my eyes away from it, and was fighting hard to overcome the desperate urge to put my face between them. Having recently become quite well acquainted with the pair, I felt qualified to say they were the most perfect tits I'd ever been in the presence of.

My gaze traveled lower, across her smooth golden curves, to the matching panties hugging her hips and cupping her ass like a second skin. More little ribbon bows were tied at the sides that I wanted to unwrap as greedily as a kid on Christmas. More goosebumps shot across her belly, and I couldn't be sure if it was from the temperature I kept it here, or from arousal under the heat of my gaze, because there was no way it wasn't blazing hot.

I was also trying to keep my rage under control, and the impulse to kill any one of those three out there who'd witnessed her dressed in this. Actually, Tanner could live another day, he'd been in his bedroom.

I picked my jaw up from where it had dropped, though my voice seemed to have regressed to that of a pre-pubescent boy, and I cleared my throat several times before I could speak. "You wore this for me?"

She nodded.

"I don't know where to start."

She took hold of my hand, and led me to the edge of the bed. "Well, seeing as you've been doing a lot of work recently, how about I start?"

I bounced onto the mattress as she pushed me back, and stood there staring down at me. I suddenly felt like I was about to lose my virginity again and made a silent prayer I didn't blow too early, because it would only take an act of God for it not to happen.

My dick straining in my pants reminded me I was still fully dressed, and held my hand up before she moved another muscle.

"Hang on."

I kicked off my sneakers as quickly as I could. She dodged out of the way before one hit her, but I was far too eager to be graceful. My shirt followed, then my trackpants, until only my boxer briefs were left.

She looked down at me with an arched brow and ill-concealed amusement. "Why stop there?"

I matched her smirk with one of my own, and eased off my briefs too. My cock sprang back with all the enthusiasm of a prisoner seeing freedom for the first time. Her eyes trained on me as I tugged the length, trying and failing to ease any of the pressure building inside me. I didn't know what was about to happen, but I had no doubt it was about to be explosive. Shifting up the bed to make room for her, the mattress dipped as she knelt down and straddled my thighs.

Oh. My. God.

I couldn't look away. I didn't dare blink as she bent and licked along the entire length of my dick, her soft pink tongue using me as her own personal lollypop. But when she sucked on the end and left a thick trail of saliva behind, I was convinced I'd died and gone to heaven.

I was too engrossed watching her spit leak slowly down my shaft to realize she'd removed her pearl necklace and had it wrapped around her fist.

No fantasy I'd ever had in my life would live up to the reality of this moment, with this glorious, sexy as fuck woman – the one with the thick, dark brown waves and smile that could stop traffic – straddled across my thighs as she took my dick in her hand and slowly began moving up and down.

I wanted to watch; I didn't want to miss a second of what she was doing to me, but I physically couldn't stop my eyes rolling back in my head.

Each individual pearl on her necklace rotated over my skin giving me a thousand simultaneous tiny dick massages, all building up to the most intense sensation I'd ever experienced.

I couldn't focus, I couldn't concentrate, I didn't know where to train my attention as her fist rolled over my dick, and cupped the end.

It was completely and entirely overwhelming.

There's no way the boys couldn't hear me groaning, deep, animalistic grunts. Noises I didn't even know existed inside me. This had to be an out-of-body experience, there was no way it was real.

My capabilities of taking a full breath had long gone; I was lightheaded, and if I wasn't already lying down, I'd have needed to.

"Fucking fuck. Wha…"

I barely managed to open eyes to witness a sly smile cresting her lip, and she increased her speed, before slowing again. Fast. Slow. Fast. Slow.

The thousand tiny massages became almost unbearable, my hips bucked into her hand, desperate for more. I didn't even know someone touching my dick could feel this good. If I had any composure at all, I'd stop what she was doing and flip her over, ass-up, and wipe that smile right off her beautiful face. But I'd lost my composure the second she touched me. All I could do was allow the adrenaline to course through my body.

My balls had turned to walnuts; rock hard. I swear actual electricity buzzed in them, and it was taking all my concentration to keep them from bursting. I needed to make this feeling last, but the pressure twisting in my spine was becoming impossible to ignore.

Then her fingers ran between my legs and squeezed my balls, and I was a goner.

My groan was all the warning she got as I shot into the air. My entire body seized like it was going through an exorcism;

every muscle clenched tight while my dick drained itself of every drop of come I had, and the rest I didn't realize I had.

I couldn't speak. I couldn't see. I couldn't breathe.

Then her perfect pink tongue ran along the end of my dick and lapped across my abs, and I died.

I was dead.

It was only her soft chuckle that brought me back to the present. I lifted an eyelid to find her grinning down at me, her stomach glistening in my come like my own goddamn canvas.

"I think you're an angel." My voice was hoarse and gruff, making her laugh again. "Actually, I take that back. A devil. Show me your tongue, I wanna see if it's forked."

She grinned, and slowly stuck it out at me. Quick as a flash I sat up, fisting through her hair and grabbing behind her head. I sucked her into my mouth, tasting my exerts along with the peaches and cream sweetness that was always present. Her groan speared right in my balls as I slipped my tongue alongside hers like we had all the time in the world, and if she hadn't been wet before, I knew she was now.

Payton might love kissing, but I was starting to love kissing her.

I gently took hold of her fist, easing off the pearls still wrapped around it. "We're keeping these for another time. They're not your grandmothers or anything, are they?"

She shook her head with a giggle, a sound I'd never heard her make before, and I added it to the list of other sounds I wanted to hear again. Starting right now.

"My turn." Placing my hands on her hips, I lifted her and set her down on the other side of the bed. "Stay there."

She did as she was told while I snatched up my backpack and pulled out the little black box I'd been searching for earlier and hid it behind my back.

"I have something for you."

She knelt forward, pulling my arm free. As she did so, her hair brushed against my chest and I took the opportunity to inhale the scent of her, something I'd swear blind I'd never consciously done before, but now the clean, floral fragrance was mingled in with the scent of us, and it fully buried itself in my brain. I knew I'd never associate anything else with that smell except this moment.

Opening the box, she eased out the packaging and tipped the contents into her palm.

Her head quirked to the left. "A vibrator?"

"It's supposed to be the best."

"Is that what Cosmo said?" she asked with a loud snort, which only made me grin wider.

"Yup."

"Isn't a battery-operated orgasm cheating? Won't it mess with your mojo or whatever you called it?"

"I'm willing to take that risk." I removed it from her open palm. "Let's see, shall we?"

Her squeal bounced off the walls and echoed around us as I pulled her legs from under her, forcing her to lay back. I'd been right that first morning together; she really was every guy's wet dream – especially mine – as she lay there decorated in my dried come.

My hands inched up her thighs until my fingers found the little bows and tugged. My eyes flooded with happiness

"They really untie!"

"Mmm hmmm." She watched as I carefully, *so carefully*, pulled the threads until the delicate lace between her thighs dropped away.

Shifting my knees forward so they nudged her thighs

wider, I ran my fingers through her slit until she was splayed out before me, a slick, glistening mess. My dick, which had been waving surrender only minutes ago, found a new lease on life.

"You're so fucking wet. Did you like watching what you were doing to me? Seeing me so totally helpless under your touch?"

She looked up, her eyes hooded, her pupils shot so big that all I could see was black, and slowly nodded.

"Say it, Payton. Use your words."

"Yes, I loved it."

"Good girl," I replied with a grin, slipping a finger inside her pussy as it clenched tight at my words. "Ready?

A gentle humming started up as I pressed the end of the vibrator. I barely touched it to her skin before her chest began heaving. I wanted to make this as excruciating as she'd made those pearls. Edging it along the top of her thigh, I moved it up to the line of her pelvis and her legs dropped wider. Tiny spasms clasped my fingers stroking inside her, and if I couldn't see the tension straining her whole body, I could feel it.

I'd never seen anything like it. Her entire pussy swelled in front of me, like it was magic. A pink glow spread across her body under a light sheen of sweat. Her toes curled, and her fists tightened around the comforter.

My hand was soaked, and my dick was throbbing again. As I buzzed a circle around her clit, she arched high off the bed, and I got to hear that moan.

My favorite sound.

Okay, I was done being a voyeur. It was time to be a participator, and I reached for the condom I'd left prepared like the good Boy Scout I'd never been.

I hovered over her, my dick nudging against her entrance

as the vibrations buzzed through both of us. I knew I was being selfish, but I wanted this orgasm on my dick. I wanted the strength of it. I wanted to feel every contraction, every clench, and I wanted it strangling me until I couldn't take any more.

"Pay... that feels so good... you feel fucking incredible... how do you feel so good all the time?" Her muscles were already fluttering and I was barely halfway in. "So wet."

"Ace... fuck... just do it," she snarled, pushing herself back on me, until her ass was on my thighs, but I held her hips fast. I knew she didn't like to surrender control, but she could survive the torture for a little longer, and this was too good to hurry. I'd make it last all night if I wasn't already on borrowed time. The tell-tale sparks of an impending orgasm were hurtling down my spine.

"Just fucking wait." I tossed the vibrator to the side, and it buzzed its way off the comforter and dropped to the floor.

Her eyes shot open to meet mine. "Wh... what? Why did you do that?"

"I'm taking credit for this," I growled, shifting her legs over my head and dropping them to the side as I sunk the rest of my dick inside her, swiping my thumb against her slick clit, which had so far remained untouched... and it was all the pressure she needed for me to have her thighs clenching hard.

"Ohhh... oh. Oh. Ace."

I pulled out and drove back in, this time with more force. "Say my name again."

"Ace."

"Again," I growled.

"ACE! FUCK!"

Her walls clamped down like a vice, cutting off my blood supply, my senses, everything, as I was yanked into her vortex and exploded for the second time. I had neither the strength nor the energy to hold myself up and collapsed breathless, winded, totally spent.

I called myself a professional athlete, but I was no match for her.

We lay there for what only felt like seconds before she shifted and eased herself away from me. Whatever it was, was far too short a time for it to now be over. As quick as I could, I ran to the bathroom to get clean, switching off the vibrator still buzzing on the floor on my way, and returned to find her curled up, her head resting on a pillow and heading to sleep.

I snuck in next to her, pulled the comforter over us and settled down so I was facing her, shifting my elbow under the pillow to scooch as close as I could get.

"Hey, guess what?"

"What?"

"It's Sunday tomorrow, which means you don't have to leave for work."

"Yeah, so?" she mumbled.

"Morning sex, Babycakes," I grinned.

Her eyes slowly blinked open as her mouth pursed and twisted, like she was thinking about it. "I might need some of those pancakes that were on the griddle earlier. Not burned ones though."

"That can be arranged."

"Then I'm sure I don't have anywhere else to be."

Her eyelids drooped until they'd shut for good, and all I could feel was her warm breath as she fell into a deep sleep.

I stayed awake, watching her features soften as she relaxed. Watching until my chest felt like it was cracking open, and I was convinced I'd never seen anything so beautiful.

It came out of nowhere, hitting me like a lightning strike.

Payton. *Cosmo*. This entire situation might have started because of a fool's errand to get my form back, but I found something else on the way.

Her.

And after tonight, I wasn't about to give it up any time soon.

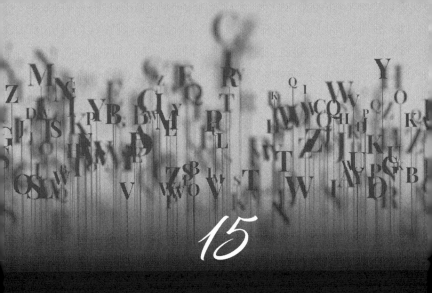

15

Payton

I opened one eye, followed by the other, and zoned into a numb, almost tingling sensation running along my entire left side.

The cause turned out to be Ace, and one of his giant thighs wedged between mine and his arm curled over my chest, twisting us together like the branches of a tree. I tried to take a deep breath, but his arm was too heavy on my lungs for me to suck one all the way in, so I lay there, staring up at the ceiling until the light dancing across it nearly sent me back to sleep. But I still had the breathing issue.

I had no clue what time it was. From the way the sunlight was hitting the ceiling, I knew it was after six a.m. but that was all. I tried to sit up a little, to see if there was a clock anywhere, but it was hard to move. It would be pointless to try and wake the lump next to me; Ace would sleep until his body clock decided it was time to get up. I didn't know what time he had to be at the grounds, but if that was lunchtime, I could see myself being trapped for the rest of the morning.

I went back to staring at the ceiling, this time with a broad smile spread across my face.

I mean, wow.

Like, holy shit. Wowzers.

I had never used the word *wowzers* to describe anything. But seriously… last night.

I had not expected *that*.

I could still feel him everywhere; the delicious aching between my thighs. His dick. His tongue. His fingers. He was a machine, a literal sex machine. I'd come so hard I was surprised my vision had returned already, because I definitely hadn't been able to see before I'd fallen asleep. I knew for a fact my vagina would never be the same.

Ace Watson had certainly taken his assignment seriously. Maybe I should send the editors at *Cosmo* a fruit basket.

I eased out of bed as carefully as I could, trying my best to move Ace as little as possible, which was hard seeing as he appeared to be glued to me. Silently tiptoeing to the bathroom, I closed the door and stood in front of the long bathroom mirror, my naked body on full display.

I'd never had a problem being naked; I loved my body, I loved the way it curved in all the right places, I loved the way my ass looked in jeans, and while I could probably lose twenty pounds, I wasn't willing to trade a great pair of tits to do so. But right now, running my fingertips over the faint marks on my hips where he'd gripped tight and thrust into me like his life depended on it, I'd never felt quite so sexy.

I turned slowly to find more on my ass.

Somehow, Ace had transformed from a guy who could

have been fucking anyone, to a guy who looked at me like he wouldn't ever get enough. It was dizzying and addictive.

It was dangerous.

A deep throb let out in my pussy, and I turned away to pee.

I was only as I was washing my hands that I realized the entire wall behind the sink was, in fact, a window, and if anyone in the buildings opposite had been awake and looking out, then they'd have had a good show. A whole wall of windows… my bathroom didn't even have a window, but this bathroom was not like the bathroom I had. I think my entire apartment could fit into it.

Also, for a twenty-three-year-old man, it was surprisingly clean and tidy. Towels hung neatly on the heated rail, there were no beard trimmings in the sink, or – as I looked – in the giant bath. An impressive selection of shampoo and body wash was lined in a row along a shelf in the shower, the labels facing out. I reached for one, twisting off the cap and taking a deep inhale. This was where the smell came from; that oaky scent that kicked up tiny pulses deep in my belly.

Stepping around the corner at the far end of the bathroom, I found myself in an equally tidy closet, organized by clothing type – t-shirts, shirts, jackets, pants – hanging on rails. I picked off the smallest t-shirt I could find, and pulled it over my head. In a drawer below I discovered boxer briefs, socks, more t-shirts, and thankfully sweats which I tugged on. Opening another door, and I was back in the bedroom; Ace hadn't even stirred.

As quietly as I could, I walked out and found myself in a dark hallway.

Arriving in his apartment had been such a blur that it took me a second to remember which way we'd come, but I followed the glow of sunlight to the cavernous main room I'd walked into off the hallway from the elevator. I stopped under the archway and peered around, just in case I wasn't alone, but I suspected Ace's roommates weren't early risers either.

My face split with a broad grin; at least I was wearing more clothes this morning.

I wasn't usually one for embarrassment, but I hadn't expected to walk in and find Lux Weston and Parker King, their eyes bugging wide and scaring the shit out of me. I wasn't sure who'd been more shocked.

Probably me.

Double height windows, just like the bathroom, stretched down one side of the living space. In the far corner near the elevator doors was the kitchen, and on the other side was another archway which I assumed led down to more bedrooms, but I wasn't about to go exploring.

I walked over to the window and stepped to the edge, ignoring the way my belly quivered as I took in the height and drop to the sidewalk. It was like being at the top of the Sears Tower, or on one of those glass walkways that assured you it could withstand the weight of a herd of elephants. But there was always that question in the back of your head – what if you were one elephant too many?

I moved back and appreciated the incredible view from a safer spot.

The sun had fully emerged over the Hudson, turning it a glowing, golden bronze color. Directly across the way, New Jersey spread out. I watched a black speed boat power up the river, leaving a white plume in its wake, and as my eyes tracked it north, I could just make out the tops of the black spears of The Lions stadium, which arched high in the cloudless sky.

Turning around, I spied a coffee machine tucked in the corner of the kitchen. Thankfully it was one I could work, not like the one at Kit's which required a PhD just to grind the beans. Opening the drawers, I discovered a neatly stacked selection of coffee pods, removed a mug from the top of the machine and stuck it underneath. While it was dripping, I continued my investigation of the living conditions of major league ball players.

What I found put me to shame.

A fridge full of neatly lined shelves, and an entire supermarket worth of fruit and vegetables. Cabinets filled with spices, seasoning and flour? I mean... *flour*? I know I used my cabinets for storing things other than food, but this was impressive and had me vowing to be more organized.

Taking my coffee, I made my way over the giant couch where I found PlayStation remotes, another edition of *Cosmo*, and a well-thumbed copy of *Don Quixote* which I picked up. I hadn't read *Don Quixote* since college, and it didn't quite seem to fit in this apartment with the basketball hoop on the wall by the giant television, and the – I counted them up – seven baseballs lying about the place. Not to mention the bats stacked by the elevator like they were umbrellas.

It was possible I was sitting in the world's most expensive frat house. It was easily the frat house with the best view, anyway.

Settling back into the couch, I sipped my coffee and began flicking through *Don Quixote;* which hadn't just been read, it had been loved. I only managed to reach page two, however, before a movement caught in the corner of my eye. I turned to find Ace leaning under the archway leading to his bedroom, wearing a smile so soft I wanted to wrap myself in it like Kit's cashmere blanket.

My belly did that thing again, like there was a butterfly emerging from its cocoon, making me feel giddy and lightheaded. And hot.

"Hey."

"Hey yourself." He pushed off the wall and walked toward me; sauntered toward me, slowly, was more like it.

I rubbed the sleep from my eyes. My heart began hammering. Maybe it was that I'd never seen him like this before; barefoot, wearing an obscenely low-slung pair of shorts that emphasized that delicious divot of muscle on his hips and thick corded abs, and nothing else. If his hair didn't always fall with that soft curl brushed away from his face, like he'd stepped off a catwalk, I'd say he'd spent half an hour styling it.

It was entirely annoying.

He stopped in front of me and dropped to his knees. I was about to make a half-hearted attempt to push him away before we started up anything his roommates could walk in on, but he merely rolled up the bottoms of the track pants I was wearing.

"I like these on you. You look cute," he grinned, looking way cuter than anything I could master, and I knew my cheeks were now pink.

What the fuck was going on with me? And why did I feel like the high-school cheerleader who'd just spent her first night with the football captain?

"Sorry, I was planning to come back," I thumbed behind me in the direction of his bedroom, "but I found…" I held up the coffee, because I'd clearly forgotten how to speak.

"I figured you would wake up early. I'm just happy you're still here."

I smiled at him, at his sincerity, but stayed silent, because what could I say to that?

"Now," his grin widened, "you can come back to bed, and I'll start your morning off right. Or I can make you pancakes first."

At that moment my stomach rumbled; I grabbed it, and he stared wide-eyed before breaking into a loud laugh. He really was cute when he laughed, and I found myself enjoying the sound – which is something I don't think I'd ever thought about before.

"I guess that's my answer," he replied and stood up, taking my coffee cup with him.

Holding his free hand out to me, I took it and allowed him to pull me to standing, where he smacked a quick kiss to my lips.

He laced our fingers together as he led me to the kitchen, pulling out one of the kitchen stools.

"Get comfy," he ordered, and I jumped onto it. "You want more coffee?"

I nodded. "Yes, please."

He flicked the coffee machine back on, before opening the fridge to pull out milk, eggs, butter, and raspberries. From the large drawer under the stove, he removed a cast iron pan, then grabbed a mixing bowl, a whisk, and what looked like a bag of chocolate chips.

Holy crap.

I wasn't even sure I *owned* a mixing bowl.

This was better than eating out.

By the time he laid it on the counter, the coffee had finished and he passed me a fresh cup. It was as he took a sip of his own that his eyes flicked up from mine, to something behind me. Some*one*, it turned out.

"Just in time. I hoped I was making enough noise to wake you."

I turned to see Lux walking toward us, wearing the same amount of clothing as Ace, and I briefly wondered if perhaps I hadn't woken up but was instead living some teenage-Payton fantasy, surrounded by two almost naked, *very hot*, guys.

"Good morning," Lux grinned, way too wide for my liking, before his eyes dropped to *Don Quixote* which I'd brought over with me from the couch. "Oh, that's where I left it."

"Is this yours?"

He nodded, taking it from me and zipped his thumb over the pages. "Yeah."

"It looks loved."

"It's my favorite book. Have you read it?"

I shook my head, "Not since college."

He stood there staring at me, unsure of what else there was to say, and I remembered why I didn't do sleepovers; the awkward roommate bump the morning after. No one should have to make polite conversation with a stranger before you'd finished your first coffee.

Finally, his eyes flicked over to Ace and down to the neat line of ingredients.

"Are you hungry?"

I nodded. "Ace was about to make breakfast."

Lux threw his head back with a loud laugh. "*I* make the breakfast."

My brows knitted together, and I looked at Ace who smirked, then rounded the island and sat next to me. "It's true. He makes breakfast, I was just getting it ready for him. But I help with the whisking."

I let out another giggle before I could slap a hand over my mouth to stop it.

"Hey," Ace murmured, his lips brushing against the shell of my ear, "don't hide that giggle. I like it."

Heat flushed my cheeks again, as my belly fluttered away.

Again. If you'd have asked me two months ago what being in Ace Watson's apartment would be like, I'd never have been able to conceive of this; two strapping major league baseball players – one in a rainbow covered apron no less – making me breakfast.

"You can put the chocolate chips into the batter," Lux said, passing me the bag.

Ace's eyes widened and he leaned in to kiss my cheek. "Wow, no one's ever allowed to pour the chocolate chips."

"*You're* not allowed," corrected Lux, "Otherwise the entire bag disappears in one go."

I picked up my coffee, peering at the pair of them over the rim of my cup. "So other girls get to pour them?"

Ace grabbed the bowl and cracked the first egg into it. "Girls don't have breakfast here. Breakfast is a sacred time."

My brow furrowed. "What does that mean?"

"We never make breakfast for girls. You're the first."

"Oh." I took another sip of my coffee, because I wasn't sure what else to do with that fact drop. "Do you guys do this every morning?"

"I do," Lux nodded, taking the bowl from Ace and whisking it at a speed I'd only seen on The Great British Bake Off, a show Kit and I used to have an unhealthy obsession with. "But if the boys aren't awake, I leave breakfast for them."

"My mama used to do it for me and my brothers before school, but Lux likes cooking so he makes it," added Ace.

"It gives me something to do before a game. I like to start the day putting effort into breakfast." Lux put the bowl of batter in front of me. "Here, add a cup of the chips."

I took the red measuring cup from Lux and scooped out one portion into the pancake mix, only for Ace to shove his fist into the bag and add another when Lux's back was turned, whispering, "Lucky Aces strikes again," with more mischief than a kid in a candy store.

"What do you normally do for breakfast?"

I shrugged. "I grab something on my way to the office. Usually a bagel. Mostly I forget, and just have coffee."

"What did you do as a kid?"

The smile I'd beamed at Ace dropped a little, and my fingers tightened around my coffee mug. "My parents were too busy fighting to have time to make me breakfast. But once they were going through a divorce, I did get double pocket money so they could out-do each other. I had a nanny for a while who used to make me egg white omelets, but they were gross."

To this day, I still can't look at an egg white omelet without thinking of Griselda, and any number of the monumental fights my parents had.

I turned to Ace, the grin he'd been wearing a second ago as he'd stuffed the chips in his mouth had vanished. Out of nowhere, a thick ball of tears pushed up my throat, and I had to work hard to swallow it down.

"I'm sorry. I didn't realize."

I shrugged, pushing it away as I always did. "Don't be. It's what I was used to, but you better believe they also sent me to a ton of child therapists so they could also convince their divorce lawyers that they were the best parent. That was fun."

"Are you close with them now?" asked Lux, snatching up the ladle from the pot of utensils.

The batter hit the hot griddle with a loud hiss, and the smell of cinnamon, sugar, and chocolate filled the air, making my stomach rumble again.

I shook my head. "Not really."

"Where do they live?"

"They're both still in Miami," I replied, really not wanting to get further into a conversation about my parents, which thankfully Ace sensed, and changed the subject.

"Hey, Weston, Payton's starting a new job this week."

He flipped one of the pancakes over and turned to me. "Oh yeah, what is it?"

"I'm a book editor. I'm moving from children's books to adult fiction."

Lux's eyes lit up. "That's cool. Do you get to read them before they hit the shelves?"

I nodded. "Yeah, as long as Simpson and Mather publish them. If you like reading, let me know what you want and I'll give them to Ace for you."

"If you can't tell, Weston here is the reader of our group."

"Hey," I reached over and patted Ace's cheek, "don't put yourself down. You read. I saw *Cosmo*, remember?"

The two of them snorted loudly and grinned at each other. I sat back in the stool as Ace got up, poured out glasses of fresh orange juice for the three of us, removed plates from the cabinet, then grabbed maple syrup before sitting down again. It was utterly domestic and wholesome, and I didn't want to think about why it was making my chest ache.

Lux placed a thick stack of pancakes in front of us, pushing it toward me with a grin, "Ladies first."

I forked one off the top. "Thank you."

"I should be thanking you for getting Watson into reading *Cosmo*. We've struck gold with that."

I coughed into my orange juice, looking up to find them smirking at me. "I'll let you know if the ladies of New York award me a service medal or something."

Lux chuckled. "No… I mean yes, that, but our game's improved since we've been reading it. All four of us."

"Come on, not you too." I rolled my eyes heavily and forked in a mouthful with a groan. Holy shit, these pancakes were good. "You're not serious?"

He scooped a handful of raspberries onto his pancakes then drowned the entire stack in maple syrup. "Deadly. I caught every ball last week."

"Isn't that what you're paid for?" I asked, which I thought was a reasonable question based on all the sports articles I'd read recently. Journalistic, definitely.

"Yes, I'm paid to catch the ball, but not just catch the ball. I play center field."

I waited for Lux to expand on that last point, but he didn't.

"She doesn't really know much about baseball," mumbled Ace through a mouthful.

My head snapped around to him. "Hey, I'm learning."

"I know, Babycakes." He patted my knee, to which I scowled, and he returned it with a grin. "Center field has the most ground to cover. They're usually furthest away from the plate, they have to be agile, have strong throwing arms, and excellent aim. Our boy Lux has it all."

"Oh." I raised a fork loaded with pancakes. "Congratulations."

"Thanks," he smirked. "I haven't missed a ball, I've been quicker, and every one I've thrown back to base has been caught."

"Okay," I nodded, because I didn't know what more to say. "Well, that's good. I'm sure Penn is happy."

"Yeah."

"But seriously, congratulations for these pancakes. They're

pretty damn good." I wiped my loaded fork around the plate to mop up the remaining syrup. "And I have to say this has been excellent service."

"You're welcome at Casa Greyskull anytime," Lux grinned, loading up his plate with another stack and pouring more syrup out.

"Where?"

"Our apartment. We're the Masters of the Baseball Universe." Lux picked up his plate and reached for his book, while I was still trying to figure out what he'd said, and looked at Ace. "I'm taking these back to bed. Leave in a couple of hours?"

"Sounds good, dude," Ace replied and winked at me. "We're going back to bed too."

Lux dropped his head with a shake and a smile. "Good to meet you, Payton."

"You too. Thank you, again, for the pancakes."

"Hey, I owed you." He saluted, and disappeared through the arch.

I stretched out in the stool with a loud groan. "I am so full."

Ace jumped off his stool and took my hands. "I'm not. Let's go."

The way he was looking at me didn't take any guesses we weren't going back to sleep.

"I'm going to get a cramp."

"Let me do the hard work. Pancakes were just the start of my breakfast." He swiped the bottle of maple syrup off the counter, and his brows raised over a devilish smirk. "I'm planning to get you all sticky, then clean you up real good in the shower."

I followed silently as he took my hand and led me back to his bedroom.

If this is what Lowe meant about taking one for the team, then sign me up.

I just wish that damn butterfly in my chest wasn't still fluttering.

16

Ace

"*O*UT!"

The umpire's right fist shot in the air.

Behind him, Parker stood, pulled up his mask, threw the ball back to me, and we walked off the field for the changeover.

"Nice work, Watson," called Coach Chase as I stepped into the dugout.

"Thanks, sir."

"You got one more inning, then Michaels is going on."

I was about to sit down, but immediately stood back up. "No, Coach, I'm good. I feel good. I don't need to come off. Lemme stay in."

But Coach shook his head. "Nope. One more. You'll have done five innings, and we're in the lead. Michaels is going in."

I threw my glove onto the pitcher's chair, which was always positioned by the water cooler. Anyone else could sit where

"Fuck's sake," I mumbled, quiet enough that Coach wouldn't hear me and subsequently fine me for swearing and/or being disrespectful about the fact he already wanted to send in one of The Lions relief pitchers. "Bullshit. That's what this is. Bullshit."

"Here."

I turned to find Parker holding out a bottle of Gatorade, and took it. I'd gulped half the bottle before he sat down next to me, and swiped my hand across my lips.

"This is bullshit, right?"

He nodded. "Yeah. He could have left you in a little longer."

"I'm still paying the price for fucking up the Opener. He doesn't trust me not to fuck up again." I tugged down on my hat, then pushed it back up to scratch hard through my hair, but nothing seemed to ease the tension and frustration which had made itself known. "I've had a great week. I feel good. I feel the best I have all season. I just wish he'd leave me in longer."

"I know, dude, you were on fire out there."

"Yeah, I fucking know," I grumbled.

"I need to talk to Rodriquez for a second, you gonna be okay?" Parker looked at me, and I nodded.

I was fine. Pissed, but fine. I planned to stay here and sulk for the rest of the game. Only as Parker got up and left, his seat was taken by someone else.

"How's it going, Watson?"

I side-eyed Jupiter. "Can't complain."

"You sure? You look like you're about to start complaining to me," he smirked.

I never used to find Jupiter annoying, but it was starting to become apparent to me that I did. Or maybe he only seemed to appear when I was in a bad mood. Like now.

"I just don't need to be pulled out," I grumbled.

He slapped me on the knee. "Happens to the best of us. Coach just wants to keep you rested and fresh."

"If I'm rested any more, I'll be unconscious."

Jupiter sat back and crossed his arms, letting out a low chuckle. Thankfully he didn't have anything more to say, and just sat there watching The Rangers find their positions.

We were currently tied at one. The Lions' run was scored off Lux smashing out a home run which reached the second tier of the stands, setting off the canons firing out gold and black paper ribbons, and a sea of black foam fingers shot into the air. The Rangers' was from Marcus Semien making it safely around the diamond, stealing one base at a time after a bloop single into right field.

I'd fielded two balls, and managed to keep two of their batters from reaching first base. My pitching had been hard and fast, which only reinforced my opinion that pulling me out now was bullshit.

I was still mulling it over when Jupiter nudged me in the ribs, way harder than he needed to.

"What was that for?" I grumbled, rubbing my side.

I followed his line of sight to where one of the coaches was on the dugout phone and beckoning us down. Or one of us down.

"Dr. Matthews wants you, she's in the tunnel," he said.

"Which one of us?" I frowned, because I had no idea why she'd want me, but summoning Jupiter in the middle of a game didn't seem her style either.

"You, Watson."

"Oh, okay. Thanks."

"Now, Ace," he urged, like I was just going to hang around and make conversation.

I wasn't.

I jogged over to where I could see Marnie, only realizing Jupiter was next to me when I got there.

"Are you following me?"

I didn't get an answer, because he was already standing in front of Marnie. "Hey, there's the most beautiful star in the sky,"

She grinned up at him. "Hey. Nice game out there today."

"Yeah? I'll catch you another ball next time we're in field." He wrapped his arms around her waist and pulled her in for a kiss.

Pretty sure there was something in the rule book about kissing field-side, and if there wasn't, there should be.

"Jupiter!" Marnie snapped, immediately jumping back up, spinning around to make sure no one had seen. "At least pretend we're professionals."

He chuckled. "Where's the fun in that?"

I turned around so I didn't have to watch their inappropriate displays of affection, though it wasn't bothering me as much as it usually did. Maybe I'd gotten too used to it. On second thoughts, was I finding it kind of… cute?

I shook that thought away and went back to the baseball.

"Anyway, Ace…"

My ears perked up, and I tore my eyes away from Saint Velasquez, The Lions' right field, who was taking his time to get to the batter's box because he and Stone Philips had a bet going on who could get there the slowest without a time penalty.

So far, Stone was in the lead with .95 of a second to spare, but this would be close.

At least Jupiter was standing further away when I turned around.

"Hey, Doc, what's up?"

"Can I check your heart monitor?"

"Sure." Pulling up my shirt, I peeled it off and handed it to her with an apologetic smile. "Sorry, it's sweaty."

"It should be," Jupiter added, leaning against the tunnel wall to watch the game as Marnie crouched down to hook the monitor up to her laptop.

When Marnie had joined The Lions last year, she'd introduced a new material which Penn immediately ordered our uniforms to be made from. The material contained tiny sensors which monitored our sweat rates, oxygen levels, and hydration, among other things, in real time, so she could adjust accordingly during the game. It's part of what had been credited to us reaching the Playoffs last year, when The Lions had never made it further from the bottom of the standings.

This year, we'd also been fitted with disposable heart monitors embedded into a patch which we stuck to our chests before each game, to monitor our blood pressure and heart rates when we were both fielding and pitching. The overall purpose had been to personalize each of our training and nutrition programs so we could optimize our capabilities.

Since we'd been following her guidance, injuries in the club were down nearly seventy-five percent.

My eyes were flicking between the diamond where Saint was now on second base and Tanner was up to bat, and Marnie's screen lit up with a graph covered in wavy green and red lines.

"Are you feeling okay?"

I nodded. "Yeah, fine, other than pissed at being pulled out."

"You don't feel faint?"

I peered down to Marnie in confusion. "No. Why would I feel faint?"

"Your heart rate is lower than it normally is. It's been lowering all week, except when you sat down just now and it shot up, which made no sense, but I guess if you're pissed, that would explain it," she mumbled, though it was so quiet I wasn't sure she was still talking to me, especially as she was still fiddling around with the screen.

"Doc?"

"Sorry." She pushed her glasses onto her head, and turned to me. "During Spring Training, your heart rate averaged around one forty when you pitched." She tapped the screen and the lines on the graph changed from green and red to blue. "See? This is March." She tapped the screen again and the red lines came back. "Now this is the beginning of the season. Opening Day and your heart rate spiked at one seventy when you were on the mound. You were pumping adrenaline." Another tap, and this time green lines reappeared. "It leveled out a bit during April, but since last Monday, it's been consistently dropping back closer to one forty. Then today, you started at one thirty-seven, but when you came off just now you were one twenty-five… until you sat down."

"You got all this from those patches?"

She nodded. "Yeah. We're still testing them, so I wanted to check if it was faulty or if you weren't feeling good. You look okay."

"I feel okay." I scratched through my beard. "What's Reeves' average?"

"Chill as fuck," he replied with a smirk.

Marnie rolled her eyes. "Jupiter's different because he's more aerobic during the games. He covers more ground. Also, you don't bat, therefore your heart rate doesn't shoot up while running bases."

"What's my heart rate saying now?" I asked.

"I'll get you a new patch, but overall, it'll be the same. Calm." Her head tilted a little and she stood up. "You do seem calmer than I've seen you in a while."

Jupiter pushed off the wall. "She's right, Watson. You have been less annoying than usual."

He grunted as Marnie nudged him hard.

"Jupiter, be quiet."

I looked back at the screen, where there in blue, green, and red was the sum of my failures and successes this season. I guess it made sense that the morning after I'd slept with Payton the second time – the successful time – was when the green lines would begin to appear, but while I knew my game had been improving, as well as my mental strength, I never expected she'd have had such a physical effect on me.

I didn't think I felt any different than I had yesterday, but the blue line said otherwise.

I took a deep breath and thought about it, I wondered if perhaps I might have felt different because this morning had been different. Having Payton in my space, wearing my clothes, sitting at the kitchen counter while we made pancakes, had been different.

The soft click of Marnie's laptop shutting brought me back to the present.

"Okay," she said, "I need to go. Good luck for the rest of the game. I'll get you a new patch."

"Nah, don't worry about it. I'm not going back in. Thanks anyway, Doc."

"You're so goddamn smart, Marn," Jupiter grinned at her, then blew her a kiss which made her cheeks redden, but when she turned to walk away, I could see a smile on her lips.

I let out a little chuckle and headed back to my seat to watch the rest of the game, just as Parker hit a home run. The crowd roared; foam fingers shot in the air as his name was chanted while he sprinted around the bases until he was safely home.

He jogged back to the dugout with a shit-eating grin, high-fiving Lux who was next up to bat.

"Awesome, buddy," I grinned, slapping him on the back. "Fucking awesome."

"King!" Coach hollered from the other end of the dugout, and gestured him over.

I sat back down, watching every guy on the team slap Parker on the back as he made his way to Coach.

"What's been going on?"

I looked at Jupiter, who was sitting next to me again. "Huh?"

"With you. What's been going on?"

Out on the field, Lux's hit managed to get him as far as second base.

"I'm not following."

"Your pitch, the lack of running your mouth off about whichever girl you hooked up with last night, you generally being more tolerable to spend time with…" He raised one thick eyebrow at me and grinned.

"I didn't ask you to follow me back here, or sit next to me," I snapped. "In fact, feel free to fuck off down the end of the benches if you're going to be a dick."

Jupiter threw his head back with a loud snort. "Easy tiger,

I'm fucking with you. Mostly. But it all smells suspiciously like you've got yourself a girl."

I stayed as still as I could, trying to school my features to give nothing away, instead of the giant smile I wanted to break out into, which would give everything away. Everything and more.

"I don't know what you're talking about."

"Sure, you don't." He sat back again, eyes on the field. "I was there in Shepherd's office, remember? You told him you were going to fix it. Looks like you have, but something tells me you didn't do it by yourself."

"I've been concentrating on getting my pitch back, and my head in the game. I'm doing it, so stop giving me a hard time. And if you really want to help, tell Coach to stop pulling me out early. I can pitch more than five innings."

Jupiter smoothed down his dark beard, twisting the longer strands between his fingers like he was fucking Columbo. No doubt he'd be patting himself on the back for a job-well-done later.

"Okay," he said as he stood up. "I need to head, I'm batting soon."

I nodded to him, watching him walk off as I thought about his words.

I was surprised he hadn't come out and accused me of taking drugs. The thing is, he wouldn't be wrong.

Except my drug of choice wasn't available on prescription.

Payton Lopez; human Prozac.

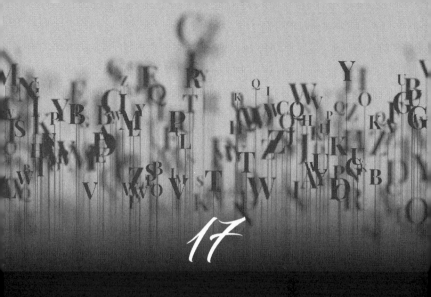

17

Payton

Ace: *Did you see it?*

Ace: *Tell me you saw it…*

Ace: *Never mind, tell me in the morning, you'll be asleep*

Ace: *It was fucking awesome though*

Ace: *Sleep tight, Babycakes. Wish I was naked with you*

I bit down on my smirk, tossed my phone to the side and stretched out. I'd had the entire bed to myself.

I should have been relishing in the space, yet something felt… different. Weird, even. A little off.

I pressed my belly. Nope, I didn't feel sick. I tried my chest, but my heart seemed to be beating just fine.

I stared up at the ceiling to see if that would help me figure came to mind, and by the time I turned my head to look at the clock, I'd been staring for twenty minutes. If I stayed in bed any longer, I'd be severely running the risk of being late for work, and I was still trying to make a good impression on the fiftieth floor.

It was as I tiptoed to the bathroom that I realized I didn't have to be quiet in case I woke the Sleeping Beauty I'd left in my bed.

Bingo. That must be it, *the quiet*. Maybe it was too quiet.

I reached for the Bluetooth speaker, switched it to *Z100 New York* and turned up the music until it was loud enough to blast the funk away I'd clearly woken up with. I could sing in the shower while I washed my hair without the embarrassment of someone listening to my hopelessly out-of-tune voice.

And when I wrapped the towel around my head and walked back through to my bedroom, Ace wasn't sitting up to watch me get dressed while he recapped every pitch and play from the night before, or ran through his stats *one more time*, or discussed his strategy for the day's game, and what he planned to improve on.

I could sit with my thoughts and dry my hair in peace.

Sweet peace.

Though as I sat down, I couldn't help but pick up my phone and click into his stream of messages. He was over on the west coast, so he'd definitely be asleep, and instead of replying, I pulled up the sports news to see what I'd missed before I texted him back.

The Lions had beaten The Giants 6–3 from multi-run home runs, courtesy of Tanner Simpson, Stone Fields, and Jupiter Reeves.

Ace had opened the pitching, and according to *ESPN*, had caught the first ball he'd thrown. He'd pitched it so hard and fast it had bounced off the bat, heading straight back to the mound, and Ace's glove. The Giant's leadoff man was out.

The second batter connected, and the rolling grounder headed back toward Ace. In less time than it took to blink, Ace dived like he was David Beckham, stopped the ball, and tossed it over to Boomer Jones on first base. The second Giant's batter walked back to the dugout.

I pulled up a clip on MLB.com to watch Ace pushing himself up off the field where the camera caught him winking to Parker with a grin I knew meant trouble.

CBS Sports, ESPN, FOX Sports, NBC Sports… all of them and more were reporting different versions of the same thing. How did Ace make that catch? How was this the same guy who'd pitched on Opening Day?

We were seven weeks into the season, and The Lions were now third in the National League East standings, behind the Phillies and the Marlins. Not only that, they were half-way up the National League standings.

In the sixth inning, the ball had smashed off the bat and flown high into the air, but it had traveled up and back, instead of out to the bleachers either side. Ace sprinted toward the dugout, powering those thighs I'd become well acquainted with, until the ball lost velocity and dropped. Ace slid along the dirt, his glove reaching high, and the ball fell straight into it.

August Chase had pulled him after that, bringing out Cory Michaels from the bullpen. But the opinions were unanimous; whatever demons Ace had been battling at the beginning of the season had been well and truly exorcised. He was becoming unstoppable. The guy from *ESPN* wrote that he expected Ace to become the first pitcher to be nominated for a Cy Young award who'd let four runs be scored off his first inning of the season.

By the time I'd finished reading everything I could find and typed out a message to Ace telling him he'd done an awesome job, I realized I'd not only taken far too long, but I'd blow-dried my hair so poorly that the only thing I could do was tie it back into a messy bun. The next three minutes allowed me to pull on the first thing I saw in my closet, which was a pair of skinny jeans, a cute sleeveless top, and pair of flat pumps, throw the green birthday Jimmy Choos into my purse next to my laptop, and sprint out the door.

I might have felt like a totally frazzled mess when I stepped into the elevator at the Greyschott building forty minutes later, but pressing the button for the fiftieth floor instead of the fortieth filled me with such a sense of calm and happiness, that when the ding went off and the doors opened, I was a real time equivalent of a before and after picture.

I stepped out with a genuine smile on my face, because for the first time in a long time, I was *loving* being at work.

The only thing I wasn't so wild about was my lack of office.

The fiftieth floor was open plan, with hot desking encouraged, so we all had lockers to dump our things in instead of littering the floor with them.

A huge black and white kitchen was stationed at one end, and a cozy looking library with floor to ceiling shelves brimming with the latest releases – some yet to be released, and Simpson and Mather classics all organized by genre – at the other. Some of the guys I'd met this week were already in here working, or reading on the squashy couches, beanbags, or chairs while they ate breakfast.

The plus side – the décor was adult, whereas the fortieth floor always reminded me of the children's wing at a hospital with its bright colors and walls covered in characters from the books we published. Maybe that was why I'd always hid in my office.

I dumped my bag, switched my shoes out, and was making my way over to the desk I'd decided I liked the most, when a voice called my name.

"Good morning, Payton."

I spun around to see Mia, one of the junior editors for adult fiction walking toward me with a mug of coffee in each hand. I'd met her on my first day last week when she told me she'd been working at Simpson and Mather just under a year, and loved historical romance and fantasy fiction.

She was cute and preppy, super enthusiastic, and I liked her immediately.

"Here." She thrust a coffee at me. "I saw you getting out of the elevator and made it for you."

My eyes widened as I inhaled the rich Arabica, and realized I had been too distracted with Ace to even make myself coffee this morning. "Thank you so much. God, I need this."

"How are you enjoying things so far?" she asked, sitting down at the desk opposite me, where her laptop was open.

I blew on the steaming mug and took as big a sip as the temperature would let me. "Good so far."

"Is it different?"

I shook my head. "Aside from the subject matter and the interior design, I'm not sure yet. I can't imagine it'll be that much different."

"These manuscripts will probably take a little longer to get through," she laughed.

"Totally. Kids' books don't stretch over that many pages," I grinned. "What are you working on right now?"

"I'm halfway through first edits of the new Callie Malone

book, so I should be done with that by the end of next week."

"Is that the next one of her Fisherwick Chronicles?"

Mia nodded, her eyes lighting up. "Yes, it's awesome. The first sold so well that we bought the rest of the series."

"I'm not really into fantasy books, but my best girlfriend read it on vacation this year and wouldn't stop talking about it."

It was true. The first Fisherwick Chronicle was one of the books Lowe had brought with her to St. Barts last New Year. She'd started it on the Tuesday morning, and hadn't spoken again until Wednesday afternoon when she finished it. After that, she proceeded to hound everyone else into reading it. The boys refused point blank, but Kit had relented followed by Beulah. I'd added it to my never ending pile of books.

"I'm loving the second, even from the first draft. I had to beg for it though; there were a lot of us on this floor who wanted it, but I got it first. Once I'm done it'll go to the senior team for editing." She grinned. "What are you working on? Have you had any submissions yet?"

I tapped the edge of my computer screen where my manuscript was open. "Actually, I have. It was one I brought with me. I got it by accident, but it's a new author and I've started reading it, and I love it. I want to run it past the team in the meeting today and see what the vibe is."

"What's the genre?"

"Small town romance, set in England."

Her eyes widened with excitement. "Oh, that'll be popular. Great work."

Our chat was interrupted by two more of the editorial team – Mateo and Tyler – who dumped their bags on their desks, dropped into their respective chairs, and propped their feet up before even acknowledging Mia and me. In fact, I wasn't even sure they'd noticed we were here at all.

I'd met them briefly last week, but since then, they'd either been sitting elsewhere or out of the office. I knew they worked in non-fiction, and I think their focus was on sports. Yeah, it was sports, something they were currently talking about very loudly.

"It was an easy catch, we should have made it," Tyler grumbled. "Then you've got Watson making catches no human should be able to make. Lux Weston is out in center field scaling the wall like he's effing Spiderman. It's not normal. They're all taking something."

"Who's Spiderman?" asked Mia, whose head had been moving between the two of them.

Both their heads snapped around to where Mia and I were sitting, and they blinked in surprise. I knew they hadn't seen us.

"Oh, hey, when did you get here?" asked Matty.

"We were here when you walked in."

"Oh."

"What are you talking about?" she asked again, as she sipped her coffee.

"Baseball. The Lions game last night. Did you watch it?"

"No." She rolled her eyes, like she had a million better things to do. "I had a date."

Matty frowned, his entire face creasing in confusion. "But all the New York teams played last night. All of them."

"What's that got to do with my date?"

"He didn't want to watch the games?" he asked, and the tone he used had me hiding a smile.

"Not everyone cares about sports to the level you to do."

Tyler scoffed, spinning his chair around until his knees

were almost touching hers, and his voice became serious. "Mia, he's lying, and if he's telling you he doesn't care about sports, it's because he wants to sleep with you. On the other hand, if he's telling the truth, then why would you want to be with him in the first place? There's something wrong with a guy who's not interested in sports."

I briefly wondered if I should introduce him to Penn. I had a feeling they'd get along. Penn Shepherd was of the same opinion about people liking or not liking sports.

My chair creaked as I leaned back into it. "And what's happening right now that you're mad about?"

"Ace Watson's comeback."

I picked up my coffee, trying to disguise the air that had stuck in my throat as a dry cough, and took the biggest sip I could manage.

"What d'you mean?"

"You know The Lions? The baseball team?"

I nodded. "Yes, I know them."

"Ace Watson is the starting pitcher for The Lions. He had the worst Opening Day I've ever seen. It was a blood bath. Utter humiliation, and a beautiful thing to watch."

I tried really hard not to shrink into my chair with each word he punched out. "You're not a Lions fan?"

"Hell no. I'm Mets all the way, baby. The Lions suck, and it doesn't matter how much money Penn Shepherd pumps in, because they will always suck. They always have."

Maybe I won't introduce him to Penn. I also refrained from asking him not to call me 'baby', because I didn't think it would make a difference.

"It's still early in the season, we'll move back up," Matty added.

I nodded silently, peering at them over the rim of my coffee mug as I sipped it. Now I understood why these two had so much attitude today. The Mets lost last night against The Orioles, and dropped below The Lions in the standings.

The bagel Matty had in his hand was making me hungry, and I debated on whether I had time to run out for one, but it seemed we weren't done talking about Ace.

Oh goody.

"Yeah, he was benched for a week," continued Tyler. "Everyone thought he had the yips, but I'm starting to think it was nothing more than a rumor put out by The Lions. No one comes back from the yips like that, and he's had a quick recovery."

"Why would they put that rumor out?" Mia asked, though she'd already gone back to her work, and I couldn't tell whether she really cared about the answer or if she was trying to fuck with the boys.

He shrugged in the way the answer should be obvious, but beats me if it was, and Mia seemed to share my opinion.

"It had to be his shoulder. There must have been a muscle or something, and he just needed to rest it," said Matty.

"Nah, it's not rest. They've injected him with something. No one makes catches like that without a little performance enhancer."

"What does that mean?" I asked, and I didn't like the line this conversation was going.

"The guy had Velcro hands last night."

"Whatever, Watson'll get caught on the next round of testing, anyway. He'll go back to being the average pitcher he is. He was mediocre at the Yankees, he's mediocre now. Shepherd paid way too much for him."

I was starting to get annoyed with these two. I'd certainly

had enough of their opinions about Ace for one day, especially as they were dead wrong. For the first time ever, I could contribute to a baseball conversation; I hadn't even realized I'd been paying that much attention to what Ace said, as my focus was usually on what his fingers, tongue, or dick was doing. But if these two were going to talk shit about him, the least I could do was make sure they got his stats correct.

"Actually, guys, even with the blip at the beginning the season, Ace has already matched his ERA from last season. If you take out the two weeks he was benched, then his average drops to nearer two-point-seven. If you take Spring Training into consideration, then it drops again. He's had a few 1-2-3 innings over the last two games, and since he's been back starting, The Lions haven't lost."

I racked my brains to see if that was everything I remembered… oh, wait.

"After last night, The Lions are now five up on The Mets in the National League, so maybe Penn Shepherd knew what he was doing with his money." Yep, that was everything, and I picked up my coffee.

The bagel Matty was about to bite down on stopped halfway to his lips. "You're a Lions' fan?"

I shrugged. "They're okay."

Tyler scoffed, scowled at me, stood up and walked away without saying another word. Matty opened his laptop and went back to his bagel, also without another word, but then seemed to think better of it. He gathered everything up in his hands and followed Tyler to wherever he'd stormed off to.

"Something I said?" I grinned at Mia as she peered around our screens.

"Now that was funny. All they do all day is talk about The Mets. I didn't realize you were a big baseball fan, but maybe

I could get on board with sports if you do that again," she grinned. "Anyway, I need the bathroom. Meet you in the editorial meeting?"

"Yeah," I replied quietly, letting out a big breath as she walked off.

I watched until she was out of sight, wondering when I'd become a baseball fan, or if I'd simply become an Ace Watson fan.

And whether I really wanted to know the answer.

18

Ace

I took the Sharpie Boobs McGee was holding out.

"Hey, Ace."

"Hey, how're you doin'?"

I tried not to breathe in the scent of her cinnamon gum as I scrawled my name across the ball she was holding directly in front of her very ample chest. There was literally nowhere else my eyes could go except to her tits. I'm surprised she didn't ask me to sign them too, something that happened way more than it ever should.

In fact, signing tits should *never* happen.

As I handed it back, she reached into her cleavage, retrieved a folded piece of paper and put it in my open palm before I could stop her.

"Um, thanks."

I didn't get the opportunity to move onto the next ball/t-shirt/poster to sign because Max Flay, the Lions coordinator who was more foghorn than human, decided to make his presence known.

"E'rybody on the bus. Let's go. Let's go. Let's goooo!"

"Jeez, Max."

I pressed down on my ear in an attempt to stop the ringing, and turned back to the line of Lions fans waiting outside the Cardinals Stadium. The excitement and screaming kicked up as they all desperately tried to get the signatures from the players they wanted before we all disappeared. Everyone's names were being shouted all at the same time and it was hard to decipher who was saying what, though I could definitely hear mine cutting through.

Ace! Ace! Ace!

We'd just finished a three-game series; lost the first, but won the second and third, so we were leaving on a high, and the fans were feeling it too. Therefore, we'd been taking our time to meet everyone who'd traveled to watch us; Boomer Jones was still signing merch, Stone Fields was taking selfies with a couple of kids, but looking around, I couldn't see any of my boys.

"What're you doing?"

I turned as a heavy arm fell over my shoulder, to find Tanner grinning at me. "Looking for you. Where are the others?"

"Coming. Parker had to run back to the locker room."

"Why?"

"Dunno," he shrugged, which I should have expected. Tanner wasn't big on detail.

"Move your asses!" came Max's voice again, and another surge of fans pressed into the barriers separating us from them.

"We're moving, calm down," Tanner grumbled as we joined the line of our teammates making our way to one of the Lions' buses heading for the airport.

I chuckled. "Dude, don't let Max hear you telling him to calm down."

"We *are* moving. I'm going as fast as I can," Tanner replied. "See? We're here now."

I stepped up into the bus, hiding my grin from both him and Max, as Max checked us off on the iPad, and I followed Tanner along the aisle to the first available seats. This wasn't like being on the school bus where the back row was exclusively for the cool kids; on the Lions' bus, you took the first seat you saw behind the coaches and rested. Therefore, first on the bus, first to sit down.

The same rules applied for the plane. Once we were past the executive seats where Penn Shepherd, any board members and exec team stopped, and past the coach's seats and the PT beds, it was a free-for-all. Except on the plane, the boys and I had taken to sitting further down the end where it was quieter and more private, which meant we could discuss our reading materials without the worry of being overheard.

Lux had hooked up with a girl last night and made a very spectacular catch off a ball which should have resulted in a hit, but somehow, he'd chased it down and managed to snatch it up. It wasn't the first time this series either. He'd spent so much time scaling the walls to snag a flying ball he could probably take on El Capitan without training.

"Tan!" I called him to a spare set of seats he'd walked straight past, which he clearly hadn't seen as his focus was on his phone screen. "Sit here."

I shook off my backpack and scooted over to the window seat, my head falling back against the rest. I should be tired tonight, we were heading off to Toronto for our final away series of this stretch, and I *should* be closing my eyes, but instead I was buzzing. This series had gotten better and better.

I'd made all my starts since we'd left New York a week ago, and gone deep into the game. I'd had a bunch of 1-2-3 innings, caught four balls straight off the bat, and we'd moved up the standings. This morning as I was walking out of the hotel, I'd spotted the Wall Street Journal sports pages on one of the end tables in the lobby and swiped it.

'The Miraculous Comeback of Ace Watson' the headline had read.

I knew the journalist.

Two months ago, he'd called me *'an overpaid pretty boy, only capable of throwing a tantrum'* and suggested I get some of those blow-up training things that kids use down the side of bowling lanes to help my aim.

I'd been about to punch the wall, but Parker had pulled me back telling me I'd only prove him right. That afternoon was the day Payton had come to the Lions parking lot.

This article, though, had been different. A full-page write-up starting with an admission of being too quick with his initial judgement, and went on to cover every pitch I'd made since Opening Day up to yesterday's game. But what had really caught my eye was the final sentence.

'Ace Watson appears to be unstoppable. If he continues at the rate he's been pitching, we will see a perfect game this season from the youngest player to have ever pitched one in the major leagues, and I want it to happen.'

I'd ripped out that final sentence, and put it in my pocket.

A perfect game. Every pitcher's dream.

I'd had two combined no-hitters games; I'd had one no-hitters game when I was in college. But a perfect game... nope. There'd only been twenty-four total recorded in the entire history of the Major Leagues. It was rarer than a pipe dream.

But this guy… the one who'd thought I was an overpaid pretty boy two months ago, now seemed to think I was capable.

And I wanted to believe he was correct.

"Dude… watch what you're doing, will you?" I shoved Tanner back into his seat and off my lap where he'd actually dropped down.

"Sorry," he mumbled, and nodded to the piece of paper Boobs McGee had handed me, which I didn't realize I was still carrying. "What's that?"

"Some girl gave it to me. Probably her number."

When I opened it to show him, however, it wasn't just her number. It was a polaroid of her wearing nothing, save for a strategically placed arm squashing her tits down.

Call me **555-638-2981**

Shellie xo

"Whoa." His eyes widened with way more enthusiasm than mine did. I had no enthusiasm for it, therefore attempted to rip it half but it's surprisingly hard to rip a polaroid, so I screwed it up as best I could and threw it in the trash.

"What are you doing?" Tanner almost yelled.

"Tossing it. What do I want with it? She probably gave one to all the guys."

"I didn't get one," he sulked, "and just because you have a girl now, doesn't mean this needs to go to waste."

He snatched it from the trash and tried to smooth it out before carefully slipping it into the front pocket of his backpack.

"Dude, we're leaving the city. In a few hours we'll be a

thousand miles away in a different country."

He shrugged. "Doesn't matter. Keep her warm for next time we're in St Louis. She might live in New York for all we know."

I didn't argue because I didn't care, and watched him open his backpack, reaching in for *Cosmo*, the one Lux had earmarked. I was reading an older edition I'd managed to get delivered on back order, because the four of us had reasoned that it was all new to us, therefore was acceptable. Parker had made the very valid point that it was like binging a box set. I was also too busy thinking about the comment he'd just made.

The one about Payton being my girl.

She'd become the first thing I thought about when I woke up, just like she'd become the last thing I thought about as I went to sleep. In the past week, it had almost become subconscious for me to reach for my phone and check my messages the second I opened my eyes... sometimes even before they'd opened. And if there wasn't a reply, it was becoming harder to ignore the disappointment.

No matter how tired I'd been, I'd jerked off every night before falling into bed, usually to the thought of her lips around my dick. Last night, I'd pictured her face as I'd used the vibrator on her, watching her mouth drop open as I slid inside her, and I swear I could still feel the way her pussy had clenched around me.

I hadn't come quite as hard as I had with her, though it hadn't been far off.

We'd been sleeping together for seven weeks and two days. I knew this because it was the length of time I'd been improving my pitch. And outside of the days I'd been traveling, we'd spent almost every night together. The days I had been traveling, we'd managed phone sex three times, because it was virtually impossible to get that type of privacy.

But *my* girl?

Doing the math, I assumed the time we spent together meant she was too busy to have sex with any other guys. If I was bringing my competitive side out, I hoped I'd tired her enough that she didn't have the energy, but the rest of me – the bit that made my chest feel like it was caving in at the thought of someone else touching her like I touched her?

Yeah, that fucking bothered me.

Did that make her my girl? Was this dating? Could it be dating if you hadn't been on a date?

I hadn't seen anything in *Cosmo* that would suggest it to be so, but the more I thought about it, the more I wanted to know.

I liked Payton. A lot. More than a lot, and I had no intention of stopping what we were doing. So yeah, she *was* my fucking girl.

I should probably tell her.

I was pulled out of my relationship thought spiral by Max's dulcet tones ordering us off the bus. I'd been so engrossed in Payton that I hadn't noticed we'd arrived outside the private terminal for where the Lions' plane had been stationed since we arrived in St Louis.

"Make sure you don't leave anything behind!" Max hollered. "That means you too, Simpson."

Tanner's head shot up from *Cosmo* with a confused frown. "What's he talking about? I don't leave stuff behind."

"Come on," I nudged him forward. "Let's find Parker and Lux."

The Lions coordination team was in charge of our passports for arriving in Canada, so once we'd stepped off the bus, we headed straight across the tarmac to the plane. I'd just taken the first step up when Parker and Lux sprinted over.

"There you two are. Where did you go?"

Parker sucked in a breath. "I forgot my phone and had to run back, then Max made us get on the second bus and the social team cornered us to make TikToks."

"Come on. Let's go and chill out."

"I'm going for a massage; my hamstrings are tight," announced Tanner.

"You'll need to wait. Stone and Boomer have already called shotgun," replied Lux.

"Course they fucking have," he grumbled as we entered the cabin and made our way to the back of the plane.

The stewards were handing out drinks, snacks, and menus for dinner once we were airborne, along with pillows and cozy blankets for anyone who wanted to sleep.

"Do you think they'll make me a BLT?" asked Parker as we passed by the coaches' seats, as well as Marnie who was already asleep on Jupiter's shoulder. I briefly glanced around but couldn't see Lowe and Beulah. Come to think of it, I hadn't seen them since we'd left San Francisco.

Lux fell in his seat with a groan, stretching out his legs under the seat opposite, forcing Parker to step over him. "I'm so tired, I cannot wait to get into bed."

"What happened with that girl last night?" I asked as the steward handed around bottles of water, protein bars, and menus.

"Do you want anything else, gentlemen?"

"I'll take a BLT, please," replied Parker, looking over the menu.

"Make that two," added Lux.

"Three."

I hadn't thought I was hungry until my stomach rumbled, so added another BLT to the order. I leaned forward as the steward moved onto the boys sitting across the aisle. "Lux, what happened?"

He removed the *Cosmo* from Tanner's hand and flicked through to the article entitled '*The Cosmo Sex Challenge: Sixty-Nine Positions for Sixty-Nine Days*', found day forty-six – which happened to be Lux's number – and passed it back.

"Wear her ankles as earrings," read out Tanner.

"Yeah, it's fucking hot," Lux nodded. "Her ass was on my thighs so she couldn't easily move, but I could reach her whole body and control it. She had to tell me what she liked and didn't like, and what she *loved*. I made her come twice before I did."

"What are you rating it?

He thought for a second. "Eight out of ten. Recommend."

Tanner folded down the page, which I had no doubt he'd be marking with a Sharpie later, while I made a mental note to try it with Payton next time I saw her. I reached around to grab my phone from my back pocket, suddenly desperate to text her.

It was midnight on a Wednesday. She told me she'd had plans with her friends, so was probably out having fun, wearing a pair of those sexy-as-fuck heels she always wore, and maybe a short little dress.

Aside from the night I'd first met her, I realized I'd never seen her in anything other than her sleep shorts, or what she wore to work, or that raincoat she'd arrived at my place in. And I wanted to. I wanted to see her on a night out. I wanted to be out with her. I wanted to take her out.

We'd start with drinks at The Polo Bar, followed by dinner

at Le Bernardin, and we'd finish with a walk around this deserted little park I found off fifty-fourth street one time when I was running. I'd hold her hand the entire evening but stay half a step behind, just so I could watch her peachy ass sway as she walked.

Then I'd kiss her and kiss her and kiss her some more, until I'd have to carry her home because her legs had given way, before I fucked her into a coma.

Fuck, I'd be the luckiest bastard alive.

Ace: *Hey, Babycakes. Whatcha doin?*

Payton: *Reading in bed*

Ace: *You didn't go out?*

Payton: *I had cocktails with the girls earlier... and saw some of the game. Some nice pitching there, Lucky Aces *smiley face**

I grinned. Ever since I'd told her the story about my name, she'd been calling be Lucky Aces, and I was fucking loving it.

Ace: *Send me a pic, I wanna see what you're wearing*

Payton: *No*

Ace: *Please, Babycakes? Give me something to get me through this flight to Toronto.*

She sent back an eyeroll emoji but it was followed with a picture.

There was nothing scandalous about it. It was Payton in bed, with a book across her lap. She was wearing that sleep shirt she'd had on the first night I'd stayed over, and her face was bare.

She was a fucking showstopper.

Ace: *You are so goddamn hot *multiple flame emojis**

The way my chest thumped as I looked at her picture again

made me realize how much I'd missed her. We'd been away over a week, and now I wanted to get home. Get back to her.

"By the Power of Greyskull, you have it bad."

I put my phone down on the table and turned to Tanner. "What?"

He turned to the boys. "If you ever catch me looking at my phone like Watson's looking at his, please hit me over the head, preferably with a sledgehammer."

"I'll hit you over the head right now if you want," I grumbled and thumped him in the arm instead.

"Ouch." He rubbed his arm, just as his face dropped. "Shit, Shepherd is heading this way."

He chucked *Cosmo* to Lux like he'd been caught passing notes in high school, and Penn was about to bust us.

"Hello, fellas."

"Sir, Mr. Shepherd," nodded Tanner. "How's it going?"

"Good. Good." He peered around the four of us, and even though we hadn't been doing anything at all, there was no way we could look more guilty if we tried.

Especially with the way Tanner's eye kept flicking to Lux, which made Penn focus more on Lux than any of us.

"What's that?" Penn nodded to *Cosmo*.

Lux cleared his throat and turned it over so the cover was in clear view.

"You're reading a girl's magazine?" he questioned and held his hand out.

Tanner groaned next to me as Lux passed it over. I'd heard Penn had an excellent poker face, and he didn't give anything away as he flicked through the pages. None of us missed his focus staying on the cartoon drawings for longer than the rest before finally handing it back.

"Anyway, I came over to congratulate you on an excellent away series. I've noticed all of you have stepped up. The plays have been phenomenal, and I want you to keep it up. Well done."

We all stumbled over each other to thank him, though we just came across as moronic... made all the more evident when Penn simply nodded, and walked off.

"Shit. Do you think he knows how we've improved... and why?" asked Tanner.

Lux shook his head. "I don't think he'd care if we'd improved from milking goats. All he cares about is improvement."

"Yeah, you're right. Nice to see our hard work is appreciated though."

"Hard work?" Lux mumbled, throwing a handful of nuts into his mouth.

Tanner's face widened with a grin. "My dick's been hard."

I chuckled, picking my phone back up because now I had an idea.

Ace: *Hey, Babycakes, what do you say about coming to the game Saturday? See your hard work in action.*

I'd expected her to have fallen asleep, but as I put my phone back down, the screen lit up.

I couldn't have snatched it quicker if I'd tried.

Payton: *Maybe, if you're lucky, Lucky Aces.*

I might have been grinning so hard it was making my ears ring, but it didn't block out Tanner next to me.

"Yep. Definitely a sledgehammer."

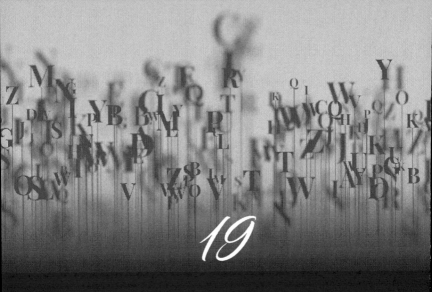

19

Payton

$\mathcal{G}$ame day at Lions Stadium is not for the faint-hearted.

It's way worse when you're already flustered from all the traffic you got stuck in, and your friend has to meet you at the executive entrance.

"Hey, buddy, watch where you're going!" I snapped at the guy who'd shoulder-barged me, following it up with an apologetic smile to the woman walking behind with her two little boys, whom I'd almost fallen into.

It wasn't usually this chaotic. Usually we took the more civilized, not to mention quieter, route to Penn's box. Except, as I kept walking, I realized we were heading in the opposite direction.

"Where are we going?

"Penn's seats behind the dugout. I thought it would be more fun," replied Lowe, marching ahead so quickly I was jogging to keep up with her, but the swarms of people lining up for beers and hot dogs made it harder to contend with.

This time I saw it coming, and dodged out of the way of a guy who thought he could carry four beers at once. Lowe was still talking as I fell back into stride with her, and we turned the corner at the top of the steps, past the pillar which had been hiding the view.

"…plus, Marnie likes to sit down there with her laptop so she can monitor what's going on with each guy, and we're keeping her company."

I stopped dead.

I hadn't been to the stadium this season, not inside to watch a game anyway, and not since the day I'd waited outside for Ace. I always forgot how huge the field was. It seemed way bigger up close with its thick, bright green stripes and terracotta diamond spread out in front of us. Groundskeepers were hosing down the dirt and wiping the bases, which were so white they look liked they'd been put in a hot wash with Clorox.

Knowing Penn, they probably had.

And maybe I hadn't noticed before because I'd never paid quite as much attention, or been so aware, but there were a lot of Watson shirts.

"Doesn't she have a whole bank of screens and her team up there?" I nodded to the boxes where we usually watched the game from.

The box was where I thought we'd be watching the game from, *hoped* we'd be watching the game from, not in the seats at the bottom of the steps I was walking down where I could smell the sweat. Where I could probably reach out and touch

Ace.

I hadn't seen him for nearly two weeks. Not IRL, anyway. Not since I'd sat in his kitchen eating pancakes, and he'd dragged me back to bed. But since then, we'd fallen into a pattern of talking every day, several times a day. In fact, I talked to him more than I talked to my family – not that *that* was an astounding feat – but two days ago, I talked to him more than I talked to Kit.

Which was astounding.

Ace had become someone I texted on the regular, and not just in reply to him. I *started* text messages. I'd laugh and tell him what Matty and Tyler had said about his latest game, or how The Mets had dropped down in the standings, and he'd reply with an update to his stats, or he'd call on the way to the game, and we'd FaceTime quickly while he *told* me his stats.

And he'd always finish with a, "See you later, Babycakes."

In the last two weeks, Ace and I had become a 'something'. I couldn't explain it, I didn't understand it… but I liked it.

And I didn't know what to do about it.

Nathalie Cheung's party was this weekend, and after that… I guess we'd go our separate ways.

A month ago, I couldn't wait for it to be over. Now though, I didn't know how to feel about it.

I neither knew what to do, or how to feel.

It had turned into quite the problem.

So, yeah, I'd been late to the game because my level of concentration today had been exactly zero, and I'd needed to catch up on my notes from the editorial meeting I'd zoned out of. Ace had messaged saying he couldn't wait to see me later, and I'd smiled so hard I'd had to get up and walk away before someone asked me what was wrong.

It was confusing, unbalancing, and thoroughly out of character.

My mind didn't seem to be my own.

"Yeah, but she also likes to be near the action – though it's probably just so she can be near Jupiter," Lowe continued, not noticing I had yet to say anything as she nodded to the seats where Kit, Beulah, and Marnie were sitting. "Oh good, the girls already got the drinks in."

I stopped at the end of the row, letting Lowe go ahead. While we currently had this section to ourselves, the rest of the stadium was filling up. All the fans I'd seen buy beers and Lions dogs were making their way to their seats. The announcers were coming in loud over the speakers, interspersed with the music blaring.

"The boys are about to come out," Kit stood up, pulling me into a hug. "You haven't missed the warmups."

"Great," I grinned, though I wasn't sure I thought it was.

I usually loved the warmups. They were almost my favorite part, but I loved them from the safety of the box *way* behind us, where you couldn't be exposed for ogling. But in these seats? We were so close to the action there was no way I could hide. I could rest my feet on top of the dugout if I wanted.

Instead, I sunk into my seat and pulled my ball cap as low as possible, taking a large gulp of the beer Kit handed me.

"I thought you'd be wearing Ace's shirt," she whispered, giving me a little nudge.

I looked down at the Lions shirt I was wearing, the *I Caught a Lion* t-shirt that Lowe's team gifted to anyone who caught a home run ball. Safe to say I got one without making a catch, because I wasn't about to hold my hand out to a ball hurtling toward me like an asteroid. With my luck, I'd miss and end up in the emergency room with a concussion and a broken nose.

"This is my Lions shirt. It's the only one I have, and the only one I'll ever wear."

She sipped her beer and raised her eyebrow in response.

My eyes flicked back to the field as the announcers fired up again.

"Number five, Jupiter Reeves!"

Marnie stuck her fingers in her mouth and whistled loudly as Jupiter jogged out through the archway and onto the field. The cheering from the five of us was no match for the crowds behind us, and we were completely drowned out.

Jupiter had never been one to acknowledge the fans, or wave, or make any indication he loved the attention, he'd simply jog to the dugout every single time. But today he looked up at Marnie, grinned wide and mouthed *I Love You* before he disappeared.

Marnie's cheeks flushed pink, especially when the rest of us all giggled and sighed like we were a bunch of highschoolers.

"Jupiter's sure changed," Kit muttered.

Saint Velazquez was next, followed by Tanner, and Boomer Jones. As each player appeared, the thudding in my chest increased, becoming loud enough to be confused with a marching band.

The final announcement came soon, and if I'd thought the cheer had been deafening with Jupiter, it was nothing compared to the noise let out now, which rivaled a Taylor Swift concert.

"Number twenty-seven, Ace Watson!"

For the second time today, I couldn't hold in the grin as I watched Ace jog out, his gloved hand held high as he waved to the home crowds. *His* home crowd.

I couldn't blink. I didn't want to miss a nanosecond of his arrival, clad in the black and gold uniform which fitted his body like a second skin, beaming out his ever-present grin. As much as I hadn't wanted him to see me ogling, I tried not to be disappointed when he didn't even notice me as he ducked under the awning and disappeared into the dugout.

The cheers didn't die down.

It had been two months since I'd been reading sports news, and in that time, Ace had gone from being vilified to being loved once more. From the volume today, it was like he'd never fucked up to begin with. It was crazy, enough to give anyone whiplash. For the first time, I understood how desperate he'd been to fix his game.

How much pressure he was under to perform.

How much rested on his ability to pitch.

It was quickly becoming clear to me that I was now surplus to requirements.

We hadn't discussed the party on Saturday or what would happen after, and the more I thought about it, the more my stomach churned. The whole thing had me reaching for the bottle of Tylenol and rubbing my temples.

I needed distraction, and peered down the row to the girls. "Hey, do you girls want hot dogs?"

Lowe nodded. "Yeah, I'm hungry. Let's get another round of beers, too."

Aside from the view, another bonus of sitting in the owner's seats were the hot dog and beer dispenser guys who appeared to be assigned to us. No sooner did I signal one over than they both appeared. By the time Lowe and I had taken five of each and handed them around, the whole lineup had run out, along with The White Sox, and were now on the field warming up.

Ace and Parker had moved to the spot in front of the bleachers on the left-hand side, where little kids were up against the railings watching them throw and catch. So obviously, that's what I did too. Every half a dozen balls, Ace would toss one over the railings and all the kids would leap in the air to catch it. By the time the boys were called off the field, he must have given ten balls away.

"That's seriously cute."

I turned to Kit to see what she was talking about, only to find she'd been watching the show I had.

"Yeah, it is," I grinned at her. "Think I've got time to pee before the game starts?"

"Totally. We're not batting first."

"I know, but I don't want to miss top of the first," I replied, hoping I wouldn't have to explain, but her frown made it clear I did because we rarely cared about the opposing team batting. "I don't want to miss Ace pitching."

A sly smile curved her lips. "Then hurry."

Thankfully I was in sneakers, therefore managed to sprint up the steps as quickly as my legs would carry me. Also, thankfully, there was a bathroom right at the top of the steps. I wasn't sure if it had been strategic so that no-one in the exec seats had to walk halfway around the stadium to pee, but I was grateful none the less because you could miss half the game looking for a bathroom in this place. The National Anthem began as I unbuttoned my jeans, and after peeing as quickly as I could, I still made it back to the seats with a minute to spare, dropping into my seat with a big puff of air.

"Okay," I started and looked down the row at the girls. "Marnie, who's going to win this game?"

She steepled her fingers together and drummed her fingertips as she thought about it. "It'll be a close score today, closer than we've seen recently. The White Sox are having a good season, but maybe we'll edge them out, seeing as we're on home ground."

"Beulah?"

"I'm going with Lions winning by one."

I looked at Lowe and Kit, who spoke for the pair of them. "Same. We're winning today, especially with you and your magic vagina as our secret weapon."

The sip of beer Marnie had just taken got snorted out, and she choked hard until she spluttered for air. Little droplets of beer foam were dripping off the end of her nose. Lowe was laughing so much that tears leaked into the creases of her eyes. In the end, Beulah slapped Marnie on the back while summoning the hot dog guy for more napkins.

"You okay, Marn?"

"Yeah," Marnie croaked. "Wasn't expecting that."

"You and me both," I grinned at her.

"Okay!" Kit clapped her hands loudly, rubbing them together. "Let's see if we're right, shall we?"

We all faced forward as The Lions took to the field.

Ace and Parker walked out, heads together for a minute before throwing up a high five and going their separate ways. Ace's face filled the jumbo screens, concentration etched over it as he stood tall and prepared to deliver.

The first White Sox guy walked to home plate.

Ace pitched.

The bat made contact… and the ball flew straight into Tanner's outstretched hand.

"Bummer for them," chuckled Lowe, before cupping her hands around her mouth and hollering, "GO LIONS!!"

It was only the third ball Ace pitched which got the White

Sox to base. Third base in fact, where the batter was now having a laugh with Jupiter. The fourth pitch went the way of the first and second balls, and unfortunately for the guy on third base, he didn't make it home before the ball, and was caught out.

The Lions walked off the field less than ten minutes after they'd arrived.

Ace was the one to leave last, too focused on whatever he and Parker were planning for next time. He looked around, searching through the crowds above us, before suddenly, out of nowhere, he focused on me. Surprise and a broad grin spread over his face. My heart came to a stuttering, spluttering stop. Even under the black rim of his baseball cap, his blue eyes pierced the darkness as he looked directly at me, and right before he stepped into the dugout, his grin widened and he threw me a wink before disappearing out of sight.

It was too much to hope no one had seen it; all four of the girls I was with let out a little sigh – the same one we'd given Marnie earlier.

"Don't," I warned Kit before she could say a word.

The butterflies returned at full flutter, just like they had in his apartment; only this time, I wished I wasn't picturing their wings crashing against glass as they tried to get back to the light.

"One down, seventeen to go," Beulah said and picked up her beer with a grin, then nodded at the jumbo screen. "Hey, Pay, you've got some competition."

The camera zoomed in on a line of girls who were clearly Ace Watson fans.

Nine of them in total, each wearing a different letter of his name. The girl in the middle, a blonde with a skirt, though that was a generous description, was holding up a large piece of cardstock that said she had a question for Ace.

Something I wholeheartedly blamed Marnie for.

"Where's the originality these days," I grumbled to no one in particular.

But then the screen split; one half still on the girl, who'd spotted herself on the screen and now looked like she was about to burst from excitement and her five seconds of fame, and one half of Ace in the dugout with Parker next to him.

I watched mutely as Parker whispered something to Ace, which had him looking up. His smile grew wider as he muttered back to Parker and had me wishing I could trade every skill in my arsenal just to know how to lip read.

Especially when Parker threw his head back in a laugh.

A thick bolt of jealously punctured me square in the chest, nearly winding me in the process. I didn't get jealous. I didn't do jealousy. It was one of those emotions that signaled nothing good. It opened you up for pain and hurt as you inhaled quarts of ice cream while you watched Nancy Meyers movies on repeat.

My mother had spent half her life being jealous, and it had got her nowhere.

As far as I was concerned, jealousy was totally pointless.

Ask any baseball fan and they'll tell you baseball is a rollercoaster of emotions, but they're likely talking about the entire game. Their focus isn't concentrated on one sole player, like mine was.

It didn't make the rollercoaster any less emotional, however.

I wanted to reply to Beulah that they were welcome to Ace, but I couldn't bring myself to.

For the rest of the game, I watched, I cheered, and I screamed when The Lions eventually won.

And tried my hardest to ignore the niggling in the back of my head, telling me something I didn't want to hear.

"*H*ey, Baby..." Ace stopped talking, his eyes widened in panic as he clocked Lowe next to me. "Payton. I mean, Payton, hello."

I'd never seen Ace look awkward before, not this awkward, as his gaze darted between me and Lowe, checking to see if he'd fucked up somehow.

My attempt at hiding a laugh didn't work, especially when Lowe snorted loudly.

"God, Ace, it's a good thing you already have a job, because your acting skills need work."

Ace shuffled his feet and looked down, though not before I saw a smile appear. "Yeah, you got that right."

Lowe turned to me. "I'll run up and find Penn. See you back here in five?"

I nodded. "Sure."

Less than a second after she disappeared up the stairs, Ace grabbed my wrist and tugged me underneath them and out of sight. Thick, strong arms roped around my waist as he pulled me against his sweaty body. I inhaled as deeply as I could; the sense of calm I'd been missing all day had made an appearance.

"Hey, Babycakes. Enjoy the game?"

I nodded. "You should be proud of yourself. You were on fire."

"It's because you were watching."

I chuckled, trying to keep the heat from my cheeks and the nerves from my belly. "No, it was you. All you."

"We'll agree to disagree." He stepped in closer, pushing up the brim of my ball cap so he could look at me properly. "I thought you were going to be in the box, and since I saw you behind the dugout, I've wanted to do something."

I didn't get the chance to ask what before his mouth found mine. The soft kiss I'd been expecting with the teasing nips he'd learned drove me crazy was gone, replaced by an insistence as his tongue thrust forward and forcefully stroked along mine. It was greedy and desperate. The air became weighted with his sweat and the steam still coming off his hard body as it pressed into me, like he could never have enough.

It was raw, masculine, and simply put, hot as fuck.

I wanted to bury myself in him and inhale until my lungs burst.

His nose ran along my jawline, his hand cupped around my chin so he could take all the time he wanted. I barely had the strength to hold myself up, let alone fight against him gaining more access to my burning skin.

Not that I wanted to fight.

His lips stopped their exploration, and he craned back a little until he was looking directly at me. "Let me take you for a late dinner."

His gaze was so penetrating that I shrunk back a little; I always thought I'd do well under cross examination but now I wasn't so sure, and I was having the hardest time concentrating.

"Wh… what?"

"I want to take you for dinner."

Flashes of those girls in their Ace Watson t-shirts scouring the city for him appeared in my head, and I shook it off. "And get myself beaten up by a load of your girly fan group? No, thanks."

That cute little smirk of his quirked his lip. "Then let me cook you dinner in a safe house of your choosing."

Those little curls of anxiety, the ones which had been present for most of the day, began stroking against my belly, curling and twisting and reminding me where I was and what I was doing.

It was on the tip of my tongue to say yes. I wanted to say yes, but somewhere in the back of my head lurked a cloud that would suffocate me if I let it.

I could cope with sex. I could definitely cope with the sex we were having; the mind blowing, delicious, bone melting sex. But dinner was… a step too far. Dinner was intimate, dinner was unnecessary for the purposes of why we were together. Dinner led down a path I *didn't* know I could cope with.

I shook my head again. "No. No dinner, thank you. Just come over when you're done here."

I could have blinked and missed it, but I definitely saw something flash across Ace's face, and when he smiled a second later, it wasn't the smile I'd become used to.

"Sure. Coming over always sounds good to me. I'll meet you at your place in an hour, Babycakes." He leaned in one last time, and this time the kiss was soft. "I gotta shower."

I watched him jog down the hallway to the locker room. Parker appeared in the far corner, and Ace threw up a high five and jumped on him. They disappeared, laughing together.

I slumped back against the wall with a deep sigh.

I couldn't deny it. This was no longer the deal we'd made.

This – whatever it was between us – had evolved way beyond a one-night-stand. I wasn't even sure if we hadn't evolved beyond fuck buddies. Truth be told, it hadn't felt like that for a while now, I just didn't want to admit it.

I might have been determined not to catch feelings; convinced that I wouldn't.

But, it seems, that hadn't stopped the feelings from catching me.

20

Ace

*L*owe thought I didn't have good acting skills, but she'd never seen me at a garden party surrounded by snooty academics and people with way too much money, and not only look interested, but have them believe I was interested.

I wasn't.

The only thing remotely interesting at this entire party was Payton, and she'd been dragged away from me almost as soon as we'd arrived. I hadn't spoken to her the entire time we'd been here.

For the past twenty minutes, I'd been watching her from my spot in this circle of guys I'd found myself in; and I was certain I'd never seen her look so beautiful. She was deep in conversation with her boss, wearing a smile brighter than the sun, blinding everyone in the vicinity with her light. The long, flowy dress with all the colored flowers she was wearing made her look like the prettiest summer garden. The whole thing was finished off with a pair of those heels that had me salivating every time she wore them.

These ones were pink, and I'd already promised myself I'd be wearing them as earrings later.

Thanks, *Cosmo*.

Her hair was curled into those big waves I hadn't seen since the first night we met, and it had my hands itching to run through them, capture the silky strands between my fingers and inhale deeply.

Payton Lopez was quite simply the most beautiful woman I'd ever seen in my entire life.

Unfortunately, the guy who'd been talking for the last twenty minutes took my smile as I watched Payton to mean I'd been listening intently to what he had to say.

I hadn't.

"What's your perspective, Ace?"

I tore my eyes away from Payton to find every other set of eyes on me. All seven sets.

"I'm sorry, I got distracted. My perspective on what?"

Barrett, the guy in the white shirt who I think was on the board of New York Education – or was on the board of something – turned around to see exactly what I'd become distracted by, and a knowing smile formed on his lips. If I wasn't convinced he was gay, I'd have punched him straight on the nose.

"On whether authors have more pressure with a follow up book or a first time, never published."

I stood there, pushing one hand down into the pocket of my chinos, just like he was doing, and rocked back on my heels.

"Well..." I began, peering around the group while I tried

to come up with a suitable answer.

Another one.

Thanks to my ability to think on my feet, and the crash course Lux had given me on books this morning, I'd been able to adequately keep up with the conversation which had been firing on all cylinders since I'd gotten here. Or in layman's terms, I'd been able to bullshit my way through them with relative ease.

Subjects I've contributed to so far included Radley Andrews attending Columbia to study English. Hadn't known that.

The record-breaking pre-sale figures for the biography of President Andrews and her campaign trail. Hadn't known anything about that either, but I hoped it didn't include me or my Opening Day disaster.

And Callie Malone's new book. Never even heard of her, or her new book, but I swear not one of them realized.

I'd done an awesome job, even if I did say so myself.

I was used to guys wanting to talk to me. I was *not* used to guys not really knowing who I am or how my season was going.

On the plus side, none of them had played last season's *The Show*.

While these guys might not have a vested interest in sports, the good thing about sports was their relatability to any situation.

Pressure, for example. Something I knew all about.

"How well did the first book sell?" I asked.

"Best seller. *New York Times, Sunday Times*. Did very well globally. Translated into forty languages."

I nodded, like I was seriously considering my answer. "Is the second book out yet?"

"No, next month."

"So it's like a sophomore season, following an MVP award. There's always going to be added pressure to meet the expectations set in the first year. It can go one of two ways – you can crumble, or you can block out the noise and keep doing what you're doing. It's a matter of mental strength," I added, like I'd done exactly that.

I'd crumbled at the first hurdle.

Crumbled until Payton saved me, and I'd long concluded she'd saved me in more ways than one.

"But sometimes," I continued, "the follow up is better than the debut. Same goes for music. Look at Nirvana, or Oasis, or Blondie. Their sophomore albums were all hailed as better than the first."

George, a guy wearing a spotty bow-tie, and sporting an impressively long handle-bar moustache that made me want to grow mine back, narrowed his already narrowed eyes, "Interesting, very interesting perspective, Ace."

"Thank you."

I took a sip of the soda water I'd been holding. Yep, nailed that one.

Thankfully, we all became distracted by the tray of a passing waiter. One good thing about this party, aside from being able to watch Payton in her natural environment, was the food. It was proper food, like sliders and fried chicken, mac and cheese, and I swiped another burger.

George was still talking, and I bit down while I tried to figure out exactly what he was talking about, but this one had me stumped. I doubted even Lux would know.

"...evolutionary structures of culture and forced scripts woven within the chapters. Fascinating book."

I stifled a yawn, even though my mouth was full, and

resisted telling him the last book I read was Harry Potter.

"Ace," called a voice from my right, and I turned to see Blake Johnson, Nathalie Cheung's husband, whom I'd met when we first arrived. The guy must have been forty-five, but he was the most handsome son-of-a-bitch I'd ever seen, and was walking toward our group with his hand on the shoulder of a little dude, who was basically his mini-me.

"Hey, man. Great party."

"Yeah?" he grinned and squinted in the way that we both knew I'd needed saving. He looked around at the group. "George, you're not talking about that book again, are you? I read it, by the way, knocked me out like a baby every single night." Blake snorted loudly with a guffaw which had his head falling back and he slapped a heavy hand on my shoulder. "Come on, guys, you're in the presence of greatness right here. He's come straight from The Lions stadium where he fired off fastball after fastball."

Everyone looked at me again, and I found myself shuffling uncomfortably, especially when they all looked confused.

"Daaaad."

Blake looked down at the little guy tugging him on the arm, "Sorry, buddy. Ace, meet my son, Chester. He's your biggest fan."

I knelt down so I was closer to Chester, and grinned at him. "No way, I've always wanted to meet my biggest fan. This is awesome."

He smiled wide, showing off a big gap where his front two teeth were missing. "Yeah. I've seen you in every game this season – and last season. I play in Little League."

"You do? What position?"

"Pitcher, like you."

"Great choice, bud." I held my hand up for a high five,

which he slapped hard, and his grin widened.

"Chester had something he wanted to say," interrupted Blake.

"Oh," Chester blushed. "Thank you for my gifts. I took the ball and glove to school for show and tell."

"You're very welcome, little dude." I grinned back, as a thought occurred to me. "Hey, do you have them here now?"

He nodded, his dark hair flopping in his face as he did. "Yeah, they're in my bedroom."

"Why don't you go and get them, and we can play a bit of catch."

His eyes flared, then he took off quicker than Lux at home base.

"You just made his year," grinned Blake.

I chuckled and stood back up. "Hey, he made mine. Don't often to get to play with my biggest fan."

"I'm warning you now, he's not that great. Neither of us can figure where this baseball obsession has come from."

"You're not into baseball?"

"Yeah, I'll watch." Blake slapped my arm with a laugh as he caught the expression on my face. "But this is a football house. The rest of the kids are at football camp this week, but all Ches wants to do is watch The Lions."

"Step aside, then. I'll teach him what he needs to know."

Blake huffed out a laugh and sipped his beer. We stood shoulder to shoulder, peering around the gathering in his yard. At the back, near where a jazz band was playing, a thin stretch of grass ran alongside the high fence adorned with twinkly lights surrounding the end of the property, along with a small basketball hoop bolted to the wall halfway down. For a New York Brownstone where space was at a premium, they managed to find somewhere with a decent sized back yard, but they must have paid upward of twenty mil for the pleasure.

Payton was now sitting on a long bench with two women and a man, listening intently. She was nodding in a way I knew meant she thought whatever was being said was bullshit; I'd learned that expression a long time ago, including the way she was now tucking her hair behind her ear.

"How long have you two been together? Nathalie hasn't stopped raving about her since they met. A book she edited last year is one of the kids' favorites."

I side-eyed Blake to see him also watching the group. It was a question I didn't have an answer for. We weren't together, not in the way Blake meant. We hadn't even talked about being together. And if you didn't count the mornings after when she'd leave me in bed, I'd never seen her in daylight before today.

Not to mention, me attending this party was the last part of our bargain.

But on the other hand, if anyone so much as looked in her direction with anything other than innocent intention, I'd want to pummel them so hard they'd be eating through a straw for a month.

You can see my predicament.

All I knew was that I wasn't ready to give her up. I wasn't sure I'd ever be ready.

"Not long."

"Settle in for the long run, bud. You're looking at her the way I looked at Nathalie when I first met her."

I was stopped from trying to figure out a response by Chester returning with more excitement in his eyes than Tanner when he first beat Parker at PlayStation.

He thrust the ball and glove at me. "Here, Ace. I got them."

"Awesome job. You wanna pitch or catch?"

Chester's smile dropped a little. "Pitch, like you, but I'm not very good."

"Oh, c'mon, I bet you are."

His head dropped as he shook it. "No, Coach said I wasn't, but I try hard."

"Well, that's gonna get you halfway there. Trying is what counts." I ruffled his hair. "Come on, let's go and practice on the grass."

I grinned at Blake as Chester ran off, and turned to the guys who'd all gone back to their conversations about books. "Good to meet you gentleman. If you'll excuse me…"

I walked over to Chester, turning his shoulders around so he was facing me, and took six paces back. "Okay, bud. Let's see what you got."

He raised his arm, twisted his little body, and threw the ball. It was only from stretching my arm out high and jumping a couple of feet in the air that I managed to catch it.

Blake and his coach had been correct, he wasn't very good, but he had power.

"Awesome! You're strong, and you have a powerful throw," I grinned at him. "Has anyone taught you how to pitch?"

He shook his head. "Not really. I learned just from what I see you do. Coach tried, but he got mad at me."

I didn't tell him that I was beginning to get mad with his Coach. He sounded like a douche.

"The first thing you need to remember is to keep your eye on where you want the ball to go, right? So don't be looking over my shoulder, you need to look right at my glove. You got that?"

He nodded, and I went back to where I'd been standing.

"Try again."

This time, the ball went straight into my glove, and I tossed it back, only for it to fall between his hands, and he ran after it as it rolled away. "Good work. Do it again."

Every time he threw the ball, it got better. Every time I caught it, his grin widened. I didn't have kids, didn't know anyone who had kids outside of the team and my eldest brother, Coby, but his was still only six months old, so hadn't mastered the throw and catch yet, but this was fun.

Watching Chester's face light up with happiness made my chest puff a little.

"Nice work, bud." I walked over and held the ball out to show him. "Now see how I'm gripping it, my fingers lined up with the seam here."

He nodded. I placed the ball in his hand and twisted it so it was positioned correctly. "Now try. And don't forget to look at my glove."

This time the throw was almost perfect from a – I took a closer look – maybe seven-year-old. I tossed it back. He got better at catching too.

"How long have you played baseball?"

"Two years. We have junior sluggers at school."

"And what's your favorite bit about baseball?"

He held onto the ball and thought for a second. "I love watching you and Parker King warm up."

"Oh yeah? So if we're your favorites, who's your third favorite?"

"Lux Weston," he replied without missing a beat. "I love when he climbs the walls. Maybe you could come and watch me in my next game."

I grinned at him. "I'll make you a deal. You come to one of the Lions games, and I'll come and watch you pitch."

His eyes widened like he'd witnessed Santa climbing down the chimney. "Oh yes! I can do that! Can I bring my mom and dad?"

I nodded.

"Can I go tell them?"

"Sure," I laughed, and he took off again.

I removed the glove, placed the ball inside and put it down on the garden bench. I guess we were done for now. I was about to sit when a shadow crossed my path, and I looked up to find Payton standing there.

My breath caught, and my chest thudded hard.

Fuck me, she was something else.

"Hey."

"Hey!" I shifted up on the bench to make room for her, and she sat. The air around me filled with the sweet scent of roses.

"What's going on?"

"Just taking a break from playing catch with a future pitcher of The Lions."

"Is that right?"

I nodded with a grin. "Yep."

"You like kids?"

I shrugged. "Yeah. I don't know many, but they're funny. What about you?"

She nodded. "I have a goddaughter who's two, and will inherit my shoe collection." She smiled, making me wish I could take a picture of her. "And my half-sisters. My dad remarried and had another family."

I didn't like the way she said 'another family', but I ignored it. "Do you see them?"

"Yeah. I fly down twice a year, but I talk to them on FaceTime. They're ten and eight, so I'm a bit cooler to them now than I was a few years ago. I'm their cool older sister," she laughed.

"I bet you're a great sister. I always wished I could've traded my brothers for one."

She laughed loudly. "Oh yeah? Which brother?"

"Stevie, most of the time. Sometimes Coby," I winked, making her laugh louder.

I glanced down at where her hands were resting near mine, and slowly so I didn't scare her, I slipped mine into hers and placed it on my knee. I held my breath, waiting to see if she'd move it, but it stayed in place.

"How's the party been for you? Has Nathalie realized how amazing you are, and promoted you to be her deputy or something?"

Payton giggled – a sound I wanted to keep in a locket around my neck. I'd never take it off.

"No, but she's told me that she loves the manuscript I've been working on."

"The one you got sent by accident?"

She nodded. "Yeah. She'd asked me to send her the first few chapters, which I did. It's way below her paygrade, but she wanted to read it.

"Because you told her it was good. She trusts you." I held her gaze, watching the reflection of the twinkly lights flicker in her brown eyes until she looked down to where her hand was still laced with mine.

"This is a big deal to be here, it means a lot to me that you came. Thank you, Ace. I'm truly grateful."

"I wouldn't have missed it," I replied truthfully.

"You haven't been bored?"

I shook my head. "No way. I've learned all about The Booker Prize winner, and some other new book I forgot the name of already. Plus, we debated on the merits and pressures of a follow up novel."

Her face split with a wide smile, her big eyes sparkling again in amusement as her hand flew up to cover her mouth. "Oh God, I'm so sorry."

"Hey, it's okay. I'm good, seriously," I replied, kissing her cheek, relishing in the way she leaned into me.

"Shall we stay at your place tonight?"

"Why?"

She shrugged. "We're always at my place, and it's so small."

"Babycakes, wherever you are, I'm happy. And your place isn't small, it's cozy," I replied, suddenly desperate to get her alone. I was done sharing her, and I certainly didn't want to share her with my roommates. "But the best thing? It's private, and I can get you to scream my name as loudly as I want."

Her eyes widened and her cheeks flushed, which in turn had me grinning. It seemed she could always make me grin. "Yeah?"

"Yeah."

She checked her watch. "Think we can get one more drink and then leave?"

"You're the boss," I replied. "Lead the way."

She stood up and took my hand, and I followed her back to the party.

Which is when it occurred to me I'd probably follow her anywhere.

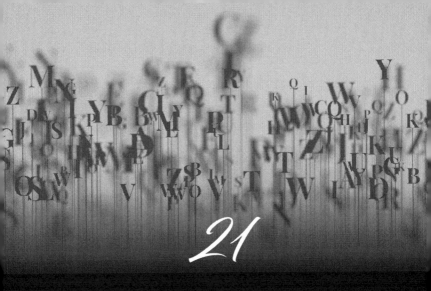

21

Payton

"Hey, Payton, reception just called and your nine a.m. is on the way up."

I put my coffee mug down on the desk and peered over the back of Mia's screen to look at her.

"What did you say?"

"Your nine a.m. is on the way up."

I brought up my calendar to find a blank space in the nine o'clock slot. "I don't have a nine a.m."

"Oh, I'm sure they said it was for you." Mia's brow dropped. "Hang on, let me call them back."

I settled in my chair and brought up the manuscript I was editing. I'd nearly finished the first draft, and I could tell this would be a best-seller. It didn't matter that I loved it, I knew the girls would love it, and the four of them were so different they were practically their own little focus group. Even without them reading, I could feel deep in my bones that everyone would go crazy for this book, especially as it was set in a little English country village with a hot AF grumpy male lead. It was cute and heartwarming, and made you want to believe in love and all the gooey shit that came with it. The fantasy of it, at least.

I wasn't going to lie and say I hadn't shed a tear or three last night when I'd been reading before Ace came over.

Which brought me back to the present.

The only other meeting I'd ever had unannounced had been Ace, and this couldn't be him. I'd left him in bed, and there's no way he'd have gotten dressed and followed me here.

Mia was still on hold with reception when the light of the elevator caught the corner of my eye. I didn't understand it, but my stomach rolled in on itself anyway. I didn't have time to theorize, as the explanation made itself known a second later. The elevator doors pinged, and out walked Penn Shepherd.

In what was likely a first for him, there was no one rushing to greet his arrival with his coffee already in hand, and take his coat, or whatever else he desired. Considering it was still early, and relatively quiet, he stood in the entrance and peered around.

There was no way this was a coincidence. He was looking for me.

I pushed out of my chair so hard it rolled into the bank of desks behind me. Ignoring the way my blood felt like it had been dipped in liquid nitrogen, I ran along the row to find him before he started hollering – which I knew he'd do if he was left any longer.

"Penn?" I smiled, again summoning my acting lessons from ninth grade and plastered on my best innocent face.

He spun around at the sound of my voice.

I'd known Penn for a couple of years now. I'd been on nights out where we'd all gotten inordinately drunk, and he'd made sure his driver had taken me home safely. I'd watched countless games of baseball with him and our mutual friends – though admittedly Penn always stood to the side and watched the field like a hawk. I'd been on vacations, weekends away, I'd been to Shepherd family galas and charity functions. I'd been Lowe's bridesmaid at their wedding last Christmas.

The point is, I'd seen him in all manner of situations, with all manner of expressions… except this one; Penn Shepherd, billionaire Baseball Club Owner on official business.

I'd been busted.

"Hello, Payton, how are you?" he kissed my cheek. "Sorry for dropping in like this, hope you don't mind. Lowe told me you finally got promoted. Nice view."

I nodded. "Thanks. Yeah, I sure busted my ass long enough."

"Mmm."

To anyone who didn't know him, they could easily claim Penn was standing in front of me looking nervous.

But I did know him.

Penn Shepherd didn't get nervous. He got what he wanted, and he did what he wanted. Anything in his way had better watch out.

I had an ominous feeling that was about to be me.

"Want a tour? Or do you want to tell me why you're really here?"

His boyish grin spread across his face. It didn't make him any less threatening though. "Touché."

"I guess you figured summoning me to your office wouldn't work."

"I figured you'd tell me to go fuck myself."

I threw my head back with a loud laugh. Penn knew me as well as I knew him.

"I guess that depends on what you have to say." I nodded to an empty meeting room along the side by the windows. It had glass walls, but whoever had designed this open-plan situation had obviously decided beggars couldn't be choosers. You either got privacy or you got quiet, not both. "Let's go in here."

Penn followed me in, and I closed the door.

He walked straight to the window, then turned around. "Is something happening between you and Ace Watson?"

"Wow, right out the gate there, aren't you?"

"Payton…"

I stood there, trying not to cross my arms over my chest and get all defensive. But even as I was trying my best, I could feel my shoulders squaring back, and a little of the defensiveness slipped out.

"I guess that would depend on what you deem as something."

"Are you sleeping together?"

My barriers were weakening, and my arms crossed over my chest. "I don't know why you think it's your business who I sleep with."

"It is my business when Ace is in the middle of the best season of his life, and it's my team he's playing for. I don't want him fucking around and messing up his head. He needs to be concentrating."

"And what makes you think he's not?"

"Because he spent his Saturday evening with you at Nathalie Cheung's summer party," he shot back.

"How did you find that out?"

"I know people who were there, and they couldn't wait to tell me they'd just met my starting pitcher – and I know it was you he winked at coming off the field last week." He narrowed his eyes at me. "What's going on? Are you in a relationship with Ace Watson?"

"No." I wasn't about to ask how he knew Ace had winked.

He narrowed his eyes even further, but I held firm. It was like a game of chicken, and I knew I was stubborn enough to not give in. I also knew Penn was equally stubborn, but suddenly the rubber band which had been slowly stretching inside me the past few months snapped hard.

I'd had enough of baseball, and baseball players, and stupid, *stupid* superstitions and theories and stats and, and, *and...*

"You know what? This is your fault in the first fucking place. You told him to do whatever it took to fix his game."

Penn's hard stare crumpled in confusion. "What does that mean?"

"He decided the way to fix his game was to sleep with me. You and your fucking stupid baseball superstitions."

He scoffed loudly. "And I bet you couldn't fucking wait to help him out!"

"Ex-fucking-cuse me, Pennington, I did not. I didn't want to sleep with him. I said no!" I managed to grit out, though I swear I'd stripped some enamel off my back teeth from how hard they were grinding together.

"Are you telling me you're the reason he's pitching so well? Are you the reason we've gone up the standing so quickly?"

"I think you're putting too much faith in me!" I snapped.

"And what do you get out of this? He'd better not be paying you." He regretted the words as soon as they fell from his lips, and it had nothing to do with the murderous rage I was firing his way. "I'm sorry, Payton, I take that back."

I didn't respond, because it was clear Penn wasn't done. He stood there, staring at me. His lips pursed as he sucked in his cheek. I could almost see the cogs whirring, and a sudden feeling of dread almost knocked the air from my lungs.

"Payton, why does Ace think you're the solution to how badly he pitched at Opening Day?"

If I was honest, I was amazed it had taken Penn this long to figure it out. For a genius, he wasn't so smart sometimes.

I wish he wouldn't stare quite so hard at me though.

"Payton, why does Ace think you're the fix?"

I shrugged. "I dunno."

"Except I think you do." He turned to look out of the window, almost muttering to himself. "The only reason you would need to fix it is if you were the cause of it in the first place. Am I right? Did you fuck up his game? Did you get in his head, somehow?"

"No, I didn't, and I object to the insinuation."

But Penn was on roll, and when he spun back around, I had the good sense to stay silent.

"Are you the reason half my starting nine is reading Cosmo?"

"No!" I yelled back.

Because I wasn't, *technically*. I didn't tell them to do it, except that's clearly not what my expression said.

"Oh, Jesus. What the fuck, Payton? We're not halfway through the season and you've got into Ace's head that you're his lucky charm!" He raked his hands through his hair and pulled hard. I'd never seen Penn get so worked up before. "We've shot up the standings because of Ace, and now we're going to plummet back to the bottom. FUCK!"

"What? Why? Why is that going to happen?"

"Because of you! You don't stick with one person for longer than a few weeks. We all know you have commitment issues. You'll get scared right before anything happens, just like you usually do and run away. Only this time, it's going to fuck with my team."

He may as well have stabbed an icicle through my heart for the effect his words had. I couldn't be sure he was right about the plummet in the standings, but he wasn't wrong about running away. And for the first time this morning, I couldn't argue with him.

Ace and I had already passed by the event in our agreement.

There was no reason for us to keep seeing each other. Anything beyond this date could be considered dating... Except it would be more than dating, and Penn was right. I would run.

I sighed deeply; deep enough I could feel it in my marrow, and the ball of tears inching up my throat. I wasn't ready to let Ace go.

Penn's face softened, and he took a step closer. I thought he was about to apologize for his savage, selfish outburst. At the very least, I thought he might apologize for bringing me to the point where my tears spilled and rolled down my cheeks.

But no.

"Payton, I'm begging you, break it off now and I can fix this before it's too late."

I snatched away another tear before it fell, but couldn't stop the snarl curving my lip. "Are you kidding? You're kidding me, right?"

"No."

"Doesn't Ace get a say in this?"

"I can fix this, Payton. I can keep us winning if you let him go now. Don't hurt Ace and hurt his game by dragging out the inevitability of you calling it quits."

I squeezed the heel of my palms against my temples, trying to rid myself of the disbelief at this conversation. But when I opened my eyes, Penn was still standing there with the same hard expression on his face.

"You're an asshole, Penn. You don't give a fuck about anything except baseball!"

"That's not true, and you know it," he snapped, "but I bought this club, and I promised the fans we would win. I promised the fans that we'd changed as a club. This is for them."

I dropped my head with a shake. "And what about Ace? What if I end this and he fucks up again?"

I couldn't believe the words were coming out of my mouth, even less than I could believe the words coming out of Penn's. Scratch that, I expected this from Penn.

These words were the epitome of Penn Shepherd.

"He'll be fine, now that I know what the cause was in the first place. I can protect him."

I fixed Penn with the coldest expression I could muster, but the tears still prickling my throat were making it hard, and Penn was giving Antarctica a run for its money right now.

"End it, Payton. We both know you don't do long term. We both know it's already run its course. Don't fuck everything else up along the way and ruin Ace's career – and this season – in the process because you can't commit to a relationship."

"Get out," I hissed. It was all I could manage.

Penn's eyes narrowed to the tiniest slits, but he said no

more as he flung open the door and stormed out without bothering to close it behind him.

Somewhere between me collapsing onto the couch and the tears making themselves known again, I heard a voice ask, "Was that Penn Shepherd?"

Mom: *Did you speak to your father? He's being an asshole, again*

Ace: *I'll be at your place in an hour*

Ace: *Make that 30, I'll shower when I get there and you can join me*

Ace: *Wanna soap my dick up?*

Mom: *I'm talking to my lawyer to renegotiate our terms. The man cannot be reasonable about anything*

Ace: *I'm on the way*

I couldn't bring myself to reply to either of them. Instead, I reached for the wine, but the bottle was empty, and in the process, I knocked over the mini bottles of tequila I'd found in the cabinet behind the empty full sized one. I mean, who puts back an empty bottle?

I couldn't have thrown it in the trash like a normal person capable of cleaning up after themselves?

Who was I kidding? Of course, I couldn't.

It totally summed up my life. My mess.

If I couldn't even keep a fully stocked kitchen to get drunk properly, how could I be expected to do any other type of adulting, like get a promotion without any help? Or summon the courage to stay in a relationship?

I always run. That's what Penn said. I get scared and run away.

Truer words had never been spoken.

A drunken lightbulb went off in the recesses of my brain. I rolled off the couch and crawled over to the cabinet on the back wall, inside which was a bottle of champagne I'd been sent for my birthday. I'd come home to find it on my doorstep, and immediately stuck it somewhere I wouldn't have to look at it. The label was still attached.

> **Sorry it's late.**
> **Happy Birthday,**
> **Dad**

Lukewarm champagne was better than nothing; needs must and all that. If I drank enough, I could forget this whole day.

The cork popped out; the champagne was already to my lips before it hit the wall.

Bang bang bang. "Payton?"

The rim of the bottle jarred against my mouth as I jolted from the noise. "Ouch, fuck."

I rolled over and pushed myself to standing, kind of, anyway.

"Payton?" *Bang bang bang.* "Open up."

Thankfully the wall was there to hold me up as I took a step to the door, followed by the next. One after the other, until my hand gripped around the doorknob and pushed it.

Oops, I needed to pull it.

I blinked at Ace, but I couldn't seem to focus. I think it was just him standing there, but I wasn't certain. There might have been two. Or three.

"Payton, are you feeling okay?"

My hand flew to my mouth to cover the hiccup, and the harsh strip light in the hallway burned my eyes as they widened.

Oh shit.

"Payton? Are you going to be…"

The word died on his lip as my body decided it no longer wanted to house everything I'd drunk over the last five hours.

Yeah, my name is Payton Lopez; the girl who broke the New York Lions starting pitcher, and subsequently fixed him.

I was also the one who'd puked on him.

22

Ace

For the first time since we started whatever it was we had started, I woke up before Payton. And let me tell you, it's an experience.

I'd been imagining some kick-ass woman bouncing out of bed before the alarm, and making the day her bitch. But today, I think I'd been short changed, or maybe I'd struck gold. I couldn't decide.

I looked down at the lump next to me as it started moving. An arm slowly reached out from under the comforter and eased it down to reveal Payton's head, reminding me of a bear emerging from hibernation.

"Good morning," I grinned at her.

Scrubbing her hand across her face, she briefly opened one eye and closed it again with a grunt. Yes, definitely a bear. A Grizzly for sure.

I reached over to the nightstand and picked up the glass

of electrolytes I'd made for Payton last night. You know, after she vomited on me and passed out.

"Drink this." I put the glass in her hand and curled her fingers around so they were gripping it properly. "It'll make you feel better."

"What is it?" she croaked with a wince. I wasn't sure if it was from her throat being sore or the volume of her voice. I lowered mine, just in case.

"Electrolytes."

She lifted her head and sniffed it carefully. Then she peered at the liquid, looking at the contents like she was convinced they might poison her, then sniffed it again. "Where did they come from?"

"I have loads of it in my bag," I replied, trying hard to hide my amusement. I'd seen some hangovers before, but I don't think I'd ever seen one like this. "Lucky for you, hey?"

"What do they do?"

"Help with the headache and the dehydration. Drink it. When you're done, I have Advil for you."

She side-eyed me again, then focused back on the glass. "Why are you here?"

"What d'you mean?"

She cleared her throat, which had her wincing again. "Please tell me we didn't have sex."

"No, Babycakes," I smirked. "After you were done puking you passed out, and you've slept like an angel ever since."

If you didn't include the snoring.

"I threw up?"

"You sure did," I nodded.

"And you saw?"

"Yes, babe. You threw up on me."

I was still trying to hide my amusement, especially at the horror crossing Payton's face. Her eyes widened, just like they had last night before she'd spewed everywhere. Only this time, her hand shot up to grab her forehead with a groan.

"I puked on *you*?" she whispered.

I nodded.

"And you're still here?"

"I wasn't going to leave you alone." I eyed the glass, watching carefully in case it tipped. I probably should have held onto it. "Babe, drink it."

Payton slowly pushed herself up until she was sitting on her haunches. She peered at the glass again.

"Drink it. Do it in one."

She looked at it again, and her lip curled. She took another sniff. But then she noticed the t-shirt she was wearing, and glanced up at me with a frown.

She pulled at the front of the shirt. "What's this?"

"It's mine, and it's clean. I didn't want to go searching around in your drawers, and I had a spare in my bag."

Truth be told, I knew exactly which drawer she kept her sleep wear in, but since that morning she'd woken up at my place and put my clothes on, I liked seeing her in my stuff.

"But what about you?"

"Payton, I will answer whatever questions you want, just drink first. You'll feel better."

She lifted the glass to her lips, and took a sip. One tiny sip, and passed the glass back to me. Her eyes widened again. Her hand slapped over her mouth.

"imgonnabesick."

She nearly fell out of bed, tripping over herself as she sprinted to the bathroom. Her speed was impressive, and before I'd had a chance to follow her, the sound of retching echoed from the bathroom.

It was amazing there was anything left inside her.

Picking up the washcloth I'd left on the sink last night, I ran it under the cold faucet and pressed it against her forehead as she slumped against the toilet bowl.

"Here, hold this."

"Ace…" she groaned again, though she looked like she was having a hard time breathing. "Why are you here?"

"Why do you keep asking me that? How about you tell me the answer you're looking for?"

She was about to respond when her head went back over the toilet bowl, and her stomach heaved. Nothing came up, but she stayed there anyway.

"Why did you stay here with me? We didn't have sex, I threw up on you, and now you're handing me cold washcloths."

"Yeah, so?"

"It's not normal." Her words echoed around the cold porcelain.

Normal? What the fuck did that mean?

When she decided there was going to be no more retching for the foreseeable future, she sat back and pressed her cheek to the cool bathroom tiles. Her long legs were stretched out in front of her, resembling more of a Raggedy Ann doll than person. I wasn't sure I'd ever seen such a sorry looking human, and I'd seen Tanner the morning after he'd lost the number of a Victoria's Secret model.

I wet the washcloth again, passed it to her, and sat down on the rim of the small bathtub.

"Thank you." She unfolded it and laid it on her face. At least she couldn't see me smirking now. "You can go, I don't need you to look after me."

"You're hugging the toilet, Babycakes. How about you tell me why you were so drunk last night? What happened yesterday? I didn't hear from you all day."

Payton muttered something from behind the washcloth, that sounded a lot like 'Penn Shepherd', though it could have easily been a groan instead. She reached into her hair, and pulled the tie out – the one I'd fashioned out of the elastic name tape labels which came attached to all our clean laundry at the club.

"Sorry, I couldn't find anything else," I replied to her confused face.

"You tied my hair up?"

I nodded, unsure why she was having such a hard time with the idea of me taking care of her. For some reason, I didn't think it had anything to do with the hangover from Hell she was sporting. "You were pretty sick, and you have a lot of hair."

"Where was I sick?"

I thumbed behind me. "In the hallway and then in here, but I cleaned it up."

There was that face again, the one which looked like she'd stepped out of the House of Horrors ride at Coney Island. "You cleaned up my puke?"

"Hey, I've birthed cattle. This was nothing."

"Where are your clothes?"

"In the trash," I grinned. "I'm not wearing them again."

She carefully rested her head back and dropped the cloth over her face again. "Ace, why are you still here? Don't you have to be somewhere?"

I frowned at her, not that she saw from behind the white terrycloth covering her face, but I was definitely fucking frowning. I shouldn't have been so excited to see what a hungover Payton would be like, because right now, it was hard to tell the difference between her and a pit Viper.

"It's seven a.m., I don't have to be anywhere unless you're trying to kick me out."

She ripped the cloth from her face and threw it in her lap. "You're not my boyfriend. Stop acting like one."

"I'm not. I'm acting like decent a human being."

"Yeah, is that what Cosmo told you to do?"

"No, it isn't," I gritted, finding it next to impossible to hide the annoyance coursing through me at the veiled insult that a. I couldn't have thought of it myself, and b. she didn't sound too happy about me being her boyfriend. On second thought, it wasn't veiled, it was a crystal-clear insult. "And what would be so bad if I *was* looking after you as a boyfriend?"

I didn't follow up with telling her there were plenty of girls desperate for me to fill that role.

"Okay," she gingerly rolled onto her knees and pushed herself to standing. I waited to see if she'd wobble, just in case I needed to catch her, but she stood firm. "Thank you for looking after me last night and cleaning up my place, I really appreciate it. I'm so sorry I puked all over you, I'll reimburse you for your clothes, just let me know what I owe you."

"Payton…"

"I think this has run its course, don't you? You fixed your game, I got my promotion. We don't need each other any more."

I turned behind me, looking to see if maybe there was a portal to a different reality, or for any indication this wasn't happening. Maybe it was one of those shitty joke shows, like Punk'd.

But her bedroom was as I'd left it, the comforter hanging half off the bed.

When I looked back, her eyes were closed and she was holding onto the sink.

She was hungover. That's all this was. The World's Worst Hangover.

"Pay, babe, why don't you go back to bed and try to sleep? You'll feel better."

"Stop telling me what to do!" she snapped, as loudly as she could manage.

"I'm not telling you what to do. I'm trying to help you feel better."

"Well, I don't need you to, and I don't need a boyfriend. I look after myself just fine."

I didn't think it was the time to remind her that she kept shoes in her kitchen cabinets, or, if I opened the fridge, there'd be a half empty carton of two percent milk and not much else.

I stood up, too annoyed to stay sitting. It was also hard to be annoyed at someone who looked like they were on the verge of dying, but I was doing my best.

"Where's this boyfriend talk coming from? Has someone said something to you? What happened yesterday?"

"No one said anything," she snapped, though I noticed she didn't look me in the eye. "I can think for myself, you know."

I had to hand it to her; I now couldn't tell if it was the hangover speaking, especially when she stormed past me into the bedroom. I followed, expecting to find her in bed, but she was standing by the bedroom door holding up my trackpants.

Guess that was my cue.

"This has been fun, and I'm really grateful for what you've done for me…"

"I haven't done anything," I snapped, snatching the pants from her hand, "and you're being ridiculous."

"*I'm* being ridiculous? Me? Me?" she pointed at her chest. "We're using each other. This whole thing started because you wanted to play better, and I wanted a promotion. It's not a relationship, Ace."

"What would you know? You've never had a relationship!"

"Neither have you!"

"No, but you know what? I want to try, and I want to see what it's like, so sue me. I like you, Payton. I more than like you – maybe not right this second – but I like you, and I know you like me, too. Don't you want to see what we'd be like together?"

"Not really," she replied, and this time I was certain she purposely looked away.

Liar.

I didn't know what was happening right now, but I knew she was lying.

"Payton, I want to have you at the games, watching me. I want to take you to dinner, and I want to hold your hand and kiss you in public. Hell, I want to see you in daylight."

She rolled her eyes, then winced from the movement. "Yeah, because you've got it in your head that you can't win without me."

I tugged my pants on and snatched up my hoodie from the floor. "No! Maybe that's how this started, but it's not why it continued. My game was fixed long ago."

"I don't want a boyfriend, Ace."

"Yeah? I call bullshit on that." I stormed past her into the living room, and waved my hands around. "All the books in this apartment are romance. They're all about finding love. No one reads that many books about love if they don't believe in it."

"I work in publishing, you dumbass!"

I shook my head. "Nice try. You didn't collect all those books in the last month. Kids don't read those kinds of books."

I think her cheeks flushed from being caught out, but she could just be about to vomit again.

"Have you been snooping, is that what you're saying?"

"You leave me in your apartment every morning, alone."

"You have been snooping!"

"No, I haven't. I walk past the bookshelves to get out of here, but I'm not going to lie and say I wasn't curious. I want to get to know you better. I want to see what's behind the bulletproof armor you wear."

"Oh, because I don't want you as a boyfriend, I must be wearing bulletproof armor. I see your ego hasn't lessened. Hope your head doesn't get stuck on the way out."

I grabbed my backpack off the kitchen counter and yanked open the front door. "I'll fit just fine, thanks."

"Glad to hear it."

I stopped as I reached the top of the stairs, and turned.

"This is bullshit, Payton, and you know it. How about you call me when you're feeling better, and you've unstuck your head from your ass? Enjoy your hangover."

"I will!" she yelled.

It didn't give me any joy knowing the sound of the door slamming behind me would have had her clasping her head again.

Okay, maybe it did... a little, but she puked on *me* and I'm the one who gets broken up with?

I never thought I'd say this, but Payton Lopez is a dick.

And I think I might be in love with her.

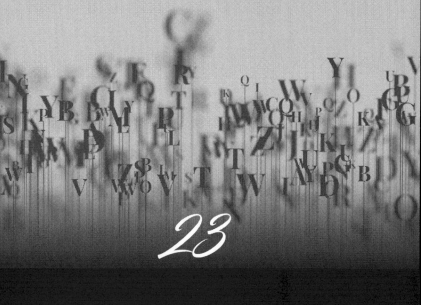

23

Payton

I've faced death and come through the other side.

I also think I'd lost ten pounds – or would have done – if I hadn't eaten my body weight in Ben and Jerry's while watching The Holiday on repeat. Anything was better than baseball.

It had taken me three days to leave my apartment. Even though I'd only walked outside, hopped in a cab, and come straight around to Kit's place, I was seeing it as a victory.

It was how I came to be sitting on a lounger on Kit's terrace, overlooking Central Park, wearing a pink bandage around my arm while a two-year-old attempted to listen to my heartbeat. However, even if the stethoscope wasn't made from finest oak, and painted with a little red and white cross, I'm not sure she'd have heard anything.

My chest was empty.

"Sick, Payton." Bell's pudgy little hand rested on mine, while simultaneously whacking me on the cheek with the end of the stethoscope. "Oops."

Kit pushed up the bandage wrapped around her head for the tenth time. "Bell, sweetheart, be careful of Auntie Payton."

I pulled a blanket around my shoulders and smiled gratefully at Kit. "Thanks."

"Come here to feel better, and you leave with concussion," she chuckled.

Maybe a concussion would knock some sense into me.

The pair of us had gotten off lighter than Barclay though, whose tail was wrapped in two green bandages while a Velcro heart rate monitor was attached to his leg. We're not sure what had happened to him, but it wasn't looking good.

Bell, wearing her white lab coat, flung the stethoscope around her neck, and trotted off to her mobile ambulance in search of the antidote to whatever she'd decided was wrong with me.

As long as it didn't involve alcohol, I'd take it.

Perhaps she'd find something to help me grow my liver back.

Resting my head on the lounger, I put my sunglasses back on and let the sunshine soak into my bones, hoping it might make me feel better. I needed something, stat. Instead, I groaned loudly enough that Barclay raised his head.

"I don't get it. Is this still the hangover talking?" asked Kit. "Are you going to tell me why you were so drunk? Not to mention you drinking without me. Rude."

I huffed a smile. It was the most I could manage. I'd possibly puked up my sense of humor – along with my dignity, and any grace I may have previously possessed. Kit was usually the one who could make me smile, but not today it seemed.

Aside from the fact I hadn't had the energy to form words until today, I was undecided on whether telling Kit about Penn's visit was a good idea. His words were still too raw, too fresh, and as much as I hated admitting it, too truthful. I also knew the second I did, she'd storm over to The Lions Stadium and give Penn Hell. It had happened before, and I think he was still a little butthurt over it.

Therefore, I didn't want to be the one to cause another fight he wouldn't win.

Even if he did deserve it.

"Ace and I called it quits," I replied, hoping it was enough information to let the subject go.

I should have known better.

"Pay, I've seen you break up with tons of guys before, and you've never had a three-day hangover from it. I've seen you move on to a new guy after nothing more than a text message to his predecessor, while on the way to a date. What happened?"

I shrugged. "Nothing."

"Wait, was he the one who broke it off? Is that why you're upset? Did you like him?"

Oh my God, so many questions my brain was starting to hurt again.

"I broke it off."

"Then why the hangover?" she pressed as Bell returned with a wooden syringe and sat down next to Barclay.

Poor Barclay.

I closed my eyes. "I just drank too much, that's all."

"Do you like Ace?" she asked again.

There was the million-dollar question.

Or rather the question she was really asking – did I like him enough to see what could happen between us? Just like he'd said.

And that was something I didn't have an answer to… Except Kit wanted one.

"Pay? Do you like Ace Watson?"

I sat up, pushing my glasses onto my head. "I don't know. Yes, I think so. But where was it going to go? What's the point?"

"What do you mean, what's the point?"

I shrugged, but she knew where this was going, because we'd already had some iteration of this conversation a thousand times over the years we'd been best friends. She got up and moved to sit on the end of my lounger.

"Not everything has to end, Pay, and you are not your parents. In fact, I'd go as far as to say you are the exact opposite. Therefore, any relationship you have you'll go into trying not to repeat their mistakes. Give yourself a break."

"It's different. I'm scared of getting to the point of relying on someone and then they leave, like my dad left my mom. I don't want to turn into my mom."

"You won't, and you know how I know that?"

"How?"

"Apart from your mom being the most selfish, self-absorbed woman I've ever met, it's because you don't want to. Therefore, you'll make the conscious effort not to. We both know they should never have been together in the first place. You're yet to find that out with Ace, but you won't if you don't try."

She made it sound so easy. I watched as a small bird landed

on one of the olive trees lining the terrace and began pecking at the branch. I wish I could fly around and eat olives all day.

"Tell me what happened with Ace." Kit used that tone I'd heard her use on Murray, or one time when I'd gone to meet her for lunch and she was talking to a student who didn't hand in his paper on time.

It was the tone that said don't mess with me.

I flung an arm over my eyes. It would be easier if I didn't have to see her face as I told her. And if I said it as quickly as possible, maybe it would be less humiliating. Ripping the Band-Aid off, so to speak.

"Penn-came-to-see-me-and-ordered-me-to-break-up-with-Ace-so-it-didn't-mess-with-his-team-because-everyone-knows-I-don't-do-relationships-so-I-got-very--drunk-Ace-came-over-and-I-threw-up-on-him-then-we-broke-up," I got out and sucked in a deep breath.

Phew.

When she still hadn't said anything after a minute, I lifted my arm to find her staring at me with her mouth wide open. She was probably trying to catch up with the speed at which I'd blurted it out.

"Kit?"

She held her hand up to silence me.

"We'll get to Penn in a minute," she managed, her brows shooting up. "You threw up on Ace? Like, you puked on him?"

I nodded, dropping my head so I couldn't see her, though I had nowhere to go. I'd hit rock bottom.

Her hand shot up, trying to stifle the laugh which burst out. "Oh my God."

"It's not funny."

"Yeah, it is," she laughed. "You puked on Ace Watson.

What did he do?"

I shrugged. "Dunno. I passed out, but he looked after me. I threw up on him, and he looked after me. When I woke up, he'd made me electrolytes and tied my hair back, and stayed to make sure I was okay."

That was the hardest part. He'd wanted to make sure I was okay, and I'd been nothing but an ungrateful brat.

"I'm telling you, if you puked on me, I'd have to seriously reevaluate our friendship," she smirked.

"Kit..." I whined, "it's not funny."

"It is, because you're being blind and a little bit stupid. And it makes me sad that you're not with someone when you have so much love to give. You're missing out on something wonderful because of your awful parents."

A thick lump formed in my throat, because she was right. I knew she was right. I'd avoided long term relationships my entire adult life because of my parents. I openly admitted it. The difference between this one and any one I'd had before was that I hadn't ended it before the feelings kicked in. Right now, I did kinda feel like I could be missing out on something, and I didn't know what to do about it.

"What happened after Ace had left?"

I sniffed, wiping my palm under my nose. Bell's head turned from where she was still attending to Barclay. "Payton sniffies? You want tissue?"

"Yes, please," I nodded, and Bell pushed off the floor and fetched a box from her trusty ambulance.

She thrust one crumpled tissue at me. "Here you go."

"Thank you, cutie pie."

"Welcome." Bell dropped back down on the floor next to Barclay.

I looked over to Kit who was grinning at her sweet, gorgeous, empathetic daughter.

"After Ace left, I crawled back to bed, called in sick, and cried. I slept all day. Those electrolytes he gave me actually did make me feel better, once I managed to keep them down."

I'd also made a half-assed attempt at seeing who was on *Tinder*, but it hadn't taken me long to realize it was a total bust. I'd tried *Bumble* and *Hinge*, but they'd been a bust as well. Swiping through dating apps had once been my favorite game, but I couldn't bring myself to go right on any of them.

Not Chad from Greenwich Village who worked on Wall Street.

Not Mike from Midtown who worked in advertising.

Not Billy from Williamsburg who owned a cold brew company – and I loved cold brew.

None of them.

Dating apps had been ruined by a six-foot-three baseball player I never wanted to have more than one night with.

"How much ice cream did you eat?" asked Kit.

I grinned. "I'm not sharing that figure."

"What are you going to do?"

I shrugged. "I don't know. I was pretty rude to him. Actually, I was very rude. I was hideous. A bitch, basically."

I wasn't sure I could even blame my hangover.

"Have you heard from him?"

I shook my head. For the first time since we'd had sex the second time, I hadn't heard from him every day, and my life felt a little quieter because of it. I missed the way he made me laugh. I missed the way he talked about our days as I got dressed. I missed the way he made me feel.

I missed him.

"He told me to call him once I'd got my head unstuck from my ass."

Kit stifled a laugh, and I couldn't even bring myself to glare at her because she was right. Ace was right.

"He sounds perfect," she smirked. "Pay, would it really be so bad? Loving someone and letting them love you back? Falling in love is the best feeling in the world."

"I don't know. It's so hard. I want to, I really do… But then what if he leaves me, or we end up hating each other?"

What if he breaks my heart?

"If he leaves you then we'll deal with it, like you would help me deal if Murray left me."

I scoffed. There was a greater chance of the sky falling in than Murray leaving Kit. The man was obsessed.

"Pay, you'd survive. You'd be stronger for it."

"My mom isn't."

"You are not your mom!" Kit gritted. "You're a strong, independent woman with an incredible job and an awesome life. Your mom didn't have those things when she met your dad. If you and Ace broke up you would see how strong you are, but you can't keep shutting yourself off just because you don't want to become a statistic."

"I guess I just always thought it would be easier to be alone."

"Being with someone doesn't mean that you have to become one person, you still have your independence."

I was an intelligent woman. I *did* have an incredible job and awesome life. Yet the one relationship model I grew up with was my parents', and no matter how smart I thought I might be, it had influenced my entire life, and it never occurred to me things could be different – even when I saw them in my friends.

However, I was good at proving people wrong. Perhaps this time, that person could be myself.

"Maybe you're right."

"I am, now what are we doing about Penn?"

"I'm not sure there's anything I can do."

"You can tell him to go fuck himself. He doesn't get to dictate who you date."

I sucked in my cheek and chewed on it, trying to push away the anxiety which had risen at the thought of Penn's words.

"He was speaking the truth."

"No, he wasn't, and he had no right to order you to break up with someone. Have you heard from Lowe? There's no way she knows about this."

Before I could answer, the sound of Murray's deep voice boomed through from the kitchen. "Columbia?" he called out, using the nickname he had for Kit. "Where are my girls?"

"Now we'll get some answers," she hissed at me, before hollering back at Murray. "We're outside. Did you know about this?"

"About what?"

We both turned as Murray appeared at the veranda doors, halting for a nanosecond as his eyes flicked to me sitting on the lounger. It was brief, but both Kit and I noticed it, and he knew we had. He also knew exactly what Kit was talking about.

Murray sighed but walked over to us, instead of running back into the apartment. "Look, it's Penn's team. It's a business. He's not running a dating agency."

"What?" snapped Kit, and tried to avoid the kiss Murray

planted on her head before he picked up Bell.

"Hello, darling girl. What are you doing? What's happened to Barclay?"

"He's sick, Papa."

Murray looked down at Barclay, whose tail was thumping against the terrace tiles in the hopes of being rescued. "I see that. Good job Doctor Bell is here to fix him then."

He kissed her cheek and put her back down. "I'm going to get a drink before we have this conversation. Do you two want wine?"

My stomach churned in a mini-cyclone of protest. It was going to be a while before I had alcohol again.

"We'll both take soda water," Kit replied, which made Murray frown, especially at me.

He returned a couple of minutes later, carrying a bottle of beer and glasses of soda water, with ice and a wedge of lemon.

"Thank you."

He sat down on the end of Kit's lounger, and pulled her legs onto his lap.

"I'm not saying what he did was right, but see it from his perspective. He's running a billion-dollar business, and he's protecting a key asset from being damaged again. He's protecting Ace."

Kit harrumphed loudly and muttered something that sounded a lot like 'ridiculous'.

Murray refrained from rolling his eyes, though I knew he wanted to, but instead he took a long swig of his beer.

"Payton, sweetheart, it's not personal, and I don't see what the big deal is. You never date anyone for long, and you've always got multiple guys on the go." He raised an eyebrow before continuing his sudden train of thought. "In fact, you said you weren't interested in Ace. I specifically recall you saying it was a one-time thing."

Murray The Memory Man, everybody.

"I didn't even know you'd started up with him." He shot an accusatory glance at Kit for not spilling the beans.

"Have you just been with Penn?" I asked.

He shook his head. "No, they're in Miami this weekend, then Chicago. They get back next Friday for the Phillies series at home."

My belly started churning again, but not from alcohol. It was from the fact Ace wasn't in the city and I hadn't known about it. I dropped my head in my hands.

I had it bad.

"What's going on? I feel like I'm missing out on some major details."

Kit answered for me, because when I opened my mouth, I didn't seem to be able to form the words I needed to.

"Payton likes Ace. Ace likes Payton and wants to try a relationship with her, but Penn had already ordered, *ordered*," Kit repeated with a snarl, "her to break up with Ace, and he was really horrible to her I might add. Payton got too drunk, puked on Ace, then broke up with him."

Murray's head moved from Kit to me and back again.

"I think I'm going to need another drink to unpack all that," he replied, downing the rest of his beer and walking off to the kitchen without another word, while I tried not to think about the fact I'd been outed for liking a boy as though I was still in high-school.

Because now I had to figure out how to get Ace back.

Along with the much easier task of telling Penn to go fuck himself.

24

Ace

"*F*ive minutes to wheels up," the steward announced over the intercom.

I picked up my phone one more time, just to check, but the screen was blank. I hadn't expected a message from Payton, but the tiny sliver of disappointment still stabbed me in the chest.

It had been a week of silence, from both of us.

I wondered if she was still hungover. It was one of the reasons I hadn't messaged her... well, that, plus my parting shot of telling her to call when she'd pulled her head from her ass. I hoped it wasn't still there.

I don't think I'd ever seen anyone so drunk, or so bad tempered.

The other reason... I wanted her to miss me.

"Dude, you okay?" Lux asked as he tossed his bag into the seat next to me. He patted down his pants pockets and shucked off his jacket before sitting opposite me with a frown.

I nodded, turning away from the window to look at him. "Yeah, I'm good."

"Because you're being real quiet."

"I'm just thinking."

"About Payton?"

I was about to answer in the affirmative when Tanner rocked up, lifted Lux's bag from the seat next to me, and put it in the empty one.

"Why didn't you just sit there?" I pointed to the formerly empty chair now housing Lux's bag.

"I don't like flying backwards."

"You can't tell."

"The clouds go the wrong way," he replied, as though that explained everything.

I didn't argue; I had too much on my mind to get into a conversation with Tanner about cloud direction. Not to mention it was the middle of the night, and therefore too dark to see anything.

"Where's Park?"

"He's coming. He got stuck with the social media chick again."

I looked down the aisle to see Parker walking slowly behind the steward handing around the pre-flight snacks and menus. Lux picked up his bag just as Parker reached us and dropped into the last empty seat.

"What took you so long?"

He shrugged. "I always get pulled over for social."

"I think it's because the girl running the social likes you," I chuckled.

My mind had been on Payton so much, and she'd made me more aware of everything going on around me. One of those things had been the very definite crush from the new social team girl on our boy, Parker. Her eyes followed wherever he went.

If that didn't speak volumes, he was quickly becoming the main character of The Lions social feed.

I seemed to be the only one who'd noticed though.

Parker sat up, straightening his shoulders. "You think? Scout?"

"Her name's Scout?"

He nodded. "Yeah. Cute, right?"

"I dunno," I shrugged, because I didn't have an opinion when it came to girls' names. Except Payton's. I fucking loved her name.

"It's from To Kill a Mockingbird," mumbled Lux, as he rummaged elbow deep in his backpack.

"What is?"

"The name Scout. She narrates the book," he replied, before annoyance took over his expression. "Have any of you seen my headphones? I can't find them."

The three of us all shook our heads as another announcement came over the intercom, requesting we get our seatbelts fastened. I pulled up the blind next to my window and peered out as the plane slowly began taxiing toward the runway.

Everyone did as they were told, except Lux, who was still searching for his headphones.

"Hey, watch where you're pointing that thing," Tanner grumbled as Lux's elbow jerked into his ribs from the jolt of the plane engines revving up. He pulled off the headphones resting around his neck and handed them over. "Here, you can use these."

"Thanks."

"What are you listening to?" he asked as Lux swiped across his phone screen.

Stretching one speaker away from his ear, he replied, "ESPN discussing our game this week. I saw a tweet on it, and wanted to catch it before we play The Cubs."

"What are they saying?" asked Tanner.

"I don't know, I haven't listened to it yet." He put the speaker back on his ear.

Parker snorted, rolling his eyes at Tanner's frown, and looked at me. "How are you doing?"

I shrugged again. "Fine."

It was the response I'd given them all week, because technically I was fine.

I was fine.

Confused, but fine.

Kind of pissed, but fine.

Missing Payton, but fine.

Fine.

"Yeah, you sure?" Pressed Parker.

"I'm sure," I replied, and I knew why he was asking, because since Payton ended things, I'd pitched once in The Yankees game, and I'd be starting tomorrow in The Cubs game. But between then and now, I'd told the boys what had happened with Payton, and ever since, they'd been sticking to me closer than a fly on horseshit.

"Because…"

"Parker, I'm sure. My head's fine, it's not about that. It's not Payton."

His brows dropped. "What then?"

I took a deep breath and stretched in my seat as the plane hurtled down the runway and its front wheels finally lifted. Holding onto my nose, I blew hard until my ears popped and the plane levelled out.

Parker was still waiting patiently for an answer.

"I mean, it's about Payton, but it's not about her. My game is fine; I know that and you know that. But I've been thinking about that morning Payton was hungover, and something wasn't right."

"What d'you mean?"

"Dude, she was so drunk. No one gets drunk on their own like that unless there's a problem. I found the empty bottles when I was cleaning. She'd sunk more than the party we threw when we moved into Casa Greyskull."

I grinned, man that was a good housewarming party. We did have to apologize to our downstairs neighbors though, and promise to warn them next time we threw another so they could go away for the night.

"Oh, come on," Parker scoffed.

"Okay, maybe not that much, but she was puking like that chick in The Exorcist."

Tanner snorted loudly. "Still can't believe you got puked on."

I ignored him, "Anyway, something was up. She didn't message me all day. She was totally normal when she left for work earlier."

I stopped talking, biting down on the grin I was trying my best not to let form as the image of Payton's full pouty lips wrapped tightly around my dick flashed through my memory.

"A morning wake-up," she'd said, and I'd come so quickly I'd gotten a headrush.

No, there'd been nothing wrong when she'd left her apartment.

"Then what?"

I jerked a shoulder and went back to looking out the window, even though it was pitch black and I couldn't see anything except the wing lights flashing. "I dunno. It's what I'm trying to figure out."

"You're starting to sound like a girl who got dumped."

"I didn't get dumped, Tan," I snapped, even though that's exactly what had happened.

He was about to reply when his focus was caught by something else.

"Heads up, Shepherd's on his way."

I glanced over Parker's head to see Penn Shepherd walking down the aisle – and he wasn't walking down having a casual check in with everyone he passed, he was heading straight for our seats. And it wasn't the first time it had happened this week, either.

I frowned. Now that I thought about it, he was another one like a fly around horseshit this week.

"Hey, have you guys noticed Shepherd paying more attention to us than normal?"

Tanner shook his head, which was no surprise, but so did Parker.

"He has, I'm telling you. Every time we've traveled, he's come to check on us. And he checked at practice yesterday, and the day before. So did Coach."

"Coach is supposed to check on you."

I shook my head. "No. He's never checked like this before.

Even at the beginning of the season when I…"

"Lost it?" Tanner interrupted unnecessarily.

"You know, you really are the worst and least supportive friend I have," I grumbled, shifting in my seat as Penn Shepherd finally reached us.

His hand gripped around the back of Parker's head rest. "Hello, boys."

"Mr. Shepherd," Tanner grinned up at him. "How are you, sir?"

"All good. Awesome, in fact. How are you all doing?" He peered around to each of us, before his eyes fixed firmly on me. "Ace, how are you? Feeling good about the game this week? You're opening tomorrow, right?" he added, like he didn't know exactly what was going on with his team.

"Yes, sir. All good," I nodded, matching his narrow-eyed stare with one of my own.

"Sure? Nothing on your mind? Have you talked to Doctor Benedict this week?"

I was still looking at Penn, but felt Tanner and Parker's stare fix on me.

"Yes, sir." I nodded again, because it was the truth.

I'd passed the good Lions' doctor in the hallway this week, and we'd shot the breeze for thirty seconds on the how the Knicks game had gone. I hadn't seen him in his professional capacity as the Lions' psychologist, however.

"Glad to hear it. You're looking good, Watson."

"Thank you, Mr. Shepherd."

His focus on me broke as the steward arrived to take our food order, and he looked around at the four of us. "The steak sandwich is really good today."

He gave us one last toothy smile, and moved out of the

way. My eyes stayed trained on his back until he was out of sight, and in the executive section where he always sat. My eyes stayed glued on the spot Penn had disappeared until Parker's fingers snapped in my face, bringing me back to the present.

"Ace. Food. Waddya want?"

"Whatever you're having, I don't care," I muttered.

Parker ordered me… I've no idea what… while I went back to thinking about how weird Penn Shepherd was acting.

"Have you really been to see Benedict this week?"

I shook my head. "No, I don't need to see a shrink. My problem was fixed."

"You told Shepherd you had."

"No, he asked if I'd talked to him, and I have. I saw him and said hello."

Parker dropped his head with a snort of amusement.

"He asked me where you were the other day. I forgot to tell you he was looking for you."

I glanced at Tanner. "The doc was looking for me?"

"No, Shepherd. You were in the bullpen with Parker, so I assumed he'd come find you." He shrugged before his focus shifted once more. "Now what?"

Even Parker turned around as I looked up, my eyes flaring when I spotted Coach Chase making his way down the plane. Shepherd was one thing, but never in the history of any Lions' plane rides had Coach Chase walked down the aisle.

"Coach." I nodded at him when he reached us.

"Gentlemen, how are you? Good game tonight. Watson, you ready for starting tomorrow?"

"Sure am." I tried my best to grin as naturally as possible, which is what I'd normally do, but this was all too weird for me to be natural. "Buzzing for it."

"That's what I like to hear." Coach peered around our group, including Lux, who'd fallen asleep. "And the four of you are keeping your heads down?"

Tanner's eyes flicked to mine, and back to Coach. "Behaving one hundred percent of the time, sir."

"Good, good," he nodded. "Come find me if you need anything."

We all watched him return to his seat, though I was waiting for Parker to turn around.

"Okay, that was weird."

I could feel the lines forming in my brow. "I told you. They've never singled me out for this much attention, even when I was pitching like shit."

"Hmm," replied Tanner, stroking his chin like he was trying to solve some great mystery, but we were interrupted by food arriving.

I picked up half my sandwich and bit down, eating in silence while my thoughts went back to Payton, and wondering what she was doing. I'd gotten so used to talking to her every day that it was hard to remember what I'd done last season during the hours outside playing ball. I must have done something, but for the life of me, my mind was blank.

I fucking missed her.

I missed her smile, her laugh, and the snort she let out when she was really amused, like the barriers she kept herself hidden behind had suddenly come down for a minute. I missed the way she was always half asleep when she'd open the door to me after a game. I missed the sliver of time every morning when I watched her get dressed. I missed the way she'd started falling asleep curled into my side.

I missed her.

"Maybe Shepherd knows you broke up, and he's checking to see if you're okay without asking about your love life."

My eyes shot to Parker's as he stuffed a handful of fries in his mouth. "Maybe, but that wouldn't explain Payton's behavior."

Tanner hadn't been wrong about acting like a girl. I'd been wracking my brain over and over, trying to pick apart our interaction, the way she kept bringing up the subject of me as her boyfriend, the way she wouldn't meet my eye.

"Maybe Shepherd told her to do it," Tanner added.

"Why would he do that?" Parker asked as he picked up his bottle of water and swigged through a smile. "As if Shepherd would care enough."

But Tanner just shrugged. "I dunno. You said they were friends, and no idea is a dumb idea, right? That's what everyone says."

"You're right, Tan," I yawned. My brain had been working overtime and now my belly was full, I was finding it hard to stay awake. From the looks of it, so were the other two. I put my plate on the table between us, and pushed my seat back. "I'm going to get some sleep for the rest of the flight."

If I was lucky, I'd dream about Payton.

"Okay, listen up. You know the drill. Buses will check you off, and you'll head to the hotel downtown. Your itinerary and instructions for tomorrow will be waiting in your rooms.

Get some sleep, gentleman."

"Max could be the guy announcing WWE if he left The Lions," whispered Parker as we made our way off the plane and into the cool Chicago midnight air.

"Yeah," I chuckled, letting out a wide yawn.

I hadn't dreamed about Payton, but somewhere in the pit of my belly, a warning began going off. I still don't know what came over me, because I'd all but forgotten what Tanner had said earlier, until I saw Penn Shepherd standing a little way off from the bottom of the plane steps talking to a couple of the PTs.

And suddenly I could hear some sense in his words.

Slapping Parker on the arm, I said, "Give me two minutes. I want to check something," and jogged in the direction Penn Shepherd was now walking.

"Hey, Mr. Shepherd, wait up."

Penn turned around, his eyes flicking from me to Parker, who'd followed, and back again. "Ace, hey, everything okay? You feeling okay?"

There was that weird tone again. It was the same one he'd used on me all this week, and it's what I hadn't been able to figure out. It was different to the way he always spoke to me before – as a boss – and this was... careful. Like I was about to break.

"I'm feeling fine," I frowned. "I'm not going to fall apart because my girlfriend broke up with me."

"Ace..." Parker's tone was low with warning, "what are you doing?"

"Your... girlfriend?" Penn cleared his throat, but I didn't miss the surprised catch in his voice. "I didn't realize you had a girlfriend."

"I do – or I did. I will have, again. I'm getting her back."

He pushed his hands into his pockets as casually as he could. "What can I help you with?"

"Some relationship advice, if that's okay?" I smiled at him. "You said to ask if I needed anything."

"Um… sure. I'll see what I can do."

"Thanks, boss." I hitched my bag further onto my shoulder. "What would you do if someone made your wife cry?"

"Lowe?" Panic flooded Penn's face as he searched the tarmac for Lowe, forgetting she hadn't been on this trip. She'd flown back to New York after Miami. "What's wrong with Lowe?"

"Nothing, I don't think. I'm asking you, what would you do if someone made her cry?"

"Oh." Penn's eyes widened, and he knew exactly why I was asking. "Um, I'd um…"

Holy shit. Tanner *was* right.

Penn Shepherd's poker face was not as good as he thought, because the only thing I could see right now was a Full House of guilt. I'd also never seen anyone look so uncomfortable.

"I'm asking because my girlfriend was very upset the other night, and someone had been the cause."

"Really? Are you sure?"

"Yep, and she can fight her own battles, but this time I don't want her to. I want her to know I will always be in her corner, and when someone makes her cry, it becomes a problem for me. Do you understand what I'm saying?"

Penn frowned, but didn't reply.

"When I find out who made her cry, there will be a steep price to pay. I'm sure you can understand." I smiled at him, though it didn't reach my eyes.

"I'm not sure I can help you." Penn fixed me with the same stare he had earlier, only this time, he held it for a little longer while he forced a smile that mirrored mine. "It sounds like you've figured it all out already, Watson. Now if I'm not mistaken, Max is hollering for you two. I'll see you in the morning."

He turned and walked off toward his car.

Parker looked at me like I'd grown another head. "Dude, what the fuck was that?"

I shook my head. "I had the craziest feeling Tanner's theory was right, so I wanted to see for myself."

"You're crazy alright," he said as we picked up the pace to jog to the buses. "Crazier that Tan was right. Now what you gonna do?"

The answer to that was easy.

"First, I'm going to pitch my ass off so Payton can see I'm not dependent on her to win. Then I'm going to get her back. Shepherd can go fuck himself."

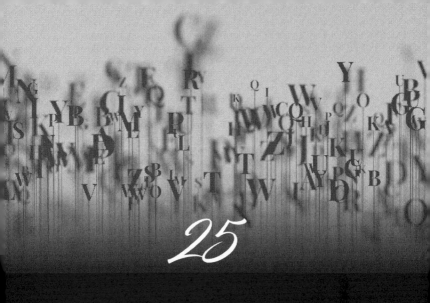

25

Payton

"What's the plan?"

I shrugged at Kit. "I don't have one."

"But you have to have one."

"I *don't* have one, though."

"Are you sure you don't want to wear a boyfriend shirt?"

"Fuck, no," I shuddered, trying hard not to burn myself with the scalding iron I currently had curled around my hair. "No offense to Marnie, but this is not being put on the big screen. No fucking way. Besides, it's a totally different situation. I'm just saying yes to him asking if we can see each other in daylight."

Kit rolled her eyes, and put down the makeup brush she'd been dusting over her face. "How romantic."

"Whatever, it's a big step for me. I'm asking him to date me."

She leaned over, planting a kiss on my head. "I know, babe. I know. I'm proud of you."

"Where's Murray?"

"He's meeting us there, and he's under strict instructions not to blab to Penn," she replied, and picked up a magazine I'd been reading and flicked through it.

"He'd better be." I didn't add that he was probably as scared of Kit as Penn was.

I went back to curling my hair in silence. As I was running my fingers through the fat waves and separating them, I caught Kit frowning in the mirror's reflection.

"What?"

She looked to the bedroom door. "I dunno. I think I heard the buzzer."

I reached over, switched off the music, and we both waited. A second later, the buzzer went again.

"Are you expecting anyone?"

I shook my head. "No, it'll be Mrs. Kellerman. She always picks up my mail by accident and then brings it down."

"I'll get it, I haven't seen her in ages. You finish deciding what to wear." She wagged her finger at me and ran off, like I hadn't already told her a million times what I was wearing.

Jeans, sneakers, and my Lions t-shirt.

I looked down at the bed, where Ace's official Lions shirt was neatly laid out with his name and number on the back. I'd bought it two days ago, after I'd come up with my plan to attend today's game against The Phillies, but I couldn't quite find the courage to wear it.

I might be putting myself on the line agreeing to see where

things could go between us, but I also knew we hadn't spoken in ten days, and the last thing I'd done was yell at him. I mean, the last thing if you didn't include the vomit situation, because, like a normal human being, I was trying my hardest to pretend it never happened.

I was buttoning up my jeans when I heard voices that didn't sound anything like my eighty-year-old upstairs neighbor, and stopped what I was doing to listen.

No, that definitely wasn't Mrs. Kellerman.

I yanked my t-shirt over my head from the sudden annoyance causing me to forget about how perfectly I'd set my hair, and stormed out to the living room to find Kit in a standoff.

I wasn't sure what was funnier – Penn looking wholly uncomfortable, not to mention scared of Kit, or the annoyance on Kit's face, with her arms rigid across her chest and her foot tapping, which was never a good sign.

Lowe was standing slightly further away, nearer the kitchen, but I think that was only so that Penn couldn't use her for protection. It was probably why the giant bunch of yellow roses he was holding gave the appearance of a very colorful and beautifully scented bulletproof vest.

Lowe and Penn's eyes shot to me as the floorboard creaked under my steps.

"Look, Pay," Kit drawled without turning around. "Mr. Baseball himself has come for a visit."

I swallowed hard because I didn't want to crack a smile and give the impression Penn wasn't sitting in the number one position on my shit list, because he was. But Kit and Penn arguing always amused me, because she was the only person I'd ever met he seemed to be wary of. In the end, Lowe was the one who stepped forward first, crossing the room and pulling me into a big hug.

"I'm so sorry, Payton. I didn't know about any of this. I'm so sorry. I wish you'd told me when it happened. I would have marched him around here sooner."

"Thanks." I offered her a smile, though my eyes narrowed at Penn. "It's not your fight though, and I didn't want to involve you. This isn't personal, right Penn?" I shot at him, and caught Lowe cringing from the corner of my eye. "How'd you find out?"

"My idiot husband told me what he'd done last night," she gritted out and Penn received another dirty look, which made the girls three for three, before Lowe turned back to me. "It's indefensible, but in his defense, he feels awful."

"As he should," snapped Kit, removing the flowers from Penn's hand. "I'll put these in water."

Without the flowers to protect him, Penn stiffened another degree and stepped closer to Lowe, who rolled her eyes as she muttered under her breath.

The three of us stood in silence.

"Those flowers are for you," Penn spoke finally. "Yellow roses mean friendship."

"I know," I replied, and crossed my arms as Kit had done, though not quite as aggressively.

"Right. Of course, you do." He looked at his feet, and as much as I wanted to enjoy this weirdly nervous Penn Shepherd, I'm not sure I liked it one bit. It felt like the equilibrium was off.

"What do you want, Penn? Shouldn't you be at the stadium?"

He shook his head. "The game doesn't start for an hour."

Right. I knew that, because I'd planned to be there to see

Ace make the first pitch. But Penn was usually at the stadium way before the game started, because he liked to watch the crowds fill the seats and soak up the atmosphere.

And today promised to be a big game.

It was the final in the Phillies series at home. It would be the first time Ace had pitched against them since Opening Day when he'd tanked. It was currently one game each in the series, and Ace would be starting for the final game. Even without talking to him, I knew this would be important.

I knew what it meant.

We'd come full-circle since that first game. So much had happened, so much had passed between us, and neither of us were the same people we'd been two months ago.

Two months ago, I would have been content to never see him again.

Now I couldn't imagine my life without him.

I didn't want to.

Hopefully I wouldn't have to.

I'd watched reruns of the Cubs game he started on Monday, and the Yankees game he'd pitched the day we'd broken up, and both times he appeared perfectly calm. He pitched better and better. Even when he sat on the bench during his rest period and the camera zoomed in as he watched the play, he looked perfectly calm, like nothing had ever happened.

He hadn't relied on me at all.

He hadn't been lying when he said his game was fixed, but of the two of us, I was the liar.

He'd never lied.

My eyes flicked back to Penn's, because I still wasn't clear exactly why he was standing in the middle of my apartment. I wasn't sure he'd ever been here.

I assumed he wanted to apologize, but apologizing was an entirely alien concept to Penn, so maybe he needed a prompter.

"You want to tell me why you're here then?"

"Yes." He cleared his throat, like he was about to deliver a great speech. "I came to apologize, and not because Lowe told me to. I wanted to come anyway, and I didn't know how to go about it and remain alive at the same time." His lip twitched, testing the waters to see if I'd laugh too, but I was still waiting for the apology. "I'm so sorry, Payton. I said some awful things to you, and I shouldn't have. It's none of my business who you date or how you choose to date, even if it is one of my players, and I'm so sorry if I made you feel anything less than the amazing woman you are."

He stopped talking, his face tense as he waited for my reaction.

My eyes widened. "Jeez, Penn. Laying it on a bit thick, aren't you?"

"I think it can be thicker!" called Kit from the kitchen where she was trimming the stems off the roses.

Penn's fists clenched and his nostrils flared through a deep breath, but he didn't argue. "Payton, you are a valued part of my life," he looked to Lowe, "of *our* life. I couldn't imagine you not being in it, and I hope that you can forgive me enough to stay in it. I'm really very, truly sorry for what I said."

Penn's mouth held in a hard line, his eyes looking nervous enough that he wasn't sure what my answer would be.

My shoulders dropped with a sigh. "Thank you for apologizing. I was planning to tell you to go fuck yourself today, so you've saved me a trip. I forgive you."

Penn's eyes flared, right before he burst out laughing. "Oh, thank God. I am sorry, Payton. I am."

"I know."

He thumbed behind him, in the direction of Kit. "Can you call off your Rottweiler now?"

"Sure," I chuckled, "once you've helped me with something, please."

"I'll help you with anything."

"I need to go to the game today, so I can find Ace and ask him on a date. Kit's coming, too."

To his credit, his expression remained unchanged. He didn't flinch or grimace or give anything away that suggested he'd rather have his fingernails pulled out than help me date one of his players.

"It would be my pleasure, Payton," he grinned, the boyish grin Penn Shepherd was famous for. "Wanna leave now?"

I glanced over to Kit who'd finished arranging the roses across several milk jugs and the three vases I owned, because who needed more than three vases?

"Yes, we're ready. Let me run to the bathroom one more time."

"Great." He held his hand out for Lowe, and she took it, winking at me as she did.

Five minutes later we were in the back of Penn's Range Rover, being driven through the New York traffic. Now Penn had apologized, his focus was back on the baseball, and I could see the tension rolling through his shoulders and clenched jaw as we stopped in yet another traffic jam.

Penn's driver had tuned the radio to the pre-game commentary. The players were on the field warming up, though given we were currently at Lincoln Square and still had to drive sixty blocks, it wasn't likely we'd see the first pitch. I also didn't want to listen to the commentators talk about Ace's pitch on Opening Day, and neither did Penn, who turned down the volume on the back speakers.

Lowe's hand was resting firmly on Penn's leg, likely to stop it from jiggling. For the first time ever, I sympathized with him and his obsession for baseball, because today, I felt the same. I wanted to see the first pitch, I wanted to see Ace as soon as was humanly possible. It couldn't come soon enough.

"Tell Payton what Ace said."

My eyes flicked over from where I was staring out of the window, to where Lowe was staring at Penn. If it was a distraction tactic, it worked very well.

Penn's gaze moved from Lowe to me. "Um, he said that I'd upset you."

"What?" I frowned. "What does that mean?"

Lowe tutted loudly, adding an eye roll. "Not that. He called you his girlfriend."

My eyes popped wide, though not as wide as Kit's when her head peered through from the back row of the car. "What?"

Lowe nudged Penn again. "Tell Payton what you told me."

"Oh, he said that someone had made his girlfriend cry and that he didn't like it, and he planned to win her back, so she knew she'd always have someone to fight in her corner, along with a veiled threat that he'd make me pay." He glanced back at Lowe and asked, "Is that it?"

She nodded, which made him grin again like a kid who'd been told 'good job'. Penn turned to me again, "but he's not why I apologized either. I truly am sorry, Payton."

"Thank you."

"Ace called you his girlfriend, Pay," Lowe whispered, almost reverently.

My teeth sunk into my lip. This was huge. I mean, for me it was huge. It might not be a big deal to any other woman, but I'd never been a girlfriend before. Not as an adult, at least.

And like a sunrise spreading across a darkened landscape, my smile broke free. I couldn't hold it back even if I wanted to. I was a girlfriend.

Or hopefully would be at the end of the day.

"Do you think we can go any faster?" I asked Penn, even though it was clear we couldn't, given the state of the traffic, but Penn always had ways of making things happen so it never hurt to ask.

Penn was about to shake his head when the driver interrupted. "Mr. Shepherd, the first pitch is about to take place."

"Can you turn up the commentary?" I asked.

"Ace Watson's looking good out there, Aaron. And we have our first pitch from him against the Phillies, just as we did two months ago on Opening Day. Let's hope it's better this time."

"I'll wager it will be, Mark."

"Can't they come up with new material, or something more original?" I grumbled.

"They're not comedians," replied Kit from the backseat.

"Shhhh," added Penn before I could.

"... and ball one is a swing and a miss."

The first Phillies player up to bat never made it to first base, returning to the dugout for the second player to attempt a better result. I listened intently as he walked to home plate, but that was as far as he got.

Same for the third.

Kit's head popped between the seats again. "That was quick. Did the Phillies not make base?"

"They didn't." Penn shook his head then looked at me.

"Your boy had a good first inning."

My boy. I turned toward the window again so none of them could see my cheeks flush from the little swirls flipping in my belly.

By the time we finally arrived at The Lions Stadium, it was top of the fourth and the Phillies were yet to make it to first base. The Lions were three up. The car screeched around the corner at the executive entrance, and Penn had opened the door before it had ground to a full halt.

"We'll go to the box. I can't watch this game from the tunnel if Ace keeps pitching like this." He jogged through the entrance before realizing the rest of us were trying to keep up with his long strides. Even when he turned you could see he was trying to be polite because he wasn't sure how far off the shit list he'd made it, but his face was also saying 'hurry the fuck up'.

"It's fine, you can go and we'll be right behind you," I said.

He gave one look to Lowe for confirmation it was still okay, then sprinted so fast he was out of sight before I'd been signed in at the reception desk.

"Why doesn't Penn want to watch from the field? I thought Ace was pitching well. The Phillies haven't scored yet," I frowned.

"He is. Penn's nervous. He'd be a nightmare by the field," Lowe replied, as we scanned through the reception gates and followed the direction Penn went.

I noticed Kit putting her phone away. "That was Murray, he's staying where he is. The boys are leaving Penn alone while he's watching, and we'll meet them later."

"Okay," I shrugged. "Let's skedaddle."

When we arrived at the box it was the bottom of the fourth, the Phillies still hadn't made first base, and we found

Penn yelling orders down the phone. "Don't take him off. I want to see how far this goes."

He slammed the receiver down and rubbed his hands together, smiling at Kit and me before pressing a kiss to Lowe's cheek and walking onto the balcony without saying another word. We were in the presence of Mr. Baseball again, and it was always better to leave him alone.

"I think we deserve a drink after all the drama today," announced Lowe, marching over to the bar where one of Penn's staff was waiting to take our order.

"I'm just going to have a soda water. I need a clear head for when I see Ace." I glanced up to the television screen, which was showing the Lions TV channel, the exact replica of what was currently on the big stadium screens.

Lux Weston was on home plate, shuffling into place and pulling on the rim of his batting helmet before readying his bat to swing. The ball made contact, flew through the air and bounced in the outfield. The Phillies center field scooped it up and threw it to second base, who caught it a split second too late. Lux was safe.

It only took Parker King one swing to hit the second home run of the game so far. By the end of the fourth inning, The Lions were up two more runs from a single by Lux and a home run from Tanner.

"Here we go again," mumbled Kit, as Ace walked to the mound during the changeover. "Come on, Ace."

I glanced at Penn who hadn't moved from the corner of the balcony he'd been standing in since we arrived.

His first pitch shot from his hand at ninety-eight miles an hour.

His second clocked in at ninety-nine.

His third, and The Phillies batter decided he was going to

attempt a swing. The ball hurtled toward the outfield where Stone Philips was running backwards, his hand stretched high. The ball nestled itself in Stone's glove, and the batter walked to the dugout.

"Two more!" Lowe jumped up from her stool, cupping her hands around her mouth and yelled, "C'mon Ace! Two more!"

She needn't have worried; the next two batters were struck out.

Ace walked off the field, his face unreadable. He didn't look at the crowds, he didn't react to any one calling his name, he didn't turn to Coach Chase as he was patted on the shoulder when he stepped inside the dugout.

Nothing.

The camera stayed trained on him as he sat down in his chair, next to the water cooler. Parker took the spot next to him and neither said a word as The Lions started at bat.

Penn walked into the suite and picked up the phone again.

"What's he doing?" I asked Lowe.

She turned to look at him. "He's probably calling the camera guys to get them to move off Ace. He won't want him distracted."

She was right. A second later, the screen changed to the crowds, and Jupiter Reeves running to second base.

The Lions were soon up six to nothing.

Which became seven to nothing.

And Ace's fifth inning turned to his sixth and seventh, still without one Phillies player making it to first base. I felt sick. Penn looked like he might be sick. Even Lowe had stopped jumping up and down, and cheering into the crowd.

The atmosphere in the stadium became eerily calm. We were on the precipice of witnessing one of the greatest feats in baseball. You could almost feel everyone wanting this for Ace, even The Phillies fans.

He stood on the mound and rolled his shoulders. The bat cracked loudly as the ball made contact, firing it high into center field. Lux sprinted back as fast as his legs would power him, Saint Velazquez sprinted from right field until they almost crashed. Lux dived forward, his glove outstretched, and rolled onto the ground.

The crowd waited.

Lux held his hand in the air, holding the ball.

New York would have been deafened from the cheer ripping around the stadium.

Kit pointed to the screen, which had frozen on the catch. "How the fuck did Lux do that? Look at his body. It's flat in the air, like he's Superman."

I shook my head. It was all I could manage.

After the first pitch, The Phillies batter seemed to crumble under the pressure.

Ace was now eight innings and twenty-four batters without a hit, walk, or hit batter. No one on The Phillies had made it to first base.

Parker, Saint, and Tanner, all hit home runs in the bottom of the eighth, like they couldn't get it over soon enough so Ace could start his quest to become only the twenty-fifth pitcher to complete a perfect game.

Ace walked slowly to the mound, his head down. I didn't know who was listening, but I sent out a prayer to anyone who might be.

Please let Ace make this. Please let Ace make this. Please let Ace make this.

The first pitch was a strikeout.

The second batter grounded to third, Jupiter Reeves snatched it up and lobbed it to Boomer Jones who caught it before the batter could pass.

"Ohmygod, ohmygod, ohmygod," Lowe squeaked.

The crowds were deadly silent. You could have heard a pin drop.

One more batter.

I turned around to find Penn sitting on a chair in the corner of the suite, head in hands, fingers in his ears. He'd given up watching in the seventh inning.

I knew exactly how he felt, but this batter could quite possibly be the one that leads to the twenty-fifth perfect game in one hundred and fifty years of the MLB, and I couldn't physically tear my eyes away from Ace.

He stood tall, his blue eyes closed as he drew in a breath. When he opened them, you could almost see the fire behind them as his arm pitched back and the ball left his hand, spinning toward the batter.

My heart thundered in my chest, my ears rang, even the nerves in my belly froze as the ball powered through the air.

Even with the loud crack of the bat, the crowds didn't make a single sound. The ball soared high into the air… but not high enough. Tanner Simpson could have been a basketball player in the moment he leapt up to catch the ball, and secured it firmly in his glove.

"Holy shit," I whispered, a nanosecond before the silence was wrenched apart by a ferocious roar of the crowds.

The entire Lions roster and coaches sprinted onto the field. Black and gold confetti rained down on the crowds, fireworks shot from the spires around the stadium and exploded over the Hudson. The Phillies and Lions fans alike were screaming themselves hoarse; they were now part of history. They'd witnessed greatness.

They'd have a story to tell their grandkids.

"HOLY SHIT!" I squealed, grabbing Lowe and Kit until we were all jumping around together, and it was only when Penn joined in that I realized I was crying.

"He did it! HE FUCKING DID IT!"

"Look!" Lowe tugged on my shirt. "Payton, look!"

I turned to Lowe to find her pointing at the big screen, which reflected back our balcony; Lowe pointing at the screen, next to Penn still hugging Kit and jumping for joy, then me trying to wipe the tears streaming down my face.

It had been brief, but my appearance was enough to get Ace's attention. I watched him spin around from where Parker and Lux were trying to hoist him onto their shoulders, and he stared directly up to the spot where I was standing. Slowly, his perfect grin split across his perfect face.

A vacuum built itself between us, drowning out all the noise and chaos we were surrounded with as he held my gaze. My heart stopped thudding, my belly stopped twisting, and calm flooded my nervous system to the point where I could finally take a deep breath.

I don't know how long we stared at each other, but it didn't break until Penn tugged me away and pulled me, along with Kit and Lowe, toward the door. "Come on, let's get down to ground level, then you can ask him on a date."

I'd never sprinted faster to an elevator, and by the time the doors opened near the entrance to the field, the players were already exiting and heading for the locker rooms. I tried to keep up with Penn hurrying down the hallway, but then I heard the one voice that could stop me in my tracks.

"… I dunno, I didn't want to think about it. Possibly after the sixth inning, because it wasn't until then I realized what was happening."

Loud laughter rumbled through the pack of reporters.

"Going from one of the worst opening games in history to a perfect game against the same club must feel good. You've joined an elite group of twenty-five."

"Any perfect game is going to feel good to a pitcher, man. It's amazing, it's exciting… but I can't really describe how I'm feeling right now. I think it's going to take a few days to settle in."

"Have you talked to your parents?"

"Dude, you grabbed me the second I came off the field," Ace laughed, "but they'll be my second call."

"Who's your first call?"

"The person responsible for getting me to this point," he answered. "Now if you'll excuse me, I need to go and find her."

Cries of Ace! Ace! Ace! were still going as he rushed out of the locker room, skidding to a stop as he spotted me standing in the corridor.

"Pay…"

"I was on my way to the field and heard your voice," I spluttered.

The smile I loved so much curved along his lips, and he took a step toward me. "I saw you watching."

"I didn't want to miss you pitching today. I wanted to come and support."

He nodded, his hands pushing into his pants pocket as he inched another step closer. His cheeks were still flushed from the pressure he'd exerted, his sweaty curls twisting around the base of his cap, but nothing could dim the piercing blue of his eyes as he stared at me.

"Is that the only reason?"

"No," I whispered and took a deep breath. "No, I wanted to see you. I wanted to apologize, and tell you how much I've been missing you."

"Okay... go on." He moved closer.

He was less than a foot away from me now, and I was finding it hard to breathe. My mind went back to the day in my office all those weeks ago when he crept as stealthily as a predator hunting prey, only this time, I didn't have any plans to put up a fight. He could catch me.

"I'm so sorry. I'm so sorry for everything. For being so horrible to you after you were so kind, for kicking you out of my apartment, for..." I winced and dropped my head so I wouldn't have to look at him, "for puking on you. I'm sorry for my behavior that morning. All of it." I swallowed the lump moving up my throat. "I'm not used to someone taking care of me. It's not an excuse and nor is being hungover, but I freaked out. You were right, I've never been in a relationship..." Fuck. My lip was throbbing from how much I was biting down on it. "I've missed you so much, Ace. I've missed you being next to me, and I've missed talking to you every day, all of it. I've missed you, and I was wondering – actually, hoping – you might have missed me, too."

He smiled at me, his bright blue eyes widening in amusement, though his silence sent me into another spiral.

"And if perhaps you have missed me, then maybe you could forgive me enough to give me another chance and let me take you on a date. The sun is still out, we can be in daylight."

I smiled, though it wasn't a wide smile like his. It was a nervous smile because I still couldn't read the expression on his face, and I was blabbering like an idiot.

He reached out, brushing his finger down the side of my cheek. "You missed me?"

I nodded and reminded myself to breathe.

"I missed you, too."

"Really?"

He grinned, that big, wide, American cookie cutter grin which had got me into this situation in the first place, and I couldn't have loved it more.

"Yes. If I hadn't seen you in the suite, I'd have run out the door and come to find you. I don't have to forgive you because there's nothing to forgive. Penn's the one who should be begging my forgiveness, especially after today. I missed you, really fucking missed you. I'm sorry I never messaged you. I wanted you to realize that I was telling the truth, that while you might have helped me fix my game, it was you I kept coming back for." He brushed his thumb against my cheek, wiping away a tear. "I missed you, Payton Lopez, and I don't plan to miss you again for a very long time… until next week on the away stretch, anyway."

"Does this mean we can go on a daylight date?"

He nodded. "Sure does, Babycakes, but first I need to do something."

His mouth finally fell onto mine, and he kissed me like he never intended to stop.

By the time we came up for air, it was possible no one was left in the stadium, and the moon had made an early appearance.

The daylight date would have to wait until tomorrow.

We would always have a tomorrow.

Epilogue

Ace

"*N*o, your leg goes here. See?" Payton slapped the page *Cosmo* was open at and twisted her ass to the left.

As she did so, the tip of my dick hit her cervix and her pussy clenched hard. It was fucking incredible, but then a spasm of pain cramped in my glutes.

"Argh, fuck! Babe," I grunted, "no."

She pushed my leg away, attempting to lift it behind her, but it was going nowhere. I might be a professional athlete, but I wasn't a fucking acrobat.

"No. No way. I'm calling it. This is impossible…" I tried to peer around her shoulder, "and you look like you're in pain."

I took both my hands to her perfect ass and squeezed it, moving her hips so I could shift her around until I was on top of her. My dick slipped out for a second, but I eased back inside her so slowly, her jaw slackened.

"Much better," I rolled my hips, adjusting myself to her

tightness, and dropped my lips down to hers. "Much, *much* better."

We might have been working our way through every edition of *Cosmo* we could find, but being here, on top of her where I could surround her and see every one of her feelings play across her face, this was and would always be my favorite position. She was so beautiful. Beneath me, her dark hair fanned out across the fluffy white pillow, the orgasmic pink glow to her cheeks that I loved so much contrasted with her deeply golden skin following the week we'd just spent in Cabo.

I don't know how I got so lucky.

Another slow roll of my hips had Payton's back arching almost subconsciously. Her perfect tits pushed into my face in the way she knew I loved, though it was more a borderline obsession. Dipping down, I took one of her taut nipples between my teeth, rolled my tongue over the hard nub and tugged gently, because I knew that's what *she* loved.

"Oh, God, Ace," she moaned loudly.

Fuck. I'd definitely become obsessed with *that;* hearing my name fall off her lips while she clenched around me.

"Tell me what you want."

Even though we'd got to the point in our relationship where I knew exactly what she wanted and needed, I still loved hearing her tell me.

"I want it slow and hard. I need to feel your dick stretching me out until I can't breathe. I want to hear my name, and I want you to show me how much you love me."

Dropping my lips to hers, I mumbled, "Good girl. I can definitely show you how much I love you."

Gathering up her fists in one of mine, I slowly ghosted my free hand along her curves until I could hitch her thigh on my hip. Every inch of her body was hypersensitive from the hour we'd already been in bed, working our way through *Cosmo*, but from the way I was now lazily moving inside her, I could sense the pressure building quickly.

Her jaw dropped, almost slack, and, cradling her face for another kiss, I knew I would never feel anything like this ever again. Slow thrust after slow thrust soon had her thighs bucking under my grip. Lightning bolts of pleasure shot down my spine, colliding with the gathering in my balls until there was no room for any more.

"Pay," I pushed up, reaching between us to tease around her clit in the same lazy manner I was driving inside her, slowly and deliberately, until her thighs began their tell-tale quivering. Since the first time we'd been together, I'd never allowed myself to come until she had, unless that pearl necklace was involved and then it was game over. "I want to feel you squeezing the life from my dick."

The trembling of her thighs moved across her entire body, until she was gasping for air. "Fuck… Ace…" she tipped her face up to me, almost pleading for release.

I wanted to make this last forever, but I was too close to explosion. My forehead dropped down to hers, my mouth capturing her mouth as I let go of her hands. Her fingers immediately pushed through my hair, pulling me into her as close as she could get.

"Now," I managed to mumble, and with one final hard drive into her, she detonated as my name fell off her lips surrounded by that moan of hers I was obsessed with.

One tight convulsion of her pussy and I followed her over the edge, my body jerking as it emptied inside her until it stole my breath too.

"I love you so much," I whispered, collapsing to the side before I crushed her, but never breaking our connection.

We stayed there silently as our heartrates settled and oxygen pumped back into our lungs. I turned my head to find her staring at me, and inched forward to kiss her nose.

She smiled, running her thumb along the fading purple bruise under my eye. "Does it still hurt?"

I shook my head and a sly grin crept up my lips. "No. It always looked worse than it felt; I just like you taking care of me."

"I still can't believe you got taken out by the Secret Service," she giggled.

"How dare you." I pushed back and sat up, my mouth dropping in mock indignation. "I didn't get taken out. I was helping my boy find love, and in the process, came to a disagreement with several armed government employees about how that should happen."

"Yeah, okay, tough guy." She pushed herself to sitting and ruffled my hair, squealing loudly as I pulled her into my lap.

"I'll show you how tough I am later. But first, we have to shower."

She peered over to the large ornate clock on the dresser along the far wall, where the time read three p.m. We had two hours to shower and dress – or Payton did, because I only needed twenty minutes – and meet the rest of The Lions team before the awards ceremony tonight.

It had been a big season for The Lions. The biggest yet. We hadn't made it to the World Series, but we'd won our division and lost in the N.L.C.S, one stage further than last year. Coach Chase had been nominated for Manager of the Year, Riley Rivers had been announced as the National League's Rookie of the Year, and tonight, I was being awarded the National League's Cy Young award – presented to the best pitchers. Following the ceremony, Penn Shepherd was throwing a little party of his own for The New York Lions, though based on last year's party, it would be anything but little.

Except this time, I wouldn't be ending up in Atlantic City. I'd be dragging Payton back to make the most of our giant hotel suite the first opportunity I got.

"What time are we meeting everyone?"

"Downstairs at five," I replied, gently kissing her cheek as I lifted her off my lap and stood up. "Shower time."

Payton swung her legs out of bed, and I let her lead the way so I could watch her ass jiggle as she walked into the bathroom and turned on the faucets.

"Are you nervous about tonight?" she asked, stepping under the showerhead and tipping her head back.

"No. Are you?"

"Why would I be nervous?"

I picked up the shampoo, squeezed a giant dollop into my hand, and twirled my finger for Payton to turn around so I could run it through her hair.

I couldn't remember exactly when this started, but it had been a few months ago, one morning before Payton went to work. She'd had a big presentation for her manuscript, and I'd gotten in the shower with her so she could practice it on me. While she was talking, I'd started washing her hair, and it soon became our thing. It was time we got to spend together every morning before she left for the office, and I went to the stadium.

It quickly became the best part of my day.

"Because you're being officially outed at my girlfriend."

"I think everyone knows, babe."

"You've handled the fame so well." I leaned in and nipped my teeth along her neck.

"Shut up," she laughed, turning around to shove me, but I caught her hand instead and pulled her into me.

"We don't have time to mess around," I muttered into her lips. "Tip your head back like the good girl I know you are."

She smirked but did as she was told so I could rinse the shampoo, and follow up with the conditioner I loved smelling on her.

"You wanna practice your speech one more time?" she asked, wiping the water from her eyes.

I pulled a face at her, because I wasn't sure I did. "I might jinx it."

She peered up at me, her big brown eyes full of love and sincerity as she took my face between her hands. "No, you've already won, and the speech is going to be amazing. I can feel it my bones."

"You wanna feel my bone?" I grinned at her, but she was having none of it.

"Be serious. I haven't heard it properly. Give me your speech."

"Okay, sit there," I sighed, and waited until she was perched on the edge of the shower bench.

Pointing the second shower head at her so she didn't get cold, I picked up a bottle of shampoo, which made an excellent stand-in microphone.

I'd been working on this speech for the best part of a month, and hadn't yet shared it with her fully. Or anyone for that matter. Lux had heard a couple of snippets when he'd walked in on me practicing, but that was it. Payton had been asking, but in what was a totally uncharacteristic move, I felt nervous.

"I've been trying to…" I peered down at her eager face. "Hang on, don't interrupt, let me get through it before you give me pointers… okay?"

She motioned her fingers zipping up her lips.

"Okay… ready?"

Payton nodded ,and her smile almost had me kissing her again.

I cleared my throat. "I've been trying to figure out where to start with my speech, because I didn't get up here by myself, and I think that honor probably has to go to Mr. Bryce Harper, smashing out his home run in the first game of Opening Day, taking The Phillies to a four-run lead against The Lions… arguably my least fine moment in fifteen years of playing baseball… but without that first game, I wouldn't be here now. That first week of the season I thought I'd hit rock bottom, and I couldn't see any way out of it. But the thing about being part of The Lions club is that no one gives up on you. Not the fans, the staff, the trainers, the coaches, my pitching coach, Coach Willis, the boss, my friends… And in the weeks that followed that first game, every single one of my opponents for putting on the best defense they could, because it all contributed to me becoming a better player, and teammate." I took a deep breath and continued, "All that being said, there's one person who's singlehandedly played the biggest part in getting me on this stage today – my girlfriend, Payton."

Her eyes widened, and she blinked through the water splashing her face. "Ace…"

I held my hand up. "No, hear me out. You promised. If you don't want to be included, I can remove it, but I want you to know how much you've done for me. How much you mean to me. At the beginning of this season I was a boy with an ego, and I realize now I had no direction, but I've become the man I want to be, and I have only you to credit for it. I wouldn't be here if it wasn't for you. I wouldn't be the player I am without you. You gave me a clarity I never had before we met. I think I'd been walking around in this fog, with my head stuck up my ass, and I never realized it. You saved me from a path I know I would never have wanted to walk down."

I sat on the bench next to her and brushed a wet strand of hair behind her ear before pulling her into my lap. Her eyes were brimming from more than the water still splashing her face, and I wrapped my arms around her to get her as close as I could, though it was never close enough.

"You're not going to say all that!" she gasped.

"No, but I'm telling you now. I wanted you to hear it," I grinned. "Don't cry."

"I'm not, it's the shower," she sniffed.

"Hey, you're not allowed to lie to me." I brushed my lips against hers. "I love you, Payton. I'm so thankful every day that I was driving down fifty-fifth that day."

"I made it happen, remember? You were my birthday wish."

"Your job was your wish."

"Potayto-potahto," she smiled. "It's a perfect speech, babe. Everyone will love it – especially Penn when you thank him for being such an awesome boss."

I let out a loud grunt. "I'm still undecided on whether I believe that. He tried to keep us apart."

Her hand cupped my cheek, looking at me from under her long, wet lashes, and I almost forgot what we'd been talking about. "Nothing would have kept us apart."

"Yeah, you're right. We're forever." I lifted her hand up between us and kissed it. "Now we need to get rinsed and out of here before we both shrivel into prunes."

An hour and a half later, I walked into the dressing room where Payton's dress had been hanging up. My heart stopped and my breath caught hard. On the hanger it had been pretty; it had been a dress. On Payton… it was a work of art.

Showstopping.

Thick black lace hugged her body from the top of her neck until it brushed the floor. I couldn't see a single inch of skin, yet she'd never looked sexier. A thick golden sash wrapped around her waist, making her curves look even curvier. I had to close my mouth before I began drooling.

"Holy shit," I gasped as she turned around. "You look unbelievable."

Lions black and gold. She really was something else.

"Thank you," she smiled, reaching up to straighten my bowtie.

"Fuck winning, I'm already the luckiest guy there tonight with you on my arm."

"Lucky Aces, right?" she laughed, making me laugh, because I could never help it whenever I heard that noise.

I picked up her golden purse from the table and held it out to her, along with my hand.

"Ready?"

"Always."

"You look so beautiful, Pay."

"So do you, award winner," she grinned, brushing her thumb across my cheek. "I love you, Ace Watson. Thank you for loving me."

"It's the easiest thing I've ever done."

I kissed her lightly so I didn't smudge her perfectly applied berry lipstick, but when I stepped into the elevator, I could see the imprint of her lips staining my beard. I had no intention of wiping it off.

She'd marked me. I was hers.

And Payton Lopez was mine.

- THE END –

ACKNOWLEDGMENTS

This is the fourth book I've written this year, and the third I've published. A year ago The New York Lions came to life in The Show and it's hard to believe that creating these characters and writing their stories is my full time job. Like, seriously... what?

It goes without saying I wouldn't be able to do any of this without YOU, my wonderful, sweet, kind, loyal readers. You are all the absolute best and I'm so *so* lucky to have you on this crazy ride. I think it on a daily, if not hourly, basis. This year I got to meet so many of you at signings, and I can't wait until I get to hug you all again in 2024, and along with new faces. I've added more incredible people to my friendship group, and clung hard onto those I'd somehow managed to find already.

Erin, thank you so so much for imparting all your baseball wisdom onto me, I'm eternally grateful that you take time out to check whether I've got National League and American League mixed up, and inning as a singular and the 17,832 times you tried to explain a hit to me. I think I got it, but probs not.

Amanda for the continued efficiency with which you run The Jupiter Reeves Fan Club - because it literally wouldn't exist without you!

Taylor who seamlessly runs my social, website and newsletter (and, readers, if you're ever in Wilmington, she owns the cutest little romance bookstore, so please go in. It's called Beach Reads Books).

To Valentine, Amy, Meagan, Kim, Sarah and everyone at Valentine PR. I'm so grateful to be working with you.

Emily Wittig. OMG. Another perfect cover!

And lastly, Georgana, my incredible agent and all round

amazing human being, WHAT A YEAR! I'm never letting you go. I can't wait until we can have an Aperol together again.

There's only so many ways to say this, but if you've made it to the bottom I also want reiterate that I'm fully aware how lucky I am. I have so much love for you all, SO SO MUCH. You give me life and fill me with so much joy, every single day.

To everyone on this journey, thank you from the bottom of my heart.

Lulu xo

ABOUT THE AUTHOR

Lulu started writing by accident, and somehow found herself stuck in a fictional world of ice hockey, baseball and billionaires. A world she has no plans to leave.

More recently she's ventured across the Atlantic to where her latest novel is set - the beautiful cities of Oxford and Cambridge, and the annual rowing showdown on the River Thames.

She's a big fan of strong heroines, because those fierce alphas need someone to keep them in check. You'll find her navigating her way through Romance Land one HEA at a time, and trying to figure out the latest social media platform she needs to post to.

She'd love to hear from you, loves hearing your opinions and thoughts, so please message her on any of the social platforms @lulumoorebooks and she'd love you to come and join her reader group on Facebook - aptly named The Jupiter Reeves Fan Club.

But if you don't want to do any of that, there's always her website - lulumoorebooks.com

ALSO BY LULU MOORE

The New York Players

Jasper

Cooper

Drew: The Vegas Edition (extended prologue)

Drew

Felix

Huck

The Tuesday Club

The Secret

The Suit

The Show

The New York Lions

The Third Baseman

The Shake Off

The Baller is coming summer 2024

The Oxbridge Series

Oar With Friends is coming March 2024

READ ON FOR MORE...

Want to know more about Kit, Beulah and Lowe? Or the origins of The New York Lions?

Find it all in my Tuesday Club Trilogy - and the three billionaires whose lives are turned upside down.

Main tropes include:

The Secret: Single dad x Nanny (Kit)

The Suit: Enemies to Lovers (Beulah)

The Show: Best friend's brother (Lowe)

Read on for an excerpt from *The Secret:*

KIT

"*E*viction?! I've just signed the lease!" I fumed at the woman on the end of the line, emphatically waving around the notice I'd been served as I'd walked out of my apartment an hour ago. "The ink can barely be dry."

"As I said, the building was sold to a private cash buyer last week and they have plans for it." Her voice was so annoying and nasally and calm that it only made me rage more. "But they've given all tenants six weeks' notice, as well as double their deposit back for any inconvenience caused."

My deep breath buoyed every shred of self-control I was currently using to not explode at her, only managing to speak through gritted teeth. "I don't want double my deposit! I want to have to not move all my things again."

I paced up and down the floor of my best friend, Payton's, apartment, where I'd stormed over to as soon as I'd opened the envelope. If there was carpet on the floor, I'd have worn it out approximately twenty minutes ago, while I was getting nowhere on the phone to this irritating representative for my landlords.

"Yes, Ma'am, I understand that." There was some shuffling down the line. "Could you please hold?"

Musak began playing through the phone before I had an opportunity to object, then it went dead.

"Hello? Hello?"

Cut off.

Ahhhrrrrrrghhhhh. My phone found itself launched across the room into the couch cushions, because even though I was angry, I wasn't about to smash it. I didn't need the hassle of sorting out a new phone as well as finding somewhere else to live.

Payton appeared with a margarita, handing it to me in silence. I gagged at the strength of it and overzealous salt edge but downed it in one, thrusting the glass back out to her for a refill from the enormous jug she was holding.

She obliged, filling it to the rim once again. "So, evicted huh?"

"Can you goddamn believe it?! I only moved in two months ago! I'm just getting used to the neighborhood; I've even found a favorite coffee shop! I've worked out the quickest route to the subway! And now I have to start all over!"

I threw myself down on the couch. Trying to find a decent, affordable apartment in New York City, which didn't require you signing the soul of your first born child over, was as easy as trying to figure out Quantum Theory or Jet Propulsion... or something else which was really hard to figure out.

Payton perched at the end of the couch opposite me, tucking her long legs underneath her. Most of her thick dark hair was twisted up in a knot on top of her head, but as always, there were still some long tendrils which had escaped, falling down the side of her face and framing her perfect cheekbones. She was one of those people who looked put together no matter if she'd just woken up and thrown on whatever she'd found on her floor – which she usually had – or if she'd spent four hours getting ready, which she'd rather die than do.

We'd met on our first day of college, where we shared the same dorm, and courses. Both studying English Literature, we'd become best friends by the end of our first class after Professor Higgins spent the entire session talking about the cleanliness of pigs, having drastically veered off the topic of George Orwell's Animal Farm, and we'd struggled to hold in the giggling.

"You can stay here for as long as you need." She sipped on her own margarita, wincing. "Oooh, I think I put too much tequila in this."

I chuckled at her reaction, and sighed. "Thank you, but hopefully I'll find somewhere else. I have six weeks. I just really, *really* didn't want to be traipsing around in the cold to find another place to live. I had plans the next few weeks; we were going to go out, I was going to start dating again, seeing as I don't have to study all hours of the day and night anymore, and now I have to change them. I love you for offering though."

"You're welcome. You know the couch always has your name on it when you need it."

"I know. You can always come apartment hunting with me again," I added, with more than a little hope in my voice. It would make it more bearable if I wasn't on my own.

"Of course," she scoffed. "I need to make sure we're closer together this time. Maybe I can persuade Mrs. Kellerman upstairs to finally move into her son's house, and then you can have her place." Her eyes lit up and she clapped her hands together. "Ohmygod, that would be amazing! Like college, but better."

"Think we can start on her today? Take her one of these," I waved my empty glass around at her, "you'd only need to give her half before she signed it over."

She leaned forward with the jug and refilled my glass with no objections from me. I'd decided it was acceptable to get drunk before noon under extenuating circumstances, and eviction certainly qualified as that.

"Yeah. We'll finish this and I'll make a fresh one," she grinned.

I took another large gulp.

"Urghhhhhh." My head fell back against the back of the couch, still smarting at the situation I was in. Reaching underneath me I discovered the culprit of what was digging into my shoulder – a well-thumbed copy of a mafia romance with a naked, tattooed torso - Payton's current literary obsession - and dropped it on the floor. "This is so frustrating.

I was supposed to be looking for a job, not an apartment."

Payton and I had graduated together six years ago, and while she'd gone straight into work for a publishing house to begin her dream of becoming a book editor, I had stayed on, earning my doctorate in Early Childhood Education. I hadn't quite figured out what I wanted to do with it yet, but I did know I wanted a career where I'd be shaping the minds of the next generations. During those six years, I'd spent time teaching in an elementary school in Brooklyn and then moved on to become a part-time nanny to save more money while I studied. And I'd saved enough so that when I graduated I had some time for a few months while I figured out the path I wanted to take - as well as catching up on sleep.

Except that had all gone to shit at approximately ten thirty-two this morning.

"Still haven't changed your mind about the Columbia position?"

I shook my head slowly. My old professor at Columbia had offered me a place as a research fellow on her program, and though it was a great opportunity and an honor in itself, I didn't want it. Or, more accurately, I didn't want to take the first job I'd been offered because I'd been her favorite student. I wanted to prove to myself all the years of study I'd put in had been worth it, which is why I'd worked so hard to save some money.

"No. Although now I'm thinking it's good I have it to fall back on." I slurped my drink. "But I probably shouldn't be making this decision until I'm sober."

A ringing stopped Payton from saying whatever she was about to, as I felt around underneath me trying to find my phone which was still wedged into the side of the couch where I'd thrown it.

"Hello?" I answered, without checking the caller ID.

"Hi, Kit, it's Marcia. How are you?"

I immediately sat up straight, my drink sloshing over the side and down my top, and tried hard to make sure my tone didn't convey the three very strong margaritas I'd just drunk on an almost empty stomach. Marcia was the owner of the nanny agency I'd been working for part-time while I studied. She ran a tight ship, like a stern English matron, and even though she couldn't see me, she had a sixth sense for when someone was misbehaving. Not that I was misbehaving. I was twenty-eight and well within my right to drink a pitcher of margaritas on a Wednesday morning if I chose to. But still, I would never slouch in Marcia's presence.

"Hey, Marcia, I'm good thanks. How are you?"

"Good, good. I've had an urgent request come in for you, for an interview this afternoon. It's a brand new assignment. Can you do a call in an hour?"

I slumped back down slightly, though not enough that she'd notice through the phone. "Not really, no. I've graduated now and you know I'm taking a break from work before I make any more decisions. Can't you offer them one of the plenty of other very qualified nannies you already have?"

"Kit, they've requested you. Just you," she reiterated firmly, as though that explained everything, and making it clear she hadn't listened to a word I'd said.

My lips pursed, because I knew I was on the losing end of a battle. This morning wasn't going to plan, at all.

"How do they even know me?"

"It's one of our current families. They remembered your résumé from when they were looking."

I sighed. "Marcia, thank you, but I really don't have time. I just got evicted and I need to look for a place to live."

"This is live-in, so it's perfect." I could have sworn I heard her clap. "And they've doubled your salary for the short notice."

Payton's eyebrows rose; she could hear everything Marcia was saying, given that Marcia didn't talk quietly. She took the silence as a reason to continue on her pitch in her trademark sing-song voice, like she was trying to give Mary Poppins a run for her money.

"It's a single father, in need of a lot of help by all accounts, not sure of the exact details. It's a brand new baby so you'll be doing nights to get a sleeping routine, which is why it's live-in. His sisters are our clients and the interview will be with them. I suggest you take it and see. They're lovely employees, they've had really good feedback, and both our nannies have extended their time twice. There are plenty of extras, including a car, expense account, travel, full membership to a gym called…" I heard a shuffle of paper, "Body by Luck." Payton's jaw dropped, mainly because she had more than a small obsession with that place. "And it's much nearer the college than where you live now, so you're closer to the city and any interviews you may have. They've also said you can have time off for interviews, plus your weekends free…"

Payton began vigorously gesturing her hands while nodding her head in a way that was both confusing and distracting.

"Sorry, Marcia, can you hold please?" I held the phone away and looked at Payton, mouthing to her. "What?"

"Take the interview," she mouthed back.

I shouldn't have picked up the phone. I'd never been able to say no to her, so I wasn't clear why I thought I could now, especially with Payton still flailing around. Damn margaritas. It was no wonder Marcia ran a business as successful as it was. She could persuade anyone to do anything.

I brought the phone to my ear again. "Okay, fine. One

interview."

"Great! Well done, Kit. I'll send the details through."

"Wait, how long is it for?" I stopped her before she hung up.

"Sixteen weeks… initially."

"And when does it start?"

"They want you immediately, but I'm sure we can arrange for something to be done about moving your things out of your current place."

"Okay, I'll take the call," I replied, thoroughly defeated. "But only sixteen weeks, Marcia. I mean it."

"Wonderful. How serendipitous."

She hung up.

Payton took a large swig of her drink. "Jesus. She could sell oil to the Texans."

I nodded. Marcia didn't take no for an answer.

"Still, she's not wrong. This sounds awesome. Plus, a Body by Luck membership! There's a huge wait list on that place. You do remember how long it took me to get that through, don't you? And now you've just been handed one! I'd take the job just for the membership! But at least now we can go together. And you never know - this single dad might be hot…" She winked with a loud guffaw as she tried to fill my glass.

I held my hand over it. "No, I need to sober up."

"I don't." She topped her own glass up. "I'm so glad I decided to work from home today, makes life so much more interesting."

I stood up. "I'm going to get some water."

* * *

"What time are they calling?"

"In five minutes."

"Here." Payton barged into the bathroom while I was sitting on the toilet, throwing a brush at me with no warning. I ducked just in time or it would have smacked me in the face. "Maybe run that through your hair."

I'd spent thirty minutes trying to drink as much water as possible in order to sober up, and then another twenty-five preventing my bladder from bursting. Not sure why I even cared. I didn't want this job, and I'd pretty much been bullied into taking the interview.

I flushed the toilet, pulled up my jeans, and stood at the sink staring at myself as I washed my hands. Payton was right; I did need to brush my hair. It was the least I could do. My hair was so thick that if I wasn't careful I could quickly take on the appearance of someone who'd been dragged through a bush.

I checked my watch.

Two minutes.

I poured a glass of water and sat down at the kitchen counter, propping my phone up on the flowerpot Payton kept there. I turned to her as she took the stool next to me.

"You're not sitting there while I'm doing this! You're distracting enough."

"I'm giving you moral support."

I pointed through to the living room. "Support me from the couch, where I can't see you."

She smirked as she moved away. "You're very uptight about a job you don't want."

The phone started ringing before I could respond to her. I answered the video chat to see two women staring back at me; one blonde, one brunette, both smiling widely. At any other time I'd have probably thought it was weird, but they seemed so genuinely happy to see me that it immediately put me at ease.

"Hello."

"Hiiii," they replied in unison.

"Thank you so much for meeting with us at such short notice. We really appreciate you making the time. I'm Wolfie," said the blonde one, in an accent that wasn't American. English? Australian, maybe? "And this is my sister, Freddie."

"I'm Kit," I smiled. "It's nice to meet you."

Freddie's bright blue eyes lit up with more enthusiasm than a kid in a candy store. "How much did Marcia explain to you? Shall we tell you a little bit about ourselves and the situation, and then we can go through questions?"

I smiled, finding it hard to hold one in against their eagerness. "Yes, thank you. That would be good. She mentioned it's a new baby and that was about it."

"Did she say it's not our baby?" Wolfie asked.

"Yes, she did actually. Your brother's?"

She nodded. "Yes, that's right. We do both have children though. I have a two-and-a-half-year-old daughter and a three-month-old son, and Freddie has a two-year-old son, with another one due soon."

I chuckled. "Sounds like a handful."

"You're not wrong, and that's how we know Marcia. She's been brilliant for us with our nannies. We love them. And when we were originally looking, we remembered your résumé, but you weren't available long-term. However, you were the first thought we had when the new baby arrived, and we contacted Marcia straight away."

"And thankfully you're available."

It didn't surprise me that Marcia hadn't told them that I wasn't actually planning to go back to nannying. But the way these two were going, it sounded like Marcia would have had as hard a time saying no to them as I did to her.

"Anyway," Wolfie continued, "this would be working for our brother, Murray. It's a bit of an unusual situation. He's recently found himself to be the father of a newborn."

I frowned, because how does one suddenly find themselves to be a parent of a brand new baby?

Freddie rolled her eyes at her sister. "Stop being diplomatic; she needs to know the truth." She looked back at me through the screen. "The baby was left with him yesterday, with a note saying she was his."

I heard Payton gasp loudly from the other room as my eyes opened wide, and I had to remind myself to blink. "What..?!"

"He didn't know," Wolfie interrupted defensively before I could say anything else, although I was struggling to figure out what else there was to say. "He wouldn't have ever let the mother of his child feel she couldn't ask for help. He came home and found the baby on the doorstep."

I'd been rendered speechless. Never, in all my years of child education or nannying, had I heard of this. I knew of Safe Haven laws, but not on the doorstep of a stranger. Or maybe not *exactly* a stranger.

But either way, that must have been the biggest shock of his life.

Freddie's laughed pulled me out of my stunned silence. "This was our reaction too."

"Is your brother okay?"

Wolfie's face softened slightly. "Yes, he is; thank you for asking. He's in shock, but our parents are coming over to help him. He just needs something permanent for the next few months to help him find a routine and adjust. He really is great with kids; he's brilliant with our three, and we have another brother in England who also has three kids. We have a big family."

I was right with the English accent thing.

"And the baby?"

"She's twelve days old."

"Her birthday is February fourteenth?"

Freddie's eyebrows shot up. "Wow, that's quick math. Yes. Valentine's Day."

I laughed. "I'd like to take credit for that, but not really. It's my birthday, too."

She tried to hold back a smile. "Interesting."

"Now that's out of the way, hopefully it explains why Murray isn't on the call and it's us interviewing." Wolfie gestured between the two of them.

I nodded.

"Your résumé is very impressive, as are your recommendations, and like I said, we remembered you from when we were looking. Do you have any questions for us?"

Considering I only found out about this an hour ago and was still slightly stunned by the baby on the doorstep revelation, my brain had frozen. I dug deep into my old list of interview questions.

"Yes, let's start with what are your expectations? Do you already have parenting methods?"

"We do, but Murray doesn't. He's great with our kids, but he's never looked after a baby properly. He needs to be shown everything and taught everything. He needs help with creating a routine so he can get back to work."

"What does he do?"

I wasn't so interested in his job but more his schedule. If he was a doctor, he'd work erratic hours which were hard for routine, but if he was a teacher, he'd work a more sociable nine to five.

"He works in finance, and he runs a company with our brother."

"Okay. And where's he based?"

"He lives up near Lincoln Square. He's not far from Columbia, which would work for you, right? Marcia told us about your college course."

I clearly hadn't been very good at hiding the surprise at them knowing that because Wolfie started talking really quickly.

"Marcia mentioned that you'd finished your degree and were taking a break to look for jobs, and we'll make sure you still have the time to do that. She also called to explain the situation with your apartment but we can help with all that, too. Freddie knows loads of good moving companies, and we can organize getting everything into storage for you, and even help with finding somewhere new for you too. If you want some of your things to come with you, that's no problem. Whatever you want."

Freddie grinned broadly. "Can you tell we really want you to take the job?"

That got me and I started giggling. "I can, and I'm flattered, really."

"We can arrange for you to speak to our current nannies, if that would help, so you can see we aren't total nut jobs. Murray is very kind and funny too, everyone loves him, and we just want to find him the best help."

I laughed again. These two were very amusing, or maybe it

was the Englishness, but they were certainly incredibly easy and likeable. I guessed it wouldn't hurt me to postpone my plans for four months. Plus the prospect of having someone help with the moving was more than enough to sway me.

"We totally understand this has been sprung on you, so take some time to think about it. However, we'd really like you to say yes. We'll get Marcia to connect you with our nannies so you can get the proper low-down."

"Sure, thank you. That would be good. Marcia mentioned you wanted a start ASAP, but what exactly does that mean?"

Wolfie winced slightly. "How about this weekend?"

Wow, it really was ASAP.

I nodded, my face neutral, because while I was probably going to say yes, I still needed to think about it.

"Okay. Is there anything else you wanted to ask?"

"Do you like dogs? Murray has a Labrador, but he's very gentle."

I grinned. "I love them. I used to have Labradors growing up, so it won't be a problem."

"And do you have a boyfriend?"

Freddie jerked sideways from the force of Wolfie's nudge following her question, but they both stared at me waiting for an answer.

"No, no I don't. But don't worry; my personal life and professional lives aren't mixed. I don't invite my friends over, even when I'm live-in."

"Oh, that's not…" Freddie earned herself another nudge.

"That's good to know, we appreciate your honesty," Wolfie interrupted. "Anyway, we'll let you go and get Marcia to connect you with our nannies. We'd really love for you to come and join our families, and we'll help get you whatever you need for your moving situation."

I smiled gratefully. "That's very kind, thank you."

They hung up and I was left staring at the phone, wondering how I'd managed to get railroaded into looking after a newborn and a single dad, when an hour ago I was worrying about sorting out my eviction.

Payton sauntered into the kitchen, perching on the stool next to me. "Wow, baby on the doorstep."

I glanced up at her. "I know, right? That's heavy shit."

Her head bobbed slowly in agreement. "You're taking it, aren't you?"

"Honestly?" I held her gaze. "They had me at movers. Plus, it's sixteen weeks with a newborn, it'll be easy, and then I can search for a proper job."

She jumped off the stool.

"Great, now that's settled, we can start drinking again."

Made in the USA
Las Vegas, NV
21 August 2024